SHEPHERD AVENUE

SHEPHERD AVENUE

Charles Carillo

The Atlantic Monthly Press
BOSTON / NEW YORK

FIRST EDITION

LIBRARY OF CONGRESS CATALOGING-IN-PUBLICATION DATA

Carillo, Charles.
  Shepherd Avenue.

  Summary: After his mother's death, a shy ten-year-old
boy must find a place for himself in his grandparents'
boisterous Italian family in New York City.
  [1. Family life—Fiction. 2. New York (N.Y.)—
Fiction] I. Title.
PS3553.A685S4 1986   813'.54 [Fic] 85-20066
ISBN 0-87113-043-2

BP
Published simultaneously in Canada
PRINTED IN THE UNITED STATES OF AMERICA

SHEPHERD AVENUE

For
CISSY, DUDY, *and* MILLIE

CHAPTER ONE

I NEVER saw my father with a newspaper in his hands.

You hear about people in aboriginal tribes who live without ever seeing a written word or hearing the story of Jesus Christ's life, but Salvatore Ambrosio traveled from Roslyn, Long Island, to midtown Manhattan each weekday to earn his living as an advertising copywriter. It was a long ride, more than an hour each way. I guess he looked out the window. It's not likely that he talked to anyone.

When he got home from work his dress pants, jacket, and tie came off and were replaced by frayed work shirts and pants. He was never casually dressed, my father. His clothing was either impeccable or absolutely shabby.

My father's aloofness toward the outside world didn't do me much good when I'd ask him to help me with current-events homework. Without batting an eye he'd say, "Just tell your teacher that people are worse than ever, and do as many terrible things to each other as they can get away with."

"Nice thing to say," my mother would comment. Then she'd trim an article out of *Newsday* and read it aloud to make sure I understood it, while my father watched with amusement as the two of us "swallowed that bilge they print in the paper."

My mother read the paper front to back. "Somebody in this house should know what's going on," she used to say. She knew in her heart that my father *cared* about people, but that he couldn't hide his disappointment in most of them.

One thing that never disappointed my father was his garden.

He loved to spend hours tending it slowly, treating our plot of land as if it were a giant jewel that needed daily polishing.

I got to know him best working beside him in silence. The big rectangles of lawns all around ours were tended by professional landscapers, men who jumped off trucks, unloaded machines, and, in furious clouds of noise and gasoline, cut lawns so fast it was like rape. My father used a four-bladed push mower. The neighbors mocked him behind his back, I'm sure.

I got an important glimpse into a secret chamber of my father's heart when I was nine years old. It was an October afternoon. We had just raked the lawn and put down fertilizer. The job done, I lay on the browning grass and fell asleep. When I awoke he was standing by our hedge, leaning against his rake just hard enough to bend the tines. A honking flock of geese flew overhead. He let the rake drop and did a perfect slow motion pantomime of their wings, flapping his arms and walking in their direction on tiptoes, backlit by the dull orange sunset. It was a startling imitation. I was sort of surprised when he didn't get airborne.

And I knew he wasn't just a nut. Something was bugging him, urging him to tear away from the circumstances of his life — something he fought internally all the time. I didn't know what it was, but I sensed that somehow I stood in his way more than my mother did. I pushed the lima beans around my plate and hardly touched the meat loaf that night.

It all came down when my mother became sick with cancer the following year. We used to visit her at the hospital early in the evenings. *She* would make *us* feel better, believe it or not.

"You guys got it backwards," she explained. "The visitors are supposed to cheer up the patient. See?" After about an hour she'd chase us out of there.

"Go feed the dog," she'd say.

"We don't have a dog, Mommy."

"Go feed the cat."

"We don't have a cat," I'd giggle.

"Go feed the ostrich."

We'd leave in laughter, then eat our dinners in Northern Boulevard diners, watching cars whiz past as we forked down cheeseburgers, french fries, and cole slaw. My father knew the rudiments of cooking, but I don't think he was able to bear the thought of a meal at our home without his wife.

She stayed at the hospital for all of April and half of May 1961. In the second week of May, he stopped taking me with him to visit. I was just ten years old but he left me alone in the house those nights and came home with take-out food in foil-lined bags.

It occurs to me that I never had a baby-sitter. Wherever my parents went — to restaurants, the movies — I came along, a son treated like a miniature adult.

Elizabeth McCullough Ambrosio died in the hospital on May 13. That night my father came home and filled a big aluminum pot with water, shook salt into it, and put the flame on full blast under it. He began opening a can of tomato paste.

"We're having spaghetti," he said as he cranked the can opener. I started to cry because I knew she was dead.

They buried my mother without a wake the day after she died. The only ones present at the cemetery were my father and me and a priest from a nearby Catholic church we'd never attended. My father was alternately sharp and polite with the priest, who didn't dare to ask my father why he'd never seen us in church.

We lived an awkward month in the house before my father put it on the market. He hired a stranger to run a garage sale and sell every stick of furniture we had.

All my mother's clothing and all his dress clothes went into a big Salvation Army hopper at a nearby shopping center. My father held me by the hips as I dropped three big bundles down the dark chute. For an instant I had a vision of him pushing me in after them.

Everything that could possibly tie him down was now gone. We lived those final June days in Roslyn like raccoons that break into summer homes through the eaves. With the rugs gone the aged oak floors groaned at every step, and even with the windows down little currents of air puffed in crazy directions.

The only thing we couldn't get rid of was the four-bladed push mower, which my father left behind in the barren garage.

5

He didn't let me in on his plan until our final night together in the house. We slept on a pair of cots dragged close together in the living room, a courtesy of the moving company that was to bring the new owner's stuff in the morning.

I hadn't asked a single question about where we were going during the scuttling of our possessions. I just sat up in my cot, waiting for him to start volunteering information.

He swallowed. He was hesitating, like a kid reluctant to tell a parent about a broken vase. "I quit my job," he said through a dry throat.

"I figured *that* out," I said, irritated. He hadn't been to work for two weeks. "So where are we going tomorrow?"

He seemed disappointed that I wasn't startled by his announcement. "I have to take off for a while."

I felt my heart plummet. I was being disposed of, too — he'd only been saving me for last!

"What do you mean? Where am I gonna go?"

"You're staying with my parents in Brooklyn."

I was stunned. "I thought we hated them," I said. "How can we stay there if we don't even *visit?*"

"We don't hate them!" my father boomed. "There have just been years and years of misunder*standing.*"

I was disgusted. "Yeah, sure, Dad."

He said weakly, "My parents are good people."

"I don't even know them!" I rolled over on the cot so I wouldn't have to look at him. Not even sure I wanted to be with him anymore I said, "Why can't I go with you?"

"Because you can't, Joseph."

"*Why?*"

"Because *no*body can," he said in a way that made it clear the matter was beyond his control, as if a demon inside him were calling the shots.

Puzzled, I rolled onto my back. Oddly, I felt my anger melting. I started thinking about how miserable this past month with my father had been. Maybe we both needed a break from each other. Somehow, I sensed that losing both parents might be easier than losing one.

"For how long?" I asked roughly.

The fact that I was talking inspired my father. "A few weeks, no more."

"And then what?"

"I don't know," he admitted.

"Where are you going?"

"Across the country in the car."

We were silent. The wind picked up, making the ancient window panes jiggle and creak in their loose putty jackets.

I felt him grasp my elbow. "Joey, don't hate me," he begged in a voice I'd never heard him use. Desperate.

"I won't," I said. I didn't take his hand but let him hold me for a few minutes before rolling onto my side and falling asleep.

Almost everything we loaded into our Comet station wagon the next morning belonged to me. My father packed one bulging canvas sack for himself, filled with shirts, pants, and underwear. That and his shaving kit were all he'd take across the United States.

When we were on the road I said, "You have to sign my report card." I dug it out of my pile of stuff. "We're supposed to mail it back to school. Maybe you don't have to if I'm not going back."

"Give it to me," he mumbled. At a red light near the Long Island Expressway he glanced at the card, hastily scrawled on it, and handed it back to me.

"Take care of it," he said, knowing I had a stamped, addressed envelope the school had provided.

I looked at the card. Through the first three marking periods Mrs. Olsen, my fifth-grade teacher, had written tiny but stinging notes in the space provided for comments: "Joseph should participate in class more often . . . Joseph needs to be more outgoing . . . Joseph holds back during sports."

And beneath each comment was my mother's light-handed, almost fluffy signature, "Mrs. Salvatore Ambrosio." She barely pressed a pen when she wrote.

I looked at the space for the last marking period.

"I suspect he can do better," Mrs. Olsen had written of my straight-B performance.

"I suspect we all can," my father wrote back before scrawling his fierce signature. It violated the boundaries of the dainty white box, and I could feel his lettering through the back side of the card, like Braille.

"There's a mailbox," I said just before we reached the entry ramp to the expressway. He braked the car. I got out and mailed the report card, sort of surprised that he'd waited instead of roaring away.

"Put your seat belt on," he said, and that was the extent of our conversation for the rest of the trip to the East New York section of Brooklyn.

He slowed the car to a crawl when we made the turn down Shepherd Avenue. We drove beneath an elevated train track structure that left a ladder-shaped shadow in the late afternoon light. Rows of sooty red brick houses, fronted with droopy maple trees that seemed to have given up trying to grow taller.

My grandmother and Uncle Victor were waiting for us on the porch. I knew them only from photographs.

Clumsy introductions outside the car door: your grand-mother, your uncle. No kisses. My father clasped his mother's hand.

"Long time," he said in a neutral voice. She nodded. Victor, after a moment's hesitation, embraced my father.

"What are we, strangers here?"

Embarrassment melted Victor's enthusiasm. He tore himself away to carry my stuff into the house. I stayed outside with my father, who kept his hand on the open car door, clinging to it as tightly as a rodeo rider grips a saddle horn.

My grandmother had planned to feed us, share one big meal together, but my father said he was already behind schedule. She urged him to stay long enough at least to see his father, who was late getting home. My father said he couldn't.

"No twenty minutes?" Constanzia Ambrosio asked. "What's this *schedule?*"

"I'm very late," my father said. "Believe me, Ma."

How strange it was to hear him use that word, and how anxious he was to get moving, as if a bomb were about to explode inside him and he wanted to put distance between himself and his family to protect us from shrapnel. He stood like a chauffeur,

8

handsome in denim jacket and jeans, misty-eyed, apologetic and arrogant at the same time. At last he hugged his mother, a collision of flesh like two human bumper cars.

"I'm sorry she died," Constanzia blurted.

"Me, too," my father said, his voice like a child's. He let go of her and put his hands under my armpits. I braced myself, anticipating a lift.

But his hands went limp against my rib cage. "No," he decided. "You're too big for that now." He crouched and hugged me, said "See you soon" in a broken voice, and split. I don't know which of us felt more relieved.

Relieved, but not for long. The switch was concise, a changing of the guard.

"You're gonna be livin' here awhile, so forget about that Grandma and Grandpa business," said Vic, my roommate, as he lugged double armfuls of my stuff to his room.

"We decided this morning," he said, breathing hard. "No titles. Just Connie and Angie and Vic."

Vic was eighteen years old, five foot ten, a hundred and ninety pounds. His hair was thick as a cluster of wire brush filaments — when he ran his hands through it, it leapt back into place. His hairline ran straight across his forehead and down the sides of his head, with no scallops at the temples. His eyes were brown, like the eyes of everyone else in the house, including me. Only my father had picked up blue eyes, through some errant gene.

Every pair of Vic's pants looked tight on him but he insisted they were comfortable and kept wearing them, despite my grandmother's warning that "They'll make you sterile." His hard belly bulged slightly, like an overinflated tire. His rump bulged in the same way. From time to time he patted his buttocks, rat-a-tat-tat, as if they were bongos.

Vic's room was sparsely furnished: a horsehair mattress on a platform bed, an army fold-out cot (for me), a crucifix on the wall, a photo of the *Journal-American*'s 1960 all-star baseball team ("I'm third from the left; that guy's hat hides my face"), a Frank Sinatra record jacket tacked to the wall, and a Victrola.

"Put that down," he said. I'd picked up his athletic cup and put it against my nose, thinking that was where it was worn. He took it from me and gestured with it.

"Listen. If we're gonna get along we can't be messing around with each other's stuff, okay?"

I nodded. "What is that thing?"

He blushed. "You wear it here," he said, holding it in front of his pants. "In case you get hit with a baseball. You like Sinatra?"

"I guess."

"You *guess?*"

"I don't listen to music much."

Shaking his head, Vic put on a record. "If you hang around here, you gotta like Sinatra." Music filled the room. Vic lay on his back, his stiff mattress crunching as he rolled with the music.

"Look," he announced when the first song ended, "I think you and me can get along real good. See, I'm a ballplayer, I need lots of sleep. Most nights I'll probably go to bed earlier than you."

"What position do you play?" I asked politely.

Vic's eyebrows arched. "You *know* baseball?"

"A little."

"I'm the shortstop. I play in between the second baseman and the third baseman."

"Oh."

"Hey, don't go thinkin' I can't hit, just because I'm an infielder. I hit better than all the outfielders on the team. If you can *call* 'em outfielders. Now listen to this part, how he does this," Vic said, leaping off the bed and cranking up the volume on the Victrola.

Down the street the elevated train rode past, partially drowning out the music. Vic muttered "Damn" and lifted the needle off the disc to play the same part again, scratching the record.

"Here it is," he said solemnly.

I forget the song but at a certain point my uncle was jumping up and down on the bed, singing along. When the song ended he stepped to the floor, pink-faced.

"Like, I get carried away," he said.

10

Connie appeared at the doorway. "I heard you jump, all the way downstairs! You're gonna come right through the floor."

"Sorry, Ma."

"Come on," Connie said. "We'll eat."

When she left, Vic grinned at me. He clasped the back of my neck and led me into the hallway, giving me a slight Indian burn.

On the way in I'd noticed a beautiful dining room where I figured dinner would be served, but Vic surprised me by leading the way to a dark, rickety staircase. Our footsteps echoed as we walked down to the cellar. There were no banisters. I put my palms against the walls for balance, feeling the scrape of rough stucco.

The basement floor was red and yellow tiles. There were windows along one wall, facing the driveway — you got a view of any approaching visitor's ankles. A long table with built-in benches stood under fluorescent lights. My grandfather's oak chair stood at the end of the table.

This was the hub of the home. During Depression years the main floor of the Ambrosio house had been rented out to boarders, so the family had gotten into the habit of using the basement. It was roomy, and always cool in the summertime.

Upstairs, the dining room might as well have been a museum — the mahogany table with its fitted glass top, a buffet table on wheels, heavy long-armed chairs. On the backs of those chairs there were doilies that stayed white year-round, and if you opened a cabinet door in the dining room there was a clicking sound, as if the long-untouched varnished surfaces had welded together. Trapped inside the cabinets were gold-rimmed teacups and saucers with paper tags still glued to their undersides.

But that room couldn't hold a candle to the character of the basement.

For one thing, the floor wasn't level, which Vic demonstrated by placing a baseball on it. The ball was still for an instant, then rolled to the opposite wall.

"Enough with that trick, already," Connie said.

The ceiling was a network of pipes and cables, painted white.

There were upright poles at strategic locations, supporting the house above us.

A bowl of spaghetti sat in the middle of the table, steam rising off it and disappearing into the fluorescents. Connie worked it with a pair of forks.

A cameo portrait of her would have displayed a slender woman. Most of her two hundred and twenty pounds hung way below her breastbone. She was fifty-five years old but her hair was black, save for a pair of white-gray stripes at either side of her part, like catfish whiskers.

Those fleshy arms rose again and again over the spaghetti, curtains of fat dangling and dancing from her upper arms. I was reminded of the flying squirrel pictures I'd seen in my science book.

Her guard was all the way up that night. "You hungry?"

"Yes," I said.

"You didn't eat so good when you and your father lived alone." A statement.

"Sometimes we ate out," I said.

"Mmmm." She was confirming her own thoughts. She put a bowl of spaghetti before me. "You remember the *last* time you ate here?"

I hesitated. "I never ate here before."

"Ah! You don't remember!"

Vic bared his teeth tightly. "*God*, Ma, he was a baby. Why do you bring that up?"

Connie ignored Vic as she loaded his dish. "That was some fight," she said. "I still get knots right here when I think about it." She made a tight fist and held it near her stomach.

"Forget the knots, let's eat," Vic said, winking and squeezing my knee.

Eating noises. Connie pointed at my side dish. "He don't like it."

I was poking my fork into something I later came to love: bread, raisins, capers, and cheese, mixed together and baked into half a red pepper. It reminded me of a little coffin and was too sharp a taste for my first day.

"You don't like it, don't eat it," Connie said, as if she didn't mind.

"This food's gotta grow on you," Vic said. "Eat a mouthful tonight, next time eat two. Before you know it you'll love it."

I held my breath and swallowed a mouthful without chewing. It went down like a giant slippery aspirin.

"I promise it won't taste so bad next time," Vic said. Already I was chasing it with a forkful of spaghetti.

"You talk like my food's poison," Connie said.

"Ah, quit acting hurt, Ma."

Connie pointed at him with a fork. "You. Don't eat so fast."

She had a point. Vic ate with the speed of an animal fleeing predators. He held his fork in his right hand and a piece of Italian bread in his left, which he used to shove food onto the fork. When the bread got mushy with sauce he took a bite off it, then resumed work with the dry bread.

"You'll bite a finger off," she warned him. "Gonna get fat."

"Ah, I burn it off fast," Vic said, a crumb flying from his mouth. He elbowed me, and I found myself smiling and nearly echoing, "Yeah, he burns it up fast," but I stopped myself. Why make an enemy of Connie when I barely knew Vic?

The rest of the meal was quiet, save for low, muffled belches out of Vic. Connie picked up a bit of food that had flown from Vic's mouth and crushed it in a paper napkin.

"Now don't go thinkin' your father don't love you," she said.

A direct hit; my eyes welled with tears. Vic stopped chewing and shot a searing look at her. Then he softened and looked my way, prodding me with an elbow.

"What team do you like, the Yankees or the Dodgers?"

I'd never even heard of the Dodgers. "Yankees."

"Me, too. My father likes the Dodgers, he's ready to kill O'Malley for sendin' 'em out west. Listen, if I make the majors, I'm gonna play for the Yanks."

"Big shot," Connie said, getting up to clear the table. The meal had lasted barely ten minutes.

Vic ignored her. "Only thing is, they got so many good players that hardly anybody gets to play every day, except for guys like

Mantle and Maris." He wiped his mouth with the back of his hand. "See, I don't wanna warm some bench when I get there."

It never occurred to my uncle that he might not make the major leagues, but only that he might get cheated out of valuable playing time once he arrived.

He folded his big hands behind his head. "The big dough's in New York. You set yourself up nice, and then you can get into, like, broadcastin'. That's how come I'm takin' a speech class in school. They remember who you are when you play in New York."

"They forget," Connie said above the thumping of hot water into the sink. "You'd be surprised how fast people forget."

Again he ignored her. His eyes narrowed suddenly. "Who hit more homers last year, Hank Aaron or Mickey Mantle?"

"Mickey Mantle," I guessed.

"Wrong!" Vic roared joyfully. "They both hit forty! See? Here's a guy hittin' homers all over the place and nobody knows about it, 'cause he doesn't play in New York. Poor guy's stuck in Milwaukee."

"Shut up already," Connie said. "Every night we hear this."

She finished washing the dishes. We climbed the stairs to the front parlor and watched TV for a while. Not once had my grandfather's absence been mentioned.

They set my cot up next to the bedroom window, which was open all the way. Warm air puffed through the screen, but you'd be exaggerating if you called it a breeze.

The sheets were stiff, having been hung to dry in the dead air of the basement because it had rained earlier in the week. Getting into bed was like climbing into an envelope.

It wasn't dark and it wasn't quiet. Light filtered in from the street lamp. Two or three radios played somewhere. There were bouts of distant laughter and the screech of brakes on Atlantic Avenue.

"Vic?"

"Yeah?"

"Is there a party going on somewhere?"

"Whatsamatter, can't you sleep?"

14

"Too much *noise*," I complained. "Is it always so bright in here?"

"Are you crazy?" He hated being awakened. "Here, sleep on this side," he said, rising.

"It'll be the same over there," I whined.

"The *same*," he mimicked. "Roll over and close your eyes."

"I already did."

"Well, just shut up."

I heard his irregular breathing across the room and imagined him hating my guts. Now and then he sucked in his breath and socked the pillow with his fist.

I had to break the silence. "My father cried when he left."

"I saw him cry once before," Vic said, startling me with his friendliness. He sat up, propping his head up with his hand.

"The time Dixie died, a long time ago. You never knew Dixie. Swell pooch. Well, anyway, he made him a coffin out of an old desk drawer and stuck him in a pillow case. Buried him right out in the backyard."

Vic flipped onto his belly. "Didn't make any noise when he cried, though. Cried and cried until his eyes got red, but . . . funny." He looked at me. "Didn't he cry when? . . ."

"When my mother died," I said, completing his sentence. "No. Not around me, anyway."

Vic let it sink in. "Weird guy." He reached around under his mattress. "Want a Milky Way?"

"We just brushed our teeth."

"Ah, it's all right, you just rub the chocolate off with your tongue. Here."

He tossed one at me. It landed in the sheets, near my knees.

"Dixie," Vic said through a mouthful of candy. "Once in a while my mother still chucks a bone out in the yard for her, where your father buried her. You can't touch the bone, either. It has to sit on the grave till it rots."

His voice grew serious. "So if you see a bone in the yard, don't touch it, 'cause it's for Dixie."

"Okay," I said.

"Especially if my mother's lookin'."

"I won't. What would I want with a dumb bone, anyhow?"

15

He flipped onto his back. "I'll tell you this — your father's all right. He was good to me when I was a shrimp."

I let his remark go without comment.

"But he was always a little crazy," Vic continued. "Remember when he got married, and everybody told him . . . jeez, do you believe this? I'm expectin' you to remember your father's wedding!"

"What did everybody tell him?"

Vic sighed. "All right. When he got married nobody was marryin' Irish girls. That's the truth. I mean it's no big deal now, but to my mother . . ."

"What?" I said. "Say it."

Vic licked his lips. "My mother thought she wasn't good enough for Sal," he said. "She apologized a million times since then," he added quickly.

The news hit my heart like dull daggers.

"God, I shouldn't have told you that," Vic said, pummeling his bedding. "Why the hell couldn't you fall asleep?"

Vic rolled away from me. I saw the black back of his head, suspected he was nowhere near sleep. I was right. When he rolled to face me again his eyes were wide open.

"Nobody could ever tell your father what to do," he said with fierce pride. "If he had his hand on a hot stove and you told him to take it off he wouldn't. A rock head. Now it's the same thing. He wants to drive away, he drives away. Understand this? Joseph?"

"Joey," I corrected. "No, I don't."

"Want another Milky Way?"

"Yeah."

This one landed on my navel. "They got married real young, they had you right away. . . . He's makin' up for lost time, I figure. Few weeks and he'll be back, guaranteed."

The bedroom door opened. Connie's form filled the doorway. "Talk soft."

"Sorry," Vic said, wincing.

She looked at me. "He keeping you awake?"

"No," I said, "I'm keeping him awake."

"Lie down and shut up," she instructed, pulling the door

closed. It was shut nearly all the way when it opened again, suddenly.

"You ain't foolin' me," she said to both of us. "I find the candy wrappers in the morning."

The door closed for good. Vic's breathing became rhythmic with sleep. I ran my tongue over my teeth to get rid of the last traces of chocolate and caramel.

The night that had given Connie "knots" was still a mystery, but that was all right. I could wait. I certainly wasn't going anywhere.

"Nowhere to go."

I hadn't meant to say it out loud. Vic rolled over.

"What'd you say?"

"Nothing."

He pushed a thick knuckle against one eye. "Aw, c'mon, kid, get used to this place and sleep, already."

CHAPTER TWO

WHEN I awoke the next morning I was alone. "Dad?" I said, then I remembered.

Sheets, blanket, and pillow lay in a thick tangle at the head of Vic's bed, and clothes were scattered on the floor. It didn't seem late. I finally found a clock under one of Vic's undershirts. It was a little after eight.

I tugged on yesterday's shirt and pants and walked into the hallway. The window at the end of the hall faced the backyard. It was a plot of black dirt about ten feet wide and fifteen feet long, next to the garage. A wild, snaggled, fruitless vine grew up the side of the wall. A few weeds speckled the dirt, and a thin beard of moss. Connie threw her decomposable garbage out there — melon rinds, coffee grounds, orange peels. The sweet smell of decay rose to the window.

I could hear water running and smelled coffee from downstairs. Still half asleep I went to the bathroom.

The door was open. I let out a yelp upon finding my grandfather, Angelo, shaving at the sink.

The whole room smelled of Rise. Angelo wore gray work pants and a sleeveless undershirt, and he was putting the final touches of lather on his face with a brush, even though the cream came from a can. He spotted me in the mirror.

"Hey." He smiled, teeth bright yellow against the snowy lather. He took a bent cigarette from the edge of the sink and puffed on it, rinsed his razor, and pinched my cheek.

"Boy, did you grow." He turned to the mirror and began scraping his cheek. "If you want to use the toilet I won't look," he promised.

"I don't have to go," I lied. My bladder was bursting.

"Didn't you just get up?"

"Yeah."

"So use it, use it," he urged. "Everybody's gotta go when they get up." He banged the razor on the edge of the sink.

I stood before the head. My cock was tinier than I'd ever seen it — I imagined a cork inside it, blocking the flow. Diplomatically, Angie started to whistle. I moaned with relief as the urine started to flow, aiming for a rust streak at the back of the bowl.

"So," he said. "You're staying here."

As if I had a choice. "Uh-huh," I said.

"Good, I'm glad."

"Where were you last night?"

He turned around to look at me. I was through pissing and shook myself, tugged the zipper. "I'm sorry. It's none of my business," I said meekly, but Angie just laughed.

"I got home three hours ago. Don't tell your grandmother."

"Didn't she wake up when you got home?"

"Nah. I'm always quiet." He finished shaving, filled the sink with cold water, and splashed his face. He rubbed it with a towel, and I noticed the furrow of eyebrow across his forehead. It was one thick line of hair, unbroken over the bridge of his nose. The hair on his head was silver but the brows were jet black. Looking him in the eye was like looking at a cobra.

With wet hands he rubbed his scalp and began combing his thick hair straight back. A grin tugged a corner of his mouth. He knew how good he looked.

I asked, "How can you get into bed with her and not wake her up?"

He shut the water off. "My room's at the other end of the hall." He flicked the comb through his hair once more and put on a plaid sport shirt. He rubbed my hair and turned to leave the bathroom, buttoning his shirt.

"Did you have a fight with her?" I asked.

"*What?*" His voice was shrill.

"I mean, how come you have different rooms?"

He tilted back his head and let out a howl. "The questions you ask!" he said. "I say she snores. She says I snore. That's how come." He reached into his shirt pocket and gave me a pack of Wrigley's Spearmint Gum with three sticks left. "See you later," he said as he left, laughing.

When I was through washing my face and brushing my teeth I went downstairs, where Connie sat with another woman.

"He finally got up," the woman announced, as if I'd kept her waiting.

Connie said, "This is my friend Grace Rothstein from next door." We exchanged stares. I even sniffed the air, sensing an enemy. She lowered her head and bared large, rodentlike teeth. She was ten years younger than Connie, tall and whipcord lean. Her hair was bleached an outrageous blond.

"Coffee," Connie said to me, moving to pour it. I'd hardly ever drunk it — my mother used to say it was bad for me. I felt flattered and doused it with sugar, pouring from a glass cylinder that obviously had been swiped from a diner.

"Where's Vic?" I asked.

"At graduation practice," Connie said.

"Where's Angie?"

"He has a plumbing job today, with Freddie Gallo. You didn't meet Freddie yet."

"Eh, I don't know how they work when they stay out late like that," Grace said.

"My husband never needed a lot of sleep."

"Thank God for that, Con, he never got any. My Rudy, he's always there, even when I don't want him."

They cackled. I sucked down the last of my coffee. There was a thick, sluggish trail of sugar at the bottom of the cup. I stuck my finger in it.

"How come you and Angie have your own rooms?"

Grace cackled with renewed vigor but Connie fell silent. She hissed something at Grace before turning to me.

"That don't concern you," she said.

My ears grew hot. "I'm sorry. My mother and father had the same room," I explained lamely, sucking my finger.

"Ahh!" Grace exclaimed, prodding Connie's side, "The Irish, they like that!"

Grace got up from the table and reached for an upright rolling cart that had been leaning against the table. "What else besides the spinach?"

"Nothing. My husband will get the bread."

"Eh. He's good for something."

Grace grunted her good-bye and left. We heard the cart wheels bang as she dragged the thing up the cellar steps. Connie moved to the stove.

"She's Italian," Connie said. "She married a Jew."

I didn't even know what a Jew was, but I knew what "Irish" meant and asked what Grace's crack about them had meant.

Without turning to face me Connie said, "My friend's a little crazy."

"She was talking about my mother."

"Yes."

"What did my mother 'like'?"

Connie's face was flushed. "Your father," she answered. "Don't make me explain Grace. Here, take more coffee."

"No, thank you."

"All right, I'll make you an egg."

"I'm not hungry."

"That's crazy, everybody's hungry when they get up in the mor —"

A gigantic engine roar from the street interrupted her. I jumped with fright but Connie didn't flinch.

"That's Johnny," she said. "He's gonna give us all heart attacks."

20

"Johnny who?"

"Johnny Gallo. Your grandfather's buddy's son. He plays with his car every day. You'll meet Freddie later. Go meet Johnny now." She pointed toward the cellar door.

Grateful for the dismissal, I cut through the furnace room, where strings of peppers hung drying. From the back door a set of steps led to the long driveway, bounded on the other side by Grace's house.

Directly across the street from where my father had dumped me was a black car surrounded by a halo of bluish smoke. Its hood was open, and a young man hunched over the engine. It roared again, seemingly of its own accord. A fresh spout of smoke surrounded the car.

By this time I was coughing. Johnny noticed me and killed the motor from where he stood.

"Bet you're Vic's nephew, the kid whose old man run off."

"My father's on a trip," I coughed.

"Whatever." He wiped his hands on a rag. A large-boned, dull-eyed girl sat on the curb, sucking noisily on half an orange. When she finished it she threw the rind across the street and watched it roll, her mouth hanging open.

Johnny jerked his thumb over his shoulder. "She's retarded," he said. "Look at her. Ya believe she's almost fifteen?"

The girl's knees were pebbled with dirty scabs. She wore a loose red dress, scuffed patent leather shoes, and thin white socks. The mouths of the socks were stretched wider than her calves. There was a wet ring around her mouth dotted with bits of orange. Her hand idly massaged curbside rubble.

The door of the house behind her opened. A frazzled-looking woman in a pink nightgown leaned on the knob as she stuck her face out.

"Louisa! Your bath is ready."

Louisa seemed to react from the feet up, and staggered to a standing position. When she was finally erect she turned and bolted up the porch stairs, like a horse flicked with a whip.

"Poor bastid," Johnny murmured. "Do me a favor, kid, start the car."

21

I slid behind the wheel, tingling with fear. "I don't have a license."

"Ah, don't worry, you ain't goin' anywhere. Don't even press the gas pedal, I can do it under here." Johnny's head disappeared, reappeared redder. "Now," he commanded.

I twisted the key. The motor squealed like a cat being strangled.

"You're killin' the battery!" Johnny screamed. A kid no bigger than me slid behind the wheel, having entered from the driver's side. The key turned. A sneakered foot pumped the gas pedal expertly, zoop-zoop-zoop.

"Faster, Johnny?" the kid called. A *girl*.

"Hold her down for a sec, Mel," Johnny shouted. The motor roared steadily for five seconds. "Okay, that's good." He slammed the hood down. I followed her out the driver's side.

Johnny wiped his hands again. "Mel, this here's Joey, he's Vic's nephew."

We stared without shaking hands. Mel wore cutoff jeans, a T-shirt, and boys' black Keds. Her hair was nearly as short as mine, parted on the left. Her broad nose made her look like a street fighter. She was skinny but muscular.

"Well Chrissakes somebody say hello," Johnny said.

"Hi," I ventured.

"See you guys later," Johnny said, getting into the car. "Sorry I yelled atcha, kid." He drove off.

Mel cracked her knuckles. Her hands were wide. I looked at my own slender hands and rested them on my hips. I felt the bulge of chewing gum in my pocket, took out the pack, and held it out.

"Gum?"

"Thanks." She took a piece. We crossed the street and sat on Connie's stoop.

"I never started a car before," I said.

"Gotta get used to it," she assured me. I watched her chew the gum. It was the first thing I'd ever shared with another child, save for the loan of my eraser at the Roslyn Country Day School.

"You sure do it good," I said.

Mel shrugged. "I'm used to it. Johnny lets me do it all the time." She tried to blow a bubble but the gum was too soft. She tucked the wad back by her molars.

"Watch 'Superman' last night?"

"No, I missed it."

"It was the one where the two guys have a fight over whose girlfriend makes the best lemon meringue pie and so they have a contest and one of the guys goes all the way to Alaska to try and steal a pie from his old girlfriend's new boyfriend."

"That's a dumb one," I said.

"I know, but it's cool when Superman crashes through the ice."

"That guy can't really fly, he's just an actor."

"Uh-*duh*. Everybody knows that." Mel cracked the gum. "How come your father ran away?"

I spat my gum out. "Why does everybody *say* that?" I screamed. "He didn't run away. He's on a *trip*."

"Yeah?" Mel challenged. "Where?"

I slumped on the steps, feeling rough bricks against my back. "I don't know."

"When's he comin' back?"

"Soon."

"Butcha don't know *when*?"

"He's got a lot of stuff to do," I said evenly.

Mel shrugged. "I got no parents. Live with my aunt and uncle up the street." She pointed.

"I'm sorry," I said.

"It ain't your fault."

"Well, I'm sorry anyway. I got no mother."

We fell silent, looking at our sneakers.

"My cousin is Vic's girlfriend," Mel said. "When they have kids the kids have to call me 'Aunt Mel' on account of I'm practically a sister, like."

"Vic didn't tell me he was getting married," I said. "When are they getting married?"

"I don't know."

"Then how do you know they are?" I challenged.

Mel stood. I was startled by the way her face darkened. The hands bunched into fists. "Listen, you, they've been goin' out for *three years*."

I hoped she wouldn't hit me. Gradually, her fists loosened. She sat again. "Everybody knows they're gonna get married, that's all."

Momentary silence. Then she said softly, "I was sick last night. I threw up. Macaroni came through my nose."

She was trying to make up. "Really? Through your *nose?*"

"Yeah."

"Ewww."

"But I feel better now." She scratched a mosquito bite on her calf. "How old are you?"

"Ten."

She smiled. "I'm eleven."

"I'll be eleven in December," I countered.

"Well, I'll be twelve in September." She touched her fingertips, counting silently. "Hey! When you're still ten I'll be twelve," she said triumphantly.

"Who cares?" I said, but she knew I did.

She pounded my shoulder. "Let's get a lemon ice. Come on, I got a quarter."

On the walk to the lemon-ice stand she softened considerably. She told me she hated her full name, Carmela Maria Di-Giovanna, and that her parents had died in a car crash, and that she'd lived in her aunt's house for two years and planned to stay at least a few more years. She hated cats, loved dogs, and hoped to play professional baseball.

"But I'm a girl," she added grimly as we reached Willie's lemon-ice stand. "I might wind up just bein' a coach. Two, Willie."

A fat, benevolent-looking man with a wide bald head scooped ice into white cups, shaping it into smooth mounds with the back of the scoop. He gave them to me while Mel fished out her quarter.

Willie gave back a nickel. "I ain't seen you before."

"This is the kid who's living with Vic whose father ran away,"

Mel explained. I was tired of giving my version of the story so I didn't.

"Pleased to meet you," Willie said. "I knew your father, he was okay."

"He's not *dead*," I snapped, sinking my teeth into the ice. It wasn't like anything I'd ever tasted before — soft and tart, with no stiffness to bite through.

Sucking our ices, we returned to Connie's stoop. "Willie's okay," Mel said, "but he was a bastard not to give us these free, you just movin' here and everything."

Then she mapped out the territory of Shepherd Avenue for me.

A block beyond the lemon-ice stand was a deli owned by Rudy Rothstein, Grace's husband.

"Vic calls her 'Aunt Grace' even though you ain't related, on account of Grace always goes to the store for your grandmother," Mel informed me. "She don't get around too good, your grandmother."

Mel lived half a block from us. In between us lived an old lady we only saw when she swept her porch, and a family with a new baby. The other families she didn't really know.

On the opposite side of the street the only people I knew so far were Louisa, the retarded girl, and Johnny Gallo. A huge part of the block was a sewing machine factory, which went all the way to Atlantic Avenue. Mel showed me a rectangular box chalked onto the brick side of that building, with a large white "X" that connected its corners.

"Our strike zone," she explained. "Vic taught me to play stickball here. I'll teach you."

"I'm not allowed to play baseball."

Mel cocked her head as if I'd just spoken in Arabic. "Whaddya mean, you're not *allowed?*"

I swallowed. "My mother told me not to."

It was the truth. Two years earlier my father, sensing something weird about the way I was growing up, signed me up in the local Little League even though I'd never even held a bat in my hands. On my first and only time at bat a spider-limbed boy named Phil McElhenny let fly with a wild pitch that conked me on the head. Luckily I was wearing a gigantic plastic helmet with earlaps that reached below my cheeks, so when I fell to my ass it was more from shock than injury.

But my mother didn't know that. She ran onto the field in hysterics, tore off the helmet, probed my skull for dents, and screamed over her shoulder at Phil. She weighed maybe a hundred pounds, but she *carried* me off that field in front of all those jeering kids and their parents, loaded me into the Comet, and ran red lights on the way to the family doctor, who informed her that not only would I live but that if I wanted to, I could go back and finish the game.

"Over my dead body," my mother said, and it was piano lessons and a new doctor for me from then on.

"Your *mother* told ya not to?" Mel said, but not maliciously. "How come?"

"I got hit in the head once, that's how come."

Mel scratched her head. "But your mother's dead. Do ya hafta obey people when they die?"

"I don't know." God, I felt alone. "*Your* parents are dead," I countered. "Do you still obey them?"

Mel shrugged. "They never told me not to do nothing." She smiled, scratching her nose. Suddenly I didn't feel so alone. "Well if ya don't play ball what do you *do?*"

I had to think it over. "I like to walk."

She laughed. "Listen, nobody around here *walks.* Look, I'll teach you stickball, it's easy. It ain't like baseball. The ball's soft. Ya won't be disobeyin' your mother. Come on."

She pointed. "If you hit a ball across the street it's a home run, except if you hit one now you lose the damn ball."

She walked me across the street to show me why. Mounds of dirt surrounded a deep, ugly hole that was to be the foundation of a fast-food hamburger joint.

We went to the lip of the hole. There was a puddle of dark water at the bottom of it, and a couple of pink Spaldeens floated on its surface like bobbing apples.

"Damn this thing," Mel crooned, spitting into the hole. I envied the way she could do that — a clean, round ball of spit

26

smacked the water like a coin. I tried but managed only a sloppy spray.

"Let's get outta here," Mel said. "The workers'll get back from lunch soon; they'll scream at us."

From down the street a shrill voice called her name.

"Get in here! You were sick last night!"

She rolled her eyes. "I'm supposed to be in bed. I sneaked out."

"Oh."

She reddened. "I . . . wanted to meet you."

"Oh."

"Well, I better go."

"Thanks for the lemon ice," I said, but she was already tearing up the block.

Vic was remarkably patient that afternoon.

"The trouble is you're lookin' at me but you ain't lookin' at the ball," he said, twirling it on his long fingers. "Keep your *eye* on this baby."

I nodded and toed the rough sidewalk with the tip of my sneaker. The stickball bat, a sawed-off broomstick handle wrapped with black tape, seemed like a big toothpick. I'd missed ten straight pitches. If I'd been in Roslyn I could have fled to the safety of my room, but this was Brooklyn.

"It's impossible," I whined.

"No, it isn't."

"The bat's too skinny."

"It don't matter how skinny the bat is because you're hittin' the ball with the middle of it, Joey."

I didn't understand that but I let it ride.

"Keep lookin' at the ball," he said. "Ted Williams says you should see the ball even when you're hittin' it."

"Who's Ted Williams?" I asked, but Vic had gone into his windup and lobbed the ball in. Behind him Mel, who'd sneaked out of her house, braced herself in anticipation of a hit. I swung and missed. Eleven pitches. Tears stung my eyes.

"I want to go in the house," I said, my voice breaking.

But Mel wouldn't let me.

"Don't throw it like that, Vic!" she shrieked. "Jesus, nobody can hit a ball like that! Just throw it regular, he'll hit it."

I wiped my eyes. Vic heeded her advice as if she were a peer. "You may be right," he said. He threw a regular fastball, and I astonished myself by hitting a clean single that Mel fielded on the short hop. She winged the ball in to Vic, who threw an identical pitch. I hit it straight at him. He could have fielded it but he let it split his legs.

"All right!" he exclaimed. "I knew you could do it! Everybody in this family can hit."

"I'm not hitting it far," I said, secretly aglow with pride.

"Ah, that's okay. You're a singles hitter. Nothing wrong with singles hitters, they make good leadoff men." He threw again and I hit it over his head. It bounced toward the open foundation but Mel fielded it at the last second.

"I ain't always gonna groove 'em like this," Vic warned, but there was pride in his voice. I could hit.

At the supper table I met Freddie Gallo. He and my grandfather had worked together that day, doing a small cement job somewhere in the neighborhood. Angie, a plumber, and Freddie, a bull of a laborer, were both retired, but they took on jobs together to pad their union pensions.

But I think they worked more for the companionship than for the extra money. They also caroused together at night — no one ever told me where.

Freddie sat at the end of the bench near Angie. They both smelled of Lava soap and their hands, hard-scrubbed, were pink. Still, there were deep lines of dirt under their fingernails and along the creases of their necks.

Still sweating from stickball, Vic and I sat next to each other.

"The kid's a natural hitter," Vic said, his hand on my back. Angie smiled neutrally at me.

"You're both sweating," Connie said.

Vic laughed. "How are we supposed to keep from sweating, Ma?"

Connie didn't answer as she ladled vegetable soup out into big bowls. It was full of beans, tomatoes, lentils, and spinach.

28

Such flavors! Connie was able to extract tastes from foods like no one I'd ever known. The vegetables seemed alive in the broth, and the soup was so thick you needed a fork and a spoon to eat it. When shreds of grated cheese hit its steaming oily surface they disappeared like snowflakes landing on a warm sidewalk.

Angie's manners were impeccable: though he was served first, he waited until everyone had food before starting. Freddie was a chowhound to rival Vic, slurping and letting out belches he only half muffled. Freddie was nearly six feet tall but he looked even taller. He was a stretched version of my grandfather, a bit leaner, with longer, stringier muscles. He wore a black T-shirt that showed off his round pectorals and pinched his upper arms. Veins and tendons coursed down his forearms like telephone cords.

Only his head looked old. His eyes were narrow and he was almost totally bald, the narrow scallop of bristly hair near his ears a close-cropped stubble.

There was no formal introduction to Freddie Gallo — he'd heard about me and I'd heard about him. A nod and a grunt sufficed.

When we finished the soup Connie cleared the table, leaving behind wine and cherry soda. Freddie and Angie rehashed the day's work while Vic idly pushed crumbs around the tablecloth.

Angie went to the back of the cool cellar and returned with enormous oranges and apples. Connie brought him a sharp knife and he began cutting the apple into sections.

He rolled an orange at me and asked me to peel it, but its skin was too hard and thick for my fingernails to penetrate. Laughing, Freddie took the orange from me.

"When you work you'll get hard hands so you can do this," he said. "When I was your age I was tyin' grapevines to poles in Naples. They hadda hire kids to do it — we fit easy between the vines."

He ripped the skin off the orange.

"You and your stories," Vic said.

Freddie tossed a piece of peel aside. "You, when are *you* gonna make a buck?"

"I'm playin' ball," Vic said calmly. "When I sign with a club I'll have more money than you ever made tyin' vines."

Freddie cackled knowingly, a sound that warned: wait, wait.

"Enough already," Angie said. He jabbed a slice of apple onto the end of his knife and offered it to me.

"Johnny makes good money working on cars," Freddie said. "Be a mechanic. If you don't make it in baseball you won't starve."

"I'll make it," Vic said. "Don't worry about it."

"I ain't the one who has to worry." Freddie pointed. "You, you could break your leg, you could get hit in the head with a pitch —"

"Oh! Shut up already!" Connie said from the sink. "You make me shiver."

Vic yawned and said, "I don't want to get my hands dirty, anyhow." He kneed me under the table to let me know he was after Freddie's goat, which he got with ease.

"Dirt is *good*," Freddie said. "A real man ain't afraid of it."

"Freddie. Your wife's callin'," Connie said, but he ignored the hint.

"How come you don't eat with your wife?" I asked. Freddie stared at me, then looked at Angie.

"What's this kid, a wise guy?"

"No," I answered. "It's not nice when people have to eat alone. My father always said that."

"Your father!" he exploded. "He should talk!"

He was sorry the moment he said it, and put a knuckly hand over his mouth.

"Let's all calm down," Angie said softly. Freddie turned to Vic and picked up the thread of the other conversation.

"I never, never — you listening? — *never* came home from work with clean hands." He passed the peeled orange to Angie and looked at me. "I got buried alive, kid. *Twice* they buried me alive."

"Here we go again," Vic sighed.

"Twice," Freddie said again, cupping his hands around his wine glass as if to warm them. "Ten feet down the first time,

fifteen the second." His eyes glittered. I was suddenly afraid of
him.

"Why?" I finally asked.

"Because I wouldn't join the union. Because the boss paid
me twenty-one bucks a day and everyone else eighteen. Well,
the guys didn't like that, so one day they say, 'Fred, join the
union.' I told 'em I was doin' okay without it."

"Eh, that's all," Connie said.

He began to nod. "Same day, late in the afternoon, the boys
are puttin' away the tools. Foreman says, 'Somebody go down
and get that goddamn pick we left behind.' I'm not doin' anything, so down I go."

He gulped wine. Connie said, "He's talkin' so much he's
dry."

"Ten feet," Freddie continued. "Even in August it's cold like
ice in that hole. You press your fist against the side and it gets
numb. Am I right, Anj?"

"Always cold in a hole," Angie said.

"Next thing I know I hear the dirt slidin'. Slidin' like somebody's pushin' it, not like it's fallin' by itself. I turn my head to
look and the dirt gets in my eyes, so now I'm blind. But I know
what's goin' on, all right."

Freddie's color changed, as if a wash of black ink had been
brushed over his face. Angie poured more wine for him. The
apple slice in front of him was browning.

"I get down on my hands and knees and put my arms around
my head to make an air pocket," he continued softly. "So's I
can keep breathin' awhile, you know?"

He demonstrated, putting his head on the table. He stayed
in place so long the top of his head went pink.

Connie snapped him out of it by saying, "You should have
joined the union."

He lifted his head. "Damn the union!"

I swallowed. "Then what?"

He grinned evilly. "What could I do but wait? I wait for the
bastards to dig, I listen for the shovels. Tons of dirt on my back,
I can't move an inch."

He leaned toward me, his face inches from mine. "Darkness," he said, the word riding to my face on a wave of wine. "Darkness like no man knows. You think you know what darkness is? Only corpses know. You shut off the light in the bedroom but the light from the street shines through the curtains. You can go in the closet but the light still comes in under the door." He prodded my shoulder. "If you wake up at three in the morning don't you see the whole room, the pictures on the walls clear as day?"

"The light bothers him at night," Vic said. Freddie snapped him an irritated look for interrupting his narrative.

"They waited till they thought I was dead," Freddie said. "But oh, how I fooled 'em! When I heard the shovels comin' close I made like I was dead. The lousy shit foreman puts his hands around my waist to pull me up and I turn around and punch him, boom! Knocked him out cold."

"Your language," Connie commented.

"He's heard worse," Freddie said, the spooky mood dissolving with the end of his story. Actually, I'd rarely heard vulgarity from either of my parents. Freddie drained his wine glass and held it out for more.

"That happened *twice*?" I said. He nodded. "How come you fell for it twice?"

Vic roared with laughter. Angie hid his face so Freddie wouldn't see him smile. Freddie waved me off.

"Ah, *you* got nothin' to worry about. You'll go to college and work in an office and have soft hands like a prince."

"Wouldn't be the worst thing in the world," Angie said.

"Feel these hands." Freddie cupped his hands around my elbow, then dragged them down toward my wrist in a snaky spiral. *"That's* how a man's hands should feel."

Connie said, "All your hard hands ever got you was buried twice. The second time you were unconscious, you almost died. So shut up."

"But I got out!" he exclaimed, releasing my wrist. "By Christ, I got out!" Blood tingled back into my hand.

"Calluses," Connie said wearily. "Your tongue oughta have

calluses, the way you talk. And in the end you joined that union."

"They made a rule," Freddie said meekly. "You can't fight a rule."

Connie clapped her hands. "Enough. All of you put on clean shirts, we have to be there in twenty minutes."

"Where?" Angie asked, his brow knotting. "What's going on?"

"The christening party for the new baby down the block. I told you about it last week."

"Another present," Angie moaned. "You take care of it?"

"We're giving money. Freddie, go home and change." She spoke as if he were a child. He climbed off the bench without thanking her for supper and cracked Vic across the back of his head with three knuckles.

"Don't be so scared of dirt, Mr. All-Star."

Vic rubbed his skull and said, "Let's compare bankbooks in a year."

The house with the baby was near the train, a sister house to my grandfather's. The only differences were green shutters instead of black ones, and a slightly less ornate wrought-iron fence in front.

The family's name was Caruso. They lived on the second floor, above the new mother's parents. As we entered the vestibule a strong, soupy odor filled our nostrils, but that smell was displaced by the tang of laundered diapers as we climbed the stairs.

I stayed close to Vic as we made our way across the crowded flat, a porpoise following a ship. He shook hands with people, dutifully pecked hairy-faced women on the cheek, and introduced me with the word, "S'mynephew."

He got us soda in paper cups. We sat on a long couch, crinkling the plastic slipcovers. The place was so jammed with covered furniture that it would have seemed crowded with no people in it. Even the long windows lent no sense of space — they were veiled in white fishnet curtains that were rough to the touch, like screens. They billowed at the faintest breeze.

I sipped my soda and gagged. "This went *bad*, Vic, it's sour," I whispered.

He sipped from my cup. "It's fine."

"That's not what Coke tastes like."

"You dope. You never had cream soda? Hey, look at this guy comin' in now, he's a real character. Junkman. Lives across the street from us."

Mel hadn't told me about Zip Aiello. He was short and wide-hipped and his thinning brown hair was slicked straight back. His mouth was set in a severe pucker, as if the tang of lemon juice were on his tongue.

He made his way toward us, hands deep in the pockets of his loose gray pants. Vic introduced me and Zip went into a nodding routine, as if some biting, ironic truth had been whispered into his ear by his Creator. I lifted my hand to shake with him, but his balled fist never left his pocket.

"I seen you from the window," he said.

Vic winked at me. "So what's happening, Zip?"

Zip shrugged. "Found a little copper," he said casually. "Thirty, forty feet. Leaders. Guy was throwin' 'em out, puttin' up new ones. Amoolinum."

"Aluminum?"

"Whatever. What are you, an English teacher?"

"Gonna sell it?"

"Sure. Everybody knows copper's better. Don't rot. Amoolinum pits. Copper turns green but it don't rot."

He walked off without saying good-bye, having gone back into his nodding routine. Connie passed by and saw him on the way to the cake table.

"Eh, but what's he thinkin' about?" she asked. "He'll wind up killin' all of us."

Vic said, "He's the champion bottle collector in the neighborhood, too. He sees a bottle in the curb, he'll jump out of a speedin' car to pick it up." There was affection in Vic's voice, then he suddenly lost his relaxed look and stiffened as a heavyset girl made her way toward us.

"This is Rosemary," he said. She hooked her arm through

his elbow. "We go out," he added, sort of apologetically. Rosemary forced a smile at me. Her face had so much makeup on it that it didn't reflect light. She pulled Vic to the other side of the room to talk with him.

Unmoored, I drifted about until Mel caught my elbow.

"They made me put this dress on." It looked awful, loose at the chest and snug at the waist. She kept tugging it down in back.

Suddenly there was a chorus of "oohs" and "aahs" throughout the room as the new mother appeared, baby in her arms. The infant was like the stamen of a flower, surrounded by blanket petals.

The mother's hair was pulled back into a ponytail. It was a few seconds before I even noticed her husband behind her, a skinny man in a dark suit. He touched a hand to the baby, then indicated the gift-laden table.

"You've been so generous," he said in a quivering voice. "It's wonderful for our Joyella to have such wonderful friends as she starts her life."

Everyone murmured approval, but as the new father was about to continue his speech there was a commotion in the stairway. A man in a three-piece white suit walked with great solemnity to the parents. His silvery hair looked freshly barbered, and a gold watch chain was looped across his round belly. There was a fat red carnation in his lapel.

"Holy shit, that's Ammiratti," Mel hissed. "He's on everyone's shit list."

With a flourish he placed an envelope on the gift table, pecked the mother on the cheek, and shook hands with the father. He apologized that his wife couldn't come — her stomach was troubling her. The father nodded without offering words of sympathy.

Crimson crept up Ammiratti's neck. He mopped his face with a handkerchief and bowed to the silent room, then left. Conversation resumed when the echo of his footsteps faded.

"A flower in his lapel," Grace Rothstein said shrilly. "Forty cents every day for a fresh flower!" She slapped her right hand into the crook of her left elbow, kinking it into an obscene right angle. Everyone but one guy laughed, and I knew he had to be her husband, "Uncle Rudy."

"Ammiratti's a rich bastard," Mel explained. "He owns a lotta houses, plus that empty lot where the hole is. *Everybody* hates him for that."

"How come?"

" 'Cause burger joints bring colored people," she said, irritated by my ignorance. "He screwed us. He sold everybody out even though he has more money than everybody else put together."

She bit into a thick cream pastry. I knew she was parroting the words of the adults she lived with.

"The balls on him," she continued, through a mouthful of cream. "Walkin' into a roomful o' people who hate you and pretendin' they love you."

Johnny Gallo came in, sticking out in that chubby crowd like a foreigner. He had no hips or buttocks, and wore black T-shirts and slacks that made him look even taller and slimmer than he was. His sideburns were shaved high and his black hair was combed straight back. He looked like a walking sperm cell.

Mel had a mild crush on Johnny, and ditched me to join him. I was marooned in the midst of all those cliques — Vic and Rosemary, Angie and Freddie, Connie and Grace. For the first time in two days I felt a real pang for my father.

The baby lay asleep in her bassinet. I felt a little jealous of her, wishing I was little enough to climb in there and lie beside her.

"You like it here okay?" Vic asked that night when the two of us were in bed.

"I guess," I said.

"When I get a little more time we'll play more stickball and stuff. I gotta practice right now, with the playoffs and everything."

"I don't mind."

"Hey. I forgot to ask you how you liked my girl Rosemary."

36

"She's nice," I lied.

"Yeah, she's somethin'," Vic said. "She got me through school, you know? Helpin' me with homework and stuff. Never yelled at me, no matter how stupid I was."

Before falling asleep I noticed Vic staring at the ceiling, smiling.

CHAPTER THREE

WHILE coffee percolated each morning, Connie combed out her hair and braided it. I would watch from the doorway to the basement, without her knowing it.

Loose, it hung to her breasts. Her expression while she worked the comb was somber, as if the stroking motion stirred up thoughts of her life's mistakes. She also looked glum because she didn't put her teeth in until she was through braiding.

Save for six brown lower teeth, the dentures were a complete set. They didn't embarrass her. She had given birth to her kids in the days before doctors knew about calcium loss, so she felt the missing teeth weren't her fault.

Besides, she took exceptional pride in her moist skin, boasting that she'd never had a pimple in her life. Three "no's" accounted for that — no restaurant food, no liquor, no makeup.

Talcum powder and aspirins were the only things in the medicine cabinet. She even made the dresses she wore, simple tentlike things with buttons at the cleavage.

Only her underwear was elaborate. She referred to her girdle as a "harness," full of hooks and straps. Hanging on the shower rod to dry, her pink slips looked like sails. They billowed when you opened the bathroom door.

She wore black nun shoes, and she didn't walk so much as she tilted from foot to foot. With each step the entire plane of her flat foot came down, thunking decisively.

Overhead, on the top floor, lived another person, who trod so lightly that I didn't even know he existed until my third day there. His name was Agosto Palmieri. We knew he was there only when he played his opera records.

With the exception of this peculiar loner, most of the other people I'd met came out to see Vic play baseball.

Even the meticulous Angie ate supper fast on game nights. On the first one I was there for Vic sat with his cap on backwards and his feet in slippers, cleats at his side. He said the hat made him feel lucky, so Angie waived standard table etiquette.

His uniform was creamy white, with blue piping down the outside of his legs and "Lane" in slow, lazy script across the chest. When he flexed his arms the piping near his biceps jumped.

Grace and Freddie arrived at the end of supper to catch a ride to the ballpark with Angie. Even Johnny Gallo stopped by, wiping his hands on a rag before shaking hands with Vic to wish him good luck.

Rosemary never came over before a game. She and Mel were waiting for us at the Franklin K. Lane bleachers when we all got there.

Vic was the same height as my father but he looked squatter because of his thickly muscled build. Shirts buttoned all the way up pinched his neck, nearly strangling him.

But he looked slimmer in a baseball uniform, graceful and confident. It was the end of his season but he was hitting an astonishing .500. He was the center of attention even during warmups with his teammates, joking and laughing, making lightning throws to first base with easy, almost casual motions.

Angie intently watched the practice session, as if it were the actual game. Connie sat back, arms folded under her breasts, a stance she maintained throughout the game.

Mel pointed at Vic. "Now you'll see a *real* ballplayer," she bragged, as if he were *her* uncle. "I'll bet he gets us free tickets when he's with the Yankees, Joey."

Rosemary sat with a woolen shawl across her shoulders, knitting needles and ball of yarn in hand. She made it clear that she was in no way a baseball fan but in *all* ways a dedicated woman, loyal enough to endure nine innings of boredom.

38

She turned to me with a smile and said, "What are you reading this summer?"

"Nothing."

The smile vanished. "Nothing? No books?"

I shrugged. "There's no school."

"That's no reason to stop reading."

I just stared back at her. She shook her head as if I were a terminal case. "You sound just like Mel," she said sadly. "I have wonderful books to lend, if you'd like them."

"Okay," I said, knowing I'd never take her up on it.

Lane won, 12 to 3. Angie sat still through his son's two diving catches on the infield dirt, his two singles, and even his eighth-inning home run, afraid that he'd jinx Vic by cheering.

That homer was something to see, a white missile soaring into the growing dusk and bouncing on the street beyond. Head bowed, Vic made the slow, heavy trot around the bases to the screams of Freddie Gallo. Mel grabbed my shoulder and couldn't stop shaking me. Rosemary, who had dozed off, asked crankily, "What happened?"

Nobody answered. I remember wanting to tell the strangers behind us who the hero was, that I shared a bedroom with him. For the first time in my life I wished I was someone else.

When the last out was made — a pop-up to Vic, fittingly enough — the team swarmed *him*, instead of the winning pitcher. Seconds after the catch Vic tore himself away from the guys and trotted to us, scrambled up the bleachers, and dutifully pecked Rosemary on the cheek.

"Be right back," he promised, hustling back to the field. His cleats left deep scars on the seats.

True to his word, Vic returned moments later, having changed from spikes into sneakers.

"Hey, Vic, come on!" one of his teammates shouted.

"Can't!" he called back, gesturing at all of us. He gave one spike to me and one to Mel, allowing us to knock the dirt out of them.

"Ah, come with us for a little while," the teammate persisted.

"I gotta go!" Vic yelled, sounding sort of timid. When the game ended so did his magic.

The ride back to Shepherd Avenue was crowded, with Mel and Rosemary added to the car. The inside of the car had a nice smell to it, a workman's smell — grease, epoxy, cement, and other things Angie carried to his jobs.

Vic sat in front, wedged between Angie and Rosemary. I sat on Freddie's bony knees. His beer breath blew warmly past my ear.

"That was your longest homer yet," Freddie said. "Madonna mi, when it went over the fence I swear it was still climbin'."

While the rest of us chorused our agreement Rosemary said, "You should have taken a shower, Vic."

"School showers are filthy," Connie said. "In five minutes he's home in his own bathroom."

Awkward silence. Mel said, "The singles were good, too."

"Yeah, well, that pitcher stunk," Vic said, uneasy with all the praise being heaped upon him.

Angie patted Vic's knee at red lights. We got a quart of lemon ice at Willie's and ate it on the porch. Vic took five minutes to shower, coming out with his wet hair slicked back. Freddie described his titanic homer to any passerby willing to listen.

The commotion excited my bladder, and when I went to the bathroom Vic's clothes were all over the floor. He'd obviously yanked down his pants and his underpants at the same time — it looked as if he'd vaporized while standing there. Crowning the pile of clothing like a cherry on a sundae was the athletic cup I'd placed against my nose during my first hour in Brooklyn.

How long ago it seemed, and yet it was only a matter of days! It was getting hard to remember the last time I'd been in a room alone.

On my way back to the porch a man in a loose green bathrobe stood in the middle of the staircase leading upstairs.

"Vic win?" he asked. I nodded. "Good," he said, and climbed back up, blinking eyes as blue as my father's.

That was my official meeting with Agosto Palmieri.

By the time I got back outside, Vic, Rosemary, and Mel had left, and things were a little calmer than before. Vic was on Rosemary's porch, practicing his diction lessons to sharpen his skills as a future sports announcer. As Rosemary did her knitting he read consonant-clogged sentences aloud. She corrected him without looking up from her work.

Freddie left minutes later. Angie and I knocked off the rest of the lemon ice. When Vic returned and went in to bed Connie finally let it out.

"And I suppose that girl smells like a rose all the time." Rosemary's shower remark had been recorded and filed indelibly.

When I went to bed a little while later Vic was fast asleep, his arms folded over his eyes. I stared at his heaving form, trying to figure out how a pile of bones and muscles cooperated to hit a baseball such a terrifying distance.

CHAPTER FOUR

With breaks for lemon ice Mel and I found things to do all day long, without plans.

My father had sneaked fifteen dollars into my pocket before leaving, a fortune spread over a summer. Punks sold at ten for a nickel, and a child with a lit punk had power. You could light a firecracker, or search for red ants in the cracked bark of sooty maples. A touch of the glowing, slow-burning punk tip turned an ant into a hissing ash.

When it got too hot to do anything we sat on my grandfather's stoop in the shade of a maple. Our conversations were always future tense, what we'd do as adults, away from homes we knew were temporary. "We'll probably get married," Mel said, in the same flat tone she used to say the Yankees would win the World Series.

Two-cent chunks of chalk the width and length of plum tomatoes were great for street artists, and the rough gray sidewalks of Shepherd Avenue provided an unlimited canvas that was washed clean after every rain. I was a better chalk artist than Mel. She was spirited but untalented, and loved to draw horses. I pointed out flaws in her drawings — she made them with hind legs bent in the same direction as the forelegs.

"That's *wrong*," I told her. "The hind legs bend the other

way." I rapidly sketched a horse. In Roslyn I'd always done well in art class.

"See?" I said when I finished. "That's how the legs are."

"You're *nuts*," Mel said. "They ain't like that."

We ran to find a copy of my grandfather's *Racing Form*, which had a drawing of a horse on it.

"See?" I said triumphantly, tracing my finger along the legs. "*Told* you."

Pow! A punch to my stomach, and I didn't see her again for days. Then she reappeared, as if nothing had happened.

On days Mel and I were apart, Connie sometimes got rid of me by sending me shopping with Grace Rothstein.

The worst thing about Grace was her eyes. They were blue but unattractive, because they bulged and seemed to jiggle, like eggs in boiling water. Her wild blond hair was pulled back and stabbed into a ball at the back of her head with a bunch of hair pins, the wide kind that don't pinch closed.

Cooking was all she seemed to care about, and her husband's deli was an excellent focus for her obsession. It was a tiny place but Angie insisted it was a gold mine for that "Real German." Being a real German had something to do with being passionless, having a capacity for cruelty, and a love of gadgetry: flashlights, precision drills, and all things battery-operated.

Once I was having a catch with Mel in the driveway when she cut her hand on the ragged Cyclone fencetop. Blood pumped from the wound as Mel ran screaming to our basement.

While everyone else yelled and tripped over things Uncle Rudy set down his coffee cup, grabbed the arm, and briefly eyed the wound before pinching it closed with his thumb and forefinger and reaching for his coffee with his other hand.

"No need for a doctor," he said. "A bit of pressure seals the wound."

He was right, but he didn't endear himself to anyone. Only a Real German could have stayed so calm.

He had been a deli man all his life, and I imagine that during their courtship — a German-Jew and an Italian-Catholic, now *there's* a combination — Rudy must have figured he'd found

42

himself a workhorse. Grace could slice a cucumber without a cutting board, using her callused thumb as the base. Without even looking at the knife she churned out an even shower of slices that fell like coins.

Angie took me with him once to fix a pipe at Rudy's. Rudy stood in front, behind the counter, his red wavy hair neatly combed, iron-rimmed glasses pressed into the flesh pockets around his eyes. His full-length white apron looked stiff — you got the impression that his body had been sprayed lightly with a coating of clear glue.

It was twenty degrees hotter in back, where Grace worked. Had the Real German stepped back there for a moment he'd have lost the starch in his apron. Grace sweated away at a cutting board, while a wonderful smell rose from a sizzling pan on the stove. The pan contained thick patties, and at one point Grace stopped cutting, scooped them out, and laid them on a tray lined with paper towels.

They looked like flat meatballs. Grace handed one to me, and when I bit into it my salivary glands became waterfalls. I sucked on my fingers when it was gone but Grace offered me no more, on account of Rudy, no doubt. The Real German made a face at the empty grease spot on the paper towel: lost business.

What ingredients went into those patties! Scraps, nothing but scraps. Pork butt ends, heels of ham and bologna loaves, curled bits of Swiss cheese, stale Italian bread — all stuff that got pushed off tablecloths and landed in most American garbage pails.

Grace all but swept the floor to catch every crumb. She raked her hand over the rough pile of food, then chopped it into dust. After that the contents went into a mixing bowl. She dripped oil into it and mixed it up with a wooden spoon.

Raw, the stuff looked like wet cardboard. Fried, it became "meat."

In warm weather the store fan blew out through the screen door toward Shepherd Avenue. By noon the smell of those patties would lure day laborers from all over the area, including the men working at the hamburger-joint site.

Connie threw a fit when she learned I'd eaten a patty. Angie protested his innocence, having been under the sink when Grace fed me.

"*Never* eat anything they make there," she warned me. "You don't know what they put in it."

I *did* know, but I didn't make a point of it. "It's delicious," I answered, but Connie waved me off.

"Never mind. Lots of stuff tastes good but it's crap. Learn to *schieve.*"

"What's that?"

"It means look out for germs. Wait till you get home, where you can eat without gettin' poisoned."

"What about lemon ice?" I said, knowing she loved the stuff. She hesitated. "Willie's okay, but that's all."

"Okay, but sometimes I get hungry."

"You ain't gonna starve. If you get hungry, come home."

Home! Was it fair to call it that?

Seconds later she was on the phone to Grace, speaking in a shrill dialect she used only when she was truly frantic. The only thing I caught from the conversation was the English sign-off: "If you give him something, at least let it be wrapped!"

The rules were different for stuff Grace made at home. I once held a starfish-shaped cookie she made, studying it before gobbling it. She had brought over a tin of such cookies to enjoy with coffee: reindeer, bows, bunny rabbits. The cookie I held was glazed yellow with egg yolk and pebbled with dots of colored sugar. When the light caught it right it gleamed like crystal.

It looked like the creation of a fairy godmother working with a magic wand instead of an oven and a cookie sheet. I sat across the table from Grace and held the cookie up to her face, closing one eye so I could see the woman and the cookie in the same dimension.

It seemed impossible for a woman who looked like that to have made such a thing of beauty. She caught me looking.

"Hey. What are you starin' at?"

I opened my other eye. "This cookie is pretty, Grace."

She blushed to the salt-and-pepper roots of her hair. "I like pretty things," she said, so softly that only I heard her. "Thank you, sonny."

Mel was visiting an aunt on Long Island. Angie was working with Freddie. I sat in the basement, watching Connie make pasta.

She beat flour and eggs into dough, rolled it into thin sheets, and sliced them into noodles. These she laid on the table edges. If she was in the right mood and I washed my hands three times, I was allowed to lay them in place.

Grace came in, a bag under her arm. She took out a cookie filled with crushed figs and raisins.

"For the bowels," she announced, handing it to me. It was oven-warm. I bit into it, the fruits swirling on my tongue in a sticky sweet mess.

I was about to compliment her when she said, "That mother of yours never fixed you nothin' like *that*."

The cookie went sour in my mouth. What brought this on? Hadn't I been nice to her? "She was too sick to cook," I said.

"Shut up, Grace," Connie said, though not harshly. She'd probably been thinking the same thing.

"I guess your father had to cook a lot, huh?" Grace asked.

A vulture of a memory landed on my brain, those greasy diners we went to after visits to the hospital. "We did fine."

"Yeah?" Grace wouldn't let it go. "Tell me what you ate."

"Lots of stuff. What do *you* care?"

Connie grinned. I'd done all right, hadn't betrayed either parent. "Eh, he's restless today, with the girl gone," she said. "Take him to the store."

The A & P was a few blocks away. We passed Zip Aiello going the other way, a Santa Claus–sized burlap sack of soda bottles on his back. He was on his way to redeem them someplace on Atlantic Avenue.

"Howard Hughes!" Grace called out. "A millionaire in nickels and dimes!"

Zip wrinkled his face as if he smelled something bad, hitched his sack higher on his shoulder, and clinked away.

45

"What a nut. He never stands straight. Always bending down to pick up shit on the street. Bottles. Pieces o' metal. You watch, they're gonna have to bury him in a curved coffin."

"Why?"

" 'Cause he's always bent over. Slow down, this ain't the Kentucky Derby."

She kept calling me back, the way a person would summon a puppy. One of the wheels of her cart was bent, so Grace had to give the thing a straightening yank every fifteen feet or so because it kept bearing away from her.

We passed under the elevated tracks just in time to meet a train roaring overhead. It made the ground tremble and then it was gone, striped sunlight back on the street. Grace reached for the back of her head.

"Madonna, my hair." She grabbed at the blond snakes of her hair. The train breeze faded, diminishing to the puff of a child's breath on birthday candles.

"That train scared you," Grace said when we were in the store. She hefted packages of chicken, poked her finger through the cellophane, and sniffed the flesh.

"I wasn't scared," I lied.

"Hey, lady, don't do that!" a man in a bloody apron said. "We spend all morning wrapping and you make holes?"

Grace pointed a bony finger at him. "You sold me a rotten bird last time. Don't threaten me. This is the only way I know it's good."

She moved like a general to the freezer case, dug around, and yanked out a TV dinner. "I bet your mother used to buy these."

"She did *not*," I said hotly. Why was Grace doing this? Because my mother threw crumbs to sparrows instead of turning them into ersatz meatballs? Because her salads were lettuce and tomatoes instead of spinach and exotic greens? Because she'd died young and had no chance to grow as ugly as Grace?

The air conditioning seemed arctic. Sawdust under my feet felt like snow. I followed Grace around, watching her cart fill with groceries. Cracked eggs topped the pile.

"They're cheaper, why pay more when they're good for baking?"

When we got to the checkout line I said, "The only time we ever had TV dinners was when she was in the hospital."

Grace's eyes glowed with triumph. "So you did have 'em."

"Yeah. What are you gonna do, put it in the newspaper?"

"You lied before."

"She *never* bought them. My father bought them."

Grace ignored the technicality. "Pass me the eggs. Be careful you don't break them."

"They're already busted." The people behind us laughed. Grace looked as if she meant to spit at me. I knew she wasn't through with me.

We turned right when we came out of the A & P.

"We live the other way," I said.

"I know," Grace said. "But let's take a little walk first."

Something fishy was up — like Mel had told me on my first morning in Brooklyn, nobody around here *walks*.

When we'd traveled three blocks the buildings grew seamy. Puerto Ricans sat on stoops shaded by the elevated tracks, sipping from bottles of neon-colored soda. Sheet metal was nailed over many of the windows. Other houses were burned out. Missing windows gaped like toothless mouths.

"Grace, let's go home."

She puffed against the weight of the cart. Her slippers slapped the broken sidewalk. "One more block."

She stopped abruptly in front of a yellow brick building with rusty fire escapes. The house beside it was rubble.

"This is where she lived," Grace said, grinning, and I understood in a flash that I was being shown the former home of my mother.

I could see all of Grace's teeth, long and brown, like those of a roasted pig. She knitted a stitch in her side with her bony fingers: the extra few blocks had taken their toll but oh, the expression on my face was worth it to her.

"The two of them," Grace said. "Oh, they were a pair, all right."

"Two?"

"Your mother and your grandmother. Your *other* grand-mother." A flash of those brown teeth. "I used to see your other grandma going to work in the morning, wearing those big hoop earrings." She made circles of her thumbs and forefingers and touched them to her earlobes. "An *ac*tress, she wanted to be! Some actress."

I'd never even seen a snapshot of my maternal grandmother. "She was an actress?"

Grace cackled. "Oh, that's what she wanted you to believe. She sang, she danced, she went to auditions. Always this far away from the big break." She held thumb and forefinger a fraction of an inch apart. "But she was just a waitress at some Howard Johnson's on Broadway."

My face felt as if it had been needled with an anesthetic. "You didn't know that, Joey?" she asked, her voice strangling with phony sweetness. "Oh, yes. She moved here from Iowa when your mother was a baby. She was divorced from her husband. Hey! Maybe your other grandfather is alive some-where."

I felt dizzy. "You're lying."

"Why should I lie?"

"Because you don't like me."

"That's true, but I ain't lyin', kid."

I licked my lips. "What else?"

"That's it. Hey, I wasn't friends with her," she said coldly. "I just remember when she died, right on the job. They say she was puttin' a plate of food in front of a customer when a vein popped in her head."

Grace put a bony fingertip to her temple. "Boom, and she was dead a minute later. Fell down in the food. Mashed potatoes all over her face. Your mother quit school and went to work. One day she met your father on the train, and that finished him. You know what happened after that."

"But —"

"I don't wanna talk about it no more," Grace said, faking a yawn. "That's the whole story. I figured you didn't know, so I told you."

My bones felt as if they were dissolving. I imagined myself melting under her gaze, like the wicked witch did in the Wizard of Oz. But Grace was that witch, not me; *she* should have been melting.

"You stink, Grace. You're . . ." I struggled, trying to think of something to say. "You're the worst person in the world."

It was the best I could do: my vocabulary didn't contain four-letter words, and for the first time in my life I felt frustrated by it. She laughed at me.

"Tough guy. Who do you think you are, anyway? You think you can just come to this neighborhood and be a wise guy?" She pointed at me. "People gotta pay for the things they do."

"What's that mean?"

"You'll find out some day, wise guy."

"So why don't you tell me?"

"I don't gotta tell you everything. Ha! A little punk like you, from Long Island." She jerked her thumb in the direction she believed to be toward Long Island. "Who wants to live out there, anyhow?"

Her anger was random, insane. "I want to go home," I said, surprising myself by calling it that. Grace caught my arm with fingers that seemed to have retained the chill of the groceries she'd handled.

"After you, mister, there couldn't be any more," she said, squeezing at the word "mister."

I felt my pulse throb against her fingers and yanked myself free. Her nails clawed my skin.

"She hadda stop havin' babies after you. Something broke in there." She patted her flat belly that had yielded no children. "You broke somethin' in there. Why do you think you got no brothers or sisters?"

"I *broke* something?" I hated my feeble voice.

She nodded gravely. "You kicked so hard when you were in there you killed all the other seeds. Seeds for the babies. Ask, ask your father. If you ever see him again. Maybe he dumped you because of what you did."

She hiked a storklike leg and waved her foot: kick, kick, kick. "Like that, you went."

The slipper fell off and I picked it up for her, an automatic polite response I'd been taught. I'd have done it for Hitler. She slid her foot into it like a knife into a scabbard.

The door to the apartment house opened. A Puerto Rican with a green cap and a thin moustache came out, carrying a transistor radio. Grace put a hand between my shoulder blades and tried to shove me inside.

"Okay, kid, she lived on the third floor. Let's climb."

I pitched forward but scampered back as soon as my balance returned. In the instant that door had been open I'd seen enough — feeble light, smashed-in mailboxes, cracked linoleum worn through to the black.

"Eh, come on, I ain't got all day," Grace said merrily. She was bluffing — no way she would leave precious groceries on the street to climb those stairs. She stroked her hair. "I'm waiting, Joey."

"You go to hell!" I screamed. My vulgarity would have been enough to fix her but I grabbed the cart, backed it up a few feet, and slammed it into the side of the building. The frame buckled as oranges and dripping eggs littered the sidewalk.

Grace was screaming but I ran away, not looking back. I ran home but kept going past the house, flopping behind a hill of dirt at the construction site. I watched the heavy traffic on Atlantic Avenue and thought about jumping into the midst of it. I climbed the hill and looked into the hamburger joint's deep foundation, a giant grave.

I knew I had to return to the building that had been my mother's home.

I walked slowly along Atlantic Avenue, so I wouldn't run into Grace. The sun was setting, making the discarded wine and whiskey bottles on the street glow as if they were precious.

I entered the apartment house and climbed stairs, linoleum creaking under my feet. I smelled bug killer, wet laundry. Somewhere overhead a baby cried: did he know, even at his age, what a dump he lived in?

On the third-floor landing there were three doors to choose from. I picked the one nearest the stairwell. It was peppered with dents — someone, maybe a jilted lover, had kicked it dozens of times at foot level. Someone had painted "3-A" on the door with cheap red paint, or maybe it was nail polish.

No bell. I knocked. My small fist barely made a sound on the dull metal.

But someone heard me — sliding, scratching, the snap of a lock. The door opened a crack, still bound by a chain. A man with dark eyes and a handlebar moustache looked out at me, the chain cutting in front of his chin.

"What?" he said. I smelled whiskey.

I swallowed. "Can I come in?"

"You sellin' somethin', kid?"

"Just let me in, please?"

His eyes narrowed. The door slammed shut. I started to turn for the stairwell but I heard the chain slide in its groove. He'd closed the door to open that final chain, and then he opened the door wide.

"Well, come on." He leaned on the doorknob as if it were a cane. He wore a sleeveless undershirt and polka-dot shorts and open-toed sandals.

"You make me open up, now you ain't comin' *in?*" he said. "Man, that's some balls."

I entered. Beer cans littered the floor. It was the same cruddy linoleum as in the hallway, just slightly less worn. There was a small TV in the middle of the room, set upon a cardboard box. Wide-open windows fronted the elevated train tracks. It looked as if you could reach out and touch them.

The paint-starved walls were the color of raw leather. Had they been painted since my mother lived here, if indeed this had been her flat? I moved to the windows, needing the air. I could smell grease from the tracks.

The man openly scratched his balls. "What business you got here, kid?" I saw bits and pieces of a uniform draped over a wooden chair — blue pants, a shirt with a badge on it, a cap with the same kind of badge.

"Are you a policeman?"

He shook his head as if it pained him. "Night watchman. You woke me up."

"I'm sorry." I hesitated. "My mother used to live here."

51

He looked at me with sudden interest. "You Puerto Rican?"

"Italian. And Irish. My mother was Irish."

"She died?"

"Yeah."

"That's tough, man." He yawned, then flopped onto an unmade bed with sheets that looked gray. Or maybe it was just the light in the apartment, the lack of it — the el blocked most sunlight.

"Where you livin' now, kid?"

"Shepherd Avenue. Is this the place where my mother lived?" I was suddenly bold. "I know she lived on this floor. Her name was McCullough —"

"I don't know who lived here last. I only been here six months."

"Oh. I'm sorry I woke you," I said. I moved to the door, but he held a hand up.

"Wait, wait around. Stick around a few more minutes, man."

"What for?"

"Just wait." He'd cocked his head toward the window, seeming to be listening for some distant sound. "Few minutes, that's all. Go by the window."

"Why?"

"Just do it . . ."

I obeyed him. Now I could hear what his ears had detected — a train was coming from deep in Brooklyn, bound for Manhattan.

The floor started to tremble. The man chuckled. It sounded as if the train would come crashing through the wall but instead it roared past the windows, casting the room into darkness.

Cheap curtains flapped like dove wings. The gust hit me and I backpedaled toward the door as if someone were shoving me.

The man was hysterical on the bed. He kicked his skinny legs in the air. I glimpsed his dick.

"Fuckin' A, man, fuckin' A," he roared. I groped for the door. There were four locks on it and *three* chains, not just one. They dangled like earrings.

The knob felt greasy. I tried turning it a few times before getting the door open, and I could hear the guy laughing all the way down the stairs.

52

I ran back to Shepherd Avenue, my heart hammering. It was impossible to imagine my mother in a place like that. Maybe it had been *nicer*, back then — fresh paint, plants, clean sheets — but how much nicer could it have been? I couldn't get that horrible man out of my mind, either. His sick laugh lingered in my ears.

I slowed to a walk a block from home, knowing Connie's hatred for human sweat. I was going to get yelled at for destroying Grace's groceries but I didn't care. Nothing could be worse than what had just happened.

In the basement, noodles filled the table. When I came in, the breeze I brought caused them to wave like fingers. Angie was there, reading the *Journal-American*.

"You look like you just saw a ghost," Connie said.

"I did," I murmured.

"What?"

"Nothing."

"Well, you sure stayed late at the park."

I was shocked. Grace had made up a lie for me, told them I'd gone to Highland Park to play.

"I forgot what time it was," I said. I was allowed to help take the noodles off the table after I'd washed my hands and Connie'd scrutinized them. She saw the scabs Grace's nails had left.

"What happened to your arm?"

"Nothing."

"Eh. What am I, blind?"

"Scraped it on the swings."

"Clumsy . . . you shaking?" she asked, still clasping my hands in search of dirt. "I feel you shaking."

"It got cold out," I lied.

CHAPTER FIVE

I was in my old room in Roslyn, under the covers of my bed, swirling my skinny legs against the cool cotton sheets, waiting for my mother to come up and tuck me in, the way she did every night. When I heard her footsteps on the carpeted stairs

53

I shoved the blankets down to my waist, so there would be something to tuck. I wore pajamas with baseball players all over them — swinging bats, catching balls, sliding. Since the time I'd gotten beaned this was as close to the game as I was allowed to get.

As she entered the room I shut my eyes and faked sleep. It was one of our favorite games.

"Are you asleep, Joseph?" she stage-whispered.

I kept my eyes shut and tightened my lips to block a smile. Suddenly her hands were tickling my ribs, almost hard enough to hurt, but not quite. She never hurt me, my mother. I shrieked with laughter, windmilling my legs and tangling up the bedding.

"Look what you did! The maid's going to be mad when she sees this bed."

"We don't have a maid, Mommy."

"Oh no? What do I look like?"

"A mommy."

"All right, smarty-pants, all right." She pulled off the sheets and blankets, shook them straight and covered me, tucking me up to my armpits. This was just the primary tuck. Before leaving my room she would tuck me all the way to my neck.

"Did you wash your hands and brush your teeth?"

"Yes."

Her hand pushed my hair away from my forehead, giving her moist lips a clean target. I smelled the residue of dishwashing soap on her hands, a sweet fake odor of some chemist's concept of lemon.

"What a face. What a beautiful face. Why, I wouldn't trade that face for a diamond ring."

Time for another nightly game, in which I tried to think of things for which she *would* trade my face.

"How about a castle?"

"No, sir."

"How about . . . a big piece of gold, like at Fort Knox?" I pulled my arms out from under the covers and held them a brick-length apart.

"No deal, buddy."

"Ummmmm . . . how about a horse?"

54

"Now where would we keep a horse?"

"In the garage. He could eat the grass. Daddy wouldn't have to mow it."

"You silly. You'll have to do better than that."

I shut my eyes tightly to help my imagination fly, then opened them suddenly. "How about a hundred dollars?"

"Hmmm." She put one hand on her elbow and cupped the other under her chin. "Well, okay. For a hundred dollars it's a deal."

"Mommy!" I tried to sit up but she kept me down by leaning on my shoulders. She kissed my strained neck.

"All right, all right, no deal," she said when I'd calmed down. "Not even for a hundred dollars."

"What can you get with a hundred dollars?"

"Anything you want, Joseph."

"*Anything?*"

"The world." She smoothed back my hair again and smiled. "You can go anywhere you want with a hundred dollars."

"Asia? Europe?" I strained to remember the other continents I'd learned during geography lessons. "Africa?"

"Uh-huh."

"Did you and Daddy have a hundred dollars when you went on your moneyhoon?"

"*Honey*moon. Yes, we did."

"Was I there?"

"In a way. You were here." She put a hand to her waist, over a hen that was embroidered on her apron. "A tiny seed, waiting to be born. Whenever we went someplace nice I lifted up my shirt so you could peek through my belly button."

"I don't remember that."

"That's because you were little. *Very* little."

"Like . . ." I recalled the dinner we'd just eaten. "A pea?"

"Oh, smaller. You could have danced on the head of a pin." She grinned at my doubting face. "It's true," she said softly. "That's how everybody starts out."

"Wow."

"But look at you *now*," she all but boomed. "You'll be even bigger than Daddy by the time you go on your honeymoon!"

"How come they call it a honeymoon?"

"Because you can take your honey all the way to the moon, if you want."

"Aw, Mommy, nobody can go to the moon."

She shrugged. "Maybe you will, someday." She dinked my nose with her fingertip. "All right, all right, no more stalling, sweetie. Go to sleep now."

"But I'm thinking about the moon."

"Think about your pillow. Pretend it's the moon."

"The kids in school say the moon is green cheese."

"When you go bring me back a piece, baby, I never tasted green cheese. Good night."

Her lips on my forehead: at their touch I closed my eyes, as usual, only this time something was wrong, very wrong. The blanket wasn't being tenderly tucked under my chin, it was crushing my neck, choking me. I opened my eyes to find myself in my mother's childhood home, flat on my back on the tacky linoleum. Grace Rothstein knelt over me, holding a stickball bat by its ends. The middle of it was pressed to my throat. She was determined to break my neck.

I couldn't even cry out. Her hair was loose, the blond snakes wiggling — they'd developed mouths that snapped on air as they lashed around, trying to bite my nose.

"Wise guy," she breathed, over and over again, barely audible over the hissing of the snakes. "Little wise guy, little wise guy . . ."

The floor trembled beneath us, and I heard the roar of a train blasting past the window. I couldn't even turn my face to look at it. I saw only Grace, whose eyes were furnaces that blazed blue fire.

She leaned harder on the bat. Bones crunched in my throat.

"Now I'll fix you."

She leaned her face close to mine. The snakes opened their mouths in unison, exposing dripping fangs. . . .

I was being shaken vigorously. I opened my eyes (weren't they already open?) and saw Vic in a sleeveless undershirt, squatting beside my cot, clenching my upper arms in his hammy hands. He held me steady for a moment, then added one more shake in annoyance before letting go of me.

"You wanna wake up the whole house? What the heck's the *matter* with you?"

I gulped air, surprised to find my throat working. "What'd I do?"

"You're moanin' and groanin' all over the place, that's what you did." His voice was whiny, cranky. He hated being awakened. "What'd you have, a nightmare?"

I shivered in response.

"Y'all right now?"

"I don't know."

"Go back to sleep, it was only a dream."

I grabbed his upper arm. Even when he was at rest, the muscle there was rock solid. "Vic. Stay with me a minute."

"Aw, Jeez! Joey, I got the last game of the year tomorrow. I gotta make an impression, you know what I'm talkin' about?" He blinked calf eyes and jutted his lower lip. "How'm I gonna hit the ball if I don't get some sleep?"

His hair stuck out in all directions, making his appearance funny enough to take away some of my fear. "Okay, I'll go to sleep," I murmured, knowing I wouldn't.

He sighed and scratched his bristly brow, where bangs would have hung if his hair hadn't been so wiry.

"Long as I'm up tell me about the nightmare."

The details were too horrible to describe. "I don't remember."

"You feelin' any better?"

"A little. . . . How come I don't have any brothers or sisters?"

The calf eyes widened. He shrugged his huge shoulders, nutbrown against the white undershirt straps. "How should I know?"

"I think you do. Grace says I killed the baby seeds in my mother when I was born."

"Oh boy." He swallowed, scratched his walnut-sized Adam's apple. "See, you were, like, what they call a *difficult* birth, ya got me?"

"What do you mean?"

"I mean ya didn't come *out* of your mother head first like

babies're supposed to. You were twisted around, like. Pointed the wrong way." He whirled his hands, then poked a forefinger into his navel. "So they hadda cut your mother open to get you. See?" The finger slid to the half-moon neckline of his undershirt. I could practically feel it on my own skin. "And that's how you were born."

Vic sighed as if he'd just delivered a lecture on nuclear physics. "That's all I know, kid."

Blood, blood — that was all I could see, flooding from the slash on my mother's belly. And me emerging from it like some kind of a swamp monster from a pond of human organs that were simultaneously beating, pumping, digesting, and croaking like bullfrogs.

Vic patted my head. "Hey. You want a glassa water?"

"No. . . . So she couldn't have more babies?"

"The way I heard it, the docs said it'd be real dangerous for her to try. So she didn't. She coulda died. Okay?" He picked mucus from his eye. "That's why they raised you so *careful*, like. I mean it's why your mother wouldn't letcha play baseball."

My revulsion turned to fury. "How did *you* know that?"

"Shhh! Keep it down, willya?"

"Mel told you that, didn't she?"

"Yeah, she told me. You told her, so it wasn't no big secret, am I right?"

I was confused about whether or not Mel deserved my anger. "Look at me," Vic said.

I obeyed. He made a fist and rapped it against his forehead. "Suppose you got killed that time you got conked on the head. God forbid, but just suppose. There'd be nobody to inherit the house and stuff. No *heirs*, see?"

"My father sold the house."

"Well, there'd be nobody to inherit his money. Me and your old man, there's two of us, so even if one of us dies there's one left to get everything here."

"What if you both die?"

Vic's eyebrows hiked up. He'd never thought about that. "Nah," he decided after five seconds of consideration. "That ain't likely. The odds are against it." He chuckled. "*I'm* gonna die? *Look* at me." He rapped his fists against his chest. "Let's turn in."

He took my chin in thumb and forefinger and twisted my face toward his.

"Do me one favor and don't go askin' my mother about this stuff, all right? And don't tell her what I told you."

"Why not?"

"Willya just *do* me that favor, Joey?" For the first time that night he was truly angry and not just annoyed.

"I won't ask." I pulled his hand off my chin. He clambered over to his bed and rumbled his way under the covers. "Two in the morning. The ball's gonna look like an aspirin." He lay still for maybe a minute, then rolled over.

"Hey, Joey. They call babies born like you cesareans."

I sat up. "Say that again."

"Say-zee-ree-yuns."

"Say-*zee*-ree-yuns?"

"You got it."

I felt a shiver of pride at the word, which suggested to me soldiers in armor wielding flashing swords.

"It's how come you got a round head," he explained. "See, you didn't have to come through what they call the *birth* canal. That's what squashes people's heads on the sides."

My hands flew to my temples. My head felt round as a basketball. "Hey, Vic, your head isn't squashed."

"It is a little. Everybody with a normal head is like that."

"I'm normal!"

"Shhh! I didn't mean *normal*, I meant . . ." he exhaled, probed the meager shelves of his vocabulary for the right word. "*Regular*," he finally said. "You ain't regular."

"I am too. What's the birth canal?"

It was too dark to see if he was blushing, but he must have been. "Can't tell you, Joey."

"Aw, come on."

Sigh. "Well. It's where a woman takes a leak."

"You're kidding me."

"No, I ain't. I swear it's true." His right hand crossed his heart. "I came through it, Joey."

"And my father?"

"Yup. Everybody in this house but you."

Isolation. The thrill of being a cesarean soldier was fading fast.

"I gotta go to the bathroom," I said.

I groped my way there, flicked on the light and looked in the mirror. It wasn't the roundness of my head I noticed, it was my slitted eyes, narrowed to protect my retinas from the sudden hundred-watt glare. I thought I looked like a Chinaman but I didn't think my head was any rounder than Vic's. I went back to the room.

"You forgot to flush."

"I didn't go. I just looked in the mirror."

"Oh, God, what did I start here?"

"Come to the bathroom with me, Vic, I wanna see your head."

"Joey, you get under those covers. I mean it."

"*Please.*"

He jumped off his bed, landing like an ape on his thick hairy legs. "Gonna strike out four times tomorrow," he groaned, but he followed me.

"God, that's bright." He covered his eyes with his hand, peeking through the fingers. I squinted at our reflection. He needed a shave. His fingers went to his temples. "See how it's dented here? You ain't got that."

If our heads were different, it was a minor difference, at best, the sort that would go unnoticed unless mentioned.

But of course everything was mentioned on Shepherd Avenue. I was a marble in a world of peanuts. I blinked back tears.

"Do you still like me, Vic?"

The hands fell from his temples. "Of course. Jerk. Whaddya think?"

Ghostlike, dentureless, unbraided hair flowing, nightgown billowing, Connie appeared at the doorway.

"What are you two doing?"

Vic scratched his chest. "Comparing our heads, Ma."

Connie looked at us as if she wondered what planet we'd be returning to. Luckily for us she was too tired to pursue it.

60

"Go to bed before I call Bellevue." She shuffled away. "Coupla nuts."

Vic giggled on the way to the room. When we were under the covers I apologized for keeping him awake.

"Ah, don't worry about it, I'll still murder the ball."

It was thrilling to hear him talk baseball, the only part of his life that swelled his ego.

"You're not gonna be mad at me tomorrow, are you, Vic?"

"Nahh. Your father never got mad at me, and I hear I was a real pain in the neck when we shared this room."

"I didn't mean to do that to my mother, you know. I didn't mean to get twisted around the wrong way."

"Course you didn't . . ."

Minutes later he was snoring, while I lay awake, rubbing my head as if it were a crystal ball.

My nighttime vigil didn't hurt Vic's batting eye in the least. He ended his high school career in a blaze of glory, blasting two home runs. He made the *Journal-American* all-star team again, this time earning a solo photo of himself taking a vicious swing at an imaginary pitch.

He got a letter from Arizona State University, offering him a full baseball scholarship. That school would later produce major league stars such as Reggie Jackson and Sal Bando.

But the pros were also interested. A scout named Jack Boswell from the Pittsburgh Pirates wanted Vic to sign a contract to play baseball that summer in their farm system, a Single-A team in West Virginia called the Nuggets. He asked to come visit the house.

Connie set the table in the upstairs dining room, arranging unchipped coffee cups with saucers and a plate of pastries. Boswell was gracious. He wore a suit and smelled as if he'd shaved a minute ago.

In a low voice he spoke of Vic's great promise. Vic would learn some fundamentals in the minors, a year or two at most just to hone his skills. He made it sound like a trifling annoyance, like getting a passport to go to Europe. He'd be in the major leagues before his twenty-first birthday.

The Pirates were the defending world champions but they were aging, Boswell noted. Players would soon retire, leaving holes to fill.

Vic interrupted to say, "You know, I always kinda wanted to be with the Yankees."

Boswell scowled. "No you don't. Hey, realistically, now — *who* are you gonna push out of that lineup? Kubek? Richardson? My gosh, the young kids on that team don't have a chance. Roberto Clemente is a big star with us now, right? If he'd signed with the Yanks he'd *still* be riding the bench."

"Roberto Clemente," Vic said reverentially.

Angie said nothing but listened intently. Connie stared at Boswell the whole time but was also silent. Boswell looked at his watch and stood.

"I've got to go," he announced. "Mr. Ambrosio, I'll see you and your son later in the week for dinner." He shook Angie's hand and turned to Connie. "I hope you'll join us, too, Mrs. Ambrosio."

Connie nodded and forced a smile. Boswell left the house, having taken just one sip of coffee. Cream dripped from the untouched pastry on his plate.

At the doorway he turned and winked at Vic. "The fences at Forbes Field are mighty cozy, son."

A few nights later Boswell took Vic and Angie out to dinner. Connie begged off, saying she had a headache. She was quiet that night in the basement as she made bread crumbs, one of her favorite activities to relieve tension. She put hunks of stale Italian bread into a meat grinder that was attached to the end of the table by screws and butterfly nuts. She let me turn the crank until it was too stiff to move.

An even brown powder dropped into a paper bag, "cheaper and better" than the "sawdust" they tried to sell at the market.

"Hey, Connie. How come that baseball guy didn't invite *me* to dinner?"

" 'Cause he don't need you to like him, that's why."

"When Vic gets to the major leagues can we go to the games for free?"

She grimaced. "What are we gonna do, move to Pittsburgh? Madonna! Move, let me crank."

She finished grinding the bread, then poured the crumbs from the bag into an empty Medaglia D'Oro coffee can, dropped a bay leaf on top, replaced the lid and burped it.

"Why'd you put that leaf in there?"

"Keeps it fresh."

"How?"

"You and your questions! I don't know, it just does." She put the can on a shelf. "What did he say to you?"

"Who?"

"Hands off the crank, it ain't a toy. . . . Vic, that's who."

"What did he say about what?"

She grew impatient. "You sleep in the same room. Did he say he was gonna sign a baseball contract?"

"He didn't say anything."

"Ah, the way you two stick together . . ." She unscrewed the crank and put it away.

"Don't you want him to sign?"

"No. He should go to NYU. They offered him half a scholarship."

"What about Arizona?"

She hesitated. "Too far away."

She was too upset to cook. She took flat, stale slices of Italian bread, wet them slightly, and cut tomatoes and cheese over them. She dripped oil over that and pronounced it supper.

When we finished eating she made me carry her rocking chair to the front porch. It was nine o'clock but the day's heat still shimmered from the bricks, and each breeze was a blessing.

The mosquitoes weren't, though — they were everywhere in the June air, having drifted over from the garbage cans. I slapped at them furiously and noticed that Connie never broke her rocking rhythm to kill any.

"Hey, how come they don't bite *you?*"

She shrugged, her gaze fixed in the distance. "Never got bit in my life. Maybe I got sour blood."

"It isn't fair." I killed one on my forearm, leaving a stain the size of a dime, my blood. "They're all coming after *me*."

She stopped rocking. "Is that nice? Do you want your grandma to get bit? Would that make you feel better?"

She resumed rocking, ignoring me. I opened my mouth, thought again, closed it. The inattention was getting to me.

"I saw where my mother lived."

Connie stopped rocking. "You saw the apartment house?"

"I went inside it, Connie."

"How'd you know where it was?"

"Grace showed me."

"Grace took you *upstairs?*"

I shook my head. "She only brought me there. I went alone."

Connie peered at me. "Why'd you do that?" she asked softly.

"I wanted to see what it was like." Smack. I killed a mosquito on my neck. She watched me flick it off the end of my fingernail.

"All Puerto Ricans in that building," she said, waiting for confirmation.

I nodded. "The guy who let me in was."

She stopped rocking again. "My God, you went in someone's flat?"

"Sure." I shrugged. I had her in the palm of my hand. "It wasn't so nice. The guy was in his underwear. He was a night watchman. He said I woke him up."

"You're lucky he didn't kill you."

"His window was right by the train."

"You should be in there when a train goes by."

"I *was*, Connie. The whole house shook." I grinned at her. For an instant she seemed frightened of me.

"Never go there again," she commanded. "They could kill you and we'd never find you."

"Nobody's going to kill me."

"*Promise* you won't go there again."

I let her hang for a moment. "Don't worry, I won't," I finally said. She began rocking again, breathing hard, as if she'd been holding her breath.

"Were you scared?"

"A little. . . . Did you know my other grandmother?"

"Used to see her on the street. But we never talked."

"Why not?"

"I didn't know her. She was already dead when your father met your mother."

"You still could have said 'hello.' "

"*She* could have said 'hello' to *me*, too," she snapped. "Madonna, that Grace has some big mouth." She rocked harder. The chair scraped forward, a centimeter at a time. "If you were so scared, why'd you do it?"

"I felt like it. Is my other grandfather alive?"

"I don't know."

"Would you tell me if you knew?"

"Of course I would. Don't you dare grill me, a shrimp like you," she said, but her voice was shaky.

"I'm not a baby, Connie." She let the crack go without comment. "Your chair's sliding. You're rockin' too hard."

"Don't worry about it."

"Connie, I'm cold."

"Go get your sweater."

"I don't want to."

"Eh, eh, eh . . ."

She slowed her rocking. The chair stopped moving. "I wish I could have met my other grandmother."

"Wishing won't do you no good."

"I still wish it."

"Who's stoppin' you?"

"I'm glad Grace showed me. I'm not afraid now."

"Afraid of what?"

I wouldn't say.

"Don't tell your grandpa where you were, he'd have a heart attack."

A train roared by down the block, bound for territories deep in Brooklyn. Connie stared at me and said, "It was nicer when your mother lived there."

"How do *you* know? You never saw it."

"I just know."

She wanted to comfort me but I wouldn't let her. I had killed about two dozen mosquitoes by the time Vic and Angie showed up after eleven o'clock, looking like strangers in their dress clothing. Angie's only suit was a real gangster-type job, with slanted pockets and thin pinstripes. Vic didn't even have a suit. He wore a salt-and-pepper jacket, a light blue shirt, and a knit tie.

The thick-knotted tie bulged at his throat like an extra Adam's apple. His face looked fat and shiny.

"Hiya, Ma," he said affectionately, kissing her cheek.

"You had a beer. You smell like a drunk."

Vic gulped. "I'm not drunk."

"We each had one beer," Angie said. "Take it easy already."

"Sure. Easy." The rocking quickened. I finally realized how dramatic a prop that rocking chair was. No wonder she'd made me lug it outside. Her staging was ingenious.

Vic said, "Ma, I signed. I'm gonna be a Pittsburgh Pirate." He tried a smile on her.

"No, you're not," she said. "You're gonna be a *Nugget*."

The smile vanished from his face. "All players start out in the minors."

"Uh-huh." Rock, rock. She looked at Angie. "You didn't even call to tell me."

Angie shrugged. "It all happened so fast. . . ."

"So why couldn't you take two minutes to call?"

"What for?" Angie exploded. "A pen? He made up his mind, he signed. End of the story."

Vic slapped at his wrist. "There's a million mosquitoes," he said, but only I was listening to him.

Connie asked, "Where'd you eat?"

"Mr. Boswell took us to the Twenty-one club," Vic said eagerly. "It cost eleven bucks for a steak."

Angie's eyes shut: here it comes, he must have said to himself. Connie's curtain of anger dropped momentarily to reveal astonishment. When she recovered she asked, "That makes you happy, that it cost so much?"

Vic was baffled. He swallowed, making his tie-knot jump. "No, Ma . . . jeez, I'm just *tellin'* ya. Nothin' was cheap at this place. The shrimp cocktail comes in a glass of ice this big." He held out his hands as if he were hefting a basketball.

66

She looked at Angie, who had opened his eyes. "You too? Steak?"

He cleared his throat. "Lobster tails."

"How much?"

"Fourteen dollars." Angie looked at his shoes.

"Mr. Boswell paid, Ma," Vic said desperately, but that only made Angie wince. "Even the chicken was eight bucks," he added.

Now Connie was nodding. In the distance a fire engine wailed. I was sure Vic and Angie would have loved to be on it, going anywhere.

"Lobster tails," she said, making the words sound like a curse. "Ain't that nice. The only way a lobster tail could get into this house would be if we had a hurricane and the ocean washed over us."

"Ma!" Vic began, but he'd done enough damage — Angie touched Vic's arm and he fell silent. It was best to let Connie get all her venom out at once. To stop or interrupt her would be to stagger the flow of poison over days, even weeks.

The lobsters were a ridiculous scapegoat. Angie let Connie handle the money with a free rein. Still he let her talk, and as she did she seemed to give off heat we could feel.

"Sure, you two with your steak and lobsters. Your grandson and me ate bread and cheese tonight, the whole meal cost maybe thirty cents. That tomato had a bad spot on it, I should have thrown the whole thing out. . . ." She paused and caught her breath before resuming the attack.

When she was through Angie kept quiet for a while, to make sure it was all out. Then he said, "Lady, there's a pound and a half of veal cutlets in your refrigerator. And besides, you were invited tonight. You pretended you had a headache. So never mind all this bread and cheese stuff."

A deadlock. Vic looked from parent to parent, his mouth open. "I got eight thousand to sign," he said.

Connie gripped the arms of the rocking chair. "It's final, then."

"Uh-huh. I leave for West Virginia in two days." He couldn't believe it himself. "Two days," he marveled.

"Come on, say something," Angie said. "Eight thousand bucks! How many kids get their hands on that kind of money? Used to take me two years to make that much."

I said, "Can I see it, Vic?" having imagined rubber-banded packets of greenbacks. He rubbed my hair and my spine tingled as I realized it was eighty hundred dollars, eighty times the magical amount my mother used to talk about. Vic could go to the moon eighty times. . . .

"They mail me a check later," he said kindly.

Connie extended a hand to be pulled out of the rocker. Vic and Angie seemed afraid to touch her, so I tried to help her up. She was dead weight, like a sack of cement. I couldn't budge her.

"Lemme rock forward, then pull."

It worked that way. She went to the door alone. "One of you carry my rocker inside. And get out of those clothes. The beer sweats through them and they stink."

She shut the door behind her. Another fire engine wailed. The three of us stood on the porch, the empty rocker still swaying. Angie put his hand out to stop it.

"Carry it in, would you, Vic? I'm beat."

Vic had never traveled and he couldn't pack worth a damn. He laid two open black suitcases on his bed, scuffed at the corners. Angie rubbed Esquire shoe polish on those areas, but up close you could still see the scraped fibers.

The first things he packed — what else? — were his glove and his spikes. He put the spikes in nails up, folded his one jacket in half and laid it on top of the spikes.

"Uh-oh . . ."

He took it out and examined the sole-shaped area of ripped threads. "Nuts, my only jacket," he said, fingering the threads. But then he laughed it off. "Heck, I'll buy a new one! I got the money."

He flopped onto his bed, between the suitcases, exhaling deeply. "You can play my records when I'm gone, Joey. And here, this can stay, too."

He jammed a Pittsburgh Pirate baseball cap Boswell had given him onto my head. My ears flattened under it.

"Can I really keep it, Vic?"

"Sure. I can't use it. I'm a Nugget, not a Pirate." Sheepish smile. "Not yet, anyhow."

"Vic. Are you going to write me letters?"

"Sure I will. Only, I ain't much of a writer."

"I'll write to you. . . ."

Why was my throat lumping up? It was crazy. I hadn't cried when my father left, and here I was choking up over a guy I'd known just a few weeks. Vic acted as if he couldn't see me misting up.

"Sleep in my bed while I'm gone, Joey, it's more comfortable."

"When are you going to visit?"

"I don't know. There's no minor leagues in New York City." Another smile. "Ya know what that means, don't ya? I'll have to get called up to the majors this season so I can visit my favorite nephew."

He winked, then his face suddenly darkened. "Wait. No. There's no National League teams left in New York."

"Damn it."

"Hey! You don't curse. Since when do you curse?"

"That was my first time. No, wait, I said 'hell' to Grace once."

"Don't get into the habit, Joey, it's bad. . . . Hey!" His mood brightened. "I got it!" He snapped his fingers. "The Yankees meet the Pirates again in the World Series, just like last year. Then I go out there and beat the Yankees. Huh?"

He cackled at his fantasy. "That'll show 'em for not signing me, huh?"

"Yeah!"

"Know what, Joey? We could wind up teammates some day, you and me."

Gooseflesh covered me from head to toe. "You mean it?"

"Sure." He shrugged. "We're, what, eight years apart? Yeah, I'd say it's possible. Very possible."

"Oh, boy!"

We shook hands formally, awkwardly. "Yeah," he mused. "Little more muscle on ya . . . we already know you got a batting eye, right? It could happen. What are you, sweating?"

He pulled his hand free and wiped it on his shirt. I did the same thing with my hand.

"You're the one who's sweating," I accused. I think we both feared the embrace that threatened to follow our handshake.

It rained the morning he left us. Boswell had arranged for a limousine to take him to the airport, and even though it was barely seven-thirty people from Shepherd Avenue were out there to say good-bye.

Angie couldn't stop with the questions: "Got the plane ticket? Got enough cash on you? You'll call soon, collect?"

Vic nodded or grunted his answers. His eyes were on Connie's bedroom window — the curtains were drawn. She'd refused to leave her room that morning.

Angie had made our breakfast. The scrambled eggs had a crust from overfrying. There was no coffee because he didn't know how to make it. Even though I didn't like the taste, I missed the smell. There was a chill in the basement the odor of coffee would have chased.

The limo was the longest and blackest car I'd ever seen. The driver wore a cap with a visor that hid his eyes.

Grace Rothstein, curlers in her wild hair, stuck an oily-bottomed bag of pepper-and-egg sandwiches in Vic's hands and kissed his cheek. "Watch what you eat," she warned.

Uncle Rudy told him to be good. Mel was sobbing out loud, but Rosemary just stood there looking solemn. Vic had visited her for hours the night before and there was nothing left to say.

Across the street, poor retarded Louisa sat on the curb, chanting and pointing: "Big car . . . big car . . . big car . . ."

Angie put his left hand on Vic's shoulder, standing away at arm's length. Vic put his right hand out to shake. He dropped it to his side as Angie extended his. They missed each other's cues a few more times before giving up and embracing.

Vic released Angie. Rosemary clutched him and turned away.

Mel ran home. I felt my own eyes wetten. Angie pushed me forward.

"Say good-bye to your uncle," he said, as if Vic were going to the gas chamber.

We shook hands. My shoulder popped when he suddenly yanked me toward him and kissed my cheek.

"Take care of Mom and Pop for me."

The impatient driver pumped the gas pedal. Vic looked for his bags. No one noticed that the driver had gotten out and loaded them. Vic got in and slammed the door. He didn't look back or wave as the car rolled away.

That night Angie came home with a fish-smelling bag. Without a word he dumped it on the basement table in front of Connie, who was shelling peas. Three confused green lobsters crawled around on the red and white checkered tablecloth. An hour later we were eating them.

The day after Vic left we heard from my father for the first time.

> *Dear Everybody,*
> *I'm in Maine. It's so cold here at night you have to wear a sweater. Yesterday I went out on a lobster boat with a man and helped him work. We made a fire on the beach and boiled the lobsters. I miss you all.*
> *Love, Sal*

Connie's hand trembled as she read. "We just ate lobsters," she said. "That's a sign." She passed the card to Angie, who read it and laughed at her notion. He slipped it to me and seemed surprised that I was able to read.

There was a picture of a lobster boat on the card — my father had gone out of his way to find something to illustrate his words.

"Why doesn't he *call?*" I complained. "Damn! He has lots of money, he could call."

"Watch that mouth," Connie warned. "And don't be fresh."

"I don't care. He could call if he wanted to. He's just a . . ." I searched for the right word. Connie and Angie braced themselves for the worst.

". . . a *cheapskate*," I finally said. They let their breath out, relieved.

Angie said, "He's way up in the country, maybe there's no phones."

"Yeah, sure," I said, tearing up the postcard before their eyes. It wasn't easy — the thin plastic coating over the lobster-boat picture wasn't easy to tear.

"Was that nice?" Connie asked. "That wasn't nice."

"Cheapskate," I repeated, stacking the little cardboard squares on the basement table.

Connie said, "You're both comin' to church with me tomorrow. No arguments. We can pray for both of my sons."

Angie nodded. "They're my sons, too."

Up until this time Connie had always gone to church alone, never nagging her husband because he didn't go. Because he was being so cooperative she didn't hassle him that night when he went out with Freddie, who blew his horn in front of the house. When Angie left she even sighed with relief.

Then Rosemary appeared at our door with a package of books tied with string. They were for me: she thought I might like reading them, even though Mel had refused to so much as glance at one page.

She sat and drank coffee with Connie while I sipped cream soda — I'd grown to like the stuff — and soon they were gossiping about Vic. Rosemary had sent him an apple-and-cinnamon cake, triple-wrapped in aluminum foil. It had cost $3.45 to mail.

Suddenly Rosemary was weeping, as if over the exhorbitant postage. She excused herself and went home.

Connie was too weary to see the girl to the door. She looked exhausted, hands resting at each side of her cup and saucer, palms up, as if in defeat.

"Why didn't Rosemary just give Vic that cake yesterday?" I asked. Connie shrugged. She glanced at the sink, hoping, I think, to find dirty pots and dishes for distraction, but the sink was clean.

At last she rose, got the cream-soda bottle from the refrigerator, uncapped it, and filled my glass. "Eh, and your father too, we don't even know where he is."

"He's in Maine," I said, a little defensively — it was all right for me to criticize my vagabond father but I felt funny when others tried it.

"We don't know *anything*," Connie said. "Maine's gigantic. Salvatore runs away and the rest of the world waits for him."

She had more to say, and I knew enough to sit still and not milk her for details. Much of my father's life was a mystery to me. On this strange evening, Connie filled in many of the holes.

She could be a spellbinding storyteller when a certain mood hit her, about as often as Halley's comet streaked across the sky.

I don't know how much was true and how much she made up, or guessed at, but the details glowed like the sparks a comet leaves behind.

My father's favorite class in school, like mine, had been art, and he displayed his talents early. At five, he made a crayon drawing of an eagle with extended talons, snaring a trout from a river.

God knows *where* he could have seen an eagle in Brooklyn, but his kindergarten teacher was so impressed she laid it under the glass plate on her desk. After that he became the only child in the class entrusted with brushes and paints. The rest of the kids struggled with crayons.

That teacher, Miss Grayson, kept tabs on Salvatore as he went through the other grades, convinced of his talent. The clincher came when he turned eight.

"Art Week" had been declared at P.S. 108, and one sunny day the entire third-grade class was taken to Highland Park under the supervision of Miss Grayson, who by then had become the school's art teacher.

The kids were told to draw objects from nature with crayons. My father drew a large maple tree entirely with dots of color. When Miss Grayson saw that he'd used dots instead of lines and blotches she was shocked. My father told her he didn't know why he'd drawn it that way. Her tone undoubtedly frightened him. He probably thought he'd broken a rule.

The next day he was summoned from recess to Miss Grayson's room, where she waited with a man in a dark suit. His tree drawing was on her desk.

The man, she explained, was from the Junior Art Institute of New York. He shook my father's hand.

"Do you know anything about an artist named Seurat, Salvatore?" he asked. (Connie pronounced it "sewer rat.") My father shook his head. He'd never even been to a museum.

"He was an artist who lived a long time ago. He used a style called pointillism. That means he used dots of color, like you did yesterday in the park. It's a very, very unusual style."

"I didn't copy," my father said.

Both adults laughed. "You're not in trouble, son," the man said. "How long have you been an artist?"

"They started giving us paper in kindergarten," my father said. "I just like to do it 'cause it's fun." They shook hands again, and my father went back to the playground.

It was far from over. Miss Grayson had found her prodigy, perhaps the one she'd hoped for all her lonely life, for she lived in a studio apartment in Flatbush with a load of books and two cats.

Early in November she had a brainstorm. She took a bunch of big sheets of white construction paper and taped them into a horseshoe around the art room classroom walls, within my father's low reach.

She assigned him to do a panorama of the Christmas season. He would have free rein to do whatever he liked. Miss Grayson had a duplicate classroom key made so my father could come in at seven each morning to work. She told the janitor not to bother the boy.

He had fine hard cakes of watercolors to work with, not the cheap grainy stuff supplied by the Board of Education. He also had a rainbow of colors to choose from, instead of the school's red-blue-yellow quota. Miss Grayson paid for the extra supplies with her own money.

74

It was a lot to thrust upon an eight-year-old. No member of his family could have understood what was going on, any more than they could have understood nuclear physics.

All they knew on Shepherd Avenue was that Sally Boy was busy with something each morning before school. Though they were curious they never asked questions.

Italian-Americans never interfered with the educational process. School was untouchable turf, as invulnerable to criticism as the church.

My father started painting from the first sheet on the far left, and like a miniature Michelangelo he inched his way around the classroom. He drew scenes straight from Shepherd Avenue, the shuttered lemon-ice stand and the elevated train.

Occasionally he put a wreath in a window but this was as close as the work ever came to being Christmasy. Miss Grayson didn't interfere until she saw him painting an enormous brick building.

"It's the sewing machine factory near my house," he told her.

"I'm not sure that has anything to do with Christmas, Salvatore."

"You said I could do this any way I want!" he exploded.

She left him alone, even more fascinated. He worked for two more weeks. There were needleless pine trees at curbsides, and wrapping paper jammed into trash cans. There was a man walking and holding the hands of his children, both of whom were crying. The curbside snow was gray slush, and when my father reached the final panel he darkened the sky and drew a sliver of moon.

A fat man in a winter coat burned a pile of Christmas trees at the curb. A tongue of orange-red fire leapt from them. A German shepherd barked at the flames. The work was done.

"Christmas isn't always happy," he told Miss Grayson. "This is what my street looks like *after* Christmas."

Every class in the school paraded past his work. Elated, Miss Grayson invited her friend back. He took one look at Sal's panorama and said it should be brought to the attention of a citywide art contest to be held in January. It was a shoo-in for honorable mention, at the very least.

Miss Grayson asked my father when his parents were going to come by for a look. He shrugged.

"They don't know about it."

She was astonished. "Didn't you tell them what you were doing every morning?"

"They never asked."

Miss Grayson phoned Connie and asked if she could come over for a talk — no, I'm not exactly your son's teacher, she said, more like a special instructor.

In the Shepherd Avenue basement Miss Grayson explained what Salvatore had accomplished and urged Connie to come and see his work. It was about to be entered in a big contest, she added; it was sure to win a prize.

Connie listened politely. When Miss Grayson finished her speech Connie said, "Yeah, well, he was always good with his hands."

Miss Grayson's eyes widened. "I'm not sure you quite understand the situation here, Mrs. Ambrosio. This is far more than good hands. Your son has a special talent that could develop into something great."

Connie raised an eyebrow. "My son is a great man?"

"I think he could be, yes. Given a chance."

"How great can an eight-year-old be?"

"Well, I'm speaking in terms of potential. We've got to consider his future."

"We?"

Miss Grayson forged ahead. "He tells me he's going to be working in a butcher shop soon, after school. I'm not convinced this is a good idea."

Miss Grayson was treading in shark-infested waters. The butcher was a close friend of Angie's.

"Nothing wrong with working there," Connie said.

"No, of course not," Miss Grayson said delicately. "But there are just so many hours in a day. A man must use them to the best possible advantage."

76

"But my son is a *kid*."

"Exactly my point," Miss Grayson said, sensing checkmate. "He's very, very impressionable."

She didn't rack up any points using a word such as "impressionable." A child was stupid or smart, fast or slow, handsome or ugly. A child had no right to be sensitive, melancholy, impressionable — let him know pain before giving him such a crutch.

What could be easier than to be a child? Who wouldn't want to be a child again?

Miss Grayson laid a pamphlet on the basement table. Connie didn't budge a muscle to touch it.

"This is from the school I'm talking about, where I think your son belongs. It's on Lexington Avenue."

"Manhattan," Connie murmured. A train to ride, a river to cross.

"The teachers there deal with children like your son. I would like, with your permission of course — my goodness, shouldn't we be talking with your husband as well?"

"He's at work. Talk to *me*."

"I would like to assemble a portfolio of Salvatore's work and take it to the admissions committee. Believe me, Mrs. Ambrosio, the process would be a formality. They key thing is your cooperation. If Salvatore thinks his parents disapprove it will certainly hurt his work."

Connie's jaw tightened. "You call painting *work*?"

Miss Grayson nodded solemnly. "The hardest kind of all."

The visit had been a disastrous humiliation for Connie. Just what was this ability to make pictures, this art? As far as Connie could tell it was a talent you had from the wrist down. You gonna set the table with that?

Still, she knew her son was different from other kids, more often alone, always a little unhappy. . . . Well, maybe not unhappy, but quiet, so quiet.

Then again, her own husband was no chatterbox, and he made his way in the world as a plumber. Could there have been truth to Miss Grayson's words? What did a dried-out virgin living alone with cats know about the world?

Such big talk about art, a plaything for the rich. Did artists raise families? Weren't they all queers?

And what about that one guy, what was his name, the one who left his wife and kids to starve while he painted nude women on an island? Was there nobility in *that*?

This woman spoke of Salvatore as if he were the second coming of Jesus Christ, and it frightened Connie. She was not ready to deal with a messiah.

Before he left for school the next day Connie said, "Your teacher, she says you paint good."

"She's not really my teacher. She kinda helps me with my art."

That word again — *art!*

"You, ah, like all this art stuff?"

He shrugged. "It's okay. I get good marks but they don't count on your report card." He was as casual about his skill as Miss Grayson was excited about it.

Bad times started. Kids in his class teased him about his work. He liked sports as much as anyone else but found himself being chosen last for games.

It worried him that Miss Grayson was pushing so hard for this special school, and that Connie was staring at him across the supper table as if he were plotting to use his talent against her in some way.

The Christmas artwork was about to be taken down and shipped to Manhattan for display and Connie hadn't even come to see it. Miss Grayson knew it would be impossible to get her to Manhattan once the work had been moved, so she phoned the house the night before and pleaded with her to come see it. Connie agreed.

When she got up the next morning she noticed that Salvatore was already out of the house. No reason for concern, he was often up early and gone. When she got to the school gate Miss Grayson stood waiting for her.

"Now you'll understand what all the fuss is about, Mrs. Ambrosio."

Together the women went to the kindergarten class. The door was open, and my father was inside. Half-a-dozen empty black paint jars were lying on the floor, rolling around. He had a full jar in his hand and was flinging it at the final panel when the women came in.

It was all destroyed. Miss Grayson fainted. Connie knelt and patted her cheeks. My father walked past them and out to the playground to play punchball.

Connie sipped from my cream soda. All that talk had left her dry. "So he grows up, he gets a good job, he quits and takes off. Figure it out." She sighed. "I shoulda let him go to that art school." She drummed her fingers along the side of the now-empty soda bottle.

"How do you know what it looked like if there was black paint all over it?" I asked.

"The teacher told me." Connie tapped her forehead. "She *memorized* the thing."

"Where are his paintings now?"

"There aren't any. That was the last thing he painted. He didn't want to touch it no more after that."

"But the eagle," I persisted. "The tree —"

"Eh, this is more than twenty years ago." She lifted her hand to dismiss me. The kitchen clock hummed over the refrigerator, a sound that was always there but suddenly became noticeable. The refrigerator kicked off an extra-loud hum, as if to join it.

"There's *nothing*?" I asked. Even to myself, my voice sounded desolate.

She stared at me, debating something within herself. "Follow me," she said abruptly, rising from the table.

We walked back to the furnace room, past the hanging peppers. Old furniture was stashed here — a three-legged chair, an end table in need of varnish, a rickety ironing board tattooed with burn marks. In one corner was a desk with an accordian-type rolltop. Connie fidgeted with its handle.

"Stuck," she said. The fat on her arms jiggled as she tried to force it open. It gave suddenly, the rolltop disappearing with the sound of a flourish down the keyboard of a xylophone.

Connie waved at the hovering dust. "Twenty years. Like opening a coffin."

On the surface of the desk was a stack of paper, browned with age along the edges. It looked as if it had been heated with matches to just below the burning point.

A clear jar contained a bunch of paintbrushes, stored bristles up. If they'd been jammed bristles down, they'd have been destroyed in the long entombment.

I eyed the goods. "It's just paper. There's nothing on it."

"I told you there weren't any pictures." She put her hand to her nose and sneezed. "Dust! That's all that's left."

She picked up a yellow metal box I hadn't noticed and opened it. Inside were circles of hard colored cakes, hunks of watercolors with tiny cracks, fissures. Each cake was a miniature desert.

"This is all the stuff that teacher gave him. The brushes, the paints, the paper . . . when he stopped using it I just shut it all up in this old thing."

"Why didn't you throw it out?"

"Mind your own business."

She patted the top of the desk. Her palm came away black with dust. I took the paint box, licked my index finger and rubbed it into a cake that looked maroon. My finger came away blood-red.

"Still good, Connie." I showed her my fingertip. "Look!"

"All these years." She shivered, though it was far from cold. I reached for a sheet of paper but it broke at my touch, delicate as the skin of ice on a puddle on the first day of winter. Paper flakes clung to my hand.

"The paper's no good. I need new paper."

Connie tilted her head. "You wanna use this stuff?"

"Yeah. If it's okay with you."

"Don't matter to me."

"Every time it rains the stuff I do on the sidewalk washes away. I got money, my father gave me a little money before he left."

"What are we, poor? We'll buy the paper, thank you very much." She tried to pick up a sheet but it crumbled just as mine had.

80

"Who ever thought . . ."

"What?" I prodded.

She took a deep breath. "Who ever thought this would get used again?"

Was she choking back a sob, or did I imagine that? Maybe the dust had made her choke. It hung in the air like fog.

"We'll get you paper," she repeated. "But go to bed now. And lay out your good clothes for the morning, we're going to the early Mass."

I climbed the stairs. It was awhile before I heard Connie's heavy feet coming up, and then I fell asleep.

CHAPTER SIX

SUNDAY morning, and Shepherd Avenue was stinging with the sharp scent of wet brick and cement, for this was the day men washed their stony domains, using hoses with gunlike handles they loved to squeeze. They began at the back of their properties and hosed up driveways, pausing for extra time at pets' droppings before washing the whole mess out into the street.

Connie had us up at six-thirty for the eight o'clock Mass, even though the church was just a few blocks away. For the first time in Brooklyn I got out my "good" clothes and was surprised at how badly they fit — the pant cuffs hiked up to my ankles, and my black shoes seemed stiff and heavy after so much time in sneakers.

I was hungry but Connie said all I could have was a glass of water. I'd never been to church before and asked Angie why we couldn't eat breakfast. He stopped rubbing polish on his shoes.

"You *never* been?"

"Nope."

"Jesus . . . well, the way it works, you're not supposed to eat before you receive."

"Receive *what*?"

"Jesus! You really don't know anything about it," he marveled. He provided a thumbnail sketch of the Catholic church in the time it took to buff his shoes.

You went there to pray; you received a piece of bread on your tongue, so thin it was like paper; you pretended it was the body of Jesus Christ, so you just *sucked* on it, without chewing; and you couldn't eat anything for hours before receiving it.

"His *body?*" I was astounded. "Why would anybody want to eat his body?"

"Good question," Angie said, putting away the shoe-shine box. "When you figure it out, you tell me. But don't tell Connie you never went to church, she thinks you did."

"Okay. But I'm hungry."

He sneaked a handful of sunflower seeds into my pocket, murmuring, "These don't count."

The three of us walked out together, cleaned and brushed, down a sidewalk that seemed to sparkle especially for us. Louisa, at curbside, looked up dumbly at us, as if our good clothes were a disguise. I felt hot and sticky and there was too much Vitalis on my hair. It dripped down my cheeks.

Mel came running up from behind, patent leather shoes flashing. "My cousin won't hurry up," she said, jerking a thumb over her shoulder at Rosemary, who made her way toward us like the Queen Mary.

Connie stopped. "We're early, we can wait for her."

"Ah, it's even hotter when you stand still," Angie said. "We'll meet you there."

"Go," Connie said, unoffended. "Sit in the middle, near the aisle. That way we don't have people crawling over us."

We abandoned Connie. "When was the last time you went to church?" Mel asked Angie in a sharp voice.

He shrugged. "Not counting weddings or funerals, maybe five years ago."

"I've never been to church," I said.

Mel's eyes widened. "Holy shit, you guys are in trouble."

"We are not," Angie said calmly. "You tell me this, Mel — do you like church?"

"It's God's house," she said dutifully.

82

Angie laughed. "What isn't?" He took a sunflower seed and split it between his teeth.

"You better not receive," Mel said musically.

"I'm not gonna, but I could if I wanted to."

"Not for three hours."

Angie rolled his eyes and poured seeds into Mel's hand. "Three hours, one hour, ten minutes — what's the difference? Some pope made up that crazy rule. What do you think happens? God gonna send down a lightning bolt because I ate one seed?" He pointed into his palm. "He's the one who made the seed, in the first place."

I took a seed from my pocket and ate it. The saltiness was agreeable, the first taste of the day.

Angie bit another seed. "You have to take this church business the right way. Otherwise you go nuts."

Mel watched us chew before biting into a seed herself. "I'll eat it, but I ain't gonna receive today."

"Just don't drop the shells on the sidewalk. If Connie sees them she'll have a fit." He jerked his thumb toward the sky, then behind his back. "I ain't afraid of Him, I'm afraid of her," he chuckled.

The church was incredibly hot. It had marble floors and high ceilings. The walls were yellow, except down low, where fake wood paneling had been painted with a coarse-bristled brush to a height of maybe five feet. Tall grinning fans spun back and forth, pushing hot air around. My pants stuck to the seat.

The priest was a fat man named Peter Valenti, and almost as soon as he began speaking I fell into a swoon. My eyes closed but Mel shoved me awake. On my other side Angie nibbled seeds on the sly. He dropped the shells into the hymnbook holder. Connie and Rosemary seemed to be paying attention, but even their eyelids drooped.

What was so great about church, I wondered. Nothing *happened!*

But suddenly we were jolted. Valenti altered his tone, snapped his prayer book shut. Heads lifted all over the place.

"Today we welcome a new man to our parish," he began. A

murmur ran through the crowd. On and on Valenti talked —
where he'd studied, how he came to arrive at Saint Rita's. I fell
into another swoon until the words ". . . so please welcome
Deacon David Sullivan."

I started to applaud, but had struck my hands together just
twice before Angie caught them. Mel hissed, "Ya never *clap* in
church, dope!" The whole congregation tittered.

The young man at the pulpit laughed and said, "Well, it's
certainly nice to know I'm welcome here."

That got me off the hook. Everyone laughed, suddenly alert,
as if a gust of cold air had blown through the church. The
deacon was six feet two and weighed no more than a hundred
and forty pounds. His arms and legs were long and thin, spidery-
looking in the black garb of his profession.

Veins bulged in his hands, which were white as a statue's.
His eyes were watery green and his nose was long and thin.
He'd just had a haircut — you could tell, because the newly
exposed scalp near his hairline gleamed even whiter than his
complexion, as if someone had traced around it with chalk.

Bony wrists jutted beyond his sleeves. He rubbed them as he
spoke, and he blinked a lot, too.

His sermon shook the foundations of that stagnant place. We
had to love one another, we should love without fear, it was
all that mattered, don't even bother *coming* here anymore, people, but make sure you love each other or everything is
useless. . . .

"My God!" he boomed. "Why do you think you're *here*?
Why do you think it takes two of you to make a new person?
You're not supposed to get through this life alone!"

On he went for twenty minutes, waving his arms, pausing to
wipe his eyes, seemingly exasperated, elated, and finally exhausted. The doors at the back of the church were opened, at
his request — "Let's *breathe*, people, God knows we have little
enough time in this world as it is."

Suddenly it was time for communion. Connie leaned toward
us, her face alive, as if she'd been hit with a pail of cold water.

"You're all receiving today," she hissed.

Mel gasped; Connie's edict had included her. My heart leapt

as the sunflower seeds in my belly turned to pebbles. I'd been a Catholic for half an hour and already I'd broken a rule.

Angie winked to assure us. "Don't worry. Listen, I'll go first. If anything happens to me you two can run out."

"Let's not," Mel pleaded.

"Eh, relax, trust me." To cement our faith in him he cracked another seed in his mouth.

Caught up in Sullivan's spirit, nearly everyone was getting on line to receive. I stood behind Angie and saw his jaws working — what defiance, to chew sunflower seeds on the way to receive! He'd show them a food-flecked tongue at the altar! I wondered what God's punishment would be — a bolt of lightning through his head, a heart attack?

Angie went to the railing, knelt — I saw the holes in his soles — received, and rose. I took my place at the altar, with Mel next to me. A boy held a gold plate under people's mouths as they received. The deacon was getting closer. I watched Mel stick her tongue out to take the wafer. I imitated her. Sullivan put it on my tongue and winked.

"How's it going, champ?" he whispered.

It tasted like cardboard but my mouth watered to dissolve it. Champ! No one had ever called me that! Valenti gave the benediction to end the Mass. Outside, people flocked around the new deacon in the brilliant sunshine. His dry, sandy hair blew in the wind. I sneaked my hand in for a quick shake and noticed how clammy it felt. His fingers somehow seemed hollow, like cigar cylinders.

Angie was waiting at the bottom of the steps, eager to get going.

"Well," Connie said. "What did you think of that?"

"Okay," Angie allowed. "Not bad."

"Even Vic would love that priest," Mel said.

"He's a deacon, not a priest," Rosemary scolded.

"Whatever he is, he's different," Angie said. "You don't get the feeling he's tryin' to keep you out of hell. I mean it ain't like he's doing you a favor. That's what I always hated about priests."

"His hand's wet," I said.

"He's too skinny," Connie said. "The only bad thing, he shouldn't have told us we don't have to go to church no more."

Angie waved at her. "That's not what he meant. You missed what he was talking about."

They argued about that, and then we broke into the groups we'd traveled in earlier. Angie, Mel, and I were nearly home when he grabbed the tops of our heads as if we were two melons.

"Hey. Didn't I tell you nothin' was gonna happen from a coupla lousy sunflower seeds? Didn't I?"

He laughed, pushed us away, and tugged off his tie, whipping us playfully with it.

Connie did more than shake Deacon Sullivan's hand — she invited him to dinner that very afternoon.

She was impossible to be around in the basement, where the pot of gravy had bubbled like a tar pit since eight that morning. She'd made fresh macaroni and stuffed them with ricotta cheese laced with bits of chopped parsley. She wanted to set the upstairs table but Angie argued that it was cooler in the basement.

"We save that room for baseball people," Connie commented as she set down a clean checkered tablecloth. She made Angie transfer wine from the gallon jug they usually used to a decanter, which would look nicer.

It was my job to rinse out the decanter. I gave it three hard shakings with soapy water and five with fresh before it seemed clean. Then I polished the silverware, gray with disuse. I blackened a bunch of rags in an hour.

I answered the door when he arrived, stunned to see him in a checkered sport shirt, slacks, and sandals. He said "hi" boyishly and rubbed my hair.

I led him down the basement steps, using the narrow staircase I'd first descended weeks earlier. "Into the catacombs," he said in a spooky voice. "Do you know what the catacombs are?"

"Uh-uh."

"They're in Italy, where they bury dead people. Hundreds of skeletons, way down in tunnels under the ground. Children your age clean the bones for the church. Am I scaring you?"

"Nah," I lied. He rubbed my hair again.

Angie was reading the sports section. At Connie's urging, he'd knotted the tie around his neck again. Connie, who had been working at the stove, whipped off her apron with the élan of a matador flourishing his cape.

It was amazing the way she changed in the presence of a clergyman. In one sentence she apologized for the heat, her appearance, and the fact that we were eating in the cellar.

She drew a long breath. "Will you . . . bless the house?"

Sullivan laughed as if he found the request quaint. "If you like," he said, casually making the sign of the cross and saying some Latin words as Angie stood by, head unbowed, cracking a sunflower seed in his teeth. He recognized no spirits that needed to be ushered into or driven from his house.

We got right down to eating. In addition to the stuffed macaroni there was roast chicken, pan-browned potatoes, spinach in olive oil, and a giant bowl of salad — not just lettuce and tomatoes but peppers, cucumbers scored with a fork, radishes, and dandelion greens.

But the deacon disappointed all of us. The wine was too harsh for his tongue and he requested scotch and water instead, innocently criticizing Freddie Gallo's homemade wine, which Angie had drunk for decades.

Sullivan came back for second and third scotches. Until he drank, his hands had been restless. He didn't seem to know where to put them — the tabletop, his knees, his pockets, everything was a hot stove. Now he calmed down.

He left macaroni and chicken behind on his plate, a mortal sin in that household. His jaws clenched noticeably at the bite of the dandelion greens. Angie's eyes narrowed each time he laid his fork beside his plate and gasped, somewhat effeminately, "I'm so *full!*"

Connie was in her glory. "Tell the truth," she said, gunning for a compliment, "when was the last time you had a meal like *this?*"

The deacon put both hands on his flat belly and narrowed his eyes, taking the question seriously.

"Not since my last birthday. My mother made my all-time favorite — fresh-killed roast duck with orange sauce." He kissed his fingertips.

"Oh," Connie said, dumbfounded.

"But this is the best I've had since then," he said, hoisting his scotch. No one else was drinking so he sipped alone. Even I knew a cheap shot when I heard one.

When Sullivan became engaged in conversation with Connie, Angie leaned over and whispered, "I'll betcha Connie kills a duck and cooks it for this guy."

After the meal Connie seemed relieved to be at the sink. Angie and the deacon sipped anisette-laced coffee and ate cannoli. A mound of walnut shells grew in front of Angie's place. He broke them, separated meat from shell, and passed the food to us.

The deacon seemed surprised to have food shared this way: despite his own steady repetition of the communion ritual, it was obviously every man for himself at the rectory dinner table. He chewed nuts in quick short bites, like a chipmunk.

Out of the clear blue he said, "Are you interested in becoming a priest, Joseph?"

"No," I said. "A baseball player."

"His uncle's a ballplayer," Connie said. "Professional, you know."

Angie looked at her. "Since when are you proud of that?" She ignored him.

"Vic and me are gonna be teammates," I proclaimed. "He said so."

Connie rolled her eyes. "Two dreamers."

Sullivan said, "In my family the tradition is for one of the male children to enter the priesthood. In my case I was an only child, so there really couldn't be any argument about it."

"What's an only child?" I asked.

"Means he's got no brothers or sisters," Connie explained. "Funny for an Irish family. Usually there's a million kids. Like rabbits, they are, am I right?"

"Hey, I'm like that, too!" I said before the deacon could react to Connie's crack. "I'm an only child!"

The deacon extended his long hand. "Well, put her there, partner." He grinned as we shook. Something felt warm and gooey in my chest as I added, "And I'm a Syrian, too."

The deacon pulled out of my grasp. "I thought you folks were Italian."

"We are," Angie said. "Joey, who told you that you were Syrian?"

Should I say? Would there be trouble if I squealed on Vic? Six eyes demanded an answer.

"Grace," I finally said. "She told me they had to cut my mother open so I could be born."

"Oh, a *cesarean!*" The deacon's laugh was shockingly falsetto and sort of cruel. Angie's mouth fell open at the sound of it and my gooey feeling went icy. The deacon's hands went to his cheeks and he actually had to wipe tears from his eyes. "Lord, that is just *precious.*"

I looked at Angie and could tell he didn't like the guy, either.

"That Grace," Connie muttered. "The mouth on her." But I knew she would never confront Grace. She needed those sturdy, bony legs to do the shopping; a fight between them would have meant no groceries coming into the house.

Then Sullivan was outlining his plans for the future, including work in Europe, when Angie interrupted him by asking, "But did you ever work?"

Sullivan's big Adam's apple twitched. Connie shut off the water and gazed at her husband. Sullivan cleared his throat.

"When I was sixteen I worked at a Howard Johnson's, making sundaes. That's why my hands feel so cold, to this very day — all that digging around in ice cream barrels."

Connie laughed politely but Angie didn't let him go.

"And now you're what?"

"Sir?"

"How old?"

"I'm twenty-six," Sullivan said evenly, finally getting the drift. Angie murmured something to himself and cracked another walnut. He squeezed the nutcracker too hard, shattering meat and shell together.

He was sweeping it off the table with the flat of his hand

when Sullivan said, "Not all forms of work can be measured by the roughness of a man's hands, Mr. Ambrosio."

Angie set the nutcracker aside. It was so quiet in the room I could hear his sweet, nutty breath wheeze through his thick nostril hairs.

"The job at Howard Johnson's was the only one I had to put money in my pocket, but in a higher sense I've been working all my life for God," Sullivan continued. "When you have The Calling it really doesn't let you rest for a single minute."

The melting ice cubes in his glass shifted, clinked. He helped himself to more scotch.

Angie flushed. "You're a priest. I guess you'd know."

Sullivan grinned. "Actually I'm a deacon."

"Whatever." Angie picked up his wineglass and touched it to Sullivan's drink.

When Sullivan left, Connie said, "You embarrassed that priest to death."

"Deacon," Angie said.

"Don't get smart! If I was him I would have left, right when you started in on him. I don't know why he stayed."

Angie tugged at his tie. "He's got guts, that's why. You see the way he stood up to me? For a church guy he's all right. Not that I like him or anything, but he's all right."

He took the tie off without pulling it all the way apart, like a noose. "From now on no tie when he comes. He don't wear one, I don't wear one."

"Don't worry about it. He'll probably never set foot here again."

But he did. Deacon Sullivan visited plenty of homes in the neighborhood, but he probably never got the sort of straight talk Angie provided. Angie even introduced Sullivan to Freddie, and the two of them warmed to each other: the deacon's father, it turned out, had been a bricklayer who'd worked on the construction of a church with Freddie.

It was Connie who grew sick of him. If we were upstairs in the front parlor and saw him coming, she'd shut off the TV and the lights so the house looked empty. The first time she suggested this trick in front of Angie he wouldn't let her pull it.

"He's got no family, we have to let him in. Where's he gonna go when he gets old?"

The TV stayed on. The doorbell sounded, and as I went to answer it Angie opened the liquor cabinet and took out the scotch.

CHAPTER SEVEN

THE letter was written on widely lined paper, the kind upon which first graders learn script. Choppy, unslanted handwriting reached from the top to the bottom of each line.

> *Dear Mom and Pop,*
> *We had four games so far but I'm not doing so hot.*
> *I only had three hits altogether. But I got robbed four*
> *times or I'd be 7 for 16 instead of 3 for 16 which is a*
> *big difference. The manager said to use a lighter bat,*
> *32 ounces instead of 34. My fielding is OK, I don't*
> *have no errors and that's what they like. I miss every-*
> *body, say hi to the kid.*
>
> love, Victor
>
> *P.S. Pop, I'm chokking up on the bat so I can make*
> *better contact. It's the manager's idea.*

Angie went wild when he read that last line.

"His power's his whole *game!*" he complained to Freddie. "Jesus, it's what makes him different, a shortstop with power!"

"The manager must know what he's doin'," Freddie said, trying to calm Angie down.

"He'll *ruin* him," Angie prophesied.

After that letter Angie was restless all the time. Connie wasn't affected by it — any way he held the bat, her baby son still wasn't around. I was just plain pissed off at the way he'd greeted me in the letter. Kid, huh? Fine, I told myself, I won't write to him.

Mel and I started choking up on our stickball bat to see how it affected our hitting. We couldn't detect a difference.

I was starting to notice Mel's looks. She knew she was never going to be beautiful by conventional standards, that her eyes were too close together and her nose was too large. This knowledge wasn't with her constantly but revealed itself from time to time. When it hit, her mood would shift abruptly, and if I happened to be nearby I would get a hard punch to my upper arm.

We remained friends through the spats, but we got tired of facing each other in stickball. We needed a new challenge, and Mel found it by setting up a game against two kids from the other side of Fulton, the shadowy street beneath the elevated tracks that split the neighborhood as effectively as a river.

Teammates, for the first time! Mel demanded that she be the pitcher — as captain, she said, this was her right. As we walked to the Fulton Street "field" — the side of a red brick building fronting a dry cleaner's parking lot — she bounced a new Spaldeen fretfully on the sidewalk.

"These guys any good?" I asked.

Mel shrugged. "I only know one of 'em. Jack's a good hitter." She stopped bouncing the ball. "You got any dough?"

"Quarter. Why? We already got a ball."

"The losers gotta buy lemon ice for the winners, Joey."

I stopped walking. "You never told me that!"

"Well, I'm tellin' ya now," she said, her anger rising.

I continued walking. "You should have told me right away. I don't like to bet."

"Damn it, Joey, this ain't betting! It's for a lousy lemon ice. You afraid we're gonna *lose?*"

"No!"

"Then stop worryin', already."

The Fulton Street boys were waiting for us. Jack Donnelly was a tall, skinny Irish kid with so many freckles around his nose that they seemed to melt into a giant one, like a birthmark on the middle of his face. His quiet teammate was named Phil, and when I heard that I had to shudder. The only other Phil I'd ever known was also a pitcher, the guy who'd beaned me.

Ducks

This one wore black shorts and black shoes pulled up high on his thick legs, and black dress shoes. He looked like a miniature old Italian.

"Got the bat?" Mel demanded. This was her greeting. Jack handed her a taped broomstick. Mel tapped its tip on the sidewalk.

"Feels funny," she said. "You sure this bat ain't cracked?"

"It ain't cracked," Jack said in a high, nasal voice. "And what if it was? You guys ain't gonna hit nothin' anyway."

"Ha-ha. Real funny, Donnelly." Mel handed me the bat. "This feel okay to you, Joey?"

I took it, shut one eye, and looked down the length of it. Then I tapped it the way Mel had. I had no idea of what I was testing it for. I passed it back to Jack without a word.

Jack cocked his head at me. "This the kid whose old man ditched him?"

A wave of hot fury washed over my body, as if the sun had suddenly plummeted to my shoulder.

"His father's away for the summer, asshole," Mel said. "He's just here for a *visit*, see?"

"That ain't what I heard," Jack said, singsongedly.

"We don't care what you heard, we're here to play ball." Mel took out a coin to flip to decide first at bats.

"Forget it," Jack said. "This is our home field. We get last licks. You guys bat first."

Mel examined the strike zone. "It looks high to me," she said, launching a new argument with Jack. Phil and I eyed each other.

"You got no Dad?" Phil asked suddenly. The deep baritone of his voice startled me but it was sympathetic.

"Sure I do. Like she said, he's away for the summer."

Phil eyed me solemnly. "My old man's an undertaker."

"What's that?"

"He takes care o' dead people. Puts clothes on 'em and combs their hair and shit. Makes 'em look good for the family."

My curiosity was aroused. My mother's casket had been closed. "What for? What's the difference if you're dead?"

93

Phil's eyes darkened. "Fuck you, man." He stalked away before I could apologize.

Phil took his warmup pitches from the sewer lid that served as a mound. Mel rubbed my shoulders as if I were a fighter about to enter the ring.

"Strike zone's a little high," she cautioned. "That son of a bitch drew it high because he's so tall, so swing even if the pitch looks high."

I nodded. "Phil's mad at me."

"Forget about him. Are *you* mad?"

"At who?"

"Jack. Don't be mad at him, otherwise you won't hit nothin'."

"I'm not mad," I lied, jerking out of her grasp. "Don't worry, I'll hit."

Phil had an awkward pitching style, a set of choppy arm and leg motions that somehow worked to deliver deceptively fast pitches. He was also a pro, through and through — I thought for sure he'd try to bean me but he didn't.

Mel and I hit nothing through the first three innings, and they were having just as much trouble trying to hit her.

Nobody spoke as we crossed one another between innings. Jack and I had nothing to do in the outfield. The game was scheduled for nine innings, and after six, the four of us agreed to break for a drink of water from a leaking hydrant a block away. Mel had a single and Jack had a double but there was still no score.

We let our opponents walk ahead of us. I felt sleepy from so much inactivity in the outfield and yawned openly. Mel saw me do it.

"Hey, wake up. Phil's gettin' tired, we're gonna start hitting him soon."

"I'm awake. Get off my back, Mel."

Wet-cheeked, Jack and Phil walked past us on the way back to the battleground. "Won't be long now," Jack said. "Man, I can just taste that sweet lemon ice."

"The game ain't over yet," Mel said. I noticed that Phil's

shoe was scraped raw on the side, where he dragged it with each pitch. I caught his elbow.

"I didn't mean nothing when I said that about your father," I said, deliberately botching my grammar. "I don't know anything about the undertaker business."

Phil nodded. "Don't worry about it."

"Come on, Phil," Jack called, annoyed at this fraternization with the enemy. Phil trotted away heavily to join Jack, who put his arm across his shoulder and whispered into his ear.

"Hey. What was all that about?" Mel wanted to know, wiping water from her mouth with the back of her wrist. She'd soaked her shirt. The small bumps of her chest showed through it.

"I just had to tell Phil something."

"He strikes you out *nine times* and you're talking to him? That's real smart, Joey, real smart."

"Hey! This isn't a war, it's a game!"

She pointed toward Shepherd Avenue. "If that's gonna be your attitude, Joey, maybe you oughta go home. Go on, I think your grandma's callin'. I'll beat these assholes by myself."

She knew just where to stick the needle. I pushed her away from the hydrant.

"Get out of my way, I'm thirsty." I squatted to drink my fill of the icy water. As I swallowed I felt her fingers through my hair. She might have been petting a shaggy dog, and I knew that she was, in her awkward way, saying she was sorry.

Bloated with water, we returned to the battlefield — another two innings, and *still* nobody scored! Mel and Phil were grunting now as they threw pitches, and all four of us groaned when we swung.

Nothing but foul tips and strikeouts. The four of us let out bulletlike curses upon third strikes: "Shit! Fuck! Damn!" I was the only one not using the "f" word.

The ninth inning. The side of Phil's left shoe was scuffed so badly by his dragging that the leather looked gray. I struck out to lead off the inning. Mel struck out and handed me the broomstick, wiping sweat from her forehead.

"Try and *hit* something," she said, in a tone that meant "for once in your life." The heat had made her cranky. The sun was setting low in the sky, hovering just above the top of the dry cleaner's — the angle of its rays in my eyes was murderous. I called for time out and rubbed my eyes while Phil was in the middle of his pitching motion.

"Quit stallin'!" Jack roared. I set myself in the batter's box. Phil wound up and threw. I swung blindly, aiming at the sun, as if it were a giant light bulb I wanted to shatter.

But instead I caught the Spaldeen solidly and glimpsed it taking off in an arc like a bee from a flower.

"Holy shit," Mel said.

"Fuck!" Phil shouted as he turned to watch the ball's flight, and then Jack was turning to chase the pink missile.

A useless chase. The ball struck the side of a building on the fly, an automatic home run. I walked straight for Mel and handed her the stick.

"Was that all right?" I deadpanned. "Now maybe you'll shut up."

She was too happy about our 1–0 lead to get mad at me. She struck out almost gleefully to end the inning.

"Nice rip," Phil said as he passed me on my way to the outfield. Jack heard him and poked him hard in the back.

"Don't talk to that lucky Wop," he said, even though Phil was also Italian. Phil looked hurt but did nothing. He reached to his calves and pulled his sinking socks up high. I grabbed Jack's bony shoulder and spun him around.

"I don't like that word," I said. In one of our nightly talks Vic had told me what it meant.

Jack knocked my hand aside. "Ah, go to the outfield, for Christ's sakes."

"You apologize first."

"I ain't gonna apologize." He was so close I could feel his hot breath in my face. He folded his thin arms across his chest. The giant freckle seemed to glow red.

A hand on my shoulder: Mel's. "Settle it later, Joey. Lemme strike out the side first."

"Fuck the game," I said, using the "f" word for the first time ever. "We'll play after he apologizes."

The surge of energy I'd felt from my home run blast still lingered in my bloodstream like a slow-moving drug. Though Jack had all those inches on me I felt no fear.

"I ain't gonna apologize," Jack repeated. His face broke into a grin. "Why should I apologize to a Wop with no Pop?"

My fist shot into his face, catching Jack in the middle of a laugh. The sound actually turned into a cry with no break in noise. I felt the cartilage in his pug nose bend against my knuckles, and then Jack's hands flew into his face and his foot kicked toward my groin almost reflexively, as if a doctor had thumped his knee with a rubber mallet.

I dodged the kick and went after him with both fists, punching at any part of him over his belt — chest, stomach, the sharp points of his elbows.

"Wop! Wop!" he yelled nasally, his hands still over his face. I couldn't call him a Mick because I was Irish, too. The frustration of the situation made me fight even harder.

My hands got sore but I didn't stop punching. Out of the corner of my eye I saw Mel and Phil seated against the strike zone, where it was shady. They might have been watching a movie.

Suddenly Jack jumped back and tore his hands away from his face. I gasped at the sight of it. I don't think I drew much blood, but the little I *had* drawn was smeared all over his face, mixed with snot and tears. He looked at his palms and shrieked.

"Fucking W*op!*" he sobbed, but by now the word meant nothing to me. I let my clenched fists drop to my sides, a pair of wrecking balls at rest. Jack fled down the street. Mel and Phil came to me. "Your knees're skakin'," Mel said. I looked down and saw that it was true, even though I couldn't feel them moving. She put a hand on my shoulder.

"God, you kicked the living shit out of him," she said, awed, as if she had just seen the Easter Bunny kill a lion. I flicked her hand off my shoulder the way a horse's tail gets rid of a fly.

"Don't touch me," I said. I was lucky that my stomach was empty because a momentary wave of nausea hit me as I finally realized what I'd done. In the distance Jack slowed to a walk, climbed a stoop, and disappeared into a house. He never looked back.

Mel turned on Phil. "We win. Your man quit so you gotta forfeit."

"*I* didn't quit," Phil said firmly. "Ain't my fault these guys started fightin'."

"You better buy us that lemon ice," Mel warned, gesturing at me as if I were her attack dog. Phil's eyes widened into shiny chunks of coal.

"Forget it," I said. "Come on, *I'll* buy the lemon ice." Mel and I started walking away. Phil stayed behind, happy to escape without a beating.

"You, too, Phil," I said, beckoning with my right hand. There were flecks of Jack Donnelly's dried blood on the knuckles. Phil swallowed.

"You ain't gonna beat me up, are ya?"

"No."

"Swear it?"

"I swear it."

"Whaddya swear it on?"

"Whaddya want me to swear it on?"

"Your balls."

"Hey," Mel said, "what are you, a wise guy?"

"Uh-uh," Phil said, his fear rising. "That's what my father always does. Puts his hand like this and swears on his balls." Phil gripped himself. "That's how my mother knows when he really means somethin'."

I gripped my groin. "I swear on my balls I won't hitcha. Now come on."

His fear vanished and he ran to catch up with us. "That Jack, sometimes he's a real asshole," Phil said, shouldering the stick-ball bat. We walked in silence toward Willie's. I noticed Mel grinning.

"What's funny?" I snapped.

She hesitated. "Was that your first fight ever?"

"Yeah . . . so what?"

"Nothing."

"How'd I do?" As if I didn't know, but I wanted to hear it from her.

She laughed out loud. "You *won*, dummy!" She mussed my hair — she couldn't stop touching me! But I let her do it, without protest, enduring it the way a champion racehorse tolerates a groom. I looked at Phil, who was frowning and looking at his feet. He kicked a pebble.

"My shoes," he said. "My fuckin' mother's gonna kill me when she sees these shoes."

I squatted at the leaky fire hydrant to wash the blood from my hand. Flecks of it were embedded in the lines of skin around my knuckles, like a mosaic. I had to scrub hard to get it off.

"If she kills you, your father can bury you for free," I said. The three of us laughed, all the way to Willie's. While we licked the ices I noticed Mel frowning.

"Hey," she said to Phil. "If your father swears on his balls, what does your mother swear on?"

He shrugged. "I dunno."

Mel gripped the loose cloth at her groin. "What a fuckin' gyp," she muttered.

We said good-bye to Phil at the el train border. Dusk was approaching, and the shadow of the tracks was angled on the buildings across the street, instead of on the street directly below.

"Let's run," I said, and Mel and I were off like jackrabbits. Everything felt right to me. The soles of my sneakers were worn just enough to feel the warmth of the pavement, my shorts felt loose at my hips, and my T-shirt flapped like a sail.

Mel peeled off at her aunt's driveway and shouted "Good night!" but I just kept going without saying anything, picking up speed. The laws of my body seemed to have reversed themselves — the faster I ran, the drier and less tired I felt. I made a hairpin turn at Angie's driveway and sprinted down that, then took the steps to the basement two at a time. I wasn't even winded.

"Don't slam the screen door!" Connie called out, too late; it boomed behind me. A big bowl of spaghetti sat in the middle of the table.

"Good timing," Angie grunted, not looking up from his newspaper. I slid onto the bench behind my dinner plate.

"Wash your hands," Connie ordered.

"They're clean," I said confidently, having rinsed them at the hydrant.

She eyed them suspiciously. "Hey, your knuckles are red. Where were you all day?"

"Playing." And fighting, I thought.

"With the crazy one?" She never used Mel's proper name.

"Yeah."

She forked the spaghetti to get a light coating of sauce all over it, to keep it from sticking to the bowl. She stopped abruptly.

"You look different. Don't he look different?" She slapped at Angie's paper to get his attention. Annoyed, Angie eyed me.

"Looks the same to me," he said after a glance.

Connie continued to study me. "He's sweating! Look, look!" She pointed at my forehead with the dripping fork. I could feel giant drops of sweat forming. I also felt out of breath — the laws of my body were catching up, demanding their due.

Connie continued pointing with the spoon as if drops of blood, not sweat, were leaking from my face.

"Ah, it's only sweat, Connie," I said, wiping my face with my forearm. "What are you getting all excited about?"

"Go wash." She pointed toward the bathroom with the fork, as if I didn't know where it was. "All the way up to *here*, mister." She tapped my elbow, leaving a red sauce streak there.

I let the water run cold for a few minutes. Meanwhile I just looked at myself in the mirror. Connie was right — I *did* look different, and not only because my face was tomato-red with heat. My eyes looked darker, deeper-set in my skull, and my head seemed longer, as if it were somehow losing its cesarean roundness.

I bared my teeth and frightened myself with my own image. I put the plug in the basin, filled it, and threw cold water on my face, knowing the red would go away but not the new look Connie had so perceptively caught.

Confidence. I'd just beaten the daylights out of a fellow human being, and was now preparing to sit down to a meal as if I'd been out shooting marbles. A feast for a conquering hero. I knew I would never be the same.

CHAPTER EIGHT

EARLY in July we were hit by a blistering heat wave. Stickball was out of the question. It was too hot to even draw on the sidewalk. All Mel and I had the energy for was lemon ice.

Angie's garage was always cool, no matter how hot it got. We went in there and pulled the sectioned door down behind us, then sat on his toolboxes to enjoy the ices. The air was rich with smells of motor oil and grease. Huge plumbing tools hung on the walls about us, looking like instruments of torture.

Enormous daddy-longleg spiders picked their way across the cinder-block walls. Mel absentmindedly caught one and began pulling its legs off, holding each severed leg in her fingers until the twitching stopped.

"Cut it out," I said. In the gloom of the garage Mel's cruel act seemed even worse than it was. It wasn't a big deal for me to challenge her, not since I'd beaten the shit out of Jack Donnelly.

"Cut what out?" She was being kittenish and continued pulling off legs until there was just one left. She held the maimed creature for an instant before flinging it toward me.

It landed smack in my lemon ice. Disgusted, I dashed it out with my fingertips, then brought my toe down on the bulbous body to take him out of his misery.

"You stupid," I said. She laughed scornfully.

"It's just a bug, Joey."

"Yeah? Well I can't eat my lemon ice now."

"Give it to me." She held one paper cup in each hand, alternating sucks. I wondered if she'd planned it all that way.

"Rosemary cried last night," she said suddenly. "Said she's gonna be an old maid."

"Why?"

" 'Cause Vic ain't writin' to her. He's gonna find someone else while he's away and fall in love."

Family loyalty rose like sap in my blood. "Vic can do whatever he wants."

"They had plans, damn it!"

"*Rosemary* had plans."

"Ah, you suck," Mel said. She noisily slurped the rest of the ices and tossed the wadded cups aside. "Well, I don't get to be a bridesmaid, then."

"Big deal."

"Joey."

"What?"

"What do you look like?"

I peered at her face, trying to catch the joke. Streaks of dirt ran down her sweaty face and her mouth was slightly open. Light that filtered through the dirty garage window made her face spooky-looking.

"I look like this," I said, confused.

But that wasn't what she meant. I'd been getting funny looks ever since I'd beaten up Jack and Phil made me swear on my balls that I wouldn't hit him. I wasn't a punk kid from Long Island anymore.

"That ain't what I mean."

"What do you mean?"

"With no clothes on."

My teeth clenched and my heart leapt. "Ja ever see a girl naked?" she whispered.

I'd never even seen a man naked. "Nope."

"Never?"

"Did you ever see a man?" I said defensively.

"Nah. I opened the door once when my uncle was takin' a bath but there were a lot of soap bubbles."

"How come you're askin' all this?"

"No reason." A menacing smile nearly hypnotized me, and then her arms flashed in a tangle of white and she whipped her shirt off. She balled it up and used it to wipe a lone drop of sweat running down the middle of her chest.

I might have been looking in a mirror. Mel was somewhat

more muscular than I was but otherwise we were the same. When she inhaled, her ribs appeared. The bumps that had shown against her wet T-shirt at the fire hydrant were hardly visible in the flesh.

"We shouldn't do this," I said.

She giggled. "We're not doin' nothin'. It's hot. Come on. You."

A challenge. Who could resist her challenges? My fingers found the back of my T-shirt. Momentarily it clung to my wet back but I managed to get it off.

"We're the same," I announced.

"Well, I'm too young to have tits," she apologized. Already her fingers were working the zipper on her pants. When she got them unzipped she pushed them down along with her underpants, one motion. She stepped out of them and knocked them aside with her foot.

I looked at her groin, a pink envelope of flesh. It was something to laugh at but I didn't. "You," she said. Half command, half suggestion.

My hands were sweat-wet, and they shook so much they kept slipping off my belt buckle. Outside cars honked, fire engines wailed. They wailed so often it seemed amazing that all of Brooklyn wasn't rubble. . . .

But they may as well have been on the moon, for all they had to do with us. I finally got the belt undone, but before taking my pants down I looked into Mel's eyes. They had never looked so *kind* before — nothing goading, nothing I-dare-you about them. She stood with a hand on her hip, as if she were awaiting a bus. I was a sparrow on the verge of flying off, so she was careful not to startle me.

Closing my eyes, I followed her example and yanked down pants and underpants at once. My scrotum had shrunk to a dried fig. My cock was like a doorbell, just the tip showing.

"It's usually bigger than that." I was talking more to myself than to her.

"Mine's always the same size. I mean, it's just sort of like a hole, ya know? I can't aim when I pee or nothin'."

"Uh-huh . . ."

"Shit. Boys always get the neatest stuff."

We were looking into each other's eyes. All we had on was our sneakers. Mel approached me, her feet crunching on the gravelly garage floor. She put out one finger and touched the tip of my cock, pressing it as if it *were* a doorbell she meant to ring.

"Wow! It's like a sponge!" she exclaimed, jerking her hand away. I covered my tingling organ with my hand and felt it shrink, as if it were having the opposite of an erection.

My other hand reached for her chest, fingers outspread. My fingertips touched the circumference of her left breast. I drew them together and let them squeeze her bud of a nipple, gently: it was hard as a coin, the size of one of those pink button candies we bit off sheets of paper. Mel shuddered as if she feared I might hurt her. I yanked my hand away.

"Well," I said.

"Well yourself."

Our voices were both shaky. "You can touch my other thing if ya want, Joey."

"Nah. We should get dressed now."

"Okay. Are you embarrassed?"

"Nah."

"Me neither." As we bent to pick up our clothes we giggled with relief.

A fist rapped on the garage door. Petrified, we looked at each other, and then the door pulled open, sections of it rattling as they slid into the metal tracks over our heads. Light caught us at our feet, knees, and torsos, just like a curtain going up on actors. We squinted at the long, thin form of Deacon David Sullivan.

"I heard voices," he began airily, but he stopped dead when he saw us. His eyes widened to baseballs. His knees even bent with momentary weakness. I think I would have felt less embarrassed if I'd been totally naked, instead of with my sneakers on. Sullivan jerked the door down halfway.

"Get dressed."

We did, rapidly. I plunged my foot into my pants three times

104

before finding the leg. Mel was crying. I would have, too, but my entire body — mouth, eyes, armpits — had gone dry.

"Are you dressed?" Sullivan demanded a minute later. I told him we were. Mel choked when she tried to talk.

He yanked the door all the way open, grabbed us by our wrists, and pulled us down the driveway. The sun felt hot on my head, as if Connie were pressing her iron on my scalp.

The deacon's strength shocked me. His thin fingers were wrapped tightly around my wrist, like piano wire. It hurt, and I'm sure Mel was hurting, too, but neither of us made a sound all the way down Shepherd Avenue, across Atlantic Avenue, and into the empty church.

Like a couple of hooked fish we were tugged to the front of the church and dumped in the front pew, directly in front of a rack filled with burning red candles in cups.

The deacon must have thought he'd stumbled upon a brand new perversion. Certainly he'd never bared himself to anyone as a child. Maybe he hadn't done it as an adult, either.

He leaned against the pew to catch his breath. "Stay here. I'll be right back." His hard heels clicked on the marble floor, echoing all the way out. The doors boomed behind him with the finality of the gates to hell. We were alone.

The church smells were deeper and cooler with the place empty. Incense blended with burning beeswax and dust to form the smell of death. Now and then we heard cars beeping in the distance and were reminded of our entrapment. Escape wasn't even a possibility to consider.

Mel finally said, "We're in trouble."

"I told you we shouldn't have," I scolded.

"But we didn't *do* it!"

"Didn't do *what?*"

She was quiet, briefly. "I don't know. But whatever it was, he thinks we did it."

"We'll tell him," I said. "We just wanted to see. He can't get mad at that."

"Don'tcha think he'll be mad *any*way? This is it, Joey, this is it!" Mel shrieked.

I didn't dare ask what "it" was. For all we knew Sullivan was out fetching an axe to chop our heads off at the altar. I looked wildly around the church. Statues leered at us. A huge crucifix behind the altar seemed grotesque, complete with blood at Christ's hands, feet, forehead, and belly.

And he was a good guy. If they did that to him, what was in store for *us?*

Mel's face dropped into her hands. "Oh, God. Oh, God."

Clumsily I laid my arm across her shoulders. She didn't respond to my touch but she didn't push me away, either. Her body was stiff as wood.

"Boy, do I hate that guy," I said. "I hated him the minute I saw him."

Her shoulders shuddered. "You're my best friend," she said into her hands.

"You're my only friend," I said. It was true. We were each saying good-bye without even knowing it.

I took my arm off Mel when I heard the church doors open. Deacon Sullivan's heels didn't sound as loud as before because he was keeping pace with two slow people, Connie and Rosemary.

The three of them stared solemnly. I felt as if I were still naked.

Rosemary was ashen. Connie's lips were tight but otherwise she looked the same as usual. I'd seen that face on her before, when she broke the yolk of an egg she was frying. There were rings of flour at her wrists, powdery bracelets where she hadn't wiped far enough.

"I didn't know where to bring them," Sullivan said. "I took them here on an impulse. Maybe I acted in haste. . . ."

His voice trailed off but neither woman urged him to continue. They probably weren't listening, anyway.

Rosemary suddenly lunged forward and grabbed Mel by the hair.

"Whaddya got to say?" she yelled. "You proud of yourself, lady?"

An incredibly shrill voice. She seemed to be imitating a parrot.

"No," Mel said, wincing in pain.

Rosemary gave the hair a tug. "I didn't *hear* you."

"No!" The single syllable boomed off the walls and the ceiling. Rosemary nodded.

"Your mother and father get killed, we take you in. Do you eat good? Do you sleep in a nice room? Do we buy you nice clothes so you can go and take them off in front of people?"

"*One* person," Mel corrected.

Rosemary let go of Mel's hair and used the same hand to slap her face. Mel's eyes watered. A moment later she was gagging and dry-heaving.

"Not in church, not in church!" Rosemary said, grabbing Mel's wrist, yanking her out of the pew, and dragging her outside.

Connie turned to Sullivan and said calmly, "You can go now."

He looked puzzled. "I hope I did the right thing —"

"Please," Connie said, "just leave." It was strange to see her taking command in the only building that could intimidate her — in effect, she was kicking Sullivan out of his own house. But he left, dismissed like a messenger.

She sat beside me. "Don't touch me," I warned — a funny thing to say, considering that she never touched me. But she laced her fingers together to show she wouldn't. I began to cry.

"We didn't *do* anything. We just took our clothes off and looked."

She noticed the flour on her wrists and dusted herself off. "Why were you in there?"

"It was hot outside. We had lemon ice."

"Didja touch each other?"

"Only a little."

She broke her unspoken promise and cupped a warm hand on my knee. Before I could protest she said, "I'm making lentil soup. Spinach and tomatoes in it, the way you like it, and then later there's ice cream."

She spoke in the same idle fashion she used to pass the time while cooking!

"Your grandfather'll be home in a few hours," she said, shifting the responsibility. "You talk to him."

"I want my mother," I sobbed, plunging my face into my hands. Even dead, she seemed more reachable than my father.

Connie patted my knee. "She's dead. Let's have soup now, you'll feel better."

Somehow, I did.

After eating I fell asleep on the basement couch. I didn't awaken until I heard the screen door bang. Angie came in and set his lunch pail down, said "Hey" to Connie in lieu of a kiss (I never saw them kiss), and asked what was wrong — he must have sensed it from her expression.

They spoke in soft tones. I feigned sleep well, lying there and watching through narrowly slit eyelids. I saw Angie's eyebrows jump.

"They do anything?" he asked.

"What could they do?" Connie hissed. "He's only ten!"

Angie chuckled. "You forget, he's Italian."

"That's disgusting!"

They talked a little while longer, and then Connie set his place at the table while he washed up.

"Wake him, talk to him," Connie said when he returned from the bathroom. A cloud of Lava soap filled my nose, and then his hand was brushing hair away from my forehead.

"Don't worry," he said. Exactly the words I needed to hear to fall back asleep.

Mel didn't do as well with her family. Three days later, she was gone from Shepherd Avenue for good.

A scenario was planned and cunningly executed. The neighbors were told that Mel's relatives out in Patchogue, Long Island, wanted her to come and live with them, since they'd bought a brand new house with lots of rooms and a big backyard. In truth the Patchogue relatives had to be bullied into taking her, the argument ending when Rosemary's mother said, "It's your turn."

I didn't even get to say good-bye. I found out about it on the fourth day. We were torn apart the way concentration camp families were by the Nazis.

I missed her and I missed myself, the self I had been before the incident in the garage. What was the matter with me? Did other kids do what I'd done? I had to get in touch with Mel.

Before going to face Rosemary I put on a clean T-shirt and wet-combed my hair. Looking down at my feet, I decided to wear my good shoes. As I rubbed black polish on them I worked out my speech:

"Please give me Mel's address so I can write her a letter."

In and out of Rosemary's house. I'd get the words out before she could slam the door in my face.

As I walked down the block my armpits felt dry, though the sun was bright and hot. The heat had chased everyone inside, and the street silence accentuated the pounding of my heart.

Mel's clumsy chalk drawings still covered the sidewalks. They would remain until the next rainfall. Stubborn to the end, she continued drawing horses with the hind legs bent the wrong way.

I climbed her old stoop and rang the bell. The door curtain parted. I glimpsed Rosemary's wide face. One eye squinted, then the curtain fell back in place.

The lock turned and the door swung inward. I was standing so close to it that I felt air being sucked in from all around me.

"What do you want?"

"Please give me Mel's address so I can send her a letter I wrote." My original speech, slightly altered. Rosemary thrust out a flour-coated arm. On one of the hottest days of the summer she was baking, probably something to send to Vic. Warm smells of butter and sugar wafted out the door. "Give me the letter, I'll send it."

"I . . . don't have it."

"What?"

"I . . . didn't write it yet."

"You just told me you wrote her a letter. Now you say you didn't. Joey, can't you stop telling *lies*?"

I bit my lip, fought for balance. My buttocks tightened. "Please just give me the address, Rosemary," I pleaded, hating the whine in my voice.

"When you finally *do* write this letter, bring it to me and I'll send it."

"I don't wanna do it that way."

"You don't trust me?"

"Why should I?"

"Then forget the whole thing." She started pushing the door shut but I caught the knob on my side and leaned forward. Rosemary was more than twice my size but she yielded easily to my push. I felt the crush of thick carpeting underfoot; I was inside.

Fear was in her eyes but she tried to act calm. "Okay. Long as you're here, come in."

She turned and walked down the dim hallway. I followed slowly, my eyes still adjusting from the bright sunshine.

We went to the room she'd shared with Mel. On one side was a cot, the thin mattress rolled up at one end like a snail shell. The network of springs reminded me of a skeleton.

On the other side of the room was a huge, overloaded bureau — saint statues, perfume bottles, toilet water. A cup with a red candle in it, the wick blackened. The overstuffed bed was stacked high with throw pillows. A doll dressed in white sat on the pillows, shiny plastic legs spread wide.

On the wall over the bed was a photo of Vic, totally out of his element — he wore a jacket and tie, the same costume he'd donned to meet the baseball scout. I wondered where it had been taken, why he'd been dressed that way.

Rosemary opened the closet on Mel's side of the room. "She left some stuff here. Maybe she didn't want it. Maybe she just forgot it. I'll give it to you. If you don't want it, throw it out."

She spoke into the closet, passing stuff behind her: a stickball bat, two scuffed Spaldeens, a brand-new box of chalk. She straightened and groaned.

"That's all of it. You can go now."

"The address," I said, cradling the stuff as if it were the corpse of a beloved pet. "I need the address."

"Go home, Joey. I'd appreciate my books back."

"You can shove those books, Rosemary."

Her open hand smacked my face. It didn't hurt but tears sprang to my eyes, liquid anger. I ran out hugging Mel's stuff to my chest.

CHAPTER NINE

Now I spent a lot of time in the house, watching Connie cook. When she wasn't looking I'd unscrew caps from her spice jars, stick my nose in and inhale deeply. Basil, thyme, rosemary — I especially liked the smell of rosemary, even though it had the same name as a person I hated with all my soul. I wondered how rosemary grew, where it grew, and if my father might be in a land where it was harvested.

I looked through Vic's old Yankee yearbooks and his paperbacks, mostly light sports reading and adventure stories. I'd stay in the bathroom so long with books like *Tarzan* that Connie would pound on the door, warning me I'd get hemorrhoids. In my fantasies I *was* Tarzan, swinging on vines, killing lion after lion, escaping from all sorts of trouble, just like my father.

When Connie managed to chase me out I'd go to the construction site and watch the men work. I had a spot on a hill where I'd sit alone for hours. They came to know me and left me alone, while other kids got chased. At lunchtime one day a worker even offered me half of his salami on pumpernickel, but I declined, remembering Connie's edict about Food Outside the Home.

I thought about looking for Phil, the kid from the stickball game, but decided not to. I couldn't bear the idea of having someone else torn from me. Nothing was worth the risk of that.

Another postcard came from my father soon after Mel was gone.

> *Dear Everybody,*
> *The picture on this card was taken right near where I'm staying. Oregon is a very beautiful place, and the trees you see here are the ones they cut down to make*

paper. I like it here but miss you all and hope everyone is fine.

                                                               Sal

"I want to tape it on my wall," I said, taking the card from Connie's hand.

"Yeah? Why? You tore up the last one."

"I know what I did," I said, irritated. But at this point I needed any contact I could get from my father, even if it was just a lousy postcard.

"He didn't sign it 'love,' " Connie said. "Would it have killed him to sign it 'love'?"

"Probably he was in a hurry." Look at who I was defending!

"Always in a hurry," Connie said. "Use tacks, tape pulls the paint off." She walked away murmuring. "Oregon, Oregon . . ."

Moments later she returned with Vic's old geography book and hunted up a map of the United States. She traced around it with her finger in search of Oregon. Her cheeks sagged as she shut the book, snap.

"He's gettin' further away," she said softly.

It seemed like a good time to probe for the truth. "But he's comin' back soon, isn't he, Connie?"

She shrugged. "Eh, what do I know?"

Jesus, it wouldn't have killed her to reassure me, but then again, why should she have bothered? She hadn't asked to get me in the first place. I decided being with people who didn't want me around was even worse than being alone — I had to escape.

But there was no escape from the brick and cement prison these peculiar people called home. Sometimes in bed I would wrap my arms around my head, trying to hatch some kind of a getaway plot. Me, a kid who'd rarely strayed past my father's hedge line in Roslyn!

The answer came to me one hot night as I stared across the room at Vic's empty bed, which I had chosen not to sleep in after he left: a hundred dollars, said the voice of my mother. With a hundred dollars you can even go to the moon. . . .

Sweat-soaked, I sat up in bed, the sheet sticking to my chest like a bandage. There it was, plain as the instructions on an aspirin bottle; get a hundred bucks and go. I was starting with nothing, because the few dollars my father had slipped me had gone toward barrels of lemon ice.

So it was prophetic that the first person I saw upon venturing outside the next morning was Zip Aiello, a sack of deposit bottles slung over his shoulder, glass cash. I ran and fell into stride with him.

"Hiya, Zip."

He gave me his lemon-sucking nod, the same one President Kennedy would have gotten had he been taking a stroll down Shepherd Avenue that morning.

"Okay if I walk with you?"

He stopped. "Why?" The word hung in the air like a dried fig.

I decided to come clean. "I wanna get money for bottles like you do. I need some money real bad."

He set his sack on the sidewalk, removed his fedora, and pushed back his hair with a yellow-nailed hand. "Why?"

"I can't tell you."

"If it ain't none of my business say, 'It ain't none of your business.'"

"It ain't none of your business."

"Fair enough." He pulled the fedora back on so that the hatband hid his eyebrows. "Kid. I got my own territory around here, unnerstand? Don't nobody touch it but me."

Uh-oh. He was afraid I'd be horning in on his turf. "Look, I'll go someplace else to find bottles. You just gotta show me where to bring them for money."

He pushed back the hat. "Another *neighborhood?*"

"Uh-huh. I promise I won't take any bottles from around here."

The lemon turned to honey in his mouth. The smile was both friendly and grim. "You leave this neighborhood, you might never come back."

"I'm not afraid," I lied.

"You oughta be. Rough streets around here."

A bit of his breakfast was irritating his gums. He took his false teeth out, ran his tongue around his gums, spat toward the curb and replaced the plates, double-clicking them in place. Those teeth were probably Zip's only possession that hadn't first been owned by someone else.

"You swear you'll stay off my territory?"

"I swear."

"You swear on your dead mother?"

He deserved a kick in the shins for that but he didn't get it. "I swear on my mother."

"Ya *dead* mother."

"My dead mother." They really made you drink your bile without a chaser when they knew they had your number on Shepherd Avenue.

Zip shouldered the bag, then looked behind as if checking for an oncoming posse of lawmen. "Awright, let's go."

We turned right on Atlantic Avenue. Seven blocks of silence, and then we went through an open garage door with the word DISTRIBUTOR over it. Crates of soda were stacked everywhere. We headed for a man in a green windowed cubicle. It was lighted by a small lamp on a desk, which cast a round circle of light on the area where he kept his charts. You forgot it was daytime back there. The man peered over the tops of his half-glasses at us.

"How many, Zip?"

"Thirty. Four big."

"You know where they go." The guy wasn't even going to bother counting them. Almost daintily, Zip removed the bottles one at a time from the sack, as if he were unpacking treasured Christmas ornaments, and set them into a shallow tin bin. When he was through the man paid him, dropping coins one at a time into his hand. The sound made my mouth water.

"Nat, this here's Joey, he's gonna bring you bottles."

Nat came out of the cubicle, tall and lanky, Lincolnesque in a white shirt with sleeves rolled to elbows, a loose stringy tie, and a vest. He had stiff hair shaped like corrugated iron. Roslyn women spent fortunes to have such patterns inflected upon their scalps. His lips were beaky and fishlike, as if he stayed alive by sucking moss off lake bottoms.

He didn't squat to meet me, and I got a good feeling shaking his hand at the end of that long arm. I was going to be taken seriously. Nat looked me in the eye as he spoke to Zip.

"Never thought I'd see the day when you took on a partner. What are you, getting old?"

"He ain't my partner. He's gonna work other streets."

"Around here? Ho! You got a gun, Joey? I'm kidding, I'm kidding. Anyway, you'll do a lot of walking, my friend. Zip has a regular Ponderosa to pick."

Neither of us laughed.

"Yiz don't watch 'Bonanza'?" Nat crooned. "Ah, well."

I pulled out of his grasp. "I don't mind walking," I said. Nat shrugged and gestured at his office. "I'm here every day but Sunday until seven. Two cents for little soda bottles, a nickel for the big ones." He clasped his hands as if to beg for mercy. "Please, booby, if the bottle's chipped you won't try and sneak it past old Nat, eh?" The hands came apart. "Bring ten at a time, at least. That way I don't look at your ugly face five times a day."

Zip and I walked out into the sunshine and squatted at curbside. Zip smoothed dirt into a blackboard and, with a Good Humor ice cream stick, diagramed his terrain. It ran in a four-block radius from his house.

He tapped his chest with the stick. "Mine. You got that?"

"I got it. Don't worry, I won't screw you," I said, using an expression Mel had taught me. I don't think she knew what it meant, either.

On the walk home he softened. "I'll give ya a sack," he said abruptly. "I got a extra one." He stopped short and grabbed my shoulder. "Look over there!" He pointed at a small paper bag, twenty yards ahead. "Whaddya see?"

Was this a trick? "A bag."

Zip got the answer he'd hoped for and smiled. "That ain't what I see." In hunched Groucho Marx steps he jogged to the bag, picked it up, and, like a magician pulling a rabbit from a hat, removed a Coke bottle.

"Just made two cents." He put the bottle into his sack, crumpled the paper bag, and threw it over his shoulder. "Ya gotta have a eye for that stuff, kid. See how the bag wasn't blowin' around in the wind? You gotta ask yourself, 'How come that bag ain't movin'?' Then you can make some money. These bottles, they like to hide, if ya know what I mean."

We made the turn on Shepherd Avenue. "You ain't gonna touch my territory, right?"

How many times did I have to tell him? "No, Zip."

"You ain't lyin', right?"

"Hey," I said, recalling another of Mel's favorite sayings, "whattaya, deaf?" I waited outside his house while he went in and got me my sack. It was wadded up in his hands. He looked both ways, yanked my shirtfront out of my pants, and stuffed the secret sack against my belly. The rough burlap fibers scratched my belly but I didn't cry out.

"Someday you'll do somethin' for me." He went inside, jingling the coins in his pocket.

My father's old painting equipment became a new source of solace for me. I spent so much time in the basement making watercolors on the good paper my grandparents had given me that Connie became fretful.

"You need sunshine," she said. "This light is no good." She pointed at the dusty, yellowy bulb that burned on the ceiling.

"I want to paint," I said, covering my work in progress with my arms.

"The sun is better light. You can set up the paper in the yard."

"I like it here," I insisted, willing her with my eyes to leave.

"You're gonna turn into a *mushroom*." She clumped away, defeated.

I was working on my masterpiece, a portrait of my mother. Incredibly, I was having trouble remembering what she looked like — had her eyes been blue or brown? Why couldn't I make a pencil outline that even *remotely* resembled her?

I tore up sheet after sheet of paper ruined by my clumsy strokes — noses too large, foreheads too small, necks too short.

The rock-hard watercolors withstood punishment, no matter how hard I scrubbed my brushes into them. I could barely deepen the crescent-moon scallops on their surfaces.

The floor beside the rolltop desk was littered with crumpled papers. It took days, but at last I succeeded in sketching a decent outline of her profile. I knew it was right because my heart leapt at the sight of it. It was her, all right.

Cautiously, I applied the paintbrush to the outline. No way I was going to botch it. Her eyes were blue, I remembered — how could I have forgotten that? I mixed yellow and brown on a sheet of scrap paper until the color of her hair seemed right.

Next, the skin. I cleaned off my softest brush, touched it to the red cake, and watered it way down before filling in her face.

Hours. When I was through I cleaned all the brushes and straightened out the desk, leaving only the portrait on its surface. I went to the bathroom and washed my hands. They were stained mostly red, as if I'd just performed surgery.

I came back to examine the work. Yes, it was still a satisfying image of her — I hadn't imagined that. Its surface, still wet with water, reflected yellow light from above.

Standing over the painting, I clasped my hands behind my back and puffed gently on the paper, urging it to dry faster. It worked. In a few minutes my mother's skin was nearly dry.

I sat and put my head in my hands. It seemed heavy as a cannonball. My back ached. My face was dropping closer and closer to the work until my lips touched her forehead in a soft kiss.

The poison-tasting watercolors jolted me back to reality. I recoiled, wiping my lips with the back of my hand.

Footsteps descending the basement steps, heavy and slow: Connie's. I made no effort to cover the painting.

I didn't turn around to look at her but felt her breath on my shoulders. An odor of garlic; she was holding a plate of macaroni for me.

"My God, it looks just like her."

Still I didn't turn around. "Sort of," I allowed.

Her hands gripped the knobs at the back of my chair. She'd put the macaroni down on the old ironing board.

"A pretty woman, she was."

"Yeah, but you never liked her, Connie."

"That's not true."

"Yes it is." I turned around. "You never visited us. Everybody around here likes to *fight*."

She refused to respond. "What are you gonna do with the picture?"

I shrugged, feeling the soreness in my shoulders. "I don't know. Hang it in my room. I mean *Vic's* room."

"It's your room too."

"No, it isn't."

Connie's eyes wettened. "Your grandfather can put a frame on it. We got one out in the garage with nothin' in it."

I was stunned. I'd never dreamed of framing my pictures, and here was Connie conferring immortality upon one, of my mother at that.

"Why didn't you like her?" I said, so softly I was nearly drowned out by the gurgle of the nearby water heater. She heard me and shrugged.

"Never really knew her."

"Whose fault was that?"

"Mine." She blinked back tears. "I didn't give her a chance. Eat the macaroni."

She went away. I didn't touch the food. It was late — I noticed the dirty cellar window was black with night. I folded my arms and fell asleep on top of the painting.

But when I awoke in the morning I was in my cot, stripped to my underpants. Angie had carried me and undressed me without awakening me. Sunlight filled the room, and when my eyes adjusted to it I saw the framed portrait of my mother hanging on the wall next to my bed.

Angie had done that, too, but I didn't thank him. I went outside to look for bottles.

Bottles. It all came down to bottles.

When I wasn't painting, I was looking for bottles, and when I wasn't doing either thing I dreamed about where the bottles and paintings would one day take me.

118

As long as I was home in time for lunch and supper I was never asked how or where I spent my daylight hours. I never tried to sneak out of the house after supper, either. What for? It was too dark to see bottles at night.

I was true to my word with Zip and never took bottles from his turf. Even if I found one right in front of the house, I'd carry it across the street and put it inside Zip's gate. This was no untainted act of generosity, of course. In return I had his promise never to tell Connie and Angie what I was doing.

"I can keep my mout shut," he said with a wink.

And he did. I gathered Nehi soda bottles from surrounding black and Puerto Rican areas without anyone but Zip Aiello knowing about it. In the world of Shepherd Avenue this, like anything else kept from public knowledge, was a minor miracle.

I became a maniac about bottles. They were the only things I could depend on not to let me down, and what or who else could that be said about?

In the basement I found an old preserves jar, the kind with the rubber-rimmed lid that clamps down with a stiff wire handle. It was very old glass, freckled with air bubbles. There was a raised pattern of a bunch of grapes on its surface. I washed the thing out, then dropped the first of my deposit bottle earnings into it.

Plink, plink, plink . . . the coins bounced noisily off the glass bottom. I figured if I could fill my jar I'd have a hundred bucks.

"A *hundred* bucks? A *hundred?*" Nat's voice was awed when I told him my goal.

"That's what I need," I said, unloading my latest haul.

Nat scratched his scalp. "That's two thousand big bottles at a nickel apiece, Joey. Five thousand little ones."

"Whatever."

"Take you a long time."

"I'm not going anywhere." *Yet*, I should have added, holding out my hand for my silvery payment.

On the street, Zip would yell to me, "Hey, kid!" He'd rub his right thumb against the other fingers of the same hand. It was question: you makin' much money?

"Pretty good." I could be as vague as that sly operator.

"You gettin' along with the Jew?" He referred to Nat that way without apparent malice. "Not bringin' him no chipped bottles or nothin', are ya?"

"Nah."

"You're lucky nobody sticks a knife in you, where you go."

If anything, the residents on my turf were awed and amused by the sight of the very little white boy with a sack on his shoulder. There wasn't a bottle I wouldn't pick up, no matter how dirty or stinking it was. My mother's warnings about germs and Connie's equivalent instructions to "schieve" things went right by the boards. If I got a disease and died from germs on bottles plucked from sewer water, it would be my father's fault. If a Puerto Rican stuck a shiv in my heart for prowling around his neighborhood, same deal. *He* would have to live with it. I wouldn't have been hunting for bottles in the first place if he hadn't ditched me.

A maniac. These wild thoughts and my quest for a hundred dollars were making me crazier all the time.

I hardly said a word at meals. There was nothing I had to say to my grandparents. As long as my appetite was good Connie let me be, and usually it was tremendous from all that walking and hauling. At night I fell asleep as soon as I got under the covers.

"I'll show you, Daddy."

Crazier and crazier. One blistering afternoon a couple of Puerto Rican painters sat on the stoop of a house eating their lunch. Behind them, the building was turning a lively pink. I was sure that if I came back at night, the place would glow in the dark.

The older men sipped coffee but the rookie of the crew drank from a big bottle of White Rock ginger ale, worth five cents empty. I stood in front of the stoop, watching and waiting. The youth noticed me staring at him.

He jerked his chin up at me. There was a thin pencil moustache on his lip that vanished from sight with his head tilted like that. "Whatchoo want, man?"

"You gonna finish that soda soon or what?"

The man who seemed to be the foreman whirled his forefinger around his ear.

"I want your bottle," I explained. I shook my sack so he could hear my bottles clink and know what I was doing. The older painters laughed but the moustached one shrugged sympathetically.

"I like to drink it slow, buddy boy."

"I'll wait."

And I did. A nickel was a nickel. When he finally finished he handed over the bottle. The White Rock girl's breasts were smudged pink. The older guys laughed as I walked off, but I heard the moustached one say, "Hey, come on, you gotta admit that took balls."

After about a week I had an inch of money at the bottom of my grape jar but then the cash flow slowed to a trickle. I had picked my territory clean. People weren't littering fast enough to suit my pace. I complained to Zip, who sympathized through his laughter.

"You gotta wait a few days, let 'em pile up."

"I don't *wanna* wait."

"Hee-hee-hee. Don't worry, you'll make money long as it stays hot."

But I had no patience. I acted as if a loan shark were at my heels.

It wasn't just my father's fault. It was Mel's fault. It was my mother's fault. It was *everybody's* fault. The only reason I was able to fall asleep during the bottle droughts was because I grew weary trying to figure out the priority of my grudges. I was mad at so many people it was hard to keep track of them all.

"You may just make that hundred, you son of a gun," Nat said. "You got the drive, all right."

It was his fault, too. He wouldn't take beer bottles and there was a fortune in brown glass going to waste in the form of those sour-smelling things I kicked aside daily.

He flashed his moss-sucking smile. "If I took beers you and Zip would take all my money and I'd have to go out of business."

"Don't bullshit me, Nat."

He shook his head at my vulgarity but he said nothing. We did business together, so I was allowed to curse like an adult, without lectures.

CHAPTER TEN

F REDDIE GALLO was going to turn seventy years old in mid-July, and Angie wanted to throw a surprise party for him. He told Freddie's wife there was more room for a party in our basement than there was in hers, and she readily agreed.

She was a small, timid woman with jumpy eyes — I never even learned her name, because all anyone ever called her was "Freddie's wife." She was a lot younger than Freddie, who had married late and fathered Johnny when he was more than fifty years old.

Once when he had a little too much wine at our house Freddie told Angie he could *still* knock up any woman around with one shot, like that, and he snapped his fingers. Connie overheard him and rapped him on the back of his head with a wooden spoon. Still, she agreed to help with the party.

Angie asked Freddie to come for a walk to nearby Highland Park on the night of his birthday. As soon as they were out of sight I was rushed to the bakery by Connie.

Ironically, the cake I picked up wasn't nearly as good as one she could have made herself. It was a sheet cake, barely two inches high, coated with white sugar icing that stood stiff for hours without wilting. Where it nudged the box it left dark, oily stains. There were pink rosebuds along its border and HAPPY BIRTHDAY in red icing across the middle.

It cost three and a half bucks. The baker packed it in a pizza-type box, which I carried on the flat of my hand. I walked home as if I were on a tightrope.

A dozen brimming cups of lemon ice were packed in the freezer, and the big white enamel coffeepot Connie saved for special occasions was on the stove. Cups and stacks of saucers stood ready, and the sugar dispenser was full.

Grace brought a bag of assorted cookies, stuffed with raisin and fig fillings and crusted with egg yolk and colored sugar dots. She never spoke to me these days, never mentioned the day she'd hauled me to my mother's home.

All the other guests were there by five to seven, because Freddie and Angie were due back by seven. Johnny Gallo arrived in dress clothes, as he had a date to keep by eight o'clock. Uncle Rudy sat at the table with his hands folded, the same stance he struck during lulls at his deli.

Rosemary arrived, a shawl across her shoulders though the night was far from cold. I went up and got the bundle of books she'd given me, still tied with string.

"You may keep them, Joseph."

"I don't want anything from you."

She shrugged elaborately and put them under the table, by her feet.

Zip had a present for Freddie he carried unwrapped — a solid brass spigot in the shape of a lion's head. Someone had thrown out an old bathtub without bothering to salvage the metal, he explained, turning the greenish thing over in his hands.

"A little polish and she'll shine like gold," he promised.

I had a present for Freddie, too — a picture of him buried alive, digging his way out like a mole. I gave him circus strong-man muscles and made his bald head resemble a light bulb. I hadn't shown it to anyone yet. I still didn't like Freddie but I did the painting to show off my skills.

Seven o'clock came, then seven-thirty. Connie served the coffee, the cookies, and the lemon ice but refused to cut the sheet cake until Angie and Freddie, *wherever* they were, got home.

Freddie's wife was a wreck but Connie said they probably stopped off at a bar and lost track of the time. But she was no actress, my grandmother — the fury in her tone blanched out the soothing words.

"Let's go to that bar and find them," Freddie's wife wailed.

"No." Connie was gracious but firm. "They ain't kids. Angie knows that people are waiting, they'll be here."

She cut and served the cake.

"Bars are evil," Freddie's wife said.

"Christ's sakes, Ma," Johnny said. He kept looking at the kitchen clock.

Zip rubbed the lion's head spigot in his hands. "If I'da known they was gonna take so long I coulda shined it up."

"You wouldn'ta shined it anyway," Connie said. He went home, leaving the spigot on the table. At five to eight Johnny left, saying there was no way he could miss this date and that he'd catch his father later. Freddie's wife gave out a little cry but she couldn't stop him.

"Work early tomorrow," Uncle Rudy said a little while later, leaving with Grace. Rosemary picked up the books and Connie told me to walk her home.

"No!" Rosemary yelped, startling Connie. "I'll be all right, it's not late." She rushed outside.

The ravaged sheet cake looked ridiculous under the fluorescents. Freddie's wife started to cry. Connie told her to go home, and then we were alone together in the basement.

She sipped coffee and stole glances at the clock. There were cups and plates to be washed but she made no move to clean up. It was the longest I'd ever seen a dirty dish remain on her table.

"Go to bed," she said to me at a quarter to ten. It sounded like a suggestion. I suspected she wanted me to wait up with her.

"When I'm tired," I said. She shrugged lightly. I *was* tired, though — my eyes closed a few times and my chin kept bumping the table and jouncing my teeth. Waiting for Angie and Freddie had become a game of endurance.

"Ah, what I put up with," Connie said with a yawn.

At twenty past ten Angie's footsteps sounded in the driveway — he was alone. I picked up my head from my folded arms, my vision still sleep-blurred. I blinked to clear my eyes. This was going to be a scene I wouldn't want to miss.

He had his hat on, but he wasn't wearing one of his sweatervests, which he usually wore in all kinds of weather because they had pockets for sunflower seeds, cigarettes, and matches. He moved without a word to his seat, like a boxer to a corner after a tough round.

He didn't remove his hat. Connie rose and gave him a cup of coffee, a dollop of milk, two spoons of sugar. She stirred it and clicked the spoon twice on the rim of his cup before laying it on the saucer. Angie stared into the coffee whirlpool.

"And where were you?" she asked tonelessly. No accusation, just a question.

His answer, given before an enormous swallow of coffee, was one word: "Hospital."

Connie's scalp jumped back, the creases in her forehead momentarily disappearing. Angie put his cup down.

"Freddie had a heart attack, right in the park. He died. He's dead."

He took another drink of coffee. I could hear him swallow.

"He has my vest," Angie said. "While we were waitin' for the ambulance to come I put my vest over him. Somebody said it's important to stay warm when you have a heart attack."

Connie reached for his hand, changed her mind, and instead folded her hands on the table.

"I didn't want to take the vest away when they put him in the ambulance." He moved to rub his hair, felt his hat and removed it.

Connie's forehead was creased again. "It was an old vest."

"That's what I figured."

"You did right."

Angie finished his coffee. "Good," he murmured into the cup, meaning the taste of the coffee. Then he looked up sharply.

"Did you hear the noise up the street? All the sirens?"

Connie lifted her hands defensively. "When don't we hear sirens?"

He thought it over. "That's right," he said. "I was just across the street with his wife. The kid's out on a date. Jesus, I'm tired."

Connie said, "You coulda called."

"I don't even know our phone number. Ain't that something? Besides, who thinks of things like that?"

Connie stood. "Maybe I better go across the street."

"No." Angie's voice was gentle but firm. "Stay with me tonight," he said, his face reddening. He looked into the cup, as

if it helped him concentrate. "He was on one o' those whud-
dyacallits, the things you walk across on your hands."

"Parallel bars," I piped in, recalling a gym activity I'd hated
at school in Roslyn. Angie looked at me, seeming to notice me
for the first time.

"Yeah, the bars," he said. "Freddie's moving across them
when all of a sudden he tells me his arms hurt. He drops off
before he reaches the end and doubles over.

"Me, I kid him about it. He always brags how he always
makes it all the way across. Then I see his face is the same
color as the sidewalk."

Angie squinted, like a man trying to remember details from
a twenty-year-old event. "He didn't die right away. I held his
hand for a while and a lady called the hospital and I rode with
him. Me, I never even *thought* about callin' the hospital. Why
should I? You don't bring an ox to the hospital, do you?"

"Okay, okay," Connie said. With a jerk of her head Angie
didn't see she motioned for me to go upstairs. This time she
meant it. I stood, trying to figure a way to say good night to
Angie.

"Freddie was stronger than *anybody*," he blurted. "My God,
they tried to bury him twice and he dug his way out of his own
grave. How could he die like that?"

"Hearts are tricky," Connie said, jerking her head at me more
urgently.

I took the lion's head spigot in my hands. "This is what Zip
was gonna give him," I said. "He says it's solid brass and it'll
shine up like gold."

Angie looked at it.

"Connie says the tile he'd have to break . . . to install this
thing'd cost . . . more than it's worth. . . ."

I was panting. Angie looked at me as if he couldn't decide
whether to beat me or hug me. Was this kid making a joke in
the face of his best friend's death?

His lips twitched. He made a hissing sound as he showed his
teeth, and then he was laughing.

God, what laughter! Connie moved behind him and shoved
me toward the stairs. I was halfway up when I heard his laughs

126

turn to sobs. I tiptoed back down for a peek. Connie stood behind him, patting both wet cheeks.

They stayed downstairs for another hour or so. In the middle of the night Angie moved from his room to Connie's. They were still asleep when I crept down to the basement the next morning. Death, it turned out, didn't affect all patterns. The kitchen was immaculately clean — dishes washed, food put away, floor swept. I went to my rolltop desk and tore up my Freddie Gallo painting without showing it to anyone.

I was infuriated when they refused to let me go to the wake. I thought it was like a party I was being kept from attending.

"You're too young," Connie said. "Stay home."

I appealed to Angie, who murmured, "Watch the house for us while we're gone, kid." I painted while they were away. When they came to the house afterward for coffee and gossip, I was permitted to listen to their stories.

How Johnny Gallo had become hysterical upon returning home at two A.M., to find his shattered mother sitting up with Deacon Sullivan.

How the undertaker — could it have been the father of Phil, the somber kid from the stickball game? — had given the Gallos a small room in the parlor, even though a dead woman hardly anyone came to visit lay in the other spacious room.

How the knot in Freddie's tie was too big and looked ridiculous anyway, because he never wore a tie when he was alive.

How Freddie's sister, a woman who hadn't spoken a word to him in fifteen years, showed up and became hysterical, grabbing Freddie's powdered hand and ordering him to "Wake up!" before the funeral director was able to pull her away.

How funny it was for a man to die on his birthday, and how odd to see the same date for the birth and the death printed on the gold plate inside the casket.

Vic made his usual collect call the next night, hours after Freddie had been buried. Connie listened while Angie talked to him about his hitting and then took the phone from him.

She began to tell about Freddie but Angie flapped his arms to stop her. Then he grabbed the phone from her.

"Your mother ran to the stove, she smelled something burning," he said. "Don't listen to that manager's advice, you just swing your swing. Yeah, we miss you, too." He hung up. Connie was staring at him.

"No sense telling him about Freddie," he said. "Ain't he already having a rough enough time?"

That was certainly true. Vic's letters got gloomier and gloomier, but they were also a shade more insightful — he wasn't just dashing them off, like a camp kid forced to write letters home. Hard times forced him to think; for once he couldn't coast on natural ability.

"How come I never get to talk to Vic?" I complained.

Connie said, "You know what it costs to call from West Virginia? Take the garbage out."

I took the greasy bag out to the can, bashing the lid down on top of it. It had contained the remnants of the birthday cake that was to have celebrated Freddie's seventieth.

"Kid," I heard someone call. "Hey, Long Island."

I knew it was Johnny Gallo. He called me that a lot, a trace of contempt in his voice. He was weaving his way across the street. It was weird to see him moving clumsily.

"Hi, Johnny," I said, scared stiff. His eyes were red and bleary and he had on a black suit he must have worn to the cemetery. He put his hand on the back of my neck, his fingers remarkably strong from all the tools he handled daily to repair engines.

"Long Island, you're all right." He belched wine breath into my face, then pointed at his house.

"My fuckin' mother, she can't stop cryin'. I had to get a load on." He straightened his tie — that is, he *thought* he was straightening it. It veered to one side of his collar, like a hangman's noose.

"Been drinkin' my father's wine," he said, in a tone that suggested he'd actually been drinking his father's blood. "My old man, he made his own wine. There's three gallons left. When we finish those . . ."

He spanked his hands together, like a magician who's just made a rabbit vanish. "No more. I don't know nothin' about makin' wine."

I shivered. "Maybe you should go to bed, Johnny."

"What do ya hear from Vic?" he said, ignoring my suggestion.

I shrugged, tried to relax. "They don't let me talk to him. He sounds kinda homesick in his letters."

"Homesick!" Johnny laughed. "For what? This fuckin' neighborhood?" He pointed toward the elevated tracks. "Spooks and spics livin' three blocks away, *three lousy blocks!* It's like a plantation over there."

He took a handkerchief out and blew his nose. "Vic's got the right idea. Stairway to the stars. Two years from now he'll have his own house, someplace nice." He clumsily pantomimed a baseball swing.

"There's *snot* on your lip, Johnny," I said, knowing how meticulous he was.

"Thanks," he said reflexively, wiping his face. "Know somethin'? I shoulda stuck to baseball. I used to play."

"I gotta go inside, Johnny."

"The fuck you do. Just sit with me awhile, here," he said, though the two of us were standing. I didn't dare move, and besides I felt a little sorry for him. He wiped his face again.

"It all off?"

He meant the snot. "You look fine."

"Oh yeah? What do you know? You're from Long Island."

"I know plenty," I said, forgetting he was drunk and that his father had just died — my feelings of anger overrode sympathy.

It didn't matter, though. Johnny had barely heard me. He held up a forefinger; something had just occurred to him.

"You know whose fault this is, don'tcha? That asshole Frank Ammiratti, that's who. He's the one who let the neighborhood go down the toilet. Buildin' that fuckin' hamburger place." He was out of breath. "My old man, he cursed that place every time he looked out the window. That's why his heart gave out."

Suddenly he ran across the street and tugged at one of the curbside cobblestones. He worked it like a loose tooth, pushing it this way and that, until it came free of the cement and packed dirt that had held it in place, probably for decades.

"What're you doing, Johnny?"

He shouldered the stone. "You're my lookout. Know what a lookout is, Long Island?"

"A lookout for *what?*"

"I'm gonna bust the fuckin' window at that burger joint. Come on."

We walked rapidly down the street, Johnny shifting the stone from hand to hand every few seconds. No one else was around.

"Do this right, Long Island," he warned. "Don't fuck up or we're both screwed."

I realized what he meant: jail for him, reform school for me. Reform school! Just like in the movies, where they shaved everybody's head and fed you gruel.

"Johnny —"

"Listen to me. When the coast is clear give me the signal and I throw this baby through the window." He tripped and dropped the stone. Cursing mildly, he picked it up. "Think you can handle that?" he asked jeeringly.

"No. I'm not gonna be your damn lookout."

"Figures."

"I want to bust a window, too."

Johnny stopped walking and put his free hand on my shoulder.

"There's *two* windows in front," I said coolly, having watched the workmen install them. "We can each bust one."

Johnny belched, faltered. "Then there's no lookout."

"We don't need one," I said, suddenly the aggressor. I grabbed his jacket lapel. "Come on, let's *do* it."

He laughed. "Long Island, I had you wrong. You got balls."

Moments later we were at the site. No street lights burned nearby but the moon was out and shone brightly. We could see each other's face and the doomed windows as well. The windows reflected the moon, forming giant glowing white eyes.

They were huge panes of glass, each four by four feet, each worth a fortune. We hid behind a hill of clay-filled soil.

"You need a rock," Johnny said. "A big rock, the fuckin' glass is this thick." He held thumb and forefinger an inch apart.

I hunted around and selected a baseball-sized stone. "Ready."

He stared at me, probably recalling the kid who'd been too

timid to start his car weeks earlier. He heard something and put a finger to his lips.

"Shh!" We ducked our heads. A man walked up the block, a huge German shepherd pulling him along on a leash.

"I thought that was your grandfather," Johnny said.

Angie — he'd be wondering where I was! I was supposed to have gone right back into the house after throwing out the garbage.

We had a quick strategy session, deciding who would break which window. The main thing was to do it fast and run like hell to Johnny's backyard.

I was amazed at how unafraid I felt. It was an alien situation, for sure, but I was also *living* with aliens, in an alien neighborhood. Let them do as they pleased if they caught me. I wasn't even afraid of reform school anymore — could it be any worse than Shepherd Avenue? At least it would be a faster getaway than waiting to collect a hundred dollars a dime at a time.

We stood side by side, ten feet from the windows. "One," Johnny counted. "Two . . ."

I thought about my father, my dead mother, Vic not writing to me . . . .

"Three!"

I shut my eyes and hurled the rock — I'd made sure I was pointed in the right direction before closing them. I opened them a split-second later, just in time to see the crash.

All that stickball practice had paid off — my throw was so hard and clean that it cut a baseball-shaped hole into the glass without shattering the rest of the window. I could see the black hole standing out in the middle of the rest of the window. Hairline cracks radiated from the hole like veins.

A heartbeat later Johnny's cobblestone hit pay dirt. He'd thrown it shot-put style, hopping toward the target before letting go.

His was a more dramatic hit than mine, shards of glass tinkling for what seemed like minutes after impact. Almost nothing remained in the frame. He yanked me by the back of my shirt.

"Christ Almighty, move it!"

We flew down the sidewalk and hopped the fence surrounding the Gallo backyard, not having bothered to open the gate.

"Jesus," Johnny kept saying. "Jesus Christ on the cross."

We listened for police sirens; nothing. A dog barked, and that was all.

I pointed at Johnny's clay-smeared pants. "Your mother's gonna kill you."

He waved his hand, still too winded to talk. "Doesn't matter. I'll take 'em to the cleaner's in the morning; she'll never know. I only gotta wear these when somebody dies." He got his breath back all the way. "Long Island, you were *great*."

"Ah, I only made a little hole. You busted the whole thing."

He shook his head. "Doesn't matter," he said gleefully. "Fuckin' Ammiratti's *still* gotta get a whole new window, even if the hole's this big." He measured off the tip of his thumb with his forefinger.

I checked my own clothes for telltale dirt, but I was clean, having stalked the dirt hills like a cat. A strange depression overtook us.

"Eh, so he buys new glass," Johnny said. "That burger joint's still gonna go up, ya know."

"JOOOO-EEEY!"

Angie's voice, calling from our driveway!

"I gotta go home," I said, but Johnny grabbed my wrist. He was barely drunk anymore, though he still reeked of his father's wine.

"Don't tell nobody about this," he warned.

I yanked myself free. "Whaddya think I am, stupid?" I ran off, not even saying good-bye. Angie saw me coming.

"Where were you? Your grandma's havin' a heart attack inside, worryin'."

"I was talkin' to Johnny."

"*Tell* us when you go visiting," he said, guiding me into the house with his hand at the small of my back. He shut the door behind us and I felt truly safe, believing I wouldn't get caught for what I'd done.

The next morning white-suited Frank Ammiratti stood in front of the wreckage and raged.

"He had it comin'," Connie said. It was as if she were commenting upon a battle that had taken place in a foreign country. Anything happening outside the walls of her house was treated this way.

"Yeah, somebody was bound to do something," Angie concluded, eyeing me. "He should have been smart enough to put the glass in last."

The next day I was startled to hear Connie murmur "Long Island" in the vestibule — had she heard Johnny call me by that nickname, and did she know what the two of us had done the night before?

No. She was just reading the return address of a letter addressed to me, from Mel.

"What do you know, the crazy one can write."

She gave me the letter as if it were something federal laws forced her to hand over, like cigarettes for prisoners. I accepted it without thanks.

"See how I didn't open it and read it first?" she said childishly. I blinked at her a few times before answering.

"You're not allowed to, Connie. It's mine. See?"

I pointed at the address, running my finger over it as if it were Braille. "My name. *My* name." I was saying it to myself as well as to her. She looked at me in astonishment, evidently trying to figure out how I'd burrowed my way into her home and what sort of pesticide or trap it would take to be rid of me. At last she just waved me off.

"Who wants to read kids' mail anyway?"

You do, I felt like saying, but instead I turned away from her and brought the letter to my cot. It was hot in the room without cross-ventilation from the hallway but I shut the door anyhow. I didn't want Connie wandering in, on the pretense of looking for laundry or something.

Mel had a wild, boyish handwriting only faintly tamed by Catholic nuns who had, according to her, tried to beat penmanship into her hand with yardstick smacks to the palm. The page was pink. I figured she had stolen it from her aunt, because it certainly wasn't a color she would have selected for herself.

Dear Joey,

Hi. It's worse here than it was in Brooklyn. No buddy plays stickball. I got no friends. My aunt has a yard but I'm not alowed to play in it. My uncle always puts ferdalizer on it, everything smells like shit. Can you come visit me? Maybe if you have any monney you could come. You could take a train. No buddy would have to drive you. We live near the stashun. Write me a letter and tell me if your comming. I'm not alowed to talk on the phone.

your friend
Mel DiGiovanna

P.S. Another thing that stinks, there's no lemon ice here.

"No lemon ice," I murmured as I stuck the letter back into the envelope — that seemed to be the saddest part of the dismal communication. I went down to the cellar and hid the letter in my art supplies, which "no buddy" ever touched. Connie was upstairs vacuuming rugs we rarely walked on. I took off my T-shirt, laid it on my painting desk, and poured out my bottle savings. The cloth of my shirt muffled the noise of the falling coins. I was afraid Connie would hear the sound (even over the noise of her Hoover upright with the bag that puffed out as it operated) and hurry down to investigate. She had the ears of a bat when it came to foreign noises in the house. She was always the first to hear a leaky faucet. Only when she slept was she oblivious to sounds, usually.

The money came to less than nine dollars, the hauling of more than four hundred bottles to Nat. It was a pittance, I knew. Disgustedly I put the coins away, put my shirt on, and, using a sketching pencil, wrote on half a sheet of my drawing paper.

Dear Mel,

It's not worse there, it's worse here. I got no friends either but Zip showed me where you can take bottles for money. The guy gives you two cents apiece and a nickel for the big ones. When I save enough money I'll

take a train to your aunt's house. I don't know when.
I would of wrote before but Rosemary hit me when I
asked for your address. I'll get even with her. Freddie
died and I didn't even get to go to the wake.
                                    your friend, Joey Ambrosio

Was this all I had to say? Something was missing.

P.S. I'm not eating any lemon ice either. I'm saving
all my money so I can see you.

Maybe that postscript would make her feel better, knowing I
too was not cooling my tongue on the wonderful ice.

I needed a stamp and an envelope. I could have shaken out
a few coins and bought them, but I decided to ask Connie
instead, knowing every penny counted in my mission to ac-
cumulate a hundred bucks. Trying to steal was out of the question. I didn't even know where her money was.

She didn't stop vacuuming when she saw me, so I waited for
her to finish. When she clicked the vacuum off, the engine
took a long time to shut up, dying from a shriek to a low baritone
whine as the bag sagged. At last there was silence.

"Pull the cord for me, it's hard for me to bend over."

I knelt, yanked, and handed her the warm pronged plug.
"Can I have a stamp and an envelope please?"

She wound the cord around the machine's shaft. "Is that your
drawing paper you wrote on?"

"Yeah."

"Hey. That's special paper, it costs a lot of money. Ask first
when you want to write a letter, we got cheap paper for that."

Who in that house ever wrote to anyone? You were lucky if
they *talked* to you. I just nodded obediently, though. I needed
what I needed.

She fetched a stamp and an envelope. I waited by the vacuum
cleaner like a customer, instead of going with her to get them.

"Thank you," I forced myself to say, and turned to go downstairs to address the thing.

"Hey," Connie called. I turned to face her. "Is the girl all
right?"

"She's fine," I lied. It was all I would say. She didn't really care, I figured. It would just be something to share with Grace Rothstein over coffee and rolls.

"Leave the letter with me. Your grandpa will mail it next time he goes out."

"I want to mail it *now*."

"You don't trust us?"

"I just don't want to wait."

"A day extra, that's no difference. She ain't going anywhere."

"Connie. I'm mailing this today." I shook the letter at her. The stiff paper didn't even flap.

The pyramid of wrinkles that suddenly vanished from her forehead told me I'd gotten my way with her for the first time.

"The mailbox is all the way down by Atlantic Avenue. You be careful, mister."

I had to swallow my snickering laughter as I walked away. She'd have had a heart attack if she'd known how far from home I strayed every day to gather the bottles sucked dry by dirty strangers.

CHAPTER ELEVEN

ANGIE slipped casually into complete retirement, declining offers for freelance plumbing jobs. He didn't want to go without Freddie.

He went days without shaving and drank loads of coffee. His beard came in pure white, though there was still some black hair on his scalp.

Suddenly he was around the house all the time — without Freddie, the racetrack didn't interest him, either. Connie had barely adjusted to having me around when suddenly there was another pain-in-the-ass male on the scene, observing her go about her daily routines with the curiosity of a schoolkid watching a lion tamer.

Once in a while he cried right in front of us, as if the realization that Freddie was gone jabbed him like a needle. His poor appetite alarmed Connie. When he used to go off to work in the morning she always fried him a big bacon-and-eggs feast, and while he ate it she assembled a lunch into his black tin pail in the order he ate it: sandwiches on top, a thermos of coffee, cake, and lastly fruit, to clean the teeth.

She packed that pail so carefully that nothing in it jiggled. Angie would finish breakfast, say "So long" and leave. Often "So long" were the first spoken words of the day in the house. Now the first words were "What are you doing?"

He wanted to know everything that went on. Eight-thirty in the morning, and Connie was frying a hunk of chuck steak.

"What are you doing?"

"It's for tonight's gravy."

"Gravy now? It's eight-thirty in the morning!"

"When'd you think I started cooking, five minutes before you got home?"

"No, but I didn't think you started an hour after I left. You have to start so early?"

She flipped the meat without answering. He rubbed his chin. "Where's the morning paper?"

"We don't get one."

"Why not?"

"We never did. What made you think we got a paper in the morning?"

He shrugged. "I just figured you read for a while after I left, or something."

"And that's what you thought I did all day while you were out, read the paper?"

"Ahh, nuts, who said all day? I just asked for the paper."

"So go buy one, you got a nickel."

He stifled a belch. "I live here all these years and I don't even know where you keep the salt."

Connie flipped the steak again. "Go shave," she said, figuring it'd at least give her five minutes of peace.

He never bugged me if I was downstairs painting, but if I was reading on my cot, he would come in and ask if the book was any good. It got trickier and trickier to sneak out with the bottle sack, but I never got caught.

*   *   *

My father finally sent a letter addressed to me alone; I was permitted to open it myself. He'd written that he was working in an apple orchard for a week or so, and would be leaving soon for another place — he wasn't sure where. The same impersonal bullshit that filled the letters he sent to "Dear Everybody."

But there were three worn dollar bills in the envelope, which I had Nat change into nickels and dimes. These I put in my money jar, the equivalent of a hundred and fifty two-cent bottles. I was only out hunting for them every third day or so, now. It just wasn't worth my while to prowl the streets daily for three or four lousy bottles.

My father had not said when he'd return. Whenever I felt bad about his absence I forced myself to think about the hidden jar in the cellar, its level of coins creeping slowly but surely toward the rim, piling up as steadily as snow on the North Pole.

Angie walked into the room scratching his crotch just as I finished reading it. "Letter?"

I nodded. "My father."

"I didn't see that one."

"He sent it to *me*."

"Oh. That mean we can't read it?"

"That's what it means," I said, immediately regretting my cruelty. "Angie, why doesn't he *call* here?"

His hand moved from his crotch to his belly, as if he were groping for a lost wallet. "Maybe he's afraid that if he hears your voice, he'll come back too soon."

He looked at the painting of my mother. "Elizabeth," he said softly, touching the glass. "You're a good artist. It looks just like her."

"How do you know?" I taunted. "When was the last time *you* saw her?"

Angie hesitated. "In the hospital, just before she died."

I sat up straight. "You visited her?"

"A few times, yeah." He seemed embarrassed. His eyes were wet but he'd been crying so much lately over Freddie Gallo that these may have been residual tears.

"Why didn't you visit me?" I demanded.

" 'Cause your father didn't think it would be a good idea, Joey. All those years in between . . ."

He put his hand out at knee level to indicate how small I'd been the last time he'd seen me. "He thought it would shock you too much, seeing me."

"Oh. So instead he makes me *live* with you. God! . . . Did Connie go to the hospital?"

"She never even knew I was goin'. She thought I was at the track."

"Didn't she care?"

"Of course she cared!"

"Then why didn't she visit?"

He picked up a Spaldeen and squeezed it. "When you're older you'll understand how it works. Okay?" His voice had grown testy.

"I don't think I'll ever figure you people out," I snapped.

Angie pointed at me. If his forefinger had been a gun the bullet would have hit my heart. "Hey, Mister. You *are* the same people as us. Don't forget that."

He looked out the window, sliding his gun hand into his pocket for a sunflower seed.

"Shit," I said, hoping to aggravate him. He didn't hear me, or maybe he just pretended he didn't.

He nibbled a seed. "Look," he said suddenly, "I'm going to the Fulton Fish Market early in the morning. I was gonna go alone, but I figured you might like to see it."

"I do," I said, as solemnly as people say it when they get married.

"It's really gonna be early," he warned. "You'll go to sleep now and feel like you're gettin' up five minutes later."

"I can get up earlier than anyone."

He chuckled. "All right. Don't be mad when I wake you up."

"Maybe I'll wake you up."

He grinned at the challenge. "Eh, we'll see about that." He left the room. I shut off my light and went to sleep curiously happy. The only other guy who'd ever gone to the market with him was Freddie Gallo.

* * *

It *did* feel as if I were being awakened five minutes later. But Angie had the gentlest touch in the world when it came to doing it; he just held my foot and barely squeezed it until my eyes opened.

The sun hadn't yet risen. His dark eyes seemed to glow in the gray light like headlights through fog.

"If you're comin', it's time to go."

"Now?" I moaned. My joints felt stiff, my blood honey-thick.

"Ah, stay, stay in bed," he whispered, holding out his hands as he backpedaled to the door. I was out of the cot a second later, yanking on my pants.

"Knew it'd work," he said.

Still afraid Angie might ditch me I urinated sloppily, hurriedly, splashing the toilet seat. I left it wet and ran to the car, which I heard revving in the driveway.

It was chilly. Our breath fogged the windshield. The inside of the car was a fragrant cloud of Colgate toothpaste and Rise lather, Angie's sweet smells. If he shaved regularly at this hour it was no wonder he was always stubbly by early afternoon.

I hadn't even washed my face. When I blinked I could feel crusts at the corners of my eyes. Angie watched me pick them out and laughed as I tried to stifle a yawn.

"Tired?"

"Nahh."

"Well *I* am, at quarter past four in the morning. Roll your window down, Joey, we gotta clear the steam. Smell this air, nice and heavy, you'll think you're back on Long Island."

Cold air blew through the car. Angie's thick fingernails tapped the steering wheel as we barreled down Atlantic Avenue.

"You busted those windows with Johnny Gallo, didn't you?"

Betrayal! He'd gotten me out of the house just for *this!*

"Yeah," I said, unable to lie at that hour. Angie just kept his eyes on the road and nodded.

"Made you feel good, huh?"

"It sure did, damn it." I was wide-awake. "You gonna tell the cops?" I glanced at the backseat, expecting to find all my stuff there — a quick dump-off at the reform school and Angie could get home in plenty of time for breakfast.

140

He chuckled. "The cops. You been watching 'The Untouchables' too much." His eyebrows knotted and he shook his head. "Just don't do it again, all right?"

"I won't." Off with just a warning. I stared at his profile. "How'd you know, anyhow?"

He shut his eyes, shrugged. "I knew, I knew. You roughed up that Donnelly kid pretty good, too, didn't you?"

I felt proud to admit that one. "Yeah," I said, trying to sound tough. "I think I busted his nose."

"No, you didn't," he said wetly. "Mostly you gave him a good scare."

"Angie, I hit him because —"

"I know all about it, I know all about it."

I believed him. He didn't probe for details. It was enough that we understood each other; however we'd arrived at that understanding was irrelevant.

But how the hell did he *know* everything?

"I get around," he said, as if I'd spoken the question aloud. We rode a few more miles in silence.

"Connie know?"

"I never told her," he said, and that was the end of the conversation. The sky remained gray for the whole ride down Atlantic Avenue. I kept looking out the passenger window. The only people around were leaden-eyed blacks and Puerto Ricans in flashy clothing, climbing out of neon-colored Cadillacs on the way home from wild nights of fun.

The car had an AM radio but I didn't turn it on. When Vic rode home from ball games and turned on music I noticed that Angie seemed vaguely insulted, as if his conversation was considered dull. I didn't want to hurt Angie's feelings — even though we weren't talking, the radio would have been an interruption. We were on the verge of a friendship we both needed, and neither of us wanted to blow it.

I fell asleep. When Angie shook my elbow we were on the entry ramp of the Brooklyn Bridge, and just as we reached the first of its spans the sun appeared.

"Ahh," we said simultaneously, in pure appreciation. We looked at each other, then down at the golden-orange water of the East River. The sun warmed us like a soft palm, all the way to South Street in Manhattan.

You smelled the fishy fog of the market long before you saw the men in long rubber boots and rubber aprons stacking all kinds of fish into cases of cracked ice, shouting and swearing and laughing, getting high on sunrise and each other's wild company and the crazy sense of urgency that pervaded everything.

In the alleys off South Street scraps of fish were tossed to the biggest sea gulls I'd ever seen, or maybe they were the same size as all gulls, but my God, they were so close, so defiant, the way they tore into the food and cawed and screamed at one another.

The place knocked me speechless. Angie just kept laughing and roweling the hair at my sideburns, just enough to make it burn slightly. He knew a few of the workmen and introduced me to them, guys who didn't shake my hand but thrust giant green-black lobsters within an inch of my face to profess friendship.

A morning of magic. When Angie and I left, the workmen were already cleaning up, using fat hoses and stiff brooms and shovels. The sun got hotter. The smell became a stench, something to flee from.

We returned to Shepherd Avenue with a basket of clams, a crate of scallops, and two big boxes of flounder fillets. It seemed as if we'd been on a long journey but it was barely past six A.M. Connie would be asleep another half hour. I'd have time to clean the toilet seat I'd fouled with my faulty aim.

"I'm up before Connie," I said. "That never happened before."

Angie nodded, understanding. "It's a neat feeling, ain't it?"

Minutes later, brushing my teeth, I felt unusually gleeful, as if I'd crammed two days of living into one and gotten away with it.

I think my friendship with Angie Ambrosio might never have been triggered if I'd rolled over and stayed in bed that morning of the Fulton Fish Market.

But now the delicate seed of a relationship was germinating, and even Connie was glad to see it happen. I took him off her hands. She had the basement kingdom all to herself again.

Angie and I were out of the house as much as possible, often taking walks to the playground at Highland Park. We really liked the swings — we had contests to see who could swing higher, and he always won. In midair on a swing the guy seemed sixteen years old.

Then one day he examined the little patch of yard he'd owned for so long, and kicked at the hard black soil with his heel.

"A waste, this land."

"My father had a garden," I said. "He grew tomatoes in Roslyn." I held out my hands as if to heft softballs. "Some of them were this big."

Angie seemed impressed. "I never knew Sal knew anything about gardening."

"He used lots of fertilizer. I guess that's how come the tomatoes got so big."

He folded his arms across his chest. "Think we could get anything planted in this place, Joey?"

I knelt and rubbed my hand over the soil, as if my palm could detect the nutrient content. "Might. But the middle of the yard is shady. My father said shade's no good."

"Nuts."

I felt a pang of sympathy for Angie. "We could plant along the edge, by the fence," I said. "It's pretty sunny there."

"Hey, maybe you're right."

Together we pulled the ragged weeds and stuffed them into a brown supermarket bag. Angie took a shovel and turned the soil over and over, until it was loamy. He didn't touch the spot where Dixie the pooch had been buried.

"We need fertilizer and stuff, Anj. That's how me and my father did it."

He picked chunks of dirt off the shovel. They were almost as hard as rocks, because the soil had gone untilled for decades. "He had it better than me. All that space in that backyard."

I shook my head. "That's not where it was. He said there was too much shade there, so he dug up part of the front yard."

"You're kidding me."

"He said grass was a waste, Anj. He said, 'If I had any guts, I'd rip out this grass and plant something really valuable.' Then he did it. He let me help him. We bought horse manure. Boy, it sure stunk bad. Nobody on the block would talk to us."

Angie smiled as he ran his fingers along the shovel's silver-edged blade. "That's probably the way he wanted it."

He knew his son, all right. I had to giggle. "The neighbors were so mad we almost hadda move. My father said he'd take us to the country, where nobody would bother us."

"And that's where he is now," Angie mused, realizing too late what he'd said to remind me of being abandoned. "Hey, Joey, I'm sorry."

"It's okay." But it wasn't. I clenched my teeth and thought about the change jar. Time spent with Angie had deprived me of bottle-hunting escapades; it had been about a week since I'd brought a load to Nat. I would have to get back to it, soon.

"Hey, listen." Angie patted my shoulder. "A guy like your father, the only way nobody'll bug him is if he goes to the moon to live. *Look!*" He pointed at the sky. "It's daytime but you can see the moon. Ain't that amazing?"

He was right. It was a half-moon, clearly visible against the bright blue sky.

"People say you can't see the moon in the daytime," he continued. "That's 'cause they all look at their feet when they walk. . . . How big was the biggest tomato you got?"

Exaggerating only slightly, I spread my hands wide enough to heft a honeydew. "This big. A guy from a newspaper wanted to take a picture of it but my father said he'd sock him on the nose if he did."

"Mad at the world, my son."

"We gonna buy fertilizer, Angie?"

He stuck the shovel in the ground. "Nuts to that. Connie's been throwin' food and coffee grounds out here for the past thirty years. If that ain't fertilizer, you tell me what is."

Connie appeared at the window and began pegging laundry onto the line. "What are you two now, farmers?"

"You got it," Angie said.

"What?"

"Tomatoes."

"The A & P is two blocks away."

"It's not the same as a fresh-grown tomato, woman!" he exclaimed, thrilling me by winking at me when he said it. Connie just shook her head and ducked back inside.

"There's things you can't tell her," Angie said before we drove off to a garden center for the seedlings.

But somehow, the Shepherd Avenue backyard looked even more pathetic with plants than it had looked barren.

"Who are we kiddin'?" Angie asked when we were through planting. He stamped his foot and ground his toe into the dirt. "We'll be lucky if we get one tomato."

I watered the last seedling in our single row. "They'll grow, Angie, I *know* about this stuff," I assured him.

"Ahhh . . ." He spat into the yard's shadowy middle. "Even if we get tomatoes there won't be many."

Strange, how the waste of space he hadn't noticed for decades was suddenly driving him crazy. Suddenly a light blazed in his eyes.

"Chickens," he announced. "We'll raise chickens."

Breathless with excitement I broke the news to Connie.

"Not too many," she said.

Zip Aiello provided the necessary lumber and chicken wire for a coop, free of charge.

"God help him if he asks for money after all the meals he's had here," Connie had forewarned.

Angie did almost all the construction work but tried to make me feel useful, letting me take the last two or three licks on a nail when it was too far into a board to be bent. While we worked, Palmieri stuck his gray head out the window and asked what we were up to.

"Chicken coop!" Angie's voice rang with delight.

Palmieri grimaced. "They bring rats." He ducked back inside. Angie laughed. "Imagine a guy like that worrying about rats? He ain't washed a dish up there in ten years!"

How this project excited him, the way my father's garden had excited *him!* They were the same man in many ways — Angie was just older, shorter, and calmer. I began to understand that I'd resulted from a network of people, not just my mother and father. Despite my alien, ultraround head, they were part of me.

I'd always imagined chickens as clean white birds that ran through green meadows and built nests in long grass, but to buy our birds we went to a place that looked like a factory. The building was cinder-block walls painted white, with small, dusty, deeply set windows. There was heavy mesh screening over them — you could barely see inside.

Over the front door was a sign lettered in red paint: ROSIELLO'S FAMOUS LIVE POULTRY. The guy had obviously not hired a pro to make the sign. The letters sloped upward and the TRY in POULTRY was wedged together.

Inside, odors of urine, dung, and feathers made my nose go wet. It seemed that a soup of those ingredients was being made out back.

There were empty feather-flecked bird crates all around. Angie called out toward the back, from where a low, throaty clucking steadily sounded.

Rosiello was a fat, sweaty man. He wore an apron with blood-stains that were so old they'd dried brown. On his head was a straw skimmer with a faded red band around it. He squinted at us as he wiped his hands on his puffy hips.

"Help you?"

"We want some birds," Angie said. "Chicks."

"Raise?"

"Yes."

Rosiello shook his head. "Got no chicks now. Only time I carry 'em's around Easter. All I got's pullets, two bucks apiece."

"What's a pullet?" I asked.

"It's a young chicken," Angie said. "Jeez, maybe pullets'd be better, they're a little stronger. How big are they?"

"Show ya. Come on."

In the back the smells were even stronger because the birds were stacked there, three or four to a crate. The crates were against the walls, leaving the center of the room clear for a work area under a single bulb dangling from a crooked black wire.

With as little room for motion as possible the birds hunched in their prisons, chins tucked into their crops. Cracked corn was scattered over the dirt floor like driveway gravel. From one of the bottom crates a lean-necked chicken stuck her neck as far as she could through the wooden bars, stretching for a kernel just out of reach. Her beak left a mark in the dirt.

I nudged the kernel toward the crate so she could get it. "Those birds are crowded. They need more room."

"No they don't," Rosiello said. He seemed to be noticing me for the first time. "Your son?"

"Grandson," Angie said.

"I thought you looked kinda old to be his father," Rosiello said. "No offense."

"They don't get any exercise," I persisted.

"Kid, Chrissakes, this ain't no Jack La Lanne I'm runnin' here." He wiped his cleaver on the apron. Behind him were a kettle of hot water, a chopping block, and a machine shaped like a box.

Steam rose off the kettle as if it contained a witch's brew. I pointed at it and asked, "What's that for?"

Rosiello sucked in a deep breath. "You ask a lotta questions. It's for pluckin' the chickens."

"The feathers come off if you just stick it in *water?*"

"No!" Rosiello stuck the cleaver into the chopping block. Big drops of sweat dripped from his forehead. He took off his hat and wiped his head. He was almost completely bald.

Angie said, "Instead of gettin' all excited, just explain it to him."

Rosiello sighed and put his hat back on. He was like the comedian Edgar Kennedy doing his famous "slow burn."

"Jesus Christ, I oughta run a school here. Okay, kid. See, before I can stick the bird into this machine, I got to —"

"What's the machine do?"

Angie ducked his head so Rosiello wouldn't see him grin. The fat man took a long breath, like the ones people take before blowing out birthday candles.

"This here machine . . . hell, lemme show ya." Rosiello took a bird from one of the crates. It cackled as he lifted her. "Maybe he shouldn't watch this part," he suggested.

"Wait outside," Angie said.

"I can watch."

Before Angie could object Rosiello shrugged, bent back the flapping bird's head, and slit its throat. A stream of bright blood rose and fell in a dying arc. Rosiello caught most of it in a bucket on the floor. Angie's hands were on my shoulders.

"Breathe deep," he urged.

"I'm all right." I really was. It had happened too fast to be repulsive. Rosiello had followed through the killing cleanly, graceful as Vic slamming a home run. He hung the bird over the pail to drain. The flapping grew feeble.

Minutes. We all waited for the bird to die, and then Rosiello took it by the feet. The blood at its neck had coagulated, and the halves of its beak were apart. The eyes seemed glued shut.

"Step one, you kill the bird," Rosiello said. "Okay. Now the hot water."

Rosiello dunked the bird into the kettle as if he were making a jelly apple. Bloody odors rose with the steam. Even Rosiello turned his head to avoid them.

Out of the water, the bird seemed swollen. Rosiello held it upside down and shook it, and the wings loosened and dropped like helicopter blades.

He gave it a final shake. "Always hated that part, the smell. Guess I shoulda gone to college, right? Okay. So now I turn this thing on to get the arms rollin'."

He was talking about spinning rubber arms inside the boxlike machine. In went the bird, head and shoulders first. With thudding sounds the feathers were stripped, her head whipping around like a rubber ball on a child's paddle toy. He cleaned the wings separately, then the legs, holding each limb the way a man holds a knife to grind it. Feathers disappeared in a white blur down a chute. Rosiello clinked off the machine.

"And that's that. 'Cept for a coupla feathers where the arms don't reach." He lifted a wing to show me the hairy little feathers under the wing pit. "Lady'll hold it over the stove and burn 'em off."

He laid the bird on his chopping block. Its head had only been partially defeathered, like a man going bald — like Rosiello, in fact.

"Hey, he looks like *you*," I couldn't help saying.

"Very funny, kid." The bird's dead eyes had been yanked open by the rollers. With two swings of his cleaver Rosiello chopped off the feet at the end of each drumstick.

"Damn shame. This lady don't want to be bothered with the feet, she don't know what good soup they make." He knocked the feet onto the floor. "I leave the head on. Let the lady cut it off herself. That way she feels like she's doin' something."

A trickle of jellyish blood oozed from the drumstick ends, but that was all. The really gory part, the removal of the internal organs, would happen while I wasn't around. Rosiello picked up the bird with real respect, as if it were a stillborn child or something.

"I gotta clean it later. Otherwise the stupid lady smashes the gall bladder and you gotta throw the whole thing out."

He took it away. I picked up the discarded feet. They were bony and yellow; except for their scaliness I might have been holding pencils. I dropped them, shuddering.

Rosiello returned. "Okay, now, pullets for youse guys." He opened a crate in the corner, slid his arm around inside it. There was a flurry of dust and feathers, and after a few moments he withdrew a flopping, squawking bird by the feet and held it upside down.

It seemed cruel to hold a *live* bird upside down, but I didn't want to bug Rosiello with more questions. He let the creature exhaust itself, until it was clucking softly, like an idling car. Then he curved his free hand around its back, pinching its wings to its sides. His touch seemed as gentle as his voice was gruff.

He swung the bird around into a sitting position in his hands. It was smaller than the one he'd just killed.

"Only a few months old. They sneak a few of these babies in every delivery, the sons of bitches."

"Hen or rooster?" Angie asked.

"Hen."

"How can you tell?" No mistrust in Angie's voice, he was just curious. A young chicken is about as asexual in appearance as any animal can be.

Rosiello rolled his eyes. "Twenty-seven years in chickens, I can tell a hen, buddy."

"No offense . . . you got more like that?"

"Hell, yeah. How many do you need?"

"I'm not sure . . . Joey?"

"How about ten?" I asked.

Angie shook his head. "Not enough room. Maybe five, tops. You have to remember the tomatoes take up room by the fence."

"You're growin' *tomatoes?*" Rosiello was incredulous.

"Sure we are."

"Tomatoes or chickens, pal. Make up your mind, you can't have both."

"The plants'll be safe," Angie said. "I got 'em fenced in."

"That's what you say now. Wait and see."

"Just give us five of your pullets."

The pullet in Rosiello's hands had been alternately struggling and relaxing, trying to catch him off guard. At last she succeeded, getting one wing free and slapping it against his arm.

"Sit still, you pain in the ass." He caught the wing and folded it back into place as if it were the seal on an envelope. "You, you don't even know you're one of the lucky ones."

"Make sure they're all hens," Angie said. "I don't want crowing at five in the morning."

"You'll get hens. Bring anything to carry them in?"

"Forgot."

"For three bucks I'll give ya a crate." Rosiello went to get one, and Angie said out of the side of his mouth, "Wouldn't you think this guy'd throw in a lousy crate?"

Rosiello continued poking around in the crates for small chickens. When his hands groped the one he wanted he pulled it out, and a chorus of riotous squawking filled the room, like a classroom of grade-schoolers when the teacher's chalk snaps against the blackboard. It took him just a few minutes to hunt up four more birds, and when he found the last one he murmured, "Well I'll be goddamned."

To heighten the suspense Rosiello kept his back to us as he held the last chicken, waiting for her to calm down. When he turned to face us he bore the thing at waist level, in both hands, the way a priest holds a chalice.

It was salt-and-pepper-colored, smaller than the other white pullets.

"Wow," I said. "She's beautiful."

Even Rosiello was beaming. "In my business this is like findin' a four-leaf clover."

Angie inspected the bird. "Her eye's bleedin'."

There was a scab I hadn't noticed, completely sealing one of the creature's eyes.

"She got attacked by the other birds," Rosiello explained. "They hate it when a special one gets in the crate, so they try to kill it."

Angie and I looked at him fishily. "Come on," Angie said.

"I ain't kiddin'. Birds of a feather and all that jazz." Rosiello's tone had grown philosophical. "It's just like people. Somebody has somethin' you don't got, you feel like killin' him."

Angie said, "If they tried to kill her here, why shouldn't they do it in my yard? I got no use for a dead chicken."

"Never happen. Not in the open. Just make sure you got room for 'em all to move around. Listen, I'll take a half a buck off on account of the eye."

"Will it get better?" I asked.

"Hell, no, kid, it's gone. Pecked right out. It'll stay shut, just like it is now. Scab'll fall off but the eye'll stay shut." He rubbed his knuckles against the bird's crop.

Angie still seemed doubtful. "Sure it's a hen?"

Rosiello laughed. "You know, jeez, I forgot to check this one." He rolled his eyes to the ceiling and reached around the bird's underside. It clucked indignantly, violated.

"Hen," Rosiello announced. "You'll give eggs even with one eye, won't you?"

But Angie said, "I still ain't sure I want a half-blind chicken."

"*She* don't know she's half blind," Rosiello said. "Hey, you want her to lay eggs or read books to you?"

"I like her," I said, casting my vote.

"Okay," Angie said. "Twelve-fifty for the works."

"Lemme get a pencil and make sure." Rosiello put the bird into our crate, then found a pencil and paper. He took off the boater in the midst of the calculations to scratch his scalp with one grimy finger.

"Right," he finally said. "Anything else?"

Angie cleared his throat. "I need a duck," he said casually. "You got ducks?"

"Sure I got ducks. Wait here."

I was excited over the prospect of another bird for the yard until I remembered that Deacon Sullivan was coming for dinner on Saturday, and that his favorite meal was fresh-killed duck.

But before I could say a word Rosiello was back with a huge cotton-white duck, which he carried as if he were a halfback cradling a football.

"Three bucks. And hell, I'll throw in her crate for nothing."

"Thanks," Angie said lamely, looking at me, knowing I knew.

"For Saturday," he said. "Your grandmother wants to make that deacon his favorite meal."

"I figured it out, Anj." The duck's feet pedaled the air. Rosiello put her in a small, one-bird crate.

They each took an end of the big crate to carry it out, while I carried the doomed duck. Everything fit on the backseat.

"Remember me Thanksgiving," Rosiello said when we were in the car. "My motto is, 'I'll kill it in front of you.' "

"We'll remember."

"You got some good deal, especially on that black one."

"Yeah, yeah, yeah, we'll see." Angie started the car and put it in reverse. Rosiello waddled back to his store.

"What a bull artist he is, Joey. These birds woulda sat in the store three months, eating his corn. He was happy to get rid of 'em." He laughed. "Everybody's a dealer."

Rosiello reappeared at his doorway. "Hey!" he shouted. "Wait!"

Angie braked suddenly. The crates jolted amid much clucking and quacking.

"Still gonna grow them tomatoes?" Rosiello yelled.

"I already got 'em in the ground!" Angie shouted back.

Rosiello wagged a finger. "They'll get to 'em," he said. "Sooner or later, stupid as they are." His shoulders shook with laughter as he went back inside.

During the slow ride home I turned around every few seconds to watch the birds. When Angie made turns, their feet slid out from under them but their heads somehow remained steady as balloons. They were fascinating to watch, especially the salt-and-pepper one. She sat in a corner and seemed quieter than the others. She tried to sleep and didn't seem maimed when her good eye was closed.

The duck was the loudest bird of all, as if she considered the presence of mere chickens beside her an insult.

"It was a deal, Joey," Angie said softly. "Your grandmother's lettin' us have the birds 'cause we're lettin' her make the duck for the deacon. Otherwise she'd be breaking our balls every day over the mess the chickens'll be makin'. Excuse my mouth."

"I gotta name the birds," I said. "That way they'll know who I'm calling. They can learn names, can't they, Angie?"

He shrugged. "I guess so." He took one hand from the steering wheel and held a finger in the air.

"Whatever you do, don't name that damn duck," he warned. I'd never heard his voice so sharp.

I defied Angie's command and secretly named the duck. Odd, how she was the only bird I would end up naming, except for "Salt and Pepper," which wasn't really a name, just a description. The others were survivors with time to go nameless.

I christened the duck Roslyn, after my old town. The name came to me halfway home from Rosiello's.

We bought the birds on a Thursday. When we let them loose in the backyard they dispersed like grammar-school children leaving a classroom for recess. I wondered if Roslyn suspected she was doomed to die in two days, or if the chickens knew how lucky they were simply because an old man had an impulse to raise birds.

The first thing Connie said when she saw them was, "How long before they start layin'?"

"Soon," Angie assured her. "I got all hens."

That night the chickens pecked at a pile of food in the middle of the yard. They may have been the only birds ever to eat pasta fagioli, macaroni with beans, leftovers Connie was going to throw out anyway because they had begun to grow mold. Meanwhile, Roslyn ate bread crumbs right from my hand.

"Don't," Angie said. He was behind me, watching.

"She's allowed to eat, isn't she?"

"Yeah, but it doesn't change nothin'."

"I know," I lied.

I went to bed that night and the next certain that Roslyn would live a long life in the backyard, lay eggs, even hatch ducklings there, if Angie could be convinced that she needed a drake for company.

Naturally the birds were the first thing on my mind on Saturday morning. I raced outside at daybreak to see how they were doing. Angie appeared soon after me, a mug of coffee in hand.

"They're all still here," I said after counting. I had made the same announcement the previous morning.

Angie chuckled. "Where were they gonna go, to church?" He sipped his coffee, then yawned theatrically. "Hey. Let's go to the movies, Joey."

The suggestion stunned me. Sit in a dark movie theater on a brilliant Saturday? No Italian in his right mind would dream of such a thing. It took an instant for everything to become clear.

"When we come back Roslyn won't be here, will she?" I asked.

Angie's eyes clouded with fury. "What did I tell you about naming that duck? Damn it!" He dashed the rest of the coffee onto the ground. The birds raced over to investigate the puddle, which sank instantly into the loamy ground.

"I hadda call her something, Angie, she ate out of my hand!" He pushed his wiry hair back. His hands came away wet with the water he had used for morning grooming. "I knew it, I knew it," he moaned. "I should have let the guy do it there."

"It ain't fresh that way," Connie said, ascending the outside cellar steps. Sunlight glinted off a long white-handled knife in her hand. It was the sharpest knife in the house, the one Angie

154

used to cut fresh Italian bread because its blade never crushed the crust.

"You're gonna kill her *here?*" I shrieked. "In front of the other birds?"

Connie looked at Angie, who instantly turned to me, as if his wife's murderous face had been too much to bear. "It's a lotta mess for inside the house."

My eyes wettened. "Can't you just buy one from the A & P?"

"No." Connie's voice was icy. "It ain't the same. Didn't you tell him about that duck?"

"He knew, he knew all along," Angie boomed.

Pleading was useless. Roslyn had joined the chickens in the middle of the yard, head down, ass in the air as she pecked at her last supper.

"All right, get her," Connie said wearily. "It's a waste that she's eating."

Angie stepped over the low fence and snared Roslyn from behind by her feet, then curled his arm over her back to contain her beating wings.

"Take him to the movies now, I'll call Grace to help," Connie said.

"He don't wanna go."

Time, time — I had to stall for time! "Wait!" I said. "Can't you take her inside to do it?"

Connie wiped the edge of the knife on her dress, as if it were already bloody. "Your grandfather already told you what a mess it is."

"But I don't want the chickens to see it."

I was surprised to hear Connie laugh. "You think they care? Watch, they won't even stop eatin'."

"All right, all right," Angie said, gripping Roslyn's throat as she went for his eye, "we'll do it over the sink for Joey. Come on, we can do that much."

Connie sighed. "Let's get it over with, already." She clumped down the cellar steps. Angie followed her, embracing Roslyn.

"Wait here," he said to me, and then the screen door slammed behind him.

I ran around to the front door and entered the house like a burglar. As I crept down the creaky cellar steps I pushed my hands against the narrow walls to take weight off my noisy feet. In the basement Connie and Angie hunched over the sink like surgeons.

Was it all over? No — I heard Roslyn cluck.

"Come on, hold her still," Connie said. "Pull that neck back. I said back! More . . . good. Now don't let go."

"Will you *do* it already?"

"Get that wing outa my face —"

Angie wrestled with Roslyn. I caught a glimpse of white wing tip as I crept up on them.

"Wait!" I screamed. Angie whipped his head around to look at me, and in that instant Connie made her fatal slash.

Roslyn squawked, a sound that turned into the gurgle of a clogged drain. Connie spun around and looked at me as if she meant to use the knife on my throat next. Roslyn flew away from all of us in an explosion of red and white.

"Damn!" Connie hissed. A line of blood streaked her cheek. The rest of the streak Connie's face had only partially interrupted reached all the way to the ceiling.

Roslyn flapped around the basement, bumping the walls and spraying them with blood. Connie remained at the sink while Angie went after the duck, who gradually lost energy. She seemed to be flapping in slow motion, like a kid's toy on weak batteries.

Angie caught Roslyn and, a cupped palm under her throat, brought her to the sink, where the rest of her lifeblood would drip into the Brooklyn sewer system.

My throat felt dry and I was too stunned to be nauseous, even when Connie brought the point of the knife to within an inch of my nose.

"See the mess you made? You know how bad blood stains?"

"I'm sorry," I said, though I felt anything but sorry. It was an automatic response. Roslyn shuddered at the sink. Angie squeezed her, coaxing blood from her white body as he would have juice from a halved orange.

"Get a wet rag, Joey," he said. "Wipe the walls fast, before the blood dries up."

I didn't budge.

"Come on, buddy, we made a deal with Connie."

She wet a rag and gave it to me. My brain felt as if it had become insulated within a jacket of fluid that wouldn't permit rage or disgust to penetrate. I wiped Roslyn's blood from the walls as if it were chalk off a blackboard.

"The floor, too. Rinse the rag first, buddy. Gimme it."

He held out a hand to take it. It was safe to do because Roslyn was just about dead. Her nearly severed head lay next to the drain. Blood leaked sluggishly from the neck, and her feathers, once beautifully aligned, seemed to be pointed in random directions. Maybe I imagined it, but she now seemed to be a shade of gray instead of brilliant white.

I cleaned the floor, then Angie took the rag from me to clean the streak on the ceiling. A toilet flushed — Connie had gone to the bathroom, and now she returned to us smelling of Ivory Soap.

"I'm warning you," she said, leaning into my face, "you ever do anything like that again . . ."

She jabbed a finger at me, an action that seemed to burst the protective jacket around my brain.

"What?" I spat. "What are you gonna do? You can't throw me out of here, you don't even know where my father is!"

Connie's finger froze in midair. I might have accused her of being a whore, judging from the expression on her face.

"Don't talk to your grandmother like that," Angie said. I felt my knees bang something hard. I looked down; I'd collapsed to the floor and knelt like an altar boy.

"I'm gonna be sick, Angie." His powerful hands slid under my armpits.

"Watch the duck, she's still movin' a little," he said to Connie as he led me by the back of the neck to the toilet. He eased me to my knees and I threw up. I'd eaten no breakfast so only saliva came out, but I couldn't stop retching.

"You knew that bird had to die," he scolded. "You knew it, you knew it, so don't expect me to feel sorry for you."

"I know," I said into the bowl. My words echoed on the porcelain. I tried to stand but my knees buckled. Angie picked me up and slung me over his shoulder. I shut my eyes as he climbed the stairs and laid me on my cot, where I fell asleep almost instantly.

It felt like afternoon when I opened my eyes. How long had I been asleep — two hours? Three hours? I could hear voices. Angie was watching television in the parlor. My shirt was soaked cold with sweat.

I went downstairs. Connie sat at the table, plucking Roslyn's feathers as if she were knitting booties for a baby. She looked up at me.

"You still sick?"

"No."

"Hungry?" Even when I was in her bad graces, I rated meals.

"No." I sat down across from her. Roslyn's body was half-stripped of feathers, the bare flesh a light pink. It wasn't a repulsive sight. It was the calm after the storm, compared to what I'd already seen. No way I was going to get nauseous again.

"Can I pull some?"

She looked at me as if I'd asked for a kiss. "*You?*"

"Yeah. I wanna try."

She held the bird's tail toward me. "Grab near the skin. Closer. Now pull."

A feather came out cleanly, a dot of blood at its tip. I pulled another, then a third.

"All right, that's enough, it'll take all year." She cradled the bird at her breast and yanked with remarkable speed.

Angie appeared. "Hey. I didn't even hear you get up. Somethin' must be wrong with my ears, I'm gettin' old." His hair had dried and looked fluffy. I'd been asleep at least long enough for his hair to dry.

"Come up and watch television with me, Joey."

"I'm watchin' this."

Connie stopped plucking to look at me. "What are you tryin' to prove?"

"Nothing." I didn't know what I was trying to prove — how tough I was, how tough she wasn't? My challenge to stay put intrigued Connie.

158

"Eh, stay, I don't care," she said, and while Angie drank coffee she pulled Roslyn's remaining feathers. The bird's head twitched with each tug as if she were still alive. Downy feathers, the ones from the wing pits and the neck, floated to the floor like hundreds of miniature parachutes.

Bored with the show, Angie went up to watch TV. When Connie was through plucking she brought the bird to the stove and burned the feathers too tiny to pick by turning Roslyn over a bare flame. The sharp smell penetrated the whole house.

"What a stink!" Angie yelled down from the parlor.

While Connie singed Roslyn I carried feathers in double fistfuls to the garbage pail. Connie grabbed a big feather and slid it into the hair at the crown of my head, the first playful gesture she ever made to me.

"Yankee Doodle," she said. "He stuck a feather in his cap and called it macaroni." I stared stonily but left the feather. "Go upstairs now, your grandfather's lonesome."

"He is not," I said. "Go ahead and do it, I can watch."

"I'm all done here."

"No, you're not." I handed her the white-handled knife. "Do it."

She put the knife down. "This one's too big. I have to use a smaller one."

While sounds of the Yankee game drifted downstairs I watched Connie butcher Roslyn.

First she spread newspapers on the table, then a paper towel directly under the bird "so the ink won't get on her skin."

Then she sawed Roslyn's head off. I picked it up and worked the yellow halves of the bill.

"Throw it out," she ordered, and I did, pitching it into the garbage pail. Her feet were sawed off at the drumstick tips, and suddenly my friend Roslyn was a store bird — nothing about her looked any different from poultry that lined refrigerator cases in supermarkets. I stacked one fist on top of the other and rested my chin on top to watch the finale.

The tip of the knife disappeared into Roslyn's belly. Connie's hand went in after it, and the sour smell of entrails filled the room as she lugged them out.

"This you gotta be careful with," Connie said, a female Rosiello now as she gestured at a green fluid-filled sac. "If this breaks inside the bird you gotta throw it out."

"Why?"

Instead of answering she jabbed the knife into the sack. A sickly odor rose from the green puddle.

"That there's the gall bladder. You got one, too, right here." She touched the knife point to a spot on my right side, just below my rib cage.

Then she found the stomach in the pile and slashed it open. Wet bread crumbs tumbled from it.

"What you fed her before. See?"

I saw. She lifted the empty bird and carried it to the sink, where she rinsed it in cold water. "That's all," she announced.

I began to fold the newspaper over the pile of guts.

"No, no, don't waste it," Connie said. "Feed it to the chickens."

"Are you crazy?" I shrieked. "They wouldn't touch this stuff."

"Yeah? Go throw it in the yard," she said casually. "Go on, do it."

I carried Roslyn's innards as if I were bearing a sacrificial offering to a pagan god. In the middle of the chicken yard I shook the bloody newspapers empty, and in an instant the five birds were all around my ankles, tearing into the stuff. One pecked at my sneaker out of sheer frenzy. The salt-and-pepper bird dragged a length of intestine away as if it were a fire hose. They even ate the barely digested bread crumbs of Roslyn's last meal.

I balled up the newspapers and threw them away in the outside pail before returning to Connie.

"Well? Was I right or what?"

"Yeah, you were right."

Connie was less pleased with her victory than I expected her to be. "It's just birds," she said, her voice almost consoling.

I sneaked out of the house with my burlap sack and spent an hour or so combing my neglected bottle turf. It was a good trip that netted me around twenty empties. Nat seemed glad to see me but I just grunted hello.

"How come you're mad every time you come here? Everybody else in the world smiles when they get money."

"Just pay me, wouldja, Nat?"

"What's with that feather in your hair?"

I started telling him about how Connie had slaughtered the duck but he made me stop, genuinely upset by it. And he hadn't even known Roslyn.

More coins into the grape preserves jar, new money on top of old: I was getting there, creeping toward my goal a dime-width at a time.

That night the stupid deacon made a huge fuss over the fresh-killed duck, the likes of which he hadn't tasted in ages. I chewed on a hamburger while Connie and Angie slowly ate their portions of Roslyn. Only the deacon took seconds.

You don't raise chickens — you keep them and they raise themselves, permitting you to watch. A chicken doesn't become loyal to his master, or protective of him. No pet ever *really* does, but chickens are honest about it. The arrangement is clear from the start: food for eggs. No confusion.

I could easily watch those five birds for hours at a time. They fought, strutted, preened. They sprinted as if they meant to run for miles but always stopped at the fence line. At night, roosting, they tucked their heads into their crops. In the darkness they looked like feathered lungs as they swelled and shrank with each breath.

Rosiello was wrong about one thing — they never did figure a way to reach the tomato plants, secure behind wire.

Angie taught me how to hypnotize a chicken. He took one of the white ones and held her head down, beak nearly touching the ground. Then he took a stick and slowly drew a straight line in the dirt within the bird's line of vision. Over it he drew a curved line, then a straight line, then another curved one.

He kept this up for a few minutes and told me to release the bird. I did, my sweaty palms clinging momentarily to the feathers. The bird stayed still as a statue.

"How come?" I whispered, watching the paralyzed bird.

"Magic." Laughing, Angie aimed a soft kick at her tail, breaking the spell in an explosion of noise and feathers.

We threw a bunch of packing straw from a crystal set Connie had into the yard for nesting materials. They made nests and sat on them for a few weeks. The nests became dung-encrusted, but no eggs. Connie began to curse the birds.

The first egg came from the salt-and-pepper bird the day after Connie threatened to make cacciatore out of the lot of them. Angie discovered it by sliding his hand under her. He pulled his hand out and made me feel it there, too. Salt and Pepper let me take it without a fuss.

It was streaked brown and white with dung. I felt repulsed until Connie straightened me out.

"Where'd you think eggs came from, their mouths?" She wiped it clean with a soft dish towel. "Nice," she admitted. "At least you bought *one* hen."

"Give the others time," Angie said.

Rosiello knew his birds, all right. Within a week all five were laying.

CHAPTER TWELVE

August. An occasional postcard from my father (Portland, Oregon, Seattle, Washington) but no word from Vic. Angie and I went for haircuts together, to the home of an old Italian who spoke almost no English. He cut my hair first, running an electric clipper up the back of my neck as if I were a sheep. It took about two minutes, then he dusted my neck generously with talcum powder. I ran my hand over the back of my head: sandpaper.

Angie got the exact same haircut, his white hair mingling with my brown on the floor. Angie said something in Italian to the barber, gesturing at me the whole while.

"Sally boy?" he asked. "Painta pick-cha too?"

"Oh yeah, he paints all the time," Angie said. "Just like his old man did."

The barber kissed me brutally on the forehead, then Angie got the same smacker. We walked jauntily back to Shepherd Avenue, the breeze cool on our identical scalps.

Rosemary was frantic because Vic wasn't writing her, despite her bombardment of letters, as well as cakes the size and heft of missiles. Connie wasn't much better as two Sundays passed without his usual collect call.

Angie and I willingly went to church with Connie. We were entertained by Deacon Sullivan, though his visits to the house now were less frequent. He had a hard time looking me in the eye.

On my own time without Angie I turned out paintings two and three a day. As much as the work itself I loved that rolltop desk and that musty corner of the cellar. No one could get me there. When I painted, Connie and Angie treated me as if I were a surgeon in the middle of an operation.

But she complained about my pale color from all those hours indoors.

"Casper the friendly ghost," she said. "What's Sally gonna say when he sees him? He'll think we kept him locked up."

"Let's take him to the beach," Angie said.

"Why? You wanna go *swimming?*"

"I don't know," Angie said. "I might go in, once we get there. Joey'll go in the water, anyway. You can't keep a kid out of the ocean."

"Well, don't expect *me* to go in," Connie said.

"You don't have to," Angie said happily, the trip assured. "I probably won't go in myself.

"So why are we goin'? We could put lawn chairs on the roof."

Angie waved her off. "Ahh, that ain't the same. There's wind at the beach, sand. We can get hot dogs. . . . For Christ's sake let's just do it. You want a breeze around here you have to go down the block and wait for the train."

Connie shrugged. "All right. Tomorrow." Angie winked at me. "But we bring lunch," she added. "Hot dogs." She shuddered. "If you knew what went into those hot dogs you wouldn't go near one."

I never saw a bathing suit like my grandmother's. It was a black thing the shape of a sofa slipcover, with narrow straps that fit over her shoulders and bit into the flesh. On her upper arm was the largest vaccination mark I'd ever seen, big as a silver dollar and raised high off the skin like a burn scar. There were few blemishes on Connie's vast expanse of skin, just a couple of red freckles like confectioners' sugar dots. The suit ended at her knees in a lacy frill.

Her bare feet were shaped exactly like her shoes. They had good-sized arches and well-formed heels, but the toes were a tangle. The big toes crossed over to the next ones, which were like shriveled cocktail frankfurters. The calluses were a thick, opaque yellow. It was as if her feet had been mangled in some vicious piece of machinery.

At Rockaway Beach cigarette butts were mixed into the sand like caraway seeds in rye bread. The place was a carnival of whites, blacks, Puerto Ricans, and radios.

We plodded through the hot sand. "If we sit near colored, we have to listen to jazz," Connie said.

"So we'll sit near white," Angie said.

"Then we'll have to listen to that rock and roll."

"We won't sit near *any*body, Con."

"It's too crowded not to sit near anybody."

Angie laughed, squatted, and scooped up two cigarette butts. "Eh, we'll stuff these in your ears, you won't hear nothin'."

"You just try it, buster."

It *was* crowded, though. There were wire litter baskets all over the place but they were crammed with junk, so beer cans and paper bags blew all over the place like tumbleweeds. Young mothers changed babies. Once in a while, when the wind was right, you smelled the ocean, but mostly the odors were suntan oil, hot dogs, perspiration.

We set the blanket down about twenty yards from the surf. Connie said, "If the tide's comin' in, we're dead."

"If it's comin' in, we'll move, we won't die," Angie said,

peeling off his T-shirt. He looked great. The hair on his chest was a cluster of steel wool so thick you couldn't see the skin beneath it. He was lightly tanned to his elbows and halfway down his neck. His legs and belly were even whiter than mine.

"Mr. America," Connie jeered. With the two of them in bathing suits it finally occurred to me that she outweighed him by quite a few pounds. If they were boxers they'd have been three weight divisions apart.

Connie pointed at me. "Funny, this one's half Irish but he's darker than you."

"I have a name, you know, Connie," I said.

"Joey," she said, as if pronouncing a word from a foreign language. "Eh, I like to just talk. No sense usin' your name when I'm lookin' right at you, am I right?"

Angie's bathing suit was black — Connie must have bought it for him — with a belt and buckle that fastened. He rubbed his palms along his ribs and took deep breaths.

"I didn't even know until now that this was what I wanted to do," he said, his eyes on the ocean. "I was wanting to do something and it was come to the beach."

"You said you wanted to come because Joey was pale," Connie said. Twice in one day, she'd said my name! It was a record never to be broken.

Angie ignored her remark. "Who's comin' with me to the water?"

"Me!" I said. Connie didn't budge.

"Swim now, then you can eat," she said.

"We won't be long unless we drown," Angie said.

"The comedian."

My experiences with swimming had been at the Roslyn pool, in bright blue water with lanes painted on the bottom. I'd learned to swim on kickboards alongside ropes strung with safety buoys.

The sight of the ocean scared me. The water looked black as ink, and the surf slammed down so hard I could feel it through my feet.

Angie took me by the elbow. "Jeez, I forgot to even ask — can you swim?"

"Sure I can swim," I said indignantly.

"Undertow's pretty strong, Joey. I'll show you what I mean."

I held his rough hand. We walked into the surf and stopped where the waves broke at my calves. After they hit, foamy water bubbled around my ankles like tiny nibbling animals. It spread like a blanket ten feet behind us, groaned, hesitated, and began rolling back to the ocean.

"Here it is," Angie said, his voice gleeful as he squeezed my hand.

The sucking sensation made me gasp out loud. Angie laughed.

"Easy, pal, she can't hurt you." Sand swirled around my feet and squeezed through my toes. Suddenly I was standing in a pair of snug holes. Another wave broke, splashing my groin. My testicles tightened and crept high into the safety of my scrotum.

Gooseflesh popped out on my arms. I was looking at a sailboat way out on the horizon, maybe half a mile away, and was certain the power of the undertow would yank me right out there and tangle me up in the seaweed at the bottom.

"Let's go back to Connie," I said.

"Already?" Angie splashed water on his back to get used to its temperature.

"I'm cold."

"Look, I'm gonna swim, I need it. Can you get back alone?"

I yanked my feet free with two loud sucks. "There's a big white and red umbrella near Connie. I'll look for it."

"Right. See ya later."

He trotted toward the approaching wave and dove right into the teeth of it. I was paralyzed by his action and didn't notice it coming at me. The beast knocked me down, gurgled water past my ears, and started drawing me toward that sailboat.

I flipped onto my belly, dug my fingers and toes into the sand. When the wave had drawn all the way back to the ocean I staggered to my feet, wiping sand and water from my eyes. I tasted salt. I thought I could hear the wave laughing.

Angie's back was to the shore. He stood up to his waist in the water, beyond the breakers. His head looked small with his hair flat to his scalp. He crouched, pushed off, and began swimming, keeping his head out of the water.

From the hard but damp sand where the tide had receded I watched his jerky strokes, white limbs swinging, silver head flashing and twisting toward alternate shoulders at each stroke, like the head of a golf course sprinkler. For a moment I thought I'd never see him again, that he'd be gone like my father and Vic and Mel.

"No," I said out loud. "He'll be back." I watched Angie swim until the sun was too bright on the water for my eyes to bear it.

With furry yellow sunspots still fading from my retinas I searched for that red and white umbrella.

Connie laughed. "You didn't last long."

"It's cold." I sat on a corner of the blanket, still shivering. "The water's dirty, too."

"It's clean enough for you. . . . Where is he?"

"Swimming."

"Johnny Weismuller." Connie seemed to be on the verge of asking for something, but she hesitated and closed her mouth.

"Rub sand on my feet," she blurted.

"*What?*"

"It's good for my calluses."

Before I could agree to do it Connie swung her feet past the edge of the blanket. I took handfuls of sand and picked them clean of cigarette butts and beer can tabs, then rubbed them against her soles until it sifted away. Her feet didn't feel like feet at all, coated in so much callus. They were more like cinder blocks with toes. Only her moans of contentment reminded me that I was working on living tissue.

I kept it up for about fifteen minutes. The way she moaned was making me feel strange.

"Hey, Connie, I don't wanna keep doing this."

"What's the matter?"

"It feels *weird*."

She cocked her head. "Weird?"

"Yeah. The way you moan."

"So stop already," she said, yanking her feet away. "Your father, he used to rub my feet for hours."

"I don't care. I'm not my father. My father's weird, too."

"What's that, your new word?" She shaded her eyes with her hand for a better look at me. "You miss him, don't you?"

I pushed sand into hills. "I don't know. A little. Those stupid postcards he sends . . . he doesn't miss me, why should I miss him?"

She took her hand away from her eyes. "You're a lot like him," she said, as if the thought had just occurred to her after all our time together.

"I am *not*," I shot back.

Connie laughed, a laugh pregnant with wisdom. "Wait, wait," she warned. "Someday you'll see. You're his thumbprint." She pressed her thumb against my stomach. "Nobody could ever tell him nothin', either." She laughed again, oddly — something about the beach had made her philosophical, a mood I knew would fade when she was back in her basement. "Oh, God," she said wearily.

"I'm bored," I announced.

"Look for money."

"Where?"

"In the sand. I brought the red sieve, it used to be Vic's."

"Aw, Connie, there's no money around here."

"Eh," she grunted, "watch me." She scooped sand into the sieve and shook it. Sand fell through the holes, leaving behind more junk, less sand, more junk, less sand. She passed me the sieve as if it were the collection plate at church.

"Look."

One by one I picked the items out of it: a piece of dull green glass, a bit of dried seaweed, a fragment of crab claw bleached rosy by the sun, a bottle cap, a bunch of cigarette butts, and, finally, a dusty penny.

I held the penny and rubbed it clean with my fingers. "You put it there," I accused.

"Do I throw money around? Shake your own, you'll see."

I hopped a few feet away, scooped twice as much sand as she

had into the sieve and shook it. This time there was a nickel under the junk.

"See? I couldn't have reached over there. You could get rich at the beach."

But I didn't need Connie's prompting. Rockaway Beach had suddenly become a prospector's paradise.

She warned, "You ain't gonna find in every load."

I found that out soon enough. I must have sifted a hundred loads of sand in that thing, shaking, pawing, throwing aside the waste, angered at the moneyless loads. I started saving beer can tabs, too, folding them into a two-foot chain.

My hands stunk from the sour tobacco of a million cigarette butts. I had a small fortune, though — half a dollar. It was mostly pennies and nickels but in part a dime, the equivalent of a twenty-five bottle haul to Nat's.

I let out a whoop when I found the dime and accidentally kicked sand on a lady buttered with suntan oil. It clung to her ribs the way bread crumbs stuck to Connie's veal cutlets.

Angie came back, breathing hard. "Swam all the way to the buoy," he announced, squatting and pointing. "Look, Con, how far I went."

"You're gettin' me wet."

"See that thing out there with the pole on it, and the red ball on top?"

Connie stretched her neck but didn't rise. "Too many umbrellas in the way."

"I'll show you when you stand up later," he panted, collapsing on the blanket. "Remind me. All the way and back!" He waved a clenched fist. "I could never do it before. Freddie could do it but not me. I didn't even hang on for a rest. The lifeguard was blowin' his whistle but I pretended I didn't hear him."

Connie said, "Remember Freddie — you'll get a heart attack just like he did."

"Not me," Angie boomed, rising and pounding his fists on his chest. "Tarzan! Come to me, woman."

"You wish." She opened her basket. "You want to eat now or later?"

"Now. I never felt better. Like I kicked off twenty years and left 'em in the surf. What's all this junk?" he asked, pointing at the stuff I'd sifted.

"I did it," I said. "Angie, look what I found." Half a buck in change made my hand bulge impressively when I was ten years old.

"Where'd you find it all, Joey?"

"Right here. Connie showed me how to shake the sand. I found these beer can things, too." I showed him the chain. He draped it over his neck.

"You'll need a tetanus shot if it cuts you," Connie cautioned.

Water dripped from his nose. "How about that, a fortune right in the sand. And me workin' all these years, like a jerk. I coulda been comin' to the beach every day." He smacked himself on the forehead. "Dope that I am!" He took the chain off his neck and flopped back onto the blanket, his rib cage heaving.

"Eggplant or veal," Connie said. "You can have either or both. Two sandwiches apiece."

Nobody wrapped food like Connie Ambrosio. The sandwiches were sealed in waxed paper *and* tinfoil. Then they were placed in plastic bags and bound in rubber bands. Angie fumbled at his sandwich with pruny hands.

"We could put these sandwiches in one of those things they make so people in the future can find them," he said. "I forget what you call them. . . ."

"Time capsules," I said, pulling the foil off an eggplant sandwich.

"That's it! Time capsules. That way people a hundred years from now can know what we ate."

"Why should they wanna know what we ate?" Connie asked.

"History."

"So who cares?" Connie was annoyed.

"*Somebody* cares," Angie mused. "Madonna, by the time I get this thing open I'll starve to death."

Connie snorted. "If you don't do this, sand gets in and you throw it all away."

The food was delicious, the bread soaked deeply with rich oils. We washed it all down with lemonade and stretched out, stuffed.

170

Then I had an idea. Connie was asleep on her back, and Angie dozed on his stomach. Without waking them I headed for the concession stand. The change I'd found grew warm in my hand.

"Yessir," the counterman said. My nose barely reached the counter.

"How much is a lemon ice?"

"Fifteen. Lemon, watermelon, and cherry."

"It costs less home."

"Kid, this ain't home."

"Lemon ice comes in other flavors?"

He sighed. "Lemon ice is lemon. I got watermelon and cherry, too, like I said."

"Give me three lemon ices."

He opened a lid behind the counter. A "phht" of cold air escaped. Three green waxed containers were plunked in front of me, and three wrapped wooden spoons.

I pointed. "That's not lemon ice."

"Sure it is. Forty-five cents."

I felt one of the rock-hard containers. "It's supposed to be soft. You're supposed to *scoop* it."

"Kid, I awreddy told you, this ain't home. Forty-five."

Coin by coin I dropped the money on the counter. "Jesus, another Rockaway treasure hunter," he muttered. I didn't mind spending that money. It was magical money that had appeared from out of thin air, unlike the deposit bottle money.

I stacked the cups and searched for the red and white umbrella as I walked. Connie was awake when I got back, sliding her feet back and forth in the sand, eroding calluses without my help.

"Where'd you go?"

I hefted the ices, my hands numb from the dry-ice cold. "Dessert," I announced, my voice triumphant.

Angie awoke, rolled over, and shielded his eyes. "Never thought I'd see the day when you'd spend money at the beach."

"Not me," she said.

Angie sat up. "The money he found? You let him spend *his* money?"

171

"It was his idea! I was asleep, I thought he was lost. Who told you to go?"

I didn't answer. I sat between them and passed out cups and spoons. Angie pinched the skinny cord at the back of my neck. I picked the lid off my ice. A young black couple walked past us, a small child on the man's shoulders.

"I wonder if the colored get sunburn," Connie mused. If not for the wind off the water they'd have heard her.

I said, "They have to pack lemon ice like this here, otherwise it gets all sandy."

Connie set her cup down. "Gonna let mine sit a minute, it's too hard." Angie and I dug into ours.

"How'd you know this was just what we needed?" he asked.

The fuss embarrassed me. "They had other flavors, too. Watermelon and cherry."

"Flavors for colored people," Connie noted.

I'd never felt prouder of myself. I was a provider for the very first time. Angie and I pointed at sailboats as we ate, and talked about where they might be going.

A huge one went by. "Maybe my father's on that one," I said.

"Naah," Angie said. "He's in Seattle, or some damn place."

"That was *last* week. He could be anywhere now."

Angie nodded. "Who knows?" he conceded.

I pointed at the same boat. "I'm gonna have a boat when I'm big. No house, just a boat. Bigger than that one, because I'm gonna live on it."

"Takes money," Connie said. "Lots of it."

I ignored her. "I'll be by myself. I won't have to worry about anybody. I can *visit* people when I want to, then just sail away by myself."

"Like your father," Angie said, completing my thought.

"That's right."

Connie said, "I thought you were gonna be a ballplayer."

"I am."

"They don't play no baseball on boats."

"I'll sail to the ballpark for games and then after I'll get back on the boat."

"Sure you will." She squeezed her ice container, testing it for softness. She began eating.

"And what about your kids?" Angie said. "They gotta go to school, it's the law."

"No kids," I said. "I already told you — nobody on board, except me." I reached the bottom of my lemon ice, where the sweetest, gooiest part was. I took a mouthful and jabbed my wooden spoon at my own narrow chest. Angie and Connie grinned at each other.

"Where you gonna get the money?" Connie said.

I thought about it. "I'll sell my pictures. I'll paint on my boat."

Connie cackled. "If the boat rocks on the waves, how you gonna *paint*?"

I crumpled my empty cup and pitched it away. "I'll think of something."

"Pick that up and put it in the garbage basket," Angie said. I obeyed.

"Eh, we'll see," Connie said. "By the time you get that boat we'll be in Saint John's anyway."

"What's Saint John's?" I asked Angie.

"The cemetery," he said softly. My stomach dropped.

"No," I declared, expanding my bony chest, but it was as if I'd just ordered the waves to stop rolling in. They both laughed. Angie said, "Relax, Joey, that's not gonna be for a long time."

"How do you know?" Connie said. "Look at Freddie."

"Shut up," he told her.

I felt drowsy and lay face down on the blanket. While I was still barely awake I heard Angie say, "The kid's okay, no matter what that deacon thinks." I drifted off to the sound of Connie's spoon scraping ice.

I must have slept for at least an hour. I felt my foot being squeezed; Angie. The afternoon sun made an orange halo shine all around his tight body. He looked like a saint, as if a baby lamb belonged around his shoulders.

"We're going home now."

We got up and shook the blanket before folding it. I picked

up my beer-tab chain but Connie made me put it in her bag. There were fewer people around, and when we were ready to leave Angie pointed at the ocean.

"See that thing? The pole with the red ball on top? That's where I swam to, Con." He looked at us like a kid trying to convince his parents he's seen a flying saucer. Salt had crusted his hair. "I did, I swear."

"Good," Connie said. "Fold the chair, we can carry it easier."

We began walking to the car. Connie fell a few steps behind. When I turned to take a final look at the ocean she beckoned to me, waiting for Angie to walk out of earshot.

"The current helped him," she said. "Don't say nothin', but the current helped him get out there." Angie's shoulders looked narrow and bony ahead of us.

We were quiet on the way back to Shepherd Avenue, the three of us so sunburned that it hurt to lean against the car's hot upholstery. My back clung to the vinyl, peeling free like Scotch tape.

"In a few days it'll turn into a tan," Angie said when I complained.

I ran to the chickens when we got home.

"Of course they're all right," Connie said. "All they need us for is food."

"Hey," Angie said, "screen door's unlocked." He pushed open the wooden door, also unlocked.

"Burglars?" Connie said.

"I'll check. Wait here."

"What if they have guns?"

"I already told you, I ain't ready for Saint John's yet."

"I'm comin' with you," Connie insisted. "Let's go."

The three of us crept inside, past my art desk, past the hanging peppers. It was dark down there, and it seemed even darker because our eyes hadn't adjusted from the sunshine.

It took awhile for my eyes to recognize the sleeping form of Vic on the battered couch.

Connie's voice awakened him.

"My God, how thin you got."

174

It was true. Vic had been sprawled on the couch with one arm dangling over the side, his face to the ceiling. His cheeks were hollow, his elbows knobby. When he heard Connie's voice he opened his eyes and sat up.

"How's it going?" His voice was slow, sleep-hoarse. His face was heavily tanned and his jeans, once snug, fit like clown's pants. I figured at first they were a pair he'd bought in West Virginia but then saw the unmistakable stitching of Connie's patchwork on the knee.

"How thin," she wailed again, her voice breaking.

Vic cleared his throat. "I lost a few pounds."

Nobody went near him. We stood in a line, elbow to elbow, as if a glass quarantine wall were bumping our noses. Sand itched inside my bathing suit.

"You lost at least thirty pounds," Connie insisted. When was someone going to hug him? We stood like hypnotized chickens.

"Twenty-four," Vic corrected. "I'm a hundred and sixty-six. Just weighed myself in a drugstore."

"You'll put it back real soon," Angie said.

"No," Vic said. "I'm just right now. I was fat before."

Finally I broke the invisible barrier and went to him. He hugged me briefly against his hard belly.

"Hey, slugger, how you hittin' 'em?"

"Good," I said, even though I hadn't played stickball since Mel had been taken away. "You guys got a game in Brooklyn?"

"No. I'm just home, that's all." He looked at his parents. "I saw Johnny Gallo outside. How come nobody told me about Freddie dying?"

Angie opened his mouth, let it close. "Your father didn't want you to worry," Connie said.

"You didn't want me to *worry*?" Vic's voice was incredulous. He shook his head. Angie looked at the floor. "So when'd we become chicken farmers?"

"Few weeks ago," Angie murmured. "Your mother wrote you about them, I thought."

"Never got it. Guess they'll forward it here."

Angie's eyebrows jumped. "Forward?"

Vic nodded. "My stuff's upstairs."

"All of it?"

"Everything."

Nobody said anything. I was wearing the Pittsburgh Pirates hat and suddenly felt ridiculous under it.

Vic walked to the stove, looking even thinner in motion. "Is that minestrone, Ma?"

"Yeah, but it's cold, we were out all day."

"Could you heat it up? Goddamn it, I'm hungry for some good food for a change."

It was unheard of for Vic to curse, but he did it so casually that it was clearly now a part of his vocabulary. He sat alone at the table and minutes later he was eating a bowl of hot soup, slowly. In the old days he'd have scarfed down three bowls and five rolls in ten minutes.

He ate as if the rest of us didn't exist, the way the chickens did, oblivious to the fence that trapped them and the captors that stared down at them.

Vic pushed the empty bowl away and stifled a belch. "Damn, that's good."

"What's with this new language?" Angie's voice was sharp. Vic didn't answer. He was running his finger around the rim of his glass, having first dipped it in cream soda. He frowned like a child.

"I was doing lousy down there."

"Well no wonder!" Angie boomed. "Vic, you're sick, look at you! A skeleton!"

Vic's eyes seemed unfocused as he watched his finger encircle the glass rim. "I'm not sick. In fact I feel better than I've ever felt in my life."

Angie wasn't believing it. "Ah, lots of guys have trouble getting started with a new team. Willie Mays couldn't hit the side of a barn his first few weeks with the Giants. . . . Nothing to worry about. Next season you give it another shot and they won't cut you."

He licked his lips, hoping Vic would say something. "It's that choking up stuff that screwed you up, Vic. I said it from the start, ask the kid."

A twinge of jealousy shot through me. Now I was back to being the kid again, with Vic around.

"No," Vic said, his voice barely audible.

"What's that?"

"No," Vic repeated. "No more shots, no next season."

I'd never heard Angie take a flat denial from anyone before. Vic pressed his finger harder and harder on the glass rim, until it started to sing. The noise made me grit my teeth. Connie reached across the table and caught his wrist.

"Enough, Victor." Her voice was gentle but when she touched his arm he flinched, as if he'd gotten a carpet shock.

"You mean," Angie said, "you got cut permanent?"

Vic sucked the soda off his finger. "Nobody *cut* me, Pop. I just don't want to play ball for anyone." He squeezed the glass so tightly his fingernails went white.

"All this shady stuff," Angie sputtered. "You got something to say, mister, just say it."

Vic grinned, his cheekbones glistening with sweat. "Okay, here it is." He stood. "I quit that team. I fucking hate baseball." His grin widened. "Happy?"

The grin intensified the shock of the word. Connie gasped, and at the same time the glass in Vic's hand shattered. Blood flowed down his palm. She took a napkin and clasped it against the wound. He stared blankly at her as she played nurse. Blood soaked the napkin.

"I've always hated it," he said more softly. Angie picked up the bits of busted glass.

"Enough," Connie said. She was crying.

Vic looked at her. "I don't know what you're cryin' about, Ma. You didn't even say good-bye, the day I left."

For a while it seemed as if Vic wasn't going to leave our room, except to use the toilet. He slept all the time, sometimes thirteen hours at a stretch.

And when he was awake he was usually stationed at the basement table, yawning over a cup of black coffee.

Food barely tempted him. At meals he ate a few thin slices

of whatever meat was being served and a mouthful of greens. It annoyed Connie and worried Angie, who couldn't imagine a man sitting down to a meal without eating at least one slice of bread.

He was more relaxed around people than he had been before. When anyone asked about his abandonment of a baseball career he answered in low, cool tones. He lit cigarettes in their faces, seeming to enjoy their astonishment at this new corrupt habit. He smoked a pack a day and inhaled all the way to his ankles.

He had little to say to me. We'd walk past the hamburger joint — by now almost completely finished, new glass and all — and he'd say, "Jesus, that went up fast." He'd sit on a crate and watch the chickens but never join in to feed them or clean the coop.

Rosemary appeared after dinner each night. The tables were turned now — *she* was ill at ease in *his* presence, while he seemed almost amused by her discomfort. Nothing she tried got him out of the house at night.

"Let's go see a movie, Vic."

"There's nothing good around, Rosemary."

"It'll do you good to get out of the house. Let's go."

"All I ever did in West Virginia was go to movies. I'd rather watch TV."

He only went out with Johnny Gallo. Once he didn't get home until four in the morning. When he crept into bed I asked where he'd been, but he just grunted "Out," grumpily.

"*Where* out?"

"If I wanted you to know I would have told you."

I was hurt. He'd never spoken so roughly to me. It was days before I even tried talking to him.

Then he stopped going out with Johnny and returned to his sleep and coffee routine. He glided around the house with haunted, accusing eyes. I wanted to break the ice but it was ten feet thick.

"Hey, Vic, how come you never wrote me a letter?"

He lit a cigarette. "I said hello to you in all my letters."

"But I never got my *own* letter."

He stubbed out the butt after just one puff. "Hey. I got my parents bugging me, I don't need you too, all right?"

I refused to give up on him. I tossed a Spaldeen at him as he lay on his bed. He practically cowered as he caught it.

"Teach me to be a power hitter, okay, Vic?"

He squeezed the ball until it seemed ready to explode, his knuckles white. "Joey. *Listen* to me. I can't teach you anything. I'm a fucking *failure*, do you understand? If you hang around me you'll get tainted."

"What's tainted?"

"It means my shit will rub off on you. And you don't need that, right?"

I gave up the battle. "We were gonna be teammates," I said, even though our dream was smashed.

Vic tossed the Spaldeen aside and lit another cigarette. "Yeah, well, now you've gotta make it to the big leagues all alone, pal, because your uncle can't cut it. I'll cheer you from the cheap seats." He scraped the match three times before it lit. "Can't even light a fuckin' match." He rolled onto his side, away from me. Only the puffs of smoke that clouded his headboard told me he was still awake.

I decided then never to become a professional ballplayer. Connie had told me I could do only one thing anyway, right? Fine. I would be a painter. Nothing but painting, the rest of the way. Painting and, for the time being, bottle collecting.

On the second Sunday after Vic's return Connie left the house after supper to see Grace Rothstein. She was gone for an hour while the rest of us watched television.

She entered the parlor and waited until we were all looking at her before speaking.

"Tomorrow you start work at Uncle Rudy's deli."

Staring at Vic, I could have sworn I saw his face turn the color of cement. Minutes passed before blood came back to his cheeks. In the space of an hour a man's fate was determined while he innocently watched television.

Every muscle in Vic's body seemed tense, ready to explode.

A vein in his neck stood out like a caterpillar, and from where he sat he could easily have kicked in the TV screen. I thought he would, but instead the tension left his face and his eyes wettened.

"Okay, Ma." Defeated. Connie turned and went to her room without saying good night.

"Well," Vic sighed. "The ball game is over."

Angie said, "It won't be too bad. Your brother worked in that deli for a while, there's a lot you can learn. You gotta do something, you know."

"I know, Pop, I understand. It doesn't matter."

But it did. It was Angie's fate as well as Vic's. Until then he'd believed Vic would pack up his gear and return to the Nuggets, eager to tear the cover off the baseball.

Now that wasn't going to happen. Connie had held her own closed court and found Victor Ambrosio guilty. His sentence was to chop celery, shred cole slaw, and peel potatoes for an indefinite length of time.

Angie and I left the parlor. Vic remained planted in front of the TV. He knew he'd be rising very early for work, but he didn't have to worry about oversleeping. He had an alarm clock named Connie, who was sure to be up at dawn to pour coffee into him and prepare him for the first regular workday of his life. She'd be tougher on him than any baseball coach he'd ever known.

There was a glazed look in Vic's eyes when he got home from his first day at Uncle Rudy's. That night he sat on the porch, smoking and drinking coffee, staring at the sky.

He stopped shaving. Grace complained to Connie that he was a sloppy image for the deli. Connie got him to shave his cheeks, at least, leaving a moustache. It grew fuller and thicker by the day, giving his face an even more emaciated appearance. Angie hated the moustache but resigned himself to it.

"Eh, he's workin' now, he can do what he wants."

Usually he couldn't sleep. He read black-bound books from the local library until dawn by the light of a small bedside lamp.

It was as if all the sleeping he'd done when he first got home made rest unnecessary now.

Connie scolded him for smoking in the bedroom, saying the smoke was bad for me, but I told her I didn't mind. I wanted his friendship back. I still couldn't figure out how I'd lost it.

That Friday Connie had the evening meal timed for Vic's arrival home. When she heard his footsteps in the driveway she broke handfuls of spaghetti and dropped them into a pot of boiling water. By the time Vic had washed up the spaghetti was cooked and in a big bowl, a light coating of sauce over it.

We sat with false heartiness, hoping to carry Vic along into the spirit. "See?" Angie said. "You worked a week already, it went fast."

Vic grunted. "I never saw so many boiled potatoes in my life. How the hell can people eat so much potato salad?"

Angie poured a generous glass of wine for him. "Forget it now, it's the weekend. And watch your mouth."

"The weekend'll be over in two days, Pop."

"Vic, if you look at it that way you'll go nuts."

"I'm *already* going nuts."

"Hey." Angie gestured with the bread knife. "I worked fifty years, I'm not crazy yet."

Connie lifted the spaghetti high on two forks and dished it into small bowls, then spooned sauce and meatballs. "You'd better give it to me now before you lose it, Vic."

He wrinkled his eyebrows, puzzled. Connie's hands were busy, so with a jerk of her head she indicated the envelope that jutted from his shirt pocket.

Vic shoved it deeper into his pocket. "I can handle it, Ma."

"Gimme, you'll lose it. Grace goes to the bank Monday, she'll take care of it."

"Oh, sure, Ma," Vic laughed. "I'm supposed to let my boss be my banker? I know how to handle money, I lived on my own."

"It's easier for Grace to —"

"I can *do* it, Ma. You act like the bank's in China." He yanked the envelope out and laid it beside his plate. Two coins rolled from its open end. Vic caught them and put them back.

Everyone but Connie started eating. "What'd you do that for?"

"What?" Vic asked.

"The envelope's open."

"So? I bought cigarettes."

"You didn't have change for cigarettes?"

Vic threw his fork on the table. "Jesus, Ma, whose money *is* this, anyway?"

"Your brother used to give the envelope without opening it."

"Good for him. I'm not my brother."

"You sure ain't."

"Well, at least you know where I am."

Silence, save for the fluorescent hum. Finally Vic forced a smile. "Ma, whatever you want from me I'll pay every week. I just don't feel like playing around, so let's make it a definite amount."

Connie looked as if she'd just been slapped. "I don't want a penny from you."

"You should, Ma, I'm all grown up." His voice was cold. "What's a fair board around here, Pop? Ten? Fifteen bucks a week?"

"Not at the table." Angie was dead serious, his voice dangerously quiet. "Put it away, Victor."

"In a sec. Let's clear this up first. What'd Sal pay when he lived here?" His voice was loud and rough, a carnival barker's. Connie looked down at the tablecloth. Angie gripped the edges of the table. Vic gently touched her wrist.

"What'd Sal give, Ma?"

"I took ten."

"Ten bucks!" He released her wrist. "Well, that was . . . what, ten years ago? So you figure with the cost of living goin' up and everything . . . how about if I give fifteen?"

Connie was weeping.

"Fifteen okay, Ma?"

"FIFTEEN IS PLENTY!" Angie slammed his fist so hard on the table that the bowls jumped. I felt like sliding under the table, but Vic just nodded and calmly pulled a ten and a five from his envelope and laid the bills beside Connie's plate.

"I swear on the cross I'll never do this at the table again."

He finished his tiny portion, rinsed his fork and bowl, and dried his hands.

"Eat fruit," Connie begged.

"I'm going out now. I need a shower, I smell like potato salad." He left, and the rest of us poked at our food. Connie stayed red-eyed for hours.

"Least he's going out," Connie said.

Angie said bitterly, "We bargained with our son like he was a Jew."

"What does that mean?"

Angie held a palm up. "Joey, do me a favor, stay out of this one, okay?"

He'd never spoken so sharply to me. Of all people, Connie said, "Hey, come on, he's just askin'."

"He's always just *askin'*. Whole family's fallin' apart and he's *askin'*." He jammed his hat on his head and stalked out of the house. I looked to Connie for more sympathetic words but that well was dry. She shrugged elaborately: what do you want from *me?*

I went up to my cot and slammed the door behind me. Vic came in so late that night that I didn't even hear him. When I left the house at dawn I was extra quiet so I wouldn't wake him up. He slept with his mouth open, gripping the pillow with both arms as if it were the side of a lifeboat.

CHAPTER THIRTEEN

SACK over my shoulder, I headed for my bottle terrain as if in search of enemies I meant to shoot dead. I would miss breakfast but I didn't care. Zip was going outside just when I was, and he seemed startled when I didn't wave back at him. All his life *he'd* been the human stone with other people.

Good, good. A taste of his own medicine.

I was in luck. There must have been a Puerto Rican block party the night before, because Nehi bottles were all over the place — on window ledges, clustered against curbstones, jammed into trash cans.

It was like coming upon a wild garden heavy with exotic fruit. It was hard to decide where to start gathering. I plucked a grape soda bottle off a window ledge just as a young woman in a blue nightgown with a bow at the neck was rolling up her shade. I heard her scream but didn't look back as I moved on to get more bottles.

Tough on her. I needed the two cents.

In no time at all I had forty bottles in my sack, the most I'd ever jammed into it. I would have taken more but I was out of room. I carried the load to Nat's, then came back and found another twenty-three.

He waited until I'd returned from the second trip to pay me. "A buck forty-five," he marveled. There'd been a few big bottles in the haul. "You'll catch up with Zip yet."

I listened to the silvery song of the nickels and dimes as they flowed into my pocket. My mouth was actually watering. Now I was sorry I'd wasted my beachcomber money on lemon ice for Connie and Angie. They were no friends of mine.

"Hey, Nat, you're a Jew, right?"

He closed his fish mouth and forced a slight smile. I could practically see the shape of his upper teeth through his tight lip. "Yes I am," he said in a formal tone. "How did you know that?"

"I heard Zip say it once. . . . What's it mean when you bargain like a Jew?"

His face was darkening as if a gray dye were being pumped into his veins. "Who said that, Zip?"

"No. My grandfather said it last night when my uncle gave him fifteen dollars for room and pord."

"*Board.*"

"Yeah, that's it."

Nat sighed and shut his eyes. "Oh dear God, let it stop," he whispered. "It just never stops."

"What never stops?"

He blinked wet eyes and focused them on me. "People hate Jews for bad reasons. . . . I should bite my tongue, for no reasons. Did you study about Hitler in school yet? No? He put Jews in ovens, just like your grandma put that duck in the oven. My mother and father went into the ovens." His eyes welled up, sparkled. "So did six million other Jews."

He pulled a handkerchief from his back pocket and wiped away a sweat moustache. Then he mopped the back of his neck.

"Low blow your grandfather threw," he said to the grimy cement floor. "Low blow." He blew his nose.

Angry as I was at Angie, I felt forced to defend him. "He's not really a bad guy, Nat. He'd never do anything like that."

"That's what everybody said about Hitler. Nice guy, cried when his canary died."

I knew he wanted me out of there. "I'm sorry, Nat." I slung my empty sack over my shoulder.

He patted the sack. "You didn't do anything, Joey. You just raked up the ashes a little. Now go, go home. This is America. Bring me more bottles, make money. Go." He swatted my ass lightly to get me started.

Nobody yelled at me for missing breakfast, and that afternoon Connie handed me another letter from Mel, again on that ridiculous pink paper.

> *Dear Joey,*
> *This place sucks. I want to bust out of here. I'm not even alowed to watch TV no more. They say I watch it too much but my fucken ant still won't let me play in the yard. When are you comming? Did you find enuf bottles to pay for the train yet? If you are comming I won't bust out. It's easy to get here. You take the train to the long eyeland railroad in jamayka and then you ask the man where the train to patchog is. It's a long ride but my ant's house is real near the stashun, I can wait for you there. I tried to look for bottles too but I hardly found any. Every buddy here brings them back themself. Don't feel bad because they didn't let*

you see Freddie when he was dead. I saw my uncle
when he died, he was just like asleep.
                    your friend Mel DiGiovanna

I got some "cheap" paper from Connie and went straight to work on my reply.

> *Dear Mel,*
> *Vic came home. He's not a good baseball player anymore and he doesn't like me anymore. Angie doesn't like me, either. He yelled at me last night. But I don't care, today I made $1.45 from bottles. The guy who gave me the money has no mother and father just like you. A guy called Hitler cooked them in a oven and also six milyun other people. Don't bust out yet. I am going to visit you when I have a lot of money. This is no bullshit. I am really going to do it.*
> *   your friend Joey Ambrosio*
> *P.S. We got five chickens in the yard now. One of them got his eye pecked out by jellis chickens. We had a duck too but Connie killed it. Angie helped her. I pulled some of her feathers out.*

When I sealed the letter in an envelope I was all but giggling with glee at having written a vulgar word — and oh, what a fit Connie would throw if she ever came across Mel's letter and read about her "fucken ant!"

I trotted to Atlantic Avenue, Nat's coins jingling in my pocket. I sort of expected an alarm to go off in the mailbox upon its acceptance of my letter with the dirty word in it, but no. Nothing ever happened to you as long as you were sneaky.

My elbow was gripped from behind: you didn't get away with everything, after all. Angie whirled me around.

"I've been lookin' all over for you. Where've you been?"

"No place."

"Don't tell me no place. . . . You mad at me?"

"No."

"Don't tell me no. I can tell you are."

A Mack truck roared by. We were shrouded in a cloud of

black oily smoke that made us cough. Angie pulled me in the direction of the house but I yanked myself out of his grasp.

"Hey, look, Joey, I was real upset last night when I talked like that. Don't be mad no more, okay?"

I slid my hand into my pocket and tickled the money so softly it didn't make noise. "You hate Jews. You're like Hitler."

He staggered back as if I'd shoved him. "I'm *what?*"

"You said something bad about them last night."

"*When?*"

His face was pure innocence. He really didn't remember, until I repeated his exact words. The skin under his white stubble went pink. He kicked a pebble into the street. "Jews are good at makin' money. *Some* Jews, anyway. It was a stupid thing to say. . . . How do you know about Hitler?"

I felt my face flame. I couldn't tell him about my secret business with Nat. "They taught us in school."

"Oh . . . how long you gonna stay mad at me?"

I thought it over briefly. "An hour."

He cracked a sunflower seed between his teeth. "Well, that sounds fair. When you're through being mad will you help me feed the chickens?"

"Yeah."

"Go on, run ahead, I'm holdin' you back."

As I ran I wondered whether I could fish my letter out and cross out the part about Angie not liking me, but in the end I decided I was content with the letter the way it was. Little grudges seemed to keep everybody going on Shepherd Avenue, and as long as I had to live there, why should I be any different?

I went to the cellar and dropped the money into the jar. When it was all in I shook the jar gently to level off the coins, and felt a tingling thrill from my spine to my scalp. Halfway full. I was getting there.

I lay in bed that night wondering how adults could cook each other. Rosemary might be able to put someone in an oven, I decided. Grace would cook me with pleasure. Connie? I was pretty sure she could make the transition from poultry to people without much trouble.

I got up and went down to inspect my escape money just one

more time, while the rest of the house slept. Moonlight leaking through the basement window guided the way. It was there, all right. I hugged it to my chest before putting it back. Now it seemed more important than ever.

The next night Vic woke me up when he came in at three A.M. and knocked a hairbrush off his dresser. Startled by the sound, I sat up. Vic was unzipping his new leather jacket, a jet-black thing Connie detested. It had cost him a week's pay.

"Sorry I woke you, kid." He hung up the jacket. All he had on underneath was his undershirt. His shoulder blades looked sharp.

"I wasn't asleep," I said.

He grinned — a genuine grin, the first one in weeks, or so it seemed. "Christ, you're like an owl. I can never catch you with your eyes shut."

I hesitated. "Where were you?"

"Highland Park. Sitting on a bench." He fingered a cigarette from his pack.

"Come on, Vic. You weren't just sitting on a bench all night."

"Yes, I was." His gentle tone, the Vic of old, threw me. I knew he wasn't lying. He looked at my painting as if noticing it for the first time.

"That your mother?"

"Uh-huh."

"You're a good artist."

I felt warm all over. Incredible. One nice sentence from him and my guard fell. "Thanks." I lay down again, propping my head up on my elbow. "You hate it where you work, huh?"

He sat on his bed with his knees apart, his arms dangling between them like lead bars. "It's all right." He wiggled his hands. "It's just that it's such a long day, and they *watch* me every second. I get the feeling Uncle Rudy doesn't trust me, the way he stares when I work. Grace, she's even worse. Like yesterday, she boiled a big pot of potatoes to make a salad, and when I peeled them some of the potato came off with the skin. You'd think I'd *killed* someone, the way she hollered. The potatoes cost maybe a buck a ton."

"I *hate* Grace," I said fervently.

Vic shrugged, yawned. "It's their store, I guess they have to worry about everything."

"You could get another job."

He shrugged. "I don't really give a shit where I work. It's not just the job, it's everything. Rosemary coming over all the time, talking. You never heard anybody *talk* so much and say nothing." He cocked his head. "You never liked her, did you?"

"She never liked *me*."

Vic nodded. "You're a good kid, you don't want to hurt my feelings. But I don't care about her anymore. I look at her and can't believe we were going to get married. What for, to make babies? Jesus, I'm a baby myself."

He squashed his cigarette out. "Those damn cakes she kept sending me." He lit a fresh one. "The way she railroaded Mel out of here." He was suddenly serious. "Don't listen to anything that deacon says. He's an asshole, you didn't do a thing wrong."

He stopped talking. We could hear Connie's loud snoring at one end of the hall and Angie's softer snoring at the opposite end. Connie's was operatic, coming in peals with lulls in between. Angie's even snoring filled the silences. They were like the auricles and ventricles of a heart, beating in perfect rhythm.

"What a marriage, huh?" Vic asked, jabbing his butt in opposite directions of the hallway.

"What do you mean?"

He chuckled. "Forget it. You'll know what I mean when you're eighteen."

"Bullshit," I said, stung by the way he'd lorded his age over mine.

"Whoa!" He blew out smoke with the sound of steam escaping from a valve. "What a mouth on you."

"I can talk that way if I want."

"Nobody's stopping you," he said calmly.

I was furious. "You'll see. Everybody'll see. Some day I'll get out of here, you watch me."

"Sure you will. Your father won't be gone forever."

189

"Yeah? Well I don't know if I'm gonna wait for him. You know?" I gulped. My throat felt parched. "Why *should* I wait for him?"

He puffed on his cigarette. "Beats me."

"You're damn right." His lack of belief in me pissed me off. Okay, okay, then, that was fine — I'd been moments away from telling him about my bottle money and the trip I was going to take to Patchogue (and beyond!), and now he'd blown it. Too bad for him.

"What are you grinning at, Joey?"

"None of your beeswax."

"You're a real wise guy since I left to play ball, you know that?"

I didn't want to talk about me anymore. I had to find out about the world beyond Shepherd Avenue.

"Hey, Vic, did you like it in West Virginia?"

He lay on his back, the ashtray on his belly. "Ahh, you could go into town if you felt like having fun. Most of the guys on the team went every night."

"What for?"

"Drink beer. Screw the town whore. I'm tired, let's go to sleep."

I was quiet for only a moment. "Vic."

"What." He finally sounded tired.

"Did you ever screw the town whore?" I spoke without knowing what it meant. Vic flicked his ashes, puffed on his cigarette again.

"Yeah, sure, I went a few times."

"Did you like it?"

He let out an exasperated breath. "Who've you been talking to, Johnny Gallo?"

"He went, too?"

Vic laughed. "Not in West Virginia, kid, they're all over the place. Where'd you think I went those nights with Johnny, the opera?"

"Well what's it like?"

He sighed, blowing ashes over his pants. He swatted them away. "It's no big deal. It's all over in about five minutes and

190

she doesn't really hug you back and the whole time you're worried about getting a disease."

"What disease?"

"The clap."

"What's that?"

"Jesus Christ, my mother ought to hear this. . . ."

"She's asleep, don't worry. Come on, Vic, did you ever have the disease?"

"Yeah. Once. It feels like your dick's on fire every time you take a leak."

Vic's imagery startled me. "It hurts when I pee. It burns a little, once in a while."

"Joey, relax, you do not have the clap."

"Maybe I got it from you."

"Impossible. We'd have to be faggots for that to happen."

"What's a fag —"

"Enough!" He sat up, held up both hands, and made erasing motions. "End of this subject. And listen, everything we said tonight stays in this room, okay? Don't tell *anyone* I had the clap."

I nodded solemnly. "You still have it?"

"Nahh. The team doc gave me shots, it went away."

"So how come you went to the whore?"

Another sigh, maybe the last one his lungs could spare that night. "You get lonely, Joey. Some of those nights I wouldn't have minded just talking to her but that ain't how it works."

He stubbed out the cigarette, put the ashtray on the floor, and lay on his side, facing me. "Everybody makes such a big deal out of it, but it's the same damn thing as food. There's got to be more to being alive than just screwing and eating."

"I'm glad you're talking to me again, Vic."

He pointed at me. "Remember, not a word of this to my mother or father. Or *Rosemary*, in case she ever tries to pump you." He thought over that possibility.

"Jesus Christ, Rosemary," he said, rolling to face the wall. "She'd be having Masses said for my soul." We fell asleep.

CHAPTER FOURTEEN

"We must always remember that we are all brothers," Deacon Sullivan said from the pulpit. "It's so easy to lose sight of this plain truth, but what we do to our brothers we do to ourselves. You cannot possibly respect yourselves if you don't respect one another."

All around the church people squirmed. Vic sat next to me. Every time he closed his eyes to catch a snooze Rosemary gave him a savage nudge. He'd open his eyes without looking over at her.

It was too hot even for idle whispering, so Sullivan's words reverberated around a silent church.

I was in agony. As usual, Connie had forced me to wear my white shirt, with its strangling collar. Men all over the church were sticking their fingers in their collars and running them around their necks.

The sermon finally ended. Deacon Sullivan had lost some of his fire — his Masses seemed less populated these days. My mind wandered during the final ten minutes of ritual prior to the distribution of communion wafers. Vic leaned to my ear.

"Kind of disgusting, don't you think, this whole business about eating somebody's body?"

My neck tingled. I didn't know what to say, though the same thought *had* occurred to me. Vic winked.

Rosemary leaned past him. "What'd he say? What'd he say?"

"None of your beeswax," I told her. I was getting good mileage out of that expression.

"Don't give me that," she said. "What'd you say, Vic?"

"I said it's very hot in this place."

"Offer it up to the souls in purgatory."

"This *is* purgatory."

From elaborate golden cabinets Sullivan brought out the flasks of wine, the sacred chalice, the huge gold goblet that held wafers for the crowd. He took a wafer the size of a cocktail coaster in both hands, murmured some words over it and broke it in half — we could hear the snap. He crunched the halves into his mouth, poured wine into the chalice and drank it down.

Connie reached across Angie's lap to prod my knee. "Let's receive."

"No," I said.

"Why not?" She squinted one eye. "Did you eat breakfast this morning?"

"No. I just don't wanna eat God's flesh."

She squeezed my kneecap as if she meant to tear it off. Angie sucked in both lips to hide a smile. She let go of my leg and shrugged lightly. If I wanted to tumble into hell along with her husband and her son, it was my business.

She got up to receive, joined by Rosemary, who left a choking scent of toilet water in her wake. Sullivan served the parishioners, most of whom were bent-over, hairy-lipped crones who clamped their mouths shut on the host as if it were a secret spy document to be swallowed for security reasons. Zip Aiello was one of the few men to receive.

"Eh, he'll eat anything that's free," Connie said when she got back to the pew.

When the last woman had been served Sullivan wiped and put away the goblets — "did the dishes," as Angie said. The doors at the back of the church were opened. A current of warm air prickled our necks, and a low groan of relief sounded. A few more minutes and we'd all be free to go home, to enjoy our cool basements with a glass of cold wine or ginger ale, then later a plate of spaghetti in thick red sauce with pieces of meat that had simmered since dawn.

Sullivan rubbed his hands, squinted toward the back of the church and cleared his throat. When he spoke the first word shot from his mouth an octave higher than the rest.

"Many of you are troubled people." He coughed; something had gone down the wrong pipe.

"What's he doing, starting over?" Angie complained.

"I got a flame on low under my gravy," Connie said.

Vic leaned past me to address his parents. "I have to get out of here. I'm dying, I mean it." A woman in front of us turned around and shot him a stare. Vic returned it in full. "What are *you* lookin' at?" The woman looked away first.

"A change is coming to this neighborhood," Sullivan said when his fit passed. "A change you all fear. This change is creating hatred, and that's the worst thing that can happen to a man." He held a fist to the pit of his chest. "It blackens his soul. Brothers must talk with one another, or there can be no love, no understanding."

Hadn't we heard this same shit already? There was impatient buzzing all over the church at this two-sermons-for-the-price-of-one special. Sullivan ignored the noise and spoke louder.

"Horrible things build up inside a man when he contains them in his soul. When you have a boil on your hand you don't put a glove over the wound to hide it, you cut it open to draw the pus."

"Disgusting," Connie said. "Now I ain't gonna be able to eat."

Sullivan cleared his throat again and waved at the back of the church. The doors, gateway to our salvation, banged shut.

"Oh, he's out to murder us," Vic said. "He definitely wants us all to suffocate."

"Shut up," Rosemary said. "Listen for a change, wise guy."

"Ah, you shut up, for once in your life."

Rosemary's startled face turned as white as the flour she was always up to her elbows in. Sullivan's words echoed, now, with the doors to deflect them.

"Your brother is here today!" he boomed. "He wishes to speak with you, to cut open his boils."

Sullivan beckoned. Behind us people turned in their pews, murmuring loudly. Frank Ammiratti, the neighborhood traitor, was coming up the aisle. It seemed to take him years to reach the pulpit.

"My poor gravy," Connie said. "The meat's gonna be like shoe leather."

While Connie bemoaned her gravy Ammiratti talked, wiped sweat off his scalp, and talked some more. He couldn't sleep at night, he told us, knowing we all thought he'd betrayed us by building the hamburger joint.

Light through stained glass shined blue on his head. He went into a speech about coming to this country poor and building himself up from nothing. He spotted Angie, pointed at him, and spoke of all the wonderful plumbing he'd installed in Ammiratti homes over the years. Angie's hands balled into loose fists but he said nothing.

Then he dropped his bombshell, reminding us that his corner lot at Shepherd and Atlantic had been vacant for so many years that we'd all forgotten it was his, not a playground. We slashed his tires, we broke his windows, but he was willing to forgive.

I slunk down low in the pew at that last sentence but Angie patted my knee reassuringly. "He don't know," he whispered.

Ammiratti forced a smile and showed us his palms. "People, why in the world do you let this restaurant upset you so? Ladies, won't it be nice to be able to buy tasty, inexpensive food without having to light the oven on these hot summer nights?"

He'd overplayed his hand; the church exploded in cries of female outrage. The women who attended the ten o'clock Mass dined out once, twice a year at most, dragged to restaurants by their Americanized kids. They wiped the silverware under the table and didn't trust that the water glasses were clean.

Ammiratti tried to save himself with a speech about how clean the place would be and how an eight-foot fence all the way around it would assure privacy for neighbors. People shouted back that the colored would come to eat, and nobody else. Outside the church, parishioners for the eleven o'clock Mass knocked on the locked doors, wondering what the hell was going on. Sullivan jumped up to the pulpit like a referee anxious to keep boxers from killing each other. He held his arms out until there was silence, save for the knocking.

Ammiratti gave his head a wipe before telling us we were all invited to Opening Day at the hamburger place, ten days from now.

"I don't want to hurt any of you."

Then he bolted out of the place. There was a moment of

noise and light when the doors opened, then muffled sounds as they closed shut behind Ammiratti.

Deacon Sullivan ran his tongue over his lips. "The Mass is ended. Go in peace."

"Thanks be to God," we whispered dutifully.

"Well," Vic said on the walk home, "that was entertaining. They ought to let Frank talk every week. Put a band behind him."

"Is that all you want out of church?" Rosemary asked. "Entertainment?"

Vic gave her an odd smile. "What else?"

Connie's gravy had not been ruined. Rosemary ate the midday meal with us, silent as a stone. Vic had more of an appetite than usual.

"Grace and Rudy are worried stiff," he said, almost joyfully. "That hamburger joint's going to rob some of their business."

"All of it," Connie corrected.

"Yeah, well, they're going to keep the store open extra hours, so they want me to work late some nights."

"What did you say to that?" Connie asked.

"What could I say? They're the bosses, you do whatever the bosses say. Right, Pop?"

"Or you get another job," Angie said. "You have a high school diploma."

"I got nothing," Vic said after a moment.

Silence. Vic lit a cigarette, careful as always to blow the smoke straight up to the ceiling. Connie began clearing the table.

"Eh, so it opens in ten days, we'll see how it goes," she sighed. "Nobody's goin' anywhere."

I hid my smile. How little they knew of my secret intentions.

Angie went to the couch to read the Sunday paper. Connie couldn't hear Rosemary over the running water when she said, "Victor, I deserve an apology."

"For what?" he said, breathing a cloud of smoke into her face.

"You told me to shut up in church."

"So I did. You've told me to shut up a million times, I don't remember you apologizing."

"You're not going to say you're sorry?"

"Hey." His eyes flicked to the sink, where water pounded, then back to her. "Fuck off, Rosemary. And I'm not sorry about that, either." He winked at her in a way that was worse than the curse.

She sat still for a moment, then took half a glass of wine and flung it at Vic. "Animal!" She rushed out of the house.

The wine looked like blood against Vic's white T-shirt. Connie was all over him, wiping with a wet rag, but Vic caught her wrist.

"Relax, Ma, we'll just soak it." He peeled off the T-shirt and took it to the bathroom.

"What'd you say to her? What did you do?"

"Nothing," Vic said. "She's nuts."

Angie said, "I never liked that girl for him, not for a second."

"You never said nothin' about it," Connie spat.

"I woulda if he tried to marry her."

"Wait till the last minute, why don'tcha?"

I scrambled off the bench. "Hey," Connie said, "where do you think you're goin'?"

"Out!" I called over my shoulder, ignoring further shouts. It was a cinch to catch up with Rosemary. She was so slow I circled her like a bee buzzing a flower. With heavy hands she swatted wildly at me, King Kong lashing out at airplanes.

"Get away from me, Joseph."

I danced on my toes, just out of reach. "Know what, Rosemary? Know what? I know where Mel is."

"You do not."

I recited the address I'd memorized from the backs of her letters. She stopped walking. "We write to each other," I taunted. "And I'm gonna visit her, too."

"You are *not*." She began moving again. I faced her profile as I followed, scissor-stepping. "You little worm. That's all you are. You can't even cross the street unless someone holds your hand. You'll never see Mel again."

My laughter was a series of shrieks. I leapt high in the air, like a ballet dancer. God, how tempting it was to tell her all about my deposit bottle money, how I'd wandered Puerto Rican streets she was too scared to even dream about.

"Stop laughing, worm."

"Yes, ma'am," I mocked. "Yes, ma'am." I saluted her, scooted around behind her, and whacked her horsey ass with a flat hand. It trembled like Jell-O and made the sound of a firecracker. I was off and running before she even had time to turn around.

"Motherless bastard!" she screamed, and instead of rage I was filled with a strange malignant joy, knowing her words would keep me out of trouble, despite what I'd done. If she told on me, I'd tell on her. The perfect crime.

"You're all sweaty!" Connie said upon my return. "Look how he's sweating! Why didn't you come back when I hollered?"

"I didn't hear you."

"You didn't hear me. They heard me in China. Go, go wash. Cold water. Break that sweat."

Like a toll gate a wooden spoon dropped in front of me on the way to the bathroom, Connie's hand at its other end.

"Why'd you run after her?"

"She forgot to say good-bye."

"Wise guy." The gate went up and I was allowed to wash. That afternoon I did a watercolor of Rosemary. I made her hog-fat and put a huge cake in her hands. I gave it to Vic, expecting him to howl with laughter, but all he did was smile sadly and say, "The poor thing." He might have been talking about a dog that had been run over.

The chickens and the tomato plants kept growing. My tiny piece of home, those plants — they were smaller than my father's had been but they smelled exactly the same. Angie and I took a folded tablecloth outside and shook it in the middle of the yard. The birds swarmed over scraps of food that otherwise would have gone into the garbage.

Across the far side of Uncle Rudy's fence we could see the completed hamburger joint. Grand opening, the arrival of the colored, was only days away.

"How are they coming, Angie?"

"Who?"

"The colored. Everybody says the colored are coming when the hamburger joint opens. Are they, like, an army?"

"No! They come like anybody who wants to buy that crap. With money in their pockets. Money is green. That's the only color anybody really worries about."

The colored: you said it in two hard syllables, kuh-lid. Once I was sitting on the sidewalk burning red ants with a punk when a tall, skinny black kid in lime-green pants came striding my way. I expected him to vault right over my head but at the last instant he veered around me, Keds squeaking, an aroma of bittersweet cologne in his wake.

I turned my head from the ants and watched him go, his high, hard buttocks leaping at each step. He was a kuh-lid, and soon he'd be an everyday sight, instead of a novelty.

Opening day at the hamburger joint.

The only Italian from the area who went inside was our tenant. Poor Palmieri was undoubtedly sick of the cold food he'd been prying from cans all his life and thought the place was a godsend. He walked out of there with his chin tucked into his shoulder, ashamed of being seen with a bagful of that crap.

Other Italians ventured as close as the far side of the street, having found reasons to walk long-neglected pets. It was easy to see everything that went on inside, through the huge windows replacing the ones Johnny Gallo and I had smashed. Almost everyone working inside was black. Ammiratti saw us through the crowd, came to the door and waved, beckoning. We dispersed like kids fleeing the truant officer.

Back at the house, they grilled me for details about the place.

"Does it look clean?" Angie asked.

"I guess so."

Connie snorted. "If it ain't clean on the first day, when can it be?" She shook a finger at me. "Don't you ever, ever go in there."

"I know, I know."

My promise didn't stop her from telling fast-food horror stories. Men who dropped burgers on the floor and served them anyway, men who fried cockroaches along with the potatoes, and of course her clincher: the man who thought he was eating a piece of fried chicken but in fact munched, in the darkness of his car, a batter-fried rat.

Boom: the sound of the screen door made me jump. Uncle Rudy had let himself in without knocking.

"Where is Victor?" he asked.

Connie's eyebrows knotted. "He's not at the store?"

Rudy shook his head. "One hour ago he spilled grease on his trousers. He said he wanted to go home and change." He consulted his pocket watch. "The trip should not take an hour." He nudged his wire-rimmed glasses further into his fat face.

"Maybe he fell asleep, he was out late last night." Connie's voice was worried. "Check his room."

I raced ahead of Angie and gasped when I got there. Vic's bed was neatly made, but the open doors of his closets revealed empty hangers. The only things inside it were two Johnny Mize bats. Angie yanked open the dresser drawers as if he expected to find Vic in one of them. They were empty, and smelled sweetly of fruitwood.

Connie and Uncle Rudy arrived last, breathing as if they'd just climbed a mountain.

"Look," Angie said, pointing to the wall over Vic's bed. A rectangle of bright paint showed where the Sinatra record jacket had hung, somehow sealing the fact of Vic's disappearance more strongly than anything else.

Connie's eyes filled with tears. Angie hefted the baseball bats, and only Uncle Rudy could find words for the situation.

"What kind of boy is that?" he said. "What kind of boy?"

"Shut up, Rudy. For God's sake." Angie put his arm across his wife's stiff shoulders.

CHAPTER FIFTEEN

TROUBLED times. Vic's departure was cause for concern but not worry; I think Connie and Angie were even a little relieved. He'd been away once, he could handle it.

The burger joint did good business and left its mark on the streets. Cardboard wrappers blew down the sidewalk, and rain turned them into dirty-looking salt-and-pepper lumps. Once I saw one at curbside, and for a horrible moment I thought our favorite chicken had been killed.

Soon after the grand opening Freddie Gallo's widow — I never learned her name, because nobody ever used it — claimed that late at night the colored were using her driveway to take leaks. She pointed out the dark stains on the brick walls of her house. Connie suggested that they could have come from the German shepherd across the street, but Freddie's widow insisted the dog couldn't possibly pee that high. Besides, she'd heard a radio playing, and no dog carried a radio.

"The rain'll wash it away," Connie said.

"It don't rain every night," Freddie's widow wailed.

One night I heard her scream and ran to the parlor window in time to see Johnny Gallo chasing a man down the street. Later Johnny said he couldn't tell if the man in their driveway had been colored.

"Sure he was," Freddie's widow insisted. "That's colored pee on the wall. Smells like a horse did it."

I asked if there was a difference between our pee and colored pee. Connie said colored pee smelled stronger because they drank so much sweet soda and beer. Angie said nobody's pee smelled good.

Trouble even touched the only truly innocent person on the block, the retarded child known to me only as Louisa.

Some time that summer, in the space of very little time, she became a woman, and a beautiful one at that. She didn't have Down's syndrome: she'd been born in the house she lived in, and because the placenta hadn't broken right away there was a lack of oxygen at birth. She looked like a model, and it seemed incredible that she could spend an entire morning with her mouth open, watching ants crawl over an ice cream stick.

I was afraid of her because she was very affectionate. Besides the rain, another reason I quit drawing on the sidewalks was because Louisa would sneak up behind me and grab me in a tight hug. The last time she did that I could feel the firm points of her swelling breasts through her loose dress.

Three weeks shy of her fifteenth birthday Louisa's mother stood on the stoop of their house, calling her name. Louisa was always within earshot, at the end of the block eating lemon ice or playing with stray cats, but this time there was no answer. Frantic with worry, she came to our door and asked Angie to find her.

I went with him. We came upon Louisa at Highland Park. She was walking aimlessly near the swings and the monkey bars, her open mouth ringed with chocolate.

When we got her home her mother said, "Where'd you get that chocolate, Louisa?"

She ran her tongue in a wide path around her mouth, from her nostrils to her chin. "Boy."

"What boy?"

"Big boy." She bolted for the door. Angie caught her and carried her back, kicking and screaming. "Call the doctor," he said, standing with legs splayed. Louisa's feet plunged the air between them.

The doctor found a red mark on her breast but otherwise, he said, she hadn't been violated. He recommended sending her to live at an upstate facility for "special" young women. The parents, awestricken by the words of a medical man, took his advice.

I watched from the parlor window as Louisa's parents — a gray-faced woman and a thin man who never let you look at his face long enough to remember it, people doing what they thought they had to do — piled her things into their car. Meanwhile, their daughter, not knowing she'd never see Shepherd Avenue again, played jacks until the trunk slammed shut.

*　*　*

Deacon Sullivan was in trouble, too, for the way he'd sided with Frank Ammiratti by letting him talk to a captive church audience, but when he came to visit us one Sunday afternoon after Vic had been gone more than a week Connie politely let him in. I'd seen him coming, through the basement window, his legs flowing in a black cassock he rarely wore. He sat at our table and, with a pained face, accepted a cup of coffee.

Connie broke off the ends of string beans and dropped them into the strainer as Sullivan sipped. Weeks earlier, she'd have sat in his presence with her hands folded in her lap, but now it was all right to get work done during his visits. On the couch Angie read the paper.

"Ahh, my sons," Connie said. "What a world. You raise them right and they wander to the end of the earth anyway." She pointed at me with a bean. "God only knows when this one'll take off. Bing-bang-boom, he won't even say good-bye."

"I'm not going anywhere," I said. "*Yet.*"

"Oh?"

"I don't have enough money."

"You wanna go, I'll give you money," she said listlessly.

"Don't kid around like that," Angie said, not looking up from his paper. He wasn't taking my hints seriously, either.

Deacon Sullivan set his coffee cup down with a gasp, as if it had become too heavy to hold. "I know where Victor is."

Angie threw down his paper. Connie put down the strainer. "Where?" she demanded. "Talk, talk."

Sullivan rubbed his eyes. "I can't say how I know, but he lives on Sullivan Street in Greenwich Village."

"The same name as you," I said.

Sullivan took out a bit of folded paper and handed it to Angie, even though Connie was closer.

"That's the address." Then, more to himself than to us, "I hope I did the right thing."

The three of us walked to the Cleveland Street station and rode the train in silence. We had to transfer once but never paid a new fare, so the truth was plain — Vic had been a subway token away all that time. Connie complained about the bumpy ride but Angie had refused to take the car, claiming the crooked streets of Greenwich Village got him all confused.

We reached our destination at West Fourth Street, and climbing those stairs from the subway was like entering a new and grossly overpopulated world. We crossed Sixth Avenue and were suddenly wandering through narrow, tree-shaded streets. Some were cobblestoned. Connie pointed, the way children do at the zoo.

"Madonna, look."

A black man with an enormous afro sat on a stoop before a blanketful of handmade jewelry. His left ear sported an earring and there was another one through a nostril.

"Hey, woman, no need to point," he drawled. "I ain't gonna *bite* you."

For once in her life Constanzia Ambrosio was dumbstruck.

"Could you please tell us how to get to Sullivan Street?" Angie asked.

The man scratched his head, then his beard. "Sullivan. Two blocks down and bang a right."

Angie thanked him and took Connie by the elbow to lead her away. The man chuckled behind us as if he knew we'd never find our destination and would wander instead into the gaping jaws of a dragon.

"Through his nose," Connie murmured. "Right through his nose!"

"Enough already," Angie said.

"What if he sneezes?"

"Stop."

She shut up, only because she was breathing hard. This was more walking than she'd done in a long time. She moved with her eyes cast groundward but Angie stared all around at the walls and roofs of the snug little buildings, each neat as a dollhouse.

"Unbelievable," he said. "Con, I can't believe we're still in New York."

"This is where the weird people live," Connie said for my benefit. "The people who don't want to work or shave or take a bath."

"Vic takes baths," I said. "He takes more baths than you."

"Well, he don't shave and he don't work. How come you always stick up for him?"

"Connie, I just —"

"Knock it off, the two of you," Angie said. "God, look at that guy!"

A skinny, shirtless man walked in the opposite direction across the street. His hands were jammed into his back pockets and he tilted forward as he moved. His beard and hair made him look like the Jesus Christ I'd come to know from statues at church. Connie was stricken by him the same way I was.

"Right off the cross," she marveled.

I studied his chest, looking for that scar from the soldier's spear Sullivan had spoken of in a sermon.

We found Sullivan Street. Nearby was Washington Square Park, from where the faint wail of saxophones, trumpets, and harmonicas could be heard. Ivy clung to the walls of the brick building Sullivan had led us to. Tendrils crept unclipped over windows.

We entered a dark vestibule and climbed wooden steps. Angie stood in front of a nameless, numberless door badly in need of paint, or at least a scrubbing.

"We don't know which apartment," he said.

"Then we try them all." Connie rang the bell and braced herself. The door opened. We were hit simultaneously with the spicy smell of incense and the sight of Vic. The growth of his new beard trailed way behind his already lush moustache.

"Jesus," he said. When the initial shock wore off he moved aside to let us in as if we were cops. No attempts at embracing anyone.

The place was a big studio. A tremendous amount of light poured in through a multipaned window that needed a good washing.

"Who was it?" Vic asked coldly. "Johnny? That damn deacon?" He smiled knowingly. "I figured the deacon would tell. They're the only two people I told, in case there was an emergency. Should have known better than to trust that deacon."

Angie said, "You told him knowing he would tell."

Vic ignored him. "Look, I was going to call you all, anyway, and invite you over in a day or two."

"Bullshit," Connie said. It was the first time I'd ever heard her use the word, and she sure knew how to say it. Vic's moustache wilted like a neglected flower. "You *never* woulda called. You'd have waited till we died."

"Aw, Ma, don't get dramatic." He spread his arms. "But what's the use of arguing? You're here now and I'm glad."

He was forcing his cheerfulness. Connie didn't move. Her shoes might have been glued to the floor, the way she stood there. Besides everything else she was cranky from all that walking.

I poked Vic's belly. "You could have said good-bye to *me*."

He nodded, rubbed my hair. "I'm sorry, Joey."

"You don't trust me."

"Oh for Christ's sake." He pulled his hand out of my hair.

Connie found her legs and began walking around, her shoes loud on the unpolished wooden floor. She gazed at a mattress in the middle of the room, a tangle of sheets and blankets at its center. No bed frame, no box spring. She made a tweezer out of thumb and forefinger and, from the midst of the mess, picked up a pair of panties, which she dropped at the sound of a toilet flushing.

The sight of the girl emerging from the bathroom, zipping the last inch of her fly, made the throb of my heart reach all the way to my throat. Her hair, shiny in the late afternoon sunlight, touched her hips. She was a butterfly, a pony, a sunbeam made human.

"Hi." A note from a flute. She moved to Vic's side and found his hand. They laced fingers. Vic cleared his throat.

"These are my parents, and my nephew, Joey. This is Jenny Sutherland."

She glided over to us on bare feet and stopped in front of me, eyes gleaming green. "Joey the painter. You make all those beautiful watercolors Vic tells me about."

She'd heard of me! It was almost more than my heart could take, and then she touched my cheek. "Your uncle talks about you all the time, how you help out with the chickens. You don't make him call you *Uncle* Vic, do you, Vic?"

"Just plain Vic," he said. He was looking at Connie.

Angie piped in for the first time. "He calls me Angie, and I'm his grandfather."

Vic, Jenny, and I burst into laughter. In the midst of it Connie swung at Vic's face with her open hand, then pulled it away suddenly, as if she'd slapped at a bee and gotten stung.

Blood gushed from Vic's nose, and now Jenny Sutherland was a cyclone, getting a handkerchief, boiling water for tea, bringing out a plate of cookies. What had started out as an invasion had turned, ridiculously, into a visit.

We sat on pillows at a low coffee table, drank orange pekoe tea, and ate salty cookies with bits of green in them — seaweed. Jenny explained that when mankind was all through ravaging the earth of its animals we would be forced to harvest the sea for food, and that she wanted to get a head start.

Connie and Angie listened politely, their breath blowing puffs of steam off their mugs. One tight muscle in Connie's throat told me she thought it was all bullshit. There was a rim of red crust around one of Vic's nostrils but otherwise he was fine, smiling and joining in the conversation.

When Jenny was through talking about nutrition from the sea Connie spoke up.

"There's plenty of cattle in the world. We can still eat all the meat we want."

Jenny smiled. "We'll see," she said softly.

"What do you do?"

"I paint, Mrs. Ambrosio. Not here, I take classes."

"You paint too!" I exclaimed. Jenny winked at me. My heart hammered as if it meant to get out of my chest.

Connie said, "You make money at this?"

Jenny shook her head. Her hair was so lush it rustled like wheat in the wind. "I work at Gristede's supermarket for money."

"Oh, oh, oh." Connie let the information sink in. "And you two ain't married."

They both laughed her off, nervously.

To change the subject, Vic said, "I'm looking for work, Ma, I got money from my baseball bonus."

"Won't they want that back?"

"Only half. I gave that much back already."

Angie hesitated. "You still have four thousand?"

"Just about."

"Long as you're keeping their money don't you think you owe baseball another shot?"

"Never, Pop." Vic's eyes got icy. "That was somebody else's merry-go-round. All I ever did with my life was try to hit a baseball over a fence. That was my big concern in life, and then I realized *I didn't give a damn.*"

Vic laced fingers with Jenny again, seemingly for strength. "Know what I used to do in the dugout, Pop? Even at Franklin K. Lane? Used to *sing* to myself, all the time. They called me Sinatra because I sang all his stuff, but all I was doing was keeping myself from going crazy."

Jenny smiled and rubbed the back of Vic's neck as if he'd just sparred a tough round. Angie waited before saying, "And you think you got it licked now, is that it?"

Vic shrugged, exasperated. "Pop, I don't know. All I know is what wasn't right for me. . . . I'll get a job. Maybe I'll take some classes at NYU. All I want to do is something I like."

"Do you think I liked plumbing?"

"Never thought about it."

"Then *think* about it!" Tea leapt from Angie's cup, scalding his wrist. Jenny reached out to wipe it but Angie pulled away from her.

"Think about what it's like to work in crawl spaces. I used to touch noses with rats. Was I happy? Did I like that? Christ!"

He buried his face in his hands, very briefly. When he took them away his eyes were red.

"You kids, you think you got the world licked. It looks easy but it's hard. Go on, play house." He turned to Connie and me. "Let's go home."

He reached for Connie's hand and pulled her to her feet. I

rose slowly, hoping to show Vic I wasn't eager to leave, wasn't his enemy.

Connie and Jenny were weeping. Vic looked as if he'd been in a car wreck. As Angie put his hand on the doorknob something in him broke. He turned, hugged his son, and then, after a moment, included Jenny in the hug.

"Oh, Mr. A.," she said.

He let them go and wiped his nose with the back of his hand. "Listen. Come to supper next week." He wrapped his arms around them again as if he meant to compress all three bodies into one being. Then he bolted out the door. Connie and I had to catch up to him.

Outside, huge gray rain clouds had blocked the sun. The sky exploded with rain just as we reached the mouth of the subway station.

For three days the rain fell, hard and steadily, keeping the three of us unusually drowsy. Drifting in and out of naps, it was hard to distinguish morning, afternoon, and dusk — only night was definite.

The backyard flooded, and the chickens huddled together on the dry island of the coop. Water ran in crooked streams down the cracked cellar steps, and the drain grate at the bottom needed a cleaning every few hours from the twigs and dirt that collected there like miniature beaver dams.

An enormous puddle formed down at the corner near the burger joint, where faulty construction had screwed up the drainage system. A residue of clay bleached it bright yellow. From the parlor we could hear unsuspecting drivers slamming their cars through the deep water, almost with the regularity of waves on a beach.

Green leaves, torn before their time from maple trees, were plastered against the sidewalk and car windshields. All the windows were shut, but an aimless draft managed to run through the house like a lost ghost.

Chill. From her cedar chest Connie dug out a blue woolen sweater that had once belonged to my father. I put it on, tainting the air around me with the smell of mothballs.

Wearing his sweater, I painted furiously in my corner of the cellar — mostly ships, on stormy oceans. Sharks devoured men who fell overboard. The blue of the sea mixed with the red of blood to make a muddy purple. I worked too fast and carelessly to keep the mess from happening. The only thing I worked on carefully during the storm was a portrait of Jenny Sutherland.

Connie came down to hang laundry on the short clothesline there. As usual, I put my brush down upon her arrival.

"My God, in that sweater you look just like him."

"You gonna be long, Connie?"

She pegged clothing. "Go ahead, I won't watch."

"Yes you will. You always *sneak* a look."

"I do not. . . . What's that, Vic's girl?"

"Connie! . . . Not yet. It will be when I'm done."

"Why are you painting *her?*"

"I *feel* like it."

"You like that girl?"

"Yeah, Connie, I like her a lot."

She sighed, returned to her laundry. "Go on, I won't look."

"I'll wait till you leave." I folded my arms.

She rolled her eyes. "Just like the father." She clumped away. I resumed work on the painting and felt a sudden SWAT! at the back of my head. She'd tiptoed back to hit me!

"That's for being a wise guy," she said, this time leaving for good.

The roof proved to be solid — there wasn't a single leak, or at least nothing that Agosto Palmieri complained about. His opera records played almost continuously, accompanied by dramatic peals of thunder — he stayed away from high-hearted jazz records during the storm.

Thoughts of my mother: could she see me now, on earth, from her place in the heavens Deacon Sullivan was always talking about? Did she know where my father was? Was she watching him drive the station wagon all over the country? As a tot, thunder had frightened me until she explained that it was just angels moving furniture. Was she moving it with them now?

In a dream my mother and I were back in our Roslyn kitchen.

I was just home from school, and she was preparing dinner. It was a peaceful time for us, my father not home yet, and too early for me to start my homework.

She brought me a glass of chocolate milk to hold me until dinnertime. She always made it, because when I tried to, the chocolate powder caked up like mud at the bottom of the glass.

She set the glass beside my hand and sat beside me, beaming, her face warm from the heat at the oven.

"Joseph, I wouldn't trade you for all the tea in China."

"How about . . . a yacht?"

"Nope."

"How about . . . the goose that laid the golden egg?"

"No, sir. Even though you have a chocolate moustache." A flick of her fingertip took it away. She licked her finger. "Mmmm."

"How about . . . a hundred dollars?"

"It's a deal, sweetie. A hundred dollars and a glass of chocolate milk." She sipped from my glass.

"Mommy!" I was going to kiss her but her stone-serious face stopped me. I'd never seen her looking like that.

"Did the milk taste bad, Mommy?"

She shook her head. "You don't like it where you are now, do you, Joseph?"

Oh God. I had to take a leak but my legs felt paralyzed. "No," I groaned. "I wanna stay here with you."

She managed a faint smile. "I'm sorry, Joseph. It wasn't my idea to die."

My heart hurt. Invisible elves hammered nails into it. "Is Daddy coming back?"

She closed her eyes and shrugged. "Sweetheart," she said vaguely.

"Mommy!" I reached to touch her cheek and she burst noiselessly, like a soap bubble, vanishing without a trace.

Then I was awake, sitting up in bed, staring at my own portrait of her. Shivering, I got out of bed and went down the hall.

Two, three A.M.? It had to have been. "Angie?"

His sheets rustled. "Joey?" His hair stood up like porcupine quills. "You sick?"

"Can I sleep in here?"

Angie's instincts were sharp, even though he was groggy. He threw back his blanket. The mother-of-pearl buttons on his fancy long johns winked in the dim light. I drifted off to sleep, his heavy, soupy breath all around me like ocean fog. No questions about it the morning after — I awoke before he did and crept back to my cot in Vic's room, where rain still spattered the window.

With the house sealed so tightly against the weather Palmieri's music penetrated to the bone, making me feel very close to death. Angie and I played lighthearted card games to buoy our spirits.

"Got any fours?"

"Go fish."

"Nuts."

"Angie?"

"I'm listening."

"After you . . . die, do you meet everybody in heaven that's already dead?"

"How should I know? I ain't died yet." Then, in afterthought: "Oh. You'll see your mother, don't worry."

But instead of death the storm brought life. Along the baseboards in the basement mushrooms sprouted, nourished by accumulated dirt in the lines of mortar, tiny pale plants with fanned undersides. All they needed was the moisture in the air.

"Perzonous," Connie warned. "Can't eat 'em."

We knocked them down and scraped them away but they grew back just as strong, with additional regiments under the shower ledge and around the base of the toilet bowl. A miracle.

On the storm's third afternoon we heard a hard splashing of water on the front stoop, as if buckets of it were being hurled from Palmieri's window. Had he gone mad up there in his lonely flat? No — the rain gutter had clogged.

I held the ladder steady while Angie removed fistfuls of black leaves and pollywogs from the thing. Soon a hard gurgling sounded all the way down the copper leader, carrying with it big flakes of rust. We'd been outside just a few minutes but went in soaked to the skin.

Connie brewed tea with lemon and honey and added a splash of whiskey to our mugs, the first alcohol of my life.

I gulped it down. Instantly my eyes filled with tears. The glow crept all the way to my hands, as if heat were emanating from a miniature sun where my heart had been, my fingertips and toes its most distant planets.

Connie tipped my empty cup. "Eh, one gulp. That's your Irish half."

That night the phone rang at ten o'clock, an unusual occurrence, especially since Vic had abandoned his baseball career. Connie stiffened when she answered it, listened awhile, and said something I couldn't hear. She motioned for Angie to turn down the volume on the TV set.

Then she held the receiver out to me in two hands, a palm under each end, cradling it as if it were a newborn infant, the extension cord its uncut umbilical.

"It's your father," she said, feigning calmness. "Hurry, take it, it's long distance."

I took it. There was a mild crackling over the wire. "Hello," I said, as if I didn't know who it was.

"Hey, Joey." The crackle grew insistent. It was as if he were calling to me across a cornfield.

"Where are you?" I asked. Angie and Connie stared at me, motionless, like a couple of kids watching a horror movie.

"Seattle," he said. "Are you okay?"

"It's raining."

He chuckled. "It rains here all the time."

"I don't care."

"Hey," he said. "That's no way to talk to me."

We listened to each other breathe. He said, "What are you doing?"

"Nothing. Painting."

"You're *what?*" The connection had gone weak for a moment.

"Painting!" I shouted. "They gave me your old paintbrushes."

"Jesus, that stuff's still around? Is it any good?"

"Some of the hairs fell out but the brushes are okay. The

paint's good, too." What the fuck were we talking about? I hadn't seen him in ages and he wanted to *chat!*

"So when are you coming back?" I asked, swallowing the words "to get me." I tried to make it sound as if I didn't care.

"Oh, a few weeks, the most . . . really, is everything okay? You sound sort of funny."

"What do *you* care?" I exploded. "You dropped me off here and drove away."

"Hey! I didn't call long distance to get yelled at! Don't you *ever* talk to your father that way!"

I held the phone against my chest while I calmed down. Maybe he heard my heart beating.

"He hang up?" Connie asked. I put the phone back to my mouth.

"What are you gonna do to me?" I asked nastily. "Hit me? You're a million miles away, Dad, I'm not afraid of you."

Silence. The man had never so much as threatened to hit me all my life.

"Joey, I didn't expect this." I'd broken him. The operator cut in.

"Forty cents for the next three minutes, please."

"Hang on," my father said, all confident again. With strangers it was easy for him to be his brassy self.

"Forty cents —"

"I *heard* you, Goddamn it!" he shrieked. Coins dropped. The phone hummed, and then he was back on the line.

"Joey?" he ventured. "Are you all right?"

I shut my eyes and pictured him dangling from a high wire by the phone he spoke into, a pool of sharks circling beneath him. If I hung up, he'd fall in.

"Yeah, I'm fine," I said. Thunder shook the house.

"What was that?"

"It's only thunder, Dad, don't be scared. . . . Take your time coming back, I like it here." If my lying would increase his pain, so much the better.

More silence, save for the damn crackling.

"Joey, don't you even *miss* me? I miss you."

I'd never heard his voice so weak. I couldn't answer him —

214

it was as if my throat were corked. I literally threw the phone to Angie, who bobbled it as if it were a hot potato. He got hold of it and passed it to Connie, who put it to her ear.

"Yeah . . . what did you expect, a brass band? . . . Sure he misses you. . . . No, don't put no more money in the phone. . . . Yeah . . . yeah . . ."

She hung up. "Madonna." She kept her hand atop the phone as if she thought it might try to leap off the hook and disgorge my father through the earpiece.

Angie gave me a pair of his long johns to wear to bed that night. I felt skinny as a scarecrow inside them. Rain hit the window like pebbles whenever the wind shifted a certain way. The clammy cold pierced even the long johns. When would this rain stop?

In the dead of night, with all of us asleep.

Before I was even fully awake the next morning I was kicking the sweaty long johns from my legs, struggling like a man in a straitjacket. Naked, I went to the window and turned my face to the sun as if I'd just discovered it.

"Oh, boy," I said aloud. I felt gladder at the sight of that sun than I ever had at the sight of a human being. I pushed my window open, and the sharp smell of brick and concrete made my tongue go wet.

Breathing behind me. Connie at the doorway, on her way to the bathroom. I covered my crack with both hands. She snorted.

"You think I never saw one before?"

I pulled on my clothes, grabbed an apple, and ran out to greet the day, though it was barely past six. The sidewalks were immaculate, as if their pebbly surfaces had been buffed. Every car parked on the street gleamed like Johnny Gallo's. There was no curbside garbage, no gasoline smells, no dog crap.

Coffee smells floated from our basement all the way to the yard, where the chickens plodded about tentatively, testing the damp ground. Their undersides were stained brown, the way ships are barnacled. When they stood still, their feet sank into mud — they seemed to be standing on yellow stilts. An undershirt had blown loose from some distant clothesline and landed in our yard, brown and wrinkled like a hunk of elephant skin.

"Two washes and it'll be good as new," Connie said.

All around me the groan of opening windows sounded. They seemed to be greeting one another. Cowering but unbroken, our tomato plants had made it, green fruit snug to the vines. Later in the day Angie and I would tie them to longer, stronger stakes with coarse hemp.

And after that I would search for bottles. There were very few around but they gleamed so brilliantly from the cleansing rain that I sort of hated trading them in for grimy coins.

"These are real clean, Nat. *Look* at 'em!"

"Clean, schmeen, the price is still the same."

The birds, Angie, Connie, and I were intact. The storm had taken away only ugliness, but just temporarily.

CHAPTER SIXTEEN

THE story of Vic's new home swept up and down Shepherd Avenue like fumes from a broken bottle of ammonia. Grace came over with Connie's groceries, offering her sympathy and at the last second slipping in a stinger about Vic's abandoning the delicatessen at the worst possible time, in the midst of their war against the hamburger joint.

"Get some other sucker to help you peddle that crap," Connie snapped. Speechless with rage, Grace left the house and didn't return for days.

But Deacon Sullivan did.

"Mr. and Mrs. Ambrosio, what can I say?" He held those white hands out, palms up. It was as if he were grieving over someone's death.

"Hey, wait a second," I said. "Vic's happy, he's with a nice lady. How come everybody's so upset?"

Connie looked at me as if I'd just told her I enjoyed murdering kittens. Her fingers squeezed and rolled a ball of dough she'd picked out of a roll. She was careless about her diet in every way but this, believing that the soft dough from bread caused heart attacks by "plugging up your veins." She wouldn't say more about it, and after meals there were always dough marbles near her dish.

"Children," she sighed. Her appetite had dimmed since seeing Vic in Greenwich Village and though her bulk was still great she'd lost weight in her face. The skin was tight over her cheekbones. Her beauty surprised me. "Get the scotch," she told me.

"No, no," Sullivan said, sounding astonished. Does a man drink whiskey at a wake? "Please, just some coffee."

Sullivan faced me at the table, Connie and Angie at either end. The coffee was scalding hot, so he couldn't even sip it.

"Ah, well," Connie finally sighed, "the other one made me suffer, why should this one be different?"

"Shut up already," Angie said into his wineglass.

"Please, now," Sullivan said, "this is the time for strength."

He leaned forward so that his chin nearly touched the table and spread his long arms as if they were condor wings. He grasped Connie and Angie by their wrists and closed his eyes as he squeezed.

"The main thing is for you to be *strong*," he said, almost hissing.

They tolerated his touch the way little kids do their mothers' grip when they cross the street. Sullivan clung as if he were a copper wire carrying a current between positive and negative electrodes.

"Whatever you do, Ambrosios, this mustn't tear you apart."

His face was contorted, seemingly in pain. The sleeves of his black jacket had yanked almost to his elbows, revealing thin wrists with knobby, coat-button like bones on their outer edges.

He let go suddenly, said a hasty good-bye, and was gone.

Angie rubbed his wrist. "He's goin' nuts, I swear to God."

Connie shuddered. "The way it felt when he grabbed me. Gave me goosebumps."

"Now you know how I felt," I said, familiar with that grip. "See why I hate him?"

Connie gave me a don't-go-hating-priests look as I left to go out and look for bottles. By now they were all grimy again.

* * *

Wednesday night. Vic and Jenny were due any minute.

Connie set down the slightly chipped rosebud-pattern bowls and plates we used every night. The upstairs dining room hadn't even been considered for this occasion.

She glanced at the clock over the refrigerator — ten minutes to six. Suddenly she walked around the table, clacking bowls on top of each other into a stack. I followed her, picking up the plates. Angie had a smile. Connie put them away and laid out the good dishes, sun yellow with blue bands around the rims.

"For my son," she emphasized. "The best for my son, not that girl."

"I didn't say nothing," Angie said.

"Yeah, but you were gonna."

I heard the back door open, and moments later Jenny poked her honey head into the room. There was an enormous glass jar in her hands and a smile on her face just as big.

"Hi!" she said, breathily but not out of breath. "Fantastic peppers hanging back there."

Angie laughed. "You know peppers?"

"Sure, only I buy mine crushed in jars. I'd love to dry them the way you folks do."

"Folks," Connie murmured. It was a foreign word from the world beyond Brooklyn. She was certain to repeat it to Grace Rothstein, once they were talking to each other again.

Vic entered timidly, as if *he* were the visitor. He nodded to Angie and hugged Connie, who didn't seem to want to let go. Jenny presented the jar to Connie, a mix of dried fruits, soybeans, and nuts. She modestly admitted it was her own blend.

I raced to my rolltop desk and brought back my present for Jenny.

"This is for you," I blurted, handing over a rolled-up, rubber-banded sheet. "It . . . I did it."

Jenny gasped with delight when she finally got my portrait of her unrolled.

"Is this me?" she squealed. I could only nod. "Oh, baby!" She hugged me and kissed me on the neck. "Vic, look, it's me! My lord, if I could have painted like this when I was ten . . .

honey, *look!*" She had to hold it open by the edges, like a pirate's treasure map.

"Kid's got talent," Vic said, rubbing my hair.

"This goes up in our house," Jenny said. "But first I'm buying a decent frame for it."

I was dizzy with delight. "You don't have to frame it," I said.

"You'd better believe I'm going to frame it," Jenny said, kissing me again. "Show me what else you've done."

I brought her to my desk and showed her the paintings I'd stacked like baseball cards. With the exception of my mother's portrait, they were all down here. Jenny studied them as if they were the undiscovered works of Vincent van Gogh. Everyone stood behind her, awaiting a verdict.

"If this boy doesn't go to art school, the world will lose out," she announced.

"My brother almost went to art school when he was a kid," Vic said. "His father."

"All right, all right, don't get into that, we gotta eat," Connie said, eager to get off that subject.

I got to sit at Jenny's left. As usual the food was good, featuring all of Vic's favorites from the days when his appetite rivaled a buffalo's: spaghetti with peanuts in the sauce, sausages, gravy meats.

Vic said very little, looking from parent to parent in search of some kind of wordless approval. His face was flushed with nervousness, the way it had been moments before he went up to accept his last baseball trophy on graduation day.

But Jenny was incredibly relaxed — what poise, what guts! She spoke freely of her life, her move to Manhattan from Kansas at the age of sixteen, her job at the supermarket ("until my own thing clicks"), the way she'd met Vic (she'd been visiting a chum from her art classes who lived in East New York and stopped by Rudy's deli for a bottle of mineral water).

Whatever came to her mind she blurted, apparently unedited. Her knowledge of food earned even Connie's grudging admiration, as she correctly identified every ingredient rolled into the *bracioles*.

I was madly in love with her. She shifted on the bench after a bout of laughter and our knees bumped. She permitted them to stay together, touching. I felt an erection growing and was grateful for the tablecloth that hid my lap.

When we were through eating Jenny jumped to help with the dishes, and Vic got up a second later.

"What are *you* doing?" asked Angie, who'd never washed a dish in his life, but Vic ignored him and reached for the loose end of Connie's dish towel. She stared at him dumbfounded and they began tug-of-warring with the towel.

"What are you doing?"

"Give me the rag, Ma."

"What —"

"For Christ's sake all I want to do is help. Come on, let go, I do this all the time when I'm home."

Connie's back arched, as if she'd received a mild electric shock — "home" was someplace else. She let go of her end.

While Jenny and Vic did the dishes Connie stretched Saran Wrap over the leftovers. Feeling left out, I got up and swept the floor. Angie stayed put, watching the scene with a dazed look on his face.

"You should all open a restaurant someplace," he said sourly.

Minutes later the work was all done.

"Well, that didn't take long," Connie said, easing herself into her chair. Angie went to the wine cellar and got his bottle of brandy. To my delight, he set out five small glasses — I was going to get a thumbnail's worth.

Vic turned to Jenny and said, "Babe, let's have some of that stuff we brought, it'll go good with the brandy." Like an old married man.

While Jenny opened the jar, Vic told Angie about the new job he was taking in a bookstore. Jenny set the jar on the table near Vic. Without even a change in the tone of his voice he reached for her waist, pulled her down into his lap, and wrapped his arms loosely over her shoulders, folding his hands together at her stomach. After a short shriek of surprised delight Jenny allowed herself to flop into Vic's lap like a Raggedy Ann doll.

Vic pushed aside the hair that hung down the side of her face and kissed the skin where Jenny's neck met her shoulder.

Burrowing his nose into her neck, he gently bit her earlobe, holding it in his teeth and wagging his head as if he meant to tear it off.

Jenny giggled all the while. Vic took his mouth off her ear, trailing a string of saliva down his beard. He bear-hugged her.

"Uhh," she said.

Connie was speechless. Angie forced a chuckle. "Vic, you could hurt her, grabbing her like that."

Vic laughed. "I do it all the time, she's used to it."

"That's the truth," Jenny giggled.

Connie squeezed her brandy glass without sipping from it. Angie gulped his brandy and poured himself more. The envy in his eyes was easy to read.

My own heart was breaking because I knew I'd never get that girl away from Vic, no matter what I tried.

We all moved upstairs to the parlor. Vic, it turned out, still had a faint interest in the game that had failed him, so he and Angie watched the Yankees while Connie and Jenny tolerated it. Vic clapped when Roger Maris smashed a home run.

"He'll break Babe Ruth's record," he said.

"He'll fold," Angie predicted.

"Want to put a buck on it?"

"You're on."

What happens to dreams? Vic lay sprawled on the parlor couch, hairy and unshaven, rooting for a team he'd all but promised to beat in the World Series that autumn. The skinny man who was still my uncle probably didn't even remember making that cocky prediction the day before he left for West Virginia.

I felt a cruel impulse to remind him of it but the sight of Jenny earnestly trying to follow the ball game stopped me. She noticed me looking at her, winked and shrugged. My insides turned to caramel. She turned her attention back to the game, and when I could find my legs I got up and tapped her wrist.

"Yes, baby?"

"Can you come downstairs with me for a sec? I want to show you something."

"She already saw your pictures," Connie said. "Let her sit." She wasn't through scrutinizing Jenny.

"Oh, I don't mind," Jenny said breezily, delighted to get away from the ball game. "I could look at his work all day long." She held out her hand. "Lead the way, Joey."

I held her hand as gently as if it were a baby bird that had fallen from a nest, but she squeezed mine on the way down the dark cellar steps.

"Can you see where you're *going*, baby?"

"I been down these steps a million times," I bragged. "I don't have to see."

"My life is in your hands."

"Don't worry, Jenny, I won't letcha get hurt."

I felt feverish as I led her to my desk. "Goody," she said, "more pictures."

But that wasn't what I had to show her. I waited a few moments to be sure no one had followed us, then I got on my knees and took my jar of coins out from its hiding place. I put it in Jenny's hands and she jounced with the weight.

"Wow," she said. "*Wow!*"

"That's thirty dollars in there," I stammered. Actually it was slightly more than twenty-eight but I didn't feel bad about my little lie. I kept looking at her small hands around the bottom of the jar. If I'd looked at her face I don't think I would have been able to talk.

"I was thinking I could . . . like, move in with you guys." I wiped sweat off my forehead and looked at her face. It was the first time I'd ever seen her not smiling. Her cheekbones seemed even sharper when she was serious. She looked older.

"Oh, baby," she sighed.

I plunged ahead, my body temperature climbing. My T-shirt stuck to my skin. "I made all this money from bottles, see? I bring back empty bottles and this guy pays me for them. That time we came to your house, I saw a lot of bottles all over the street. I could make a lot of money. I mean . . ." I swallowed. "I wouldn't cost you anything."

Jenny's eyes filled up as she put the jar on my desktop. My wildest thoughts became spoken words.

"I got this friend, she lives on Long Island now, she could move in too. We could *both* find bottles. She doesn't like it where she lives, either."

Jenny wiped her eyes and puffed out her cheeks as she sat on the wooden stump.

"So I was thinkin', if we can make a lot of money from bottles and give it to you and Vic, maybe you guys could sort of . . . you know . . ."

"Adopt you?"

"That's it. Yeah. And you know those windows in your house? Well I could wash those windows. I know how to do it good. You use a newspaper instead of a rag. Connie let me help her do it once."

At last Jenny's smile returned, if only faintly. "We've been meaning to wash those windows." She ran her finger over the grape pattern on the jar. "You don't like it here, huh?"

"Not much. Angie's okay but Connie doesn't like me. They wouldn't care if I left."

"Oh, baby, they would, they *would*."

"You wanna bet?"

"No, I don't want to bet." She beckoned for me, arms outstretched. I expected a hug but she grabbed my shoulders and squeezed them at arms' length. "Now listen, Joey. In the first place you're not an orphan. Your Daddy's still alive."

"Fuck him."

Her hands tightened. "In the second place," she began quietly, "why" — she giggled and cried at the same time — "why, I'm not even old enough to be your *mother!* Do you know that? I just turned eighteen!"

"That doesn't matter."

"Oh, it matters, it *matters*. In a lot of ways I'm just a child myself. See?"

"No. Let go of me."

She let her hands drop. "You're mad. I can understand that, but please try and understand *me*, too. Will you?" She reached for my face with both hands and held my cheeks. "My God, you're hot as a fire." She rubbed my cheeks and my neck, smiling and blinking back tears. "My friend. My very special friend." At last she hugged me but I could feel a strain across her chest, a strain I'd never detected in my mother when she used to hug me. We used to sort of melt into each other.

I pushed lightly at Jenny's hips. She let me go.

"Are you and Vic gonna get married?"

"It's way too soon to know, Joey. *Way* too soon."

"Vic used to be a great baseball player but now he stinks."

"I know all about it. That doesn't matter to me. Listen, Joey." She took my right hand and shook it conventionally. "I got an idea. I can be your big sister. How about that? We can be friends and you can come visit me whenever you like. Would that be good?"

"Sure." I half meant it and half didn't give a damn. She startled me by grabbing my cheeks again and planting a loud kiss on my forehead. "Salty. You're sweating." She cranked her smile up all the way. "Should we go upstairs now, brother?"

"I'll come up in a second. I gotta put my money away. I never showed my money jar to anybody, you know. Not even Vic. You're the only one who knows about it."

"I'm very honored."

"You are not."

"Go on, be mad awhile, get it out of your system. I'll turn around while you hide it and then you can guide me back up those scary stairs."

"Nahh. You don't have to wait. I'll put the light on for you." I went to the bottom of the stairs and flicked a switch I never bothered using when I was alone.

"Go on up, Jenny, I'll meet ya there."

With a stricken look on her face she climbed the stairs while I put my jar away.

Fuck her. Fuck Vic. Fuck the world. Why was it taking so long for me to fill up that jar? Had Connie discovered it and begun skimming off the top? A quarter here, half a buck there — who would notice? I took it out again and made a mark on the outside of it with a red grease pencil. If the cash level fell any lower than that, I would know there was a thief in the house.

I joined them in the parlor and pouted through the rest of the ball game, sitting on the floor yoga-style. Inning by inning

Jenny moved closer to me, until at last she was beside me. She put her hand on top of mine and we looked each other in the eye.

"I'm your big sister, okay?" she whispered.

"Okay, Jenny." It was impossible to stay mad at her. Roger Maris hit another home run. Vic whooped.

"That buck is in the bag."

When the game ended we walked them to the vestibule. Jenny shook hands with Connie and Angie, then took me in an embrace that nearly knocked the wind out of me. I was just starting to get that melting feeling I used to have with my mother when Connie ruined it with her inimitable timing.

"Go home already before the sun sets and the colored come out with their knives."

The two of them were out the door and running, not trotting, toward the elevated train. I watched them go, rubbing my hands up and down my torso to keep that feeling alive, but it was no use. It went away with a tingling sensation, like when your foot falls asleep and blood is just starting to flow again.

"Thanks a lot, Connie," I said angrily, but she didn't even look at me. She just kept watching Jenny and Vic until they turned the corner.

"It's my fault they met," she said to Angie. "I got him the job at Rudy's, she walked in and grabbed him."

Angie made a croaky sound in his throat. "Maybe they grabbed each other." He went away.

"I was married when I was her age," she said. "Married a year. Did I know what I was doin'? Eh, eh, eh." She pulled the door shut and walked past me to the parlor. She hadn't been speaking to me. She'd barely been speaking to herself.

In all the excitement we'd forgotten to feed the chickens. While I threw food at them Angie watered the tomatoes, which were big and green.

"I like Vic's girl," I said, my voice fervent. "If I ever get married, that's the kind of girl I want."

Angie grinned. "What about your boat? You were gonna live on a big boat all by yourself."

"If the lady was like Jenny I'd take her with me. . . . Think they're gonna get married?"

"Jesus, I hope not."

My heart sank. "Why not?"

Angie pushed aside the leaves of a tomato plant so he could water the roots directly. A chicken pecked his pant cuff. He kicked it away softly. "Joey, you're so young."

My heart sank deeper at the way he was putting me down. He could tell I was hurt.

"Look," he said, "I like the girl, and I love Vic, but they're too happy together. You get what I mean?"

"No."

"Your father ever burn up an old Christmas tree?"

"Yeah."

"Remember how fast it went up?"

"Sure, and it smelled good. So what?"

"It burnt up in ten seconds, but those punks you buy at the candy store, they take all day to burn up. See? That's how it's gotta go when you get married. Everything's gotta go slow. It's gotta last." He shook his head. "Vic, he's goin' too fast with that girl. All that happiness . . ." His voice trailed off.

"Angie, that doesn't make sense."

He clapped dirt from his hands. "Maybe you'll see what I mean someday. I just hope nothin' happens. I hope to Christ they're careful."

CHAPTER SEVENTEEN

My father's cryptic postcard read as if we'd never had our disastrous telephone conversation.

> Dear Joey,
>   I'm on a farm in upstate New York and will be back before school starts in September. I think about you and miss you a lot.
>
> love, Dad

"Do you *believe* this guy?" I said after reading it aloud. "He acts like everything is okay."

"He's your father, not a guy," Connie said. "And what's not okay?"

Connie never thought there was anything wrong unless blood was flowing or a bone was sticking out through your skin. I didn't even try to answer her.

"Eh, all right, good," she continued. "September is next month. He'll be here before you know it. And he's gettin' closer all the time. Upstate New York ain't far."

"What's farther away, upstate New York or Patchogue?"

She squinted at me. "Why you askin'?"

"No reason," I said airily, crumpling up the postcard.

"How nice you used to save your father's postcards. Shame on you."

September. My mother taking me to Stride Rite and making me try on pair after pair of shoes, judging from the look on my face whether they fit. Book covers made from Bohack paper bags, new bookbags, pencil cases with Batman and Superman on them.

Where would my schooling continue? Angie and Connie never mentioned it, and here it was, the end of August. It was just as well, I decided — after all, I was going to run away.

As if to remind me of my mission's urgency there was a letter from Mel the next day.

> *Dear Joey,*
>
> *You ain't ever comming here are you? I bet you got a new girlfriend and forgot all about me. You don't care about me no more, you asshole. Fuck you in that case and fuck your chickens too. If I'm wrong you better tell me. Hurry up.*
>
> *Mel*

How had she detected Jenny Sutherland, through telepathy? I raced to my desk to write an answer.

Dear Mel,

No I do not have a new girlfriend. Vic has a new girlfriend and she is great, not like your ant Rosemary. Rosemary threw wine at Vic and I hit her in the ass. I alreddy told you I'm saving up money from bottles till there's lots. It's harder to make money now because everybody buys sodas from the hamberger place in cups. You can't get money for cups. I am still coming to see you, don't worry.

I read over what I'd written. It had a whimpering tone I hated, so in a slashing scrawl I added:

This is all true. If you don't believe me then fuck you.

Joey Ambrosio

The pencil felt flame-hot as I dropped it and sealed the letter. Until then I'd thought that *saying* the "f" word was the worst thing a person could do, and here I'd actually *written* it. I felt dizzy walking to the mailbox, connected to nothing and no one, like a helium balloon on a thread that could break at the slightest strain. I'd float up into the emptiness of the sky and drift forever among the clouds.

"You sick or something?" Angie said when I walked in.

"I want to see my house."

He gestured at the walls. "This *is* your house."

"My old house."

On the ride to Roslyn I stared out my window, counting light poles. I felt his hand poking my rib cage.

"Gum?" He held out a pack of Wrigley's, one stick jutting like a cigarette. I declined it, but moments later he poked me again.

"Seeds?" In his cupped palm were sunflower seeds, bleached white. He dropped them into my hand and I noticed how thick his calluses were, from a lifetime of twisting wrenches and pipes to bring people water. There was furry hair on the back of his hand that resembled steel wool.

228

Was it my imagination, or were Angie's ears and nose larger than they'd been at the start of the summer? It seemed as if a mainspring inside his body had loosened, causing everything to sag. Or maybe it was just the way the afternoon sun poured through the windshield and lighted his face.

He caught me staring. "What's the matter?" His voice was sharp.

"Nothing," I said, embarrassed. "I was just thinking."

"About what?"

I hesitated. "You're old, Angie."

He laughed. "That's news?"

I cracked seeds in my teeth and threw the shells out the window.

"Don't count on seein' your father out here," Angie said. "He wouldn't come home without telling you, that's for sure."

"I know that," I said. "The house ain't ours anymore, he sold it. I just want to *see* it."

Angie swerved to avoid running over a dead dog in our lane. "The house *isn't* yours," he corrected gently. "Don't say 'ain't.' You talk good English, don't let us wreck it."

We reached the Roslyn exit on the Long Island Expressway. "You gotta guide me from here."

I did, curtly. "Left . . . right . . . another left, by that big tree . . ."

I kept it up until he said, "I know where we are now."

"You do? How?" He wouldn't say. He pulled the car up along the curb in front of the house but didn't cut the motor. It idled erratically, like a troubled stomach.

"Needs a tune-up," he said, lighting a cigarette. He seemed nervous. "You want to get out, or what?"

"Let's just sit here a sec, Angie."

"Should I shut off the motor?"

"No," I said, but the car belched and died of its own accord. We looked at each other, wide-eyed.

"She conks like that," Angie said. "The second you stop feedin' her gas, she conks." But he didn't start the engine again. He turned off the ignition and removed the key, slipping it into a vest pocket. He rolled down the window to let the smoke from his cigarette out.

The house looked grayer, shabbier, and smaller than I'd remembered it. The paint on the trim was peeling but the lawn seemed well-kept, obviously tended by professional gardeners. It bore the wheel marks of heavy machinery.

The patch of soil that had been my father's crazy garden was sodded over, a quilt of dark green grass squares that stood out as plainly as an area rug.

"You been here before, Angie?"

"Once. You were a baby. Told Connie I was at the track."

"We shoulda been friends all that time, instead of waiting for my mother to die."

"You're tellin' me."

I fumbled with the door, my hand shaky.

"Where you goin'?"

"I'm just gonna get out for a while, Angie."

I stood leaning against the passenger door. Two boys on bikes pedaled toward me on the sidewalk. One I didn't know but the other was Phil McElhenny, the kid who'd conked me on the head in my one and only Little League game. At the sight of me he screeched on his foot brake and pointed with a long arm.

"Hey, Henry, this is the guy I was tellin' ya about," Phil said excitedly. "I hit him on the head and his mother *carried* him home!"

Henry was a fireplug of a boy with a squarish head and the shortest crewcut I'd ever seen. "Baby, baby, stick your head in gravy," he said, barely trying to sing it.

Phil pursed his lips. "How's his widdle head, huh? Does his widdle head hurt?"

Angie got out of the car and rapped the roof with his knuckles to get my attention. "Come on, Joey, get in the car."

I didn't turn to look at him. "In a minute."

Phil pointed. "Who's that old geezer?"

I stepped toward Phil. Angie called my name so sharply I turned around to look at him. "No fighting for you, Joey, I mean it."

"I won't, Angie. Just stay out of this."

"But —"

"*You* get in the car, Angie."

He obeyed me. As I walked toward Phil McElhenny I felt absolutely no fear. The incident Phil remembered so vividly was like ancient history to me, something that had happened to another boy on a remote planet. I was only mad at him for the name he'd called Angie. As Mel might have said, it was time to "teach him a lesson."

And I was going to keep my word with Angie, thanks to Johnny Gallo, who'd given me some advice the day after I clobbered Jack Donnelly.

"Lemme show ya how to fight without fighting, Long Island," he'd said, and then he grabbed my shirtfront and, holding it tightly, walked straight ahead, forcing me to stumble backwards. After a few strides I went down painlessly on my ass. Johnny glowered down at me, then his face broke into a smile.

"See? You're scared of me and you ain't even hurt. Just remember to keep walking and hold on to the sucker's shirt real tight, like."

But first I had to dismount Phil, whose hands gripped and twisted the bicycle handles as if he were on a motorcycle. He made a kissing sound that Henry echoed. I ignored the fat boy.

"Get off the bike, Phil."

My soft tone surprised him. His lips lost their pucker. He asked Henry to hold the bike, then walked lazily toward me. I didn't even notice his face. All that mattered to me was his loose striped short-sleeved shirt.

It was easy to grab, and he was so stunned by my sudden leap that he did nothing to defend himself. His hands hung at his sides as I walked. Angie blew the car horn.

"*Hey*," Phil said, "*hey!*"

I tightened my grip, felt skin pinch in the cloth. Phil yelped like a puppy whose ears have been pulled. I backed him into the side of the bike, then let go of the shirt with a shove. Down he went, and so did his bike, and so did Henry on top of *his* bike: dominoes. Angie blew the horn again but I wasn't quite through. Bike wheels were still spinning on air with a clicking sound when I said, "You guys get the hell out of here."

I tried to imitate Johnny Gallo's frozen face, and it worked, because the guys couldn't take their eyes off me, even as they struggled to their feet, climbed on their bikes and rode off.

At last I shook with the fear I should have felt earlier. I got back into the car. Angie's hands trembled as he lit a cigarette with the dashboard lighter.

"What are you, a nut? I was havin' a heart attack here."

"I didn't hit him. . . . Ya see how scared they were?"

"That what you want? People to be scared of you?"

"Yeah."

"You nut . . . you ever do that again, I'll put you over my knee. Old as I am." He puffed on his cig, pointed, and patted my shoulder. "Look, there's a kid goin' toward your house. Go say hello. Maybe he lives here now."

I went out, at last noticing the smells I'd gone without all summer — cool suburban air, grass clippings, the salty nearness of Long Island Sound. I breathed in as deeply as I could, as if I were about to shout from one mountain peak to another.

"Hey, you!"

The boy, a thin kid in flowered swimming trunks that hung to his knees, stopped in the middle of the path to the front door. I approached him and sniffed chlorine. He'd obviously just come from a swim at the pool. His tight curls were wet and his eyes were as red as his hair.

"What do you want?" he asked, sounding scared.

I tried to smile. "I used to live in this house."

His eyes widened. "No kidding?"

"I moved out in June."

"That's right," the kid said, his last traces of suspicion vanishing. "That's when we moved in." Little puddles formed around his feet as he dripped. "Where do you live now?"

"Brooklyn." The word sounded rough coming from my mouth. Maybe nobody can say it gently.

"I was there, once." He shivered. "My name is Francis."

"Joey."

He extended his hand, cold and pruny from swimming, and I shook it. I'd all but forgotten the simple formality of a handshake — people from Shepherd Avenue eyed each other upon introduction the way animals size each other up in the jungle.

"Do you sleep in my old room?"

"Which one?"

"The one with the window near the tree."

"Sure, that's my room. . . . You want to come in or something?"

"Yeah," I said, and without even a look back to poor Angie I followed Francis into his house. My house. The house.

"MA!" Francis had a shrill yell that shook me.

"Stand there on the mat, Francis, I'll get a towel," a female voice called from upstairs. I looked at the alien furniture around the room I'd known so well.

Footsteps down the staircase. "Francis, you'll *destroy* the woodwork with those wet feet — oh. Hello, there. Francis, who's your friend?"

"He used to live here," Francis said, his teeth chattering. "His name's Joey."

Francis's mother dropped to her knees on the mat to wipe the water on her son's legs, as if he were a Thoroughbred in need of a rubdown. The smell of her perfume filled the foyer.

She looked up at me, her face chubby and heart-shaped. "How did you get here, Joey?"

"My grandfather's out front."

She hung the towel across her son's shoulders. "Invite him in for coffee, Francis."

Francis ran to get Angie while I followed the woman into the kitchen. Late afternoon sunshine shimmered over everything as she brought a tall white coffeepot to the table and set out cups, saucers, and a plate of homemade chocolate chip cookies. She even set out linen napkins that were so white they made the coffeepot look dingy.

"You look so much like your daddy," she said. "Around the eyes. It's remarkable."

"No I don't."

She stopped folding napkins. "I beg your pardon?"

"I don't look like him. I don't look like him at all."

"Is that right? I wonder who you look like."

"Nobody." The smile left her face as if a mask had fallen from it. "I don't look like anybody. Just *me*."

She knelt to pick up a dropped napkin, and while she was down there she found the smile and put it back on.

Then the mood shifted with airy, lighthearted questions about my new home. She was smart enough not to ask about my father. I answered numbly, in blurts: "It's okay . . . I guess so . . . I dunno . . ."

She sat next to me, her long pink dress crinkling with starch. When had I become seated? I couldn't remember. I felt as if I were underwater.

"Could I . . ." I halted. Francis's mother touched my knee. "Yes?"

Her touch triggered it. I plunged my face into her dress, between her breasts, each of which felt firm against my cheeks. The source of the perfume smell — White Shoulders, the same stuff my mother used to wear — was here!

Footsteps into the kitchen, one set padded, the other hard-heeled: Angie's.

"Gee, Ma, what's the matter with him?"

"He's all right," she said cheerily. Her hands were at the back of my head, holding me in place as she stroked my hair.

"I'm Angelo," I heard my grandfather say. "I'm sorry, he's been upset all day —"

He stopped talking, abruptly. One of her hands had left the back of my head — she must have waved for him to be silent — and then the hand returned to stroke me.

"Pour coffee for Angelo," she instructed. I heard and felt her voice through her breasts, which cupped me like headphones. I wasn't crying. I was happier than I'd been since my mother was alive. This was the kind of hug I used to get from her, only Francis's mother's breasts were bigger. My soul swelled.

I stayed there ten, maybe fifteen minutes. I heard whistles for the Long Island Rail Road. I heard Angie sipping coffee, and making polite conversation.

Suddenly I jerked away from her, the way a gasoline hose

234

jolts when a gas tank is full. My vision was blurry. I'd pressed against her so hard and long it took time for me to focus.

"I'm sorry," I said.

"Don't be silly." She squeezed my earlobes.

"He gonna throw up, Ma?"

I turned to look at Francis, the luckiest guy in the world. His hair had dried, the curls puffing away from his head. He and Angie sat stiffly, like people in a hospital waiting room.

"I'm fine," I announced to the room. Angie stood and jerked his head toward the front door.

"We'll go now," he said. I noticed that he'd combed his hair straight back, the way it usually was when he left the bathroom in the morning. He must have kept a comb in the glove compartment.

On the way to the front door Francis's mother said, "Would you like to see your old room before you go?"

"No. . . . Is it okay if I look in the garage?"

"What *for?*" Francis asked.

"Of course you may," she said. "Francis, take him there."

"I know where it is."

Our old four-bladed push mower stood in the same place on the oily floor where my father had left it after cutting the lawn for the last time. No other tools in sight; the mower was a prisoner in solitary confinement. I brushed off whitish-yellow blades of dried grass before wheeling the thing outside.

"Ma, he's *crazy!*" Francis was even more scared of me than Phil and Henry had been.

"What are you doing, Joseph?" Angie asked, but he left me alone.

With a grunt I began pushing the mower over the grass, starting next to the driveway, the same way my father used to do it, cutting a strip and then overlapping it halfway on the return cut to make sure that even the stubborn grasses got shorn.

But it was useless. The grass was so short that nothing got cut, the blades spinning inches over its surface. All the mower did was make noise, because it needed oil.

"They cut the grass *yesterday*," Francis said. "Ma, how come he's doing that?"

"Hush, Francis, just hush."

I pushed it over ten strips of grass, up to the edge where the garden had been, before I stopped, sweat-soaked, out of breath. I dragged the mower to the garage like a sled, put it back where I'd found it, and went to the car without saying good-bye.

It started on the first try, to Angie's relief.

"I was afraid she wouldn't go," he said, patting the red dashboard as if it were the neck of a favorite but aging horse.

He didn't speak again until we were on the expressway.

"Feel better?"

"I feel like an ass."

His hand went to my neck and squeezed the cord there. "Joseph." We were quiet the rest of the way to Shepherd Avenue.

"How was it?" Connie asked.

"We just looked at the place from the car," Angie said, pleasing and surprising me. I was going to miss him when I ran away.

CHAPTER EIGHTEEN

DURING breakfast the next morning the phone rang. Connie spoke a few cryptic sentences before hanging up on Jenny Sutherland, who was inviting me to spend the day with her and Vic in the Village.

I gulped a mouthful of coffee. By this time I had trained myself to endure the stuff. "My sister," I murmured sarcastically.

Connie cocked her head. "What'd you call her?"

"Nothing . . . why do they want me?"

She shrugged. "Maybe they like you. Go figure it. Anyway, you ain't going."

"Why not?"

"You could get lost on the train. A colored could stab you. A Pee-Arr could steal your money. You could get kidnapped."

"I could run away," I interrupted.

"Yeah, sure, tomorrow. *Run away*. I'll pack your things."

"Don't kid around like that," Angie said. Connie still didn't take my hints seriously but Angie wasn't just brushing them off anymore. It was nice to have the extra attention since Vic's departure but at the same time, I had to be careful. He was light as an angel on his feet, and if he decided to follow me to my money jar someday I'd never hear him stalking me.

Maybe the day in Roslyn had taken something out of him and he was anxious to have me out of his hair. "Let him go," he said.

Connie frowned. "You think she sets a good example for a little boy?"

So that was it. She wasn't really worried about me getting lost, stabbed, robbed, or kidnapped — she feared I'd be forever tainted by Jenny's loose morals.

Angie laughed her off. "What's she gonna do, teach him to murder?"

Connie shuffled back to the phone, where Vic's number was scrawled on a scrap of a macaroni box that was wedged between the phone and the wall. "Funny. Milton Berle should worry about his job." She began dialing.

Astronauts bound for Mars couldn't have a more detailed list of instructions than the one Connie recited for my solo journey to Manhattan:

Ride in a subway car with a cop, look before you sit, don't touch the seat with your hands, don't get caught in the doors, don't stare at no one, don't eat any candy you find.

Angie and I laughed together at that last one.

"You really think he'd eat candy he finds on the train? What is he, a monkey?"

"It don't hurt to say it," Connie said.

"What about fruit?" I teased. "Can I eat an apple if I find one on the train, Connie?"

She gave me a black stare and pressed the price of two tokens into my hand. "Walk him to the train," she commanded. On the way Angie slipped me a buck.

"Treat your uncle and the girl to ice cream," he said, turning for home at the bottom of the el staircase.

Angie's decision not to wait for the train surprised me, and then it hit me, like the puff of wind from the train that came minutes later: he was no kid anymore, and stairs weren't easy to manage. That impression I'd gotten on the ride to Roslyn was no illusion.

I made the trip without a hitch, remembering the right place to transfer and riding the whole way with my hands on my lap. There was a half-eaten O! Henry bar on the floor of the train I never would have dreamed of eating if not for Connie's warning. I let it lie, wondering how the hell she knew it would be there.

When I emerged into the sunlight of West Fourth Street I was surprised to find Jenny waiting for me by the Waverly movie theater. Vic had staked out the other subway exit, across the street. I was a little disappointed because I'd wanted to see their home again. Vic, hairier than ever, said they were afraid I'd get lost among the crooked streets.

It was a bullshit reason. He knew that if I saw the house, Connie would grill me as intensely as cops do a murder suspect once I got back to Brooklyn: Was the bed made? Were there dishes in the sink? Did you see any cockroaches (this question accompanied by the inimitable twitching of her fingertips)?

No *wonder* she finally decided to let me go! Little did she suspect her son's quick thinking would foil her. She'd be as frustrated as a tourist who takes snapshots of an exotic land but forgets to remove the lens cap.

It was a brilliant day. There were so many people on Sixth Avenue that we couldn't walk three abreast, so Vic led the way, snake-style, holding Jenny's hand while she held mine. She looked back at me from time to time, laughing at nothing in particular.

The first stop was for soft ice cream cones, which I paid for, telling them it was Angie's money.

"He's so *honest*," Jenny said.

Next we headed for Washington Square Park, where musicians played in front of upended hats. One guy stretched a rope between two young trees, and while he walked along it he juggled three tennis balls. A magician cut a piece of string with

238

a scissors, held the cut ends in his fingertips, and produced one long string again.

Jenny pulled me aside while Vic became absorbed in the act. I let a wild joy flood my being, anticipating what I'd hoped for on that long train ride: a change of heart in Jenny, who was about to ask me — no, *beg* me — to move in with them, along with my pal Mel. We'd have the world beat, as long as people were too lazy to bring back soda bottles for deposit money.

She stroked my face, her thumbs rubbing where sideburns would one day grow. "Baby, you're not mad at me anymore, are you? I mean you understand why we can't all live together, don't you?"

I thought I could hear my heart turn over behind my ribs, as if it had been flipped with a spatula and pressed flat to fry faster.

"Joey?" She clapped my cheeks lightly. "You understand, right?"

"Sure." I clenched my teeth and pursed my lips, a living Portrait of Zip Aiello as a Young Man. Her hands fell from my face.

"Oh, baby —"

"It's okay because I'm going away pretty soon anyway."

"You are? *Where?*"

First my money jar, now my half-baked dream of departure — I spilled my darkest secrets to this child-woman without any prompting. It was important to make her believe I didn't need her.

"Long Island," I said. "Patchogue. That friend I told you about, she's waiting for me. She's kinda mad at me now, though. I gotta see if she's still my friend."

"Of course she's still your friend."

"Shut up. You don't even know her."

Jenny didn't get mad. "When are you going?"

"When I make some more money."

"But how will you get there?"

"Trains. It's easy. I ride trains all by myself," I bragged, having ridden alone for the first time an hour earlier.

It was remarkable, how seriously Jenny was taking me. She'd

been on her own from such a young age that everything I said sounded plausible. She chewed her lower lip before saying, "But what will you do when you get there? Live with *her* family?"

"Nah. They don't like her and she doesn't like them."

"So where will you go?"

"I dunno yet. I ain't even sure I want to take her with me."

She dared to take my cheeks in her hands again. "Oh, baby, I never tell *anyone* what to do but please please *please* be careful."

"Don't worry about me." I took her wrists and pulled her hands off me. Vic turned to us, shaking his head in wonder.

"Every week I watch that guy cut the rope and I still don't know how he does it."

We walked away, dodging footballs and baseballs that crisscrossed the air over our heads. One errant baseball headed our way. Natural shortstop that he was, Vic snared it on the short hop in one hand. He gazed at it for a moment, as if it were a tiny planet populated with wonderful people, before tossing it back.

Jenny squeezed his hand. "Miss baseball?"

Vic smiled, teeth showing white through his beard. "Nahh."

Vic and Jenny wore matching sandals. I could go a lot faster in my sneakers and had to slow down to their shuffling sandal pace. Jenny sensed my urgency and tugged on my hand.

"He's like a wild stallion!" she laughed, yanking me to her hard chest and kissing the top of my head. "I've never seen so much *energy* in anybody!"

"Yeah, he gets worked up," Vic said. "Used to take him hours just to fall asleep."

Jenny passed her palm down my forehead, past my nose and chin. Then she ran it across my shoulders.

"Uh-huh," she said, confirming her own thoughts. "He's going to be very tall, Vic. Taller than you. The size of his head — I can tell."

"I'm a cesarean," I proclaimed, proud of it now, proud of anything that set me apart from the rest of the creatures in my cage. "I didn't come through the birth canal. They hadda cut my mother open so I could be borned."

I'd intended to frighten Jenny but she smiled. "It was worth it, little brother."

Good God Almighty, what did a young male have to do to stay mad at her? I hadn't a clue, and Vic probably didn't, either.

"You really think I'll be tall, Jenny?"

"I know you will."

Vic pushed back his shaggy hair. "Don't be in such a rush to grow up, kid," he advised. "You have all the time in the world."

"Don't call me 'kid,' " I snapped.

Vic was surprised. "Hey, I didn't mean it. I call everybody 'kid.' "

"I'm not a kid anymore. . . . Call me Joe."

"Not Joey?"

"No," I insisted. "Just Joe. Joe's my name from now on."

"Joe it is," Vic said, reaching for a low branch of a maple tree and grabbing a leaf. "Sure, like Joe DiMaggio."

"Don't pull the leaves. . . . Who's that?" Jenny asked, but Vic only hugged her and winked at me. I didn't return the wink because his hug had pulled Jenny's hand from mine, where I'd wanted it to remain all day long. As soon as he let go of her I grabbed her hand again.

"You trying to steal my woman, Joe?"

"Yeah."

Jenny laughed gleefully and did a little two-step in the air. "Dear me," she gasped, "my two handsome men! I'm the envy of New York City today!"

They decided that my sneakers were too hot to wear on a summer day and led me to a basement shop on a side street. The air in there was rank with the smell of cowhide but it was much cooler than the street.

A skinny man with a goatlike beard came out from a back room, wearing a leather apron. His hands were dye-stained.

"How they fit?" he asked Jenny, his voice filled with suspicion.

"Oh, ours are fine," Jenny said, twinkling her toes. "We want a pair for our son."

Vic's mouth dropped open. I stared at Jenny, then at Vic — what was *this* all about? But Jenny's eyes told it all: Don't let on, let him think you are!

"Yeah," Vic said when his composure had returned. "Make my son a pair like ours."

The cobbler had barely given me a look. His eyes were on my feet. "Take the sneakers off. Socks too."

He made me stand on sheets of white paper and traced around them with a pencil.

"Stand still!"

"It tickles."

Jenny giggled. Vic rolled his eyes to the ceiling, the tolerant husband indulging his giddy wife.

"Same color?" the cobbler asked.

"It's up to him," Jenny said.

"I want mine the same as yours, Mom," I said. Jenny buried her face in Vic's shoulder. At last the cobbler rose, a hand to his crooked spine.

"This is your kid?"

"Our firstborn," Vic said straight-faced.

He eyed us, tugged his beard. "Well my God, you must have had him when you were twelve!" He cackled shrilly. "All right, come back in an hour."

We left the shop, roaring with laughter, and wandered around the park some more. Vic was anxious to watch the magician cut rope again, vowing "This time, I'll catch the trick."

While he was absorbed in the show Jenny said to me, "Sometimes it's fun to pretend, isn't it, Joey? I mean Joe."

Why did she have to remind me it had only been a game? My airy mood burst and turned leaden. "Pretending is for babies."

"Aww. But every *once* in a while —"

"You're not my mother, Jenny. She's dead. And you're not even really my sister."

She caught a windblown wisp of her own hair and twirled it in her fingers, holding its tip and gesturing with it like a teacher with chalk.

"I'll tell you what," she said. "If I ever *do* have a child, I hope he's exactly like you."

My back tingled as if the tip of a feather were being dragged lightly along the bumps of my spine.

"Exactly?"

"To a tee. I mean that."

"They'd have to cut you open to get him, you know. I bet it would hurt."

"I wouldn't mind." She dropped her hair, crossed her heart, kissed her fingertip, and touched my nose. "I swear I wouldn't."

The crowd applauded the magician. We were the only ones not watching him.

"How about if it hurt . . . like a toothache?"

"I'd still have him."

"How about if it hurt . . . like an earache?"

"I'd still have him."

"How about . . ." I shut up, swallowed, and rubbed the sudden gooseflesh on my arms. This was one game I'd never expected to play again.

"You cold, baby? On a hot day like this?" I let her hug me until it was time to get my sandals. All those people watching the guy cutting rope were missing out on the real magic of Jenny Sutherland, right behind them.

The sandals fit perfectly and cost ten dollars, which Jenny paid out of her pocketbook. I think she held the money for both of them.

"Thanks," I said. "This is one of the best days of my life," I added, surprised to hear my voice crack.

"Aw, it's our pleasure, Joe," Vic said, emphasizing my new name.

"All right, enough of this," Jenny said. "We're all starving so let's go home and eat."

Vic looked alarmed. "I thought we were gonna eat Chinese."

"Right, at home," Jenny said. "We've been out all day and I want to try our new wok."

"What's a wok?" I asked.

"A Chinese frying pan. Let's go home."

I would get to see their house after all! I slung my sneakers over my shoulder the way David must have carried his slingshot after killing Goliath. They were tied at the lace tips and bumped my back like an exterior heartbeat as I walked.

"Let's go!" I shouted, unable to contain my joy. Maybe I would get to stay the night. If it worked out, maybe I could stay for good. . . .

I led the way to Sullivan Street, along Sixth Avenue. I was in the middle, holding their hands. The Waverly was directly across the street from where we were now, and at a tiny newsstand in front of the subway stairs I'd climbed earlier I saw my father buy a pack of gum.

His blue eyes looked past us, maybe at the pickup basketball games behind us. He had a gruff beard, even thicker than Vic's. It was devoid of gray, unlike the salt-and-pepper of his thick hair. His face was suntanned. His blue jeans were low-slung on his hips. He unwrapped a stick of gum, folded it into his mouth, and bit it hard.

Those teeth: perfect, even, defiant, unmistakable.

I dropped their hands. "Sal!" I screamed, instead of "Dad." He moved casually down the subway steps. I made it halfway across the avenue and then there was a screech of brakes, a bump to my left hip. I was flying through the air. I rolled for a while, seeing a succession of alternate images: sky-street, sky-street, sky-street. Jenny screamed my name, and then I lost consciousness.

When I came to the first face I saw was Connie's, hovering over me like a harvest moon.

"He's alive," she said, then put a hand to her mouth at even the thought that I might not be.

"Of course he is." Angie appeared at her side. "Hey, you." He tickled my toes through a bed sheet.

"Jenny Sutherland, her face tear-streaked, took my hand. "Baby, are you all right? Oh, baby, baby!"

Behind her stood Vic, looking like a naughty schoolboy. He probably hadn't been yelled at by his parents yet. Now that I was conscious the fireworks could begin.

"What happened? Where am I?" My tongue clung to the roof of my mouth as if it had been glued.

"You're in Saint Vincent's Hospital," Vic said. "You got hit by a cab near here. Don't you remember?"

"I didn't see any cab."

"He didn't see you either. You ran out there like a maniac."

"Get the doctor," Angie snapped. "Where the hell's the doctor?" Vic left the room and returned moments later with a tall, thin man in hospital whites. He parted his way through everybody without touching them. They made way for him as if he were a fire engine.

"How are you feeling?" he asked gently.

I swallowed. "I'm thirsty."

"Do you remember what happened?"

"I saw my father across the street," I said groggily. The doctor looked at Connie for an explanation.

"His father's gone, he thought he saw him," Connie said.

I sat up. "I *did* see him, Connie." My hip throbbed. The doctor leaned close to me.

"You're all right," he said. "You've had a mild concussion — that's sort of like a big headache. You're a very lucky boy."

"My hip hurts."

"But it isn't broken. We took X rays." He straightened to stand back with the others. "He's incredibly lucky. That cab could have killed him but all he got was a few bruises. Do you know what the odds are against that?"

"Hey," Angie said, "what do I look like, a bookie?"

"Can I have some water?" I whined. The doctor passed me a white plastic cup with a straw jutting from its lid.

"Sip it slowly," he instructed. "And rest." He patted my head. I slid my hand under the sheet to feel my hip and learned I was naked.

The doctor huddled with Connie and Angie near the doorway while Vic and Jenny stayed with me. Vic manfully tried to blink back tears, without much luck.

"Give him air," Connie commanded. The doctor had gone away. They were at the mercy of her wrath.

"Keep your voice down," Angie said, pointing to the other side of the room where a boy with a bandaged head slept.

Everyone was quiet, but it was the eye of the storm. I heard cars honking out on Seventh Avenue and felt oddly safe in this room, out of their range.

I sucked on the straw. The water was deliciously cold. "I'm okay," I assured them.

Angie pointed at Jenny and Vic. "You two, you should have watched him."

"You're blaming *us* for this, Pop?"

Angie held his hands out, palms up. "All I know is, we had him all summer, he never got hurt. You have him one day . . ." His voice trailed off.

"That cab knocked his sneakers right off his feet," Connie said, fueling the argument. "The ambulance driver said they were ten feet away."

"It didn't knock 'em off, Ma, he was *carrying* his sneakers."

Connie's eyes widened. "You let him go barefoot?"

"He was wearing sandals. We got him sandals like ours."

Connie looked down at their feet. "Ten years old and you're turning him into a beatnik?"

"Oh, stop it, Ma, just cut it out."

"Don't blame them," I piped in. "They didn't *push* me into the street, I was chasing my father. How many times do I have to tell you?"

I stopped talking because my head throbbed. Connie smiled at me in a sickeningly sweet way.

"Don't do that, Connie, I'm not crazy," I said. "That was my father going to the subway."

"Did you two see Sal?" Angie asked Vic and Jenny.

Vic rolled his eyes. "Christ, Pop, there were a million people around," he boomed, flapping his arms.

Jenny Sutherland opened her mouth and hesitated before saying, "I don't even know what his father looks like." But her words, the chirp of a sparrow amid the roar of lions, were barely acknowledged.

Connie turned back to me. "Okay, what did he look like?"

"You know what he looks like. Except he had a beard."

"Everybody in this crazy neighborhood has a beard. What else?"

"I don't know." My head throbbed harder. "I just know it was him."

"What makes you so *sure?*" Connie persisted. "You ain't seen him in months and you ain't never seen him with a beard."

"I'd know that fucker *anywhere*," I shot back.

My words stunned them. Next to me the bandaged boy groaned and rolled over.

"All right, all right, it's the drugs they gave him," Angie said. "He didn't mean it."

Connie couldn't have been more shocked if I'd spit in her eye. She backed away from the bed as if I'd turned into a cobra.

"It's all so terrible," Jenny said, reaching for Vic's hand.

Connie said, "You, can't you keep your hands off him for *one second?*" The women exchanged steel-melting gazes. If they'd begun socking each other no one would have been surprised. Jenny gave up and began pulling her hand away but Vic wouldn't let her.

"*Never* talk to my lady like that, Ma." His voice was chilling. "My lady can do whatever she wants."

To everyone's relief the doctor returned and put a hand to my forehead. It was cool as a raw steak. "We want to keep Joseph here for the night, just for observation."

"No!" I knocked his hand away. "Please, please, don't let them keep me here, Angie."

"You said nothing was broken," Angie said.

"Well that's true, but he's experienced —"

"We got pillows and blankets in my car," Angie said in an iron voice. "We are taking him home, sir."

The doctor shrugged. "It might be best at that." What a jellyfish! He left the room and called for a nurse to make out the papers.

"Thanks, Angie, thanks," I said, as if I'd just been spared from the electric chair.

Vic said, "Our house is closer."

"Forget it," Angie said. "You've done enough."

They made me ride a wheelchair to the sidewalk. Angie had

driven into the city, despite the crooked streets that confused him. Vic carried me to the car. Jenny kissed me on my forehead.

"We'll call you tomorrow, sweetheart."

Connie arranged blankets and pillows in the back, and then we began the long, slow ride back to Shepherd Avenue, Angie braking frequently to avoid potholes.

"I thought you never drove to Manhattan," I said, half asleep. "That's what you told me, Angie."

"This was an emergency," he said, reaching back to pat my knee. I shut my eyes. The last voice I heard before falling asleep was his.

"If that *was* Sal, what the hell is he doing in the city?"

I woke up the next morning in Vic's bed. My head throbbing, I went across to my cot. I must have slept for sixteen hours straight.

"No running around today," Connie ordered, forbidding me even from my paintbrushes. I was annoyed, because it had been days since I'd gone bottle hunting. I was sure there were at least a dozen on my turf with my name on them.

Of all people, Grace Rothstein made me a wonderful baked Alaska. I ate the whole thing by myself. She sat stroking my back and cooing while I spooned the sweetness down. I remembered Vic telling me how she went hot and cold with children. Until now, I'd never believed it. I told her the story of the accident, and then Connie said, "You're so mad at your father, why'd you run after him?"

I licked my spoon clean before answering. "I was gonna tell him not to come back for me."

Grace gasped. Angie said, "You weren't really gonna do that, were you?"

I shrugged and dug into the rest of the baked Alaska.

Even Rosemary came to see me. Could she have forgotten the time I'd whacked her on the ass? No, but nothing cleansed Shepherd Avenue sins like a brush with death. She brought me a fistful of Superman comics, which was really incredible, knowing how trashy she thought they were. The buzz around the neighborhood was that she was dating a dentist from Woodhaven. Connie was polite to her face but after she went home she murmured, "Bet she had her eye on that dentist while Vic was away playin' ball."

The only real disappointment that day came when Vic called to see how I was. No, he said, Jenny couldn't come to the phone because she wasn't around. Some "sister."

My last visitor of the day was Freddie Gallo's widow, but even as I told her about getting hit by a car — the description improved with each rendition — I could tell she wasn't paying attention.

"And then I stopped rolling and that's all I remember," I said.

"Good," Freddie's widow murmured absently, as if I'd just described my first day at school. She was quiet for a moment and then the news was out suddenly.

"Johnny's engaged." Her voice was artificially bright. "Nice girl, from Cobble Hill. Has her own apartment."

Connie hiked an eyebrow. "She lives alone?"

"Oh, yes, she's real independent. My Johnny always liked independent women." Her hands squirmed in her lap. Angie found the manners that had deserted Connie.

"Congratulations," he said, squeezing her hand and kissing her damp forehead. I was annoyed, having lost center stage.

"The reason I came over . . . I mean I wanted to see if the boy was okay, but . . . there should be a party or something." She swallowed. "I don't know how to put no party together."

Before she could start bawling Angie and Connie assured her our basement would be a perfect place for the party, and that she could invite anyone she wanted. She was on her way out when Connie asked, "Does Johnny have a choice?"

Freddie's widow didn't turn around but stopped dead and arched her back, catlike, as if someone had caught her between the shoulder blades with a dart.

"No."

CHAPTER NINETEEN

ANOTHER party. Same cake, same lemon ice, most of the same people.

Johnny Gallo's fiancée didn't invite anyone from her side. Her name was Nancy. She was dark-haired, dark-eyed, very thin. She seemed bored, or scared, as if she expected to get yelled at. She was very quiet, with none of Jenny Sutherland's bounce. My heart jumped in anticipation of Jenny's arrival with Vic; I was no longer mad that she hadn't called me.

When at last Vic came down the rickety basement stairs — for some reason he'd used the front door, something he never did — he was greeted with shouts and even applause. Only I didn't clap. Jenny wasn't with him.

Grace yelled, "Hey, where's this American girl you ran out on your job like a bum for?"

Vic smiled weakly, tolerantly. "She didn't feel so hot, she decided to stay behind." He shifted his weight from foot to foot. "She says hello to everybody."

"She don't even know us," Grace mumbled.

Zip Aiello said, "Shave that beard already — what are you, a Jew?" Uncle Rudy gave Zip a hard look but said nothing.

I was nearly in tears over Jenny's absence and intercepted Vic on his way to greet Johnny.

"How's your head and your leg, Joe?"

"Fine. . . . Is she okay, Vic?"

"Sure she's okay. Leave me alone for a while, okay?" He rubbed my hair as he nudged me aside.

Vic and Johnny were stony-faced as they approached each other. They stuck out their hands to shake but on a simultaneous impulse dropped them and embraced for a good ten seconds. Then Johnny made a clumsy, formal introduction of his bride-to-be.

"Didn't notice your car outside, Johnny," Vic said.

Johnny nodded grimly. "Sold it. The wedding, the new apartment . . . I can use the bucks, ya know?" He rubbed his nose. "Maris and Mantle, they're sure knocking the shit out of the ball, ain't they?"

Vic nodded, though he probably hadn't watched a game since his last time here with Jenny. Johnny touched his cheek. "Beard looks good. Maybe I'll grow one."

Nancy said, "Please don't do that, Johnny, you'll scratch me."

Johnny gestured at Vic with his beer bottle. "His woman don't complain." Vic walked away gray-faced.

Grace was disappointed in being gypped out of a chance to inspect Jenny. "All the times I felt bad I still went to parties, I didn't want to spoil nobody's fun," she said.

Uncle Rudy, gadget-lover that he was, had brought along his movie camera and asked the engaged couple to strut for him. Johnny and Nancy obliged, trudging like robots toward his blazing row of hand-held lights.

Was that a pot belly that Johnny, of all people, was growing? He moved as if he'd had an operation to remove springs from his heels.

Zip obligingly spooned cake and gulped wine for the camera, and then Rudy beamed his lights on Connie. She squinted and put her hands over her eyes.

"You're melting the icing on the cake, Rudy."

He didn't stop filming. "It's a movie, *do* something," he urged frantically as precious film spun through the sprockets.

Connie lifted the cake and slid it forward a few inches, then pulled it back to its original spot. "Satisfied? Pain in the ass German," she said. Grace laughed shrilly.

Rudy killed the lights. "None of you *move* for me."

"Madonna, I see purple flowers," Connie said, rubbing her eyes.

Rudy twisted a key to wind his camera. "Where's Angelo? I have a few feet of film left, let's get him in the movie."

Connie rolled her eyes and said to me, "Make your Uncle Rudy happy, go find your grandfather and tell him to come be in the movie."

I ran upstairs. It was unusually quiet, no sound of radio or

TV — Angie liked to sneak away from crowds to catch ball games. He wasn't in the parlor or the upstairs kitchen. I pushed open the door to Angie's room without knocking.

He and Vic were seated side by side on his bed. Vic's arms dangled low between his knees. They looked at me.

"Taking movies downstairs," I said.

No answer. I sat on the end of the bed, next to Vic. He reached around for the back of my neck but didn't squeeze it with his usual vigor. The fingers felt damp.

"She just split, Pop," he said in a voice of wonder. "I get back from the bookstore Thursday and all her stuff's gone, all her clothes. That same morning she asked me if I wanted chili that night. I told her sure."

Vic shook his head, the way a man does to clear it after taking a knock. "The note just said, 'I had to go.' Bing, like that. Not even her name, she signed. Who was I, the milkman?"

Angie's breath whistled through his nostrils. "What do you want from me?"

"Tell me what I did wrong!"

"Vic, I was here, you were there."

"Pop, she said she was gonna cook *chili!* You tell someone you're gonna do something and then you disappear? That's lying." Fierce tears flooded his eyes. "I swear I don't know what I did wrong."

Angie waited for a wailing police car to pass before saying, "Maybe the way you lived was like lying."

Vic stiffened. "Hey, I wanted to marry that girl."

"Did she know that?"

"I only told her a million times. She used to laugh it off, so I did, too. I figured there was time. . . ."

Angie's grin was odd, half sympathy, half mockery. "You scared her off."

Vic was crying harder. His beard was wet. "I only meant her good. God, for the first time in my life . . ."

He buried his face in Angie's shirtfront and squeezed my neck with renewed strength. He needed us, *both* of us. I'd never felt so close to Victor Ambrosio.

But Angie wasn't drawn into the passion of it all. He kept his

252

head high, as if a rising flood were approaching his nose. "Tell you a story," he said. "When I was a kid I saw a dog walking funny once, right in this damn neighborhood. I get a little closer, I see his hind leg is practically ripped off — the bone's sticking through the skin, he's bleeding to death."

"Dixie?" I guessed.

"No, not Dixie. Joey, don't interrupt." He narrowed his eyes in concentration. "Car must have winged the pooch. I went after him but he ran faster on three legs than I did on two. But finally he falls down, and I get to him. And he bites my hand."

Angie tapped his stomach. "Fourteen shots for rabies, right in my gut. One worse than the other."

Vic sniffed. "What's this got to do with me?"

"I only meant him good."

Snot bubbled from Vic's nose. "Jesus, Pop, you compare my girl to some rabid *dog?*"

"Wild is wild, Victor. That don't mean bad."

Vic sighed as if it hurt to breathe. "That story doesn't do me any good."

"I'm sorry. It's all I got. Now you figure it out and live with it, one way or the other. Blow your nose, we have to be in a movie."

Vic rose, wiping his face. "I'd better wash first, I'm a mess."

"Movin' back in?"

"I'd like that, Pop."

"Good, good." Angie held up a finger. "But this is it. You leave again, you stay gone. This ain't the YMCA. Fair enough?"

Vic nodded.

"You all right now?"

"I'll live."

"Hurry up, wash your face. Twenty years from now you don't want somebody lookin' at this stupid movie and askin' why you were crying."

We followed Vic to the bathroom, as if he couldn't handle the task alone. "This Jenny, she couldn't be pregnant, could she?" Angie asked casually.

Vic opened both spigots at the sink, doused his face. "No. We were real careful about that."

"Too bad Johnny wasn't, the poor kid." Angie went downstairs.

Vic threw more water on his face. He looked at himself in the medicine cabinet mirror to watch it drip off the beard.

"Hey, Vic?"

"I'm right here, Joe." He kept looking at himself. Maybe he was trying to figure out if his appearance had chased her off.

"How about me, Vic?"

He looked at me. "*You? What about you?*"

I handed him a towel. He rubbed his face as if he meant to erase his features. "Did Jenny say anything about me before she left?"

His laugh exploded like a sneeze into the towel, which he balled up and threw against the wall. The hairs of his beard pointed wildly in all directions.

"*I* didn't even rate a good-bye, ya think *you* were gonna get one? Come on. All she did was leave, buddy." He snapped his fingers. "Pick up the towel, would you?"

I hung it on the rack. "I just thought . . ."

"What? *What?* Talk louder, for Christ's sakes."

"I THOUGHT SHE LIKED ME!" While the "L" sound was still rolling off my tongue I didn't know what I was going to say. I'd come within a vowel of "loved."

Vic laughed again and smacked the mirror with his palm, putting a hairline crack in the glass. "Sure she liked you, Joe. How she cried all *night* when that cab hit you . . ." He wrinkled his face in mock sorrow and dragged a forefinger from the corner of his eye down his hairy cheek. "She was your sister, right, and your mother, too, huh?"

He pounded his chest. "And what about me, huh? God, what a wizard at playing house, lemme tell you. Cook, sew, *fuck* —"

"Shut up! You shut up about her!"

"No. You hear this, Joe, now's as good a time as any." He clapped his hands once, hard, a teacher getting the attention of a sleepy student.

"Important lesson, here, for a young man." He put a heavy

254

hand on my shoulder. "Learn how to spot a flake when you meet one. Lesson *two*." The other hand slammed down on my other shoulder. "Stay the hell away from her."

The hands came off my shoulders and I felt light enough to float, all of me but my heart, which plummeted like a rock dropped in a vat of pudding.

Downstairs, they called for us. "We're coming!" Vic shouted through cupped hands. I pushed his chest.

"You're a liar, Vic. You don't mean that about Jenny."

"Every word of it I mean." He suddenly seemed so old-world Italian — his anger, his dramatics, the placement of nouns first in his sentences. He shoved me aside. "Come on, they're waiting for us."

I couldn't find an outlet for my rage. "You'll get yelled at for busting that mirror!" I sputtered at his back.

The party — if you could call it that — was over before ten o'clock. Vic went to bed right away. Connie folded the cake box in half and wedged it into a bulging garbage bag, then handed it to me to take outside. She was paranoid about roaches and never let trash stay inside overnight.

When I got outside with the oily bag I noticed someone standing with his hand gripped around the NO PARKING pole a little way down the block. I pushed the bag into the can and went over to check it out.

It was Zip Aiello, rocking on his heels as if he were on a sailboat during a squall. "Come over here, kid."

He beckoned with his free hand. I got close enough to smell his breath, sour from all the wine he'd drunk.

"C'mon, get on the train," he urged. "Hurry, she's gonna pull outta the station."

Tingling, I gripped the pole under his hand. His breath wheezed through my hair. For the first time since Mel was gone, somebody wanted to play make-believe!

"Careful, it gets shaky goin' over the river." Zip's heels clattered on the sidewalk. With his free hand he held his battered fedora to his head, as if there were a wind.

"You figure I'm nuts."

"No, I don't," I said, but of course that's exactly what I thought.

"You like me?"

"Yeah."

"Bullshit . . . really?"

"Except for that time you broke my balls and made me swear on my dead mother."

"I doan remember that." He frowned. "Nobody likes me. They invite me to these parties 'cause they feel sorry for me."

"Zip, I like you, you're just weird."

He grinned at my honesty. "You, maybe, but the rest of 'em . . . I ain't crazy. *They're* crazy." He gestured at the house, the block, the world.

"You better go home, Zip."

"Lemme ride the train awhile." He rocked on his heels again. Down the block the real train roared by. He smiled.

"So whaddya gonna do with all that dough you made?"

"None of your beeswax."

"Ah, is that a way to talk? Who got you started in this here bottle deal, huh? Thanks to me you got forty bucks."

"I do not."

"The Jew says you do. It don't matter, I gotcha beat."

A flame of competitive spirit heated my guts. "Yeah? How much did *you* make?"

"None o' ya business. Ha!" He didn't know it yet, but his knees had begun to bend. He finally caught himself when he'd just about sunk to his ass, then he pulled himself back up, hand over hand on the pole.

He squinted at me. "What are you, crying?" He made it sound like a disease.

I wiped my eyes. The tears felt bacon-fat slippery on my cheeks. "This stinks."

"*What* stinks?"

"Everything."

His laughter sounded like choking. "You just found out, huh?"

"Yeah. 'Cause it used to be nice when my mother was alive."

256

He took one of his hands off the pole and waved it at me, a move that nearly cost him his balance. "Your mother didn't do you no favors, lettin' you have it soft. Sooner or later you was gonna find out how bad this world is."

He said it as if there were another world we could flee to, but of course there wasn't. Hell, there wasn't even a whole world. There was only Shepherd Avenue, and nobody really left that street unless they didn't want to go.

Another train went by down the block, in the opposite direction of the last one. I was feeling better, somehow. I really don't know why. Maybe because I thought I'd hit bottom, and it wasn't so damn bad after all. True, I was crying in front of a drunken maniac who pretended to be riding a subway, but I still had my jar of money, no matter who didn't care whether I lived or died.

Death: I'd come within an inch of it days earlier, and if I'd died no one would have found my fortune! When I found that empty jar it sported a furry jacket of dust that must have taken at least a decade to grow. Undoubtedly it would have grown an equally luxuriant jacket and my coins in it would have tarnished to the color of coal before someone stumbled upon it, maybe another kid like me. . . .

But I hadn't died. Sorry, everybody. The money was there to serve *me*, and there suddenly seemed to be no more time to waste, even though I was less than halfway to my goal.

"Hey, Zip, which train takes you to Jamaica Station?"

"This here one I'm on." He stamped his foot, eager to continue the subway illusion. "Few more stops and we're there, kid."

"Come on, the *real* train. Which way?"

He pointed. "Why? You got a date someplace?"

"Nah. I just gotta know for my plan."

Gossip; how he loved it. He squared his shoulders. "Is that so?"

"Yup."

He let go of the pole, both hands, so interested that he forgot about the train he was on. "You gonna tell me more or what?"

"You promise not to tell anyone?"

He made a zipping motion across his lips; was that how he'd gotten his nickname? "Come on, kid, give."

"Okay. I'm runnin' away."

He seemed disappointed, as if he'd expected something more exciting. "When?"

"Real soon. I'm gonna make a little more money and then I'm going."

"All by yaself?"

"Yeah . . . *no.*" Even as I spoke with him my plan was undergoing mutations. "First I'm gonna go out to Long Island and get Mel. Then we're both running away. I was gonna visit her anyway. . . ."

Now his brow was knotted in concentration. I'd never seen him do that before. It was a funny sight.

"That little tomboy with the big nose what got naked witchoo in your grandpa's garage?"

"Yeah, her."

He laughed low and mockingly, hee-hee-hee. "Whaddya gonna do, get married and have *bay-beez?*" He gripped the elbows of his shabby jacket and made a rocking motion.

"Maybe we will. I don't know. You quit laughing, Zip."

He let go of his elbows. His pantomime had been so real I gasped at the thought of the imaginary baby plunging to the sidewalk. He stopped laughing, though.

"Gonna buy a house?" he said. "A house and a car with them forty bucks?"

"No. A boat. We're gonna live on a sailboat and sail all over the place. And if people ain't nice we'll sail someplace else."

"Hee-hee-hee. And they say I'm crazy. . . . What about them chickens you like so much?"

I hadn't thought of that. "They're coming with us."

"On a *boat?*"

"Sure. You can do that. Long as you have food for them."

He let fly with the biggest belch I'd ever heard. I swear, it was a five-syllable job. "Forget about the boat, forget about the boat. How you gonna load 'em all on that train?" He pointed down the block, toward Step One of my trip to freedom.

He had me there. No way I could carry all those crates up the steps of the el.

"Okay," I conceded. "So I'll just bring Salt and Pepper, then. The rest can stay with Angie. They like him."

"Huh. That grandpa o' yours, he's okay. Your grandma?" he held out a flat hand and rotated it at the wrist, the *mezzo-mezzo* sign. "And what about all your udda stuff? How ya gonna carry the money, ya clothes?"

I gulped. I didn't even have a suitcase — my father had just loaded my stuff onto the backseat of the car.

"My sack!" I said brightly. "I can use my bottle sack!"

Zip frowned. "I gave you that sack, remember."

"I know."

"Well." His voice got sheepish. "Now you got money," he said, blinking and toeing the sidewalk.

I let him suffer a few minutes before saying, "How much you want for it?"

He picked his nose, flicked a bugger toward the street. "Half a buck'd do it."

"Wait here."

I got two quarters from my grape jar, my first withdrawal of the summer. I felt a weird twinge doing that, a sensation that my plans were backsliding. Then I ran back out and put the coins into Zip's puffy palm. He grinned as his fingers closed over the money. The poor guy had probably agonized over that freebie burlap sack all summer.

"Now we're square, Joey." He tapped my cheek softly with his fist, the coins as snug in there as seeds in an apple.

"Don't you tell anybody my secret plan."

"Mmm. Someday you take me for a ride on that boat o' yours. I never been on a boat. Tried to join the Navy but my feet's flat. . . . Hey. You tell me somethin'." His eyes gleamed wet in the light from the street lamp. "You ever know a guy who found as much good stuff as me?"

"Uh-uh." It was the truth, and he knew I meant it.

"There's gold in the garbage, Joey. I found a TV set one time that needed one lousy tube. Worked perfect for years."

"Wow."

He winked a wet eye, forcing a tear down his cheek. "People don't know what they're throwin' out is why."

He shut his eyes and clung tighter than ever to the pole. Backpedaling away from him, I bumped into Angie.

"Every time you take out the garbage you're gone a week."

"I was talking with Zip, Angie." I was a little pissed at him for the way he'd shut me up during his lecture to Vic.

Zip had slid into a sitting position, still holding the pole. "He doing that train ride bit?" Angie asked.

"You *know* it?"

Angie shrugged. "It's an old routine, every time he drinks."

I felt a twinge of sympathy for Zip, who after all had made my fortune possible. "Let's take him home, Angie."

Zip snored. "Ahh, we'll leave him," Angie said quietly. "He gets mad if you wake him up before the last stop."

CHAPTER TWENTY

UNCLE Rudy knew when he was licked and gave up the fight against the hamburger joint, selling his deli to a man with plans to turn it into a liquor store.

The buyer had foresight. In an Italian neighborhood a liquor store would have starved, but changes were coming to Shepherd Avenue, which was like an island that sinks a little further into the ocean with each tide.

Grace collapsed on the sidewalk while lugging shelf goods out of the deli. An ambulance took her to the Brooklyn Hospital, where she had to stay a week to recover from exhaustion. Rudy rode with her to the hospital and returned to Shepherd Avenue in time to sell his leftover shelf goods back to the wholesaler.

Vic wouldn't let Angie help him move his things back to the house, insisting on doing it alone by subway. All he brought back was two giant boxes tied with rough hemp that bit into the cardboard. They contained books and clothing, plus my portrait of Jenny, now framed.

"She didn't take it with her?" I asked. Even out of my life she was finding ways to break my heart.

Cool weather, the coming of autumn. Connie put heavier blankets on our beds. I pulled mine up to my chin and rolled onto my side. There were things I needed to know before I blazed my path across the world.

"Vic?"

"What."

Every time you spoke to him these days, you felt as if you were interrupting a daydream.

"What's a whore?"

"For Christ's sakes, didn't we go through this already?"

"You never *told* me what a whore *was*. You just told me about the clap and all that other stuff."

I heard him swallow. "A girl who treats a guy crummy. Or a guy who treats a girl crummy."

"That's all?"

"Yes."

"Are you sure?"

He was through talking. I hesitated before saying, "The opposite of a whore is a virgin."

"Wrong." He sat up. "A virgin's just a girl who never slept with a guy. You can be a virgin and a whore, both."

I stared at the ceiling, soaking in this new knowledge. "Well if that's all a whore is how come nobody ever told me?"

"I don't know, Joe," he said. "Maybe they didn't know."

"You gonna hang my picture of Jenny up in here?"

"I'm thinking about burning it."

"Fuck you, Vic."

In the morning I got a letter from another person I'd cursed that way. It shocked me to see Mel so vulnerable on the page, and it was impossible for me to imagine her saying the words she'd written.

Dear Joey,
Im sorry I said fuck you. I dint mean it. You are my friend. We have to be friends, there aint nobody else. Are you sorry you said fuck you to me? Tell me

*you are sorry. Dont keep saving monney. This is taking
too long. You can sneak on the train and hide under
the seat. I did that one time, they dont yell at you if
they katch you cause your little.*

*I cant remember what you look like. Your face I
mean. I wish we never went in the garage that time.
I wish somebody wood blow up that garage with a
bom. It is going to be my birthday on Septemmber 12,
I will be 12 years old. What I wood like is if you com
here on my birthday. Say you will. You have to cause
I miss you. A lot. If you need more monney you should
go in your gramas pockabook. I have wrote down all
the trains that come here from Jamayka. All you have
to do is tell me witch one your takeing on my birthday.*

love, Mel DiGiovanna

Love! She'd signed the thing "love," in letters wavier than
the rest of the letter. Not since my mother died had anyone
used the word with me. The letter became slippery in my hands,
and then I saw that my fingers were all sweaty. I dried them on
a towel before I started writing.

Dear Mel,

*I'm sorry I said fuck you too. I will come and see
you on your birthday. My father is in New York but
he doesn't want me. I don't want him eether. I saw
him across the street, then I got hit by a car but I
didn't get killed.*

*Here is what you have to do. Put some clothes in a
bag when you come to meet me. Then we will get on
another train and go for a nice honeymoon. I mean
it. This isn't bullshit so don't laugh. I have enuf money
for a wile but when we need more we can look for
bottles. I know how, I am a expert. I don't have to
steel Connie's money. I am bringing a chicken with
one eye who is my pet. I think your alowed to bring
it on the subway. I will cover his cage with a blankit.*

If any buddy tries to stop us I will beat him up like

I beat up Jack that time. Even if it's a cop I will beat him up. Even if it's my father. I am going to take the seven aclock in the morning train so I won't wake them up.

I hesitated before hastily scrawling the word, thrilling myself as I did it.

love, Joe Ambrosio
P.S. From now on I'm Joe, not Joey

The walk to the mailbox: the plan and my feelings for Mel wouldn't become real until I dropped the letter through the slot. I opened the red metal flap and noticed its edge was rusting, resembling a row of rotted teeth. The dark mouth beckoned.

"Yes," I said as I scaled the letter in. I heard it hit bottom, the faint thud of paper on paper as soft as a chickadee landing on a telephone wire.

My proclamation of love for Mel frightened me as much as the journey itself. It would only be a matter of days before she found out everything, however long it took the U.S. mail to deliver my letter. It was all just a little more than a week away.

Little did I suspect that I would not be the first to escape.

I should have seen it coming. We all should have. There was something wrong about the way he was so quiet, how he let Connie get away with relentless ball-breaking. It was mild ball-breaking, like a low-grade fever that wouldn't break.

His beard. His hair. The bookstore job he rode to each day on the trains. The way he'd lost four thousand dollars by quitting the baseball team.

"That's a lotta hours in a bookstore."

Deeper and deeper the needle sank. She got around to reminding him of the college scholarships he'd snubbed to go pro. She told him about Rosemary and the dentist from Woodhaven. She teased him about how Jenny ate seaweed.

"Who were you livin' with, a goldfish?"

He'd just get up and walk away from her. Sometimes he

cleaned the house to vent his feelings. Once he washed all the upstairs windows, reducing an entire edition of the *Journal-American* to dirty, wet wads.

"Jeez, Vic, I didn't even get to see the sports section," Angie said.

"Me neither," Vic answered. "Who cares?"

"*You* sure did, the times you had your picture in it."

Then one night he got out of bed in the middle of the night and spent half an hour in the bathroom without flushing the toilet. He came back clean-shaven, his cheeks seeming to gleam white. The closet door opened, and I heard his suitcase slide. That clean-shaven face would make him more streamlined for travel.

"Where?" I whispered.

He didn't break stride in his packing. "Boston, for a while. Guy I knew from the Nuggets lives there, his old man runs a bar I can work in."

"Angie said you can't come back if you run away."

"Got no plans to come back, kid."

"Joe."

"No! *Kid!* Because that's all you are. Someday you'll understand, these fucking people are *crazy*, man, they're so sick and fucked up it's not even funny."

"Quit it, Vic!" I was frightened. It was as if Vic's warmth and compassion had vanished with his whiskers, the way Samson's strength abandoned him when his hair was cut.

He hurled his pillow against the wall. "No, I won't quit it. Kid, you might as well know the truth. Your mother was maybe the sweetest fucking woman I ever knew, but that Connie, boy, she wouldn't give her a break."

"Why?"

"Ask her sometime! No, don't bother, she wouldn't give you a straight answer." He narrowed his eyes. "Do you know how long it takes to make a baby, Joseph?" His voice was scornful.

"Nine months," I spat. "We had that in science."

"Science." Vic chuckled. "Do you know how long after they got married your mother had *you?*"

I was silent. My blood tingled like seltzer water.

"Eight and a half months," Vic snapped. "That's how long they were married when they had to cut your mother open. You were *premature*, understand me? You hardly weighed five fucking pounds, you were in an incubator for two weeks."

"So what?"

"So *nothing*. But Connie, oh, Jesus, that was all she needed to start calling Elizabeth a whore. She said she trapped your father into getting married. Right downstairs in this house, she said it."

"You're lying, Vic."

"Nine months a virgin, eight months a whore. Connie's very words, may I be struck dead if they weren't."

"I *hate* you."

"Go ahead, hate me." He tossed rolled socks into his suitcase. "Think that changes the truth?" He pointed at me. "*You* were there, too, only you can't remember. The day your father left you off here, Connie asked if you remembered the last time you ate here, and I made her shut up. . . . Remember?"

"Yeah . . ."

"You were in a high chair, that's why you don't remember." Now Vic was laughing. "You want to know the funniest part? This whole stupid, fucking, crazy war happened over a bowl of lentil soup."

With each subsequent sentence Vic bent back a finger to make a point.

"*Connie* put a bowl of soup on your high chair. Your *mother* said it was too much for you. Connie said you were small because you didn't get enough to *eat*. Your *mother* said you were tiny 'cause you were a preemie. That's when Connie told her to cut out that bullshit story, that she knew the *real truth*."

Vic let go of his fingers. "And that's the whole story. You guys split from the house and never came back. Because of a damn bowl of soup. And you want to know why *I'm* splitting."

He was out of breath but he lit a cigarette. "Fucking madhouse," he kept murmuring. "Fucking *madhouse*."

He bent over to rummage through a drawer. His tight T-shirt clung to his ribs, which stuck out like ladder rungs. I stood on his rough mattress, horsehair crinkling under my feet, and then

I sailed through the air and landed on his back. Upon impact I wrapped my arms around his hard torso. Vic plunged forward and cracked his forehead against the dresser mirror, but it didn't break. He only lost his balance momentarily.

"What the f—"

"Asshole, asshole, asshole!" I hissed. I made a fist and punched at his head. I hit his ear, his cheek, his mouth. I felt a stab of pain shoot through my middle knuckle as I caught a tooth.

Vic backpedaled to his bed and shook me off. The fall seemed to take forever, and when I landed I felt the wind get knocked from my lungs.

He pinned me down by my wrists. I tried to kick his balls but he crossed his lower leg over my knees to hold me in place. His bare teeth were clenched.

"You're getting mad at the wrong guy, Joe. I'm just feeding you the truth."

I spat at him. He hadn't expected that, and put a hand to his wet eye. I made a fist and caught him on the chin with a punch. He drew his fist back behind his head. His eyes were wild with rage, but suddenly he loosened his fist and let his arm drop.

"What am I, crazy?" he asked himself. "God, as if you haven't been through enough."

And suddenly my fury was gone, too, as if I'd been injected with a calming drug. Vic released my other wrist and took his leg off me. He moved his chin from side to side, checking for busted bones. "We Ambrosios," he said. "We should each live alone on a mountaintop, I think."

I lay limp on the bed, not answering him.

"You got some punch," he commented. "I'm tastin' blood here."

"I'm leaving too, Vic."

"Not with me you aren't."

"I don't wanna go with you. I got my own money and everything. I'm going in a few days."

"Lotsa luck, Joe. Drive carefully."

Right to the end he didn't believe me. Good, good — it was just as well. He'd find out I hadn't been kidding the first time

266

he got in touch with Connie and Angie. *If* he ever intended to get in touch with them.

"Angie'll miss you," I said.

Vic nodded and wiped his eyes with the back of his hand. "I'll miss him, too. I got nothing against my old man, or you."

I blinked bleary eyes at him. "Sorry I spit at you."

"It wipes right off. . . . Christ, is that smoke I smell?"

He yanked the dresser away from the wall. The whole house seemed to shudder with the wood-scraping sound. "My fucking cig went down there when you jumped me!" He knelt and pounded the floor with his palm, then mashed the butt out in an ashtray.

"That woulda been some going-away present, to burn the house down. Mighta done some good, in this crazy place."

He pushed the dresser back in place, wincing at the noise it made. It was incredible how Connie and Angie could sleep through all the ruckus.

"You seen my leather jacket?"

"You left it in the basement."

He went to get it. I went to Angie's room and shook him awake.

"You sick?"

"No. Listen, Angie, in a coupla minutes come to our room."

"What's goin' on?"

"Just come. Pretend you got up to get a glass of water."

I made it back to my cot before Vic returned with the jacket, my entire body drumskin-tight. Angie arrived slit-eyed, rubbing his crotch. Slightly overacted, I thought.

"Hey, what's goin' on?"

Vic froze, shot a stare at me. I peered back at him and feigned wide-eyed innocence. He zipped his jacket.

"I'm going to Boston, Pop."

Angie's shoulders sagged inside his loose undershirt. He didn't seem too surprised. "You shaved that beard. Did the hair go down my drain?"

"Nah, I did it over the wastebasket."

Vic let Angie touch his face. "Soft as a baby's. Your mother would pay a million bucks to see it again. Wait till morning."

"Forget it."

"Come on. She ain't a monster."

"I don't want to see her and that's it."

Angie shrugged. There didn't seem to be any fight left in him. He plopped onto the edge of Vic's bed, making the springs squeak. Vic stuck his head out the door and looked in the direction of Connie's room, but she was still snoring.

"Don't try to wake her up like that, Pop, that's sneaky."

"It was an accident. . . . You're a grown man. You wanna go, go."

Vic nodded, closed his suitcase and wet his lips. "I lied, Pop. I never hated baseball. It kills me that I couldn't cut it." He put his face in his hands. "Whenever I struck out down there it was like I could hear God *laughing* at me."

Angie stood and patted Vic's shoulder. "So? He's laughin' at all of us. Why do you think he put us here? For kicks, that's why."

Vic seemed startled. "You be*lieve* that?"

Angie pushed his hair back. "After this summer I don't know what I believe. But what I said before still sticks — you leave now, that's it. *Visit* all you want, *call* all you want. But you can't call this place home no more."

"It's a deal."

Vic told Angie about the job waiting for him in Boston. Angie didn't even seem to be listening, and then he said, "At least leave her a note, a short letter. Takes five minutes to write."

"No."

"Victor. Don't you think you owe your mother a good-bye?"

The whites in Vic's eyes gleamed. "Did she say good-bye when I left for West Virginia? Huh? How the hell was I supposed to concentrate on baseball when I didn't even have my mother behind me? You got any idea what it's like when your favorite person in the world . . ."

A sob that was almost feminine bubbled from Vic. He swallowed it and opened his eyes wide again. "Where was she?" he asked. "Where was she when the rest of Shepherd Avenue was

268

out in front of the house the day I left? Am I supposed to forget that?"

"Nobody in this house ever forgot anything," Angie hissed. "We got memories like *elephants*. Come on, Victor, be different."

But Vic shook his head. "I'm no pioneer, Pop. Just let me go." He wiped his eyes and took a long breath. "I'm sorry I lied about hating baseball."

They embraced, Vic's leather jacket crinkling.

"Do one thing for me," Angie said over Vic's shoulder. "Don't hate her. Love her. Can you promise me that?"

"Sure."

"No, no, you answered too quick. When you're gone think of the good stuff, then call her up. Okay?"

Vic nodded, too willingly to be convincing, but by that time Angie was eager to believe anything. They pulled away from each other.

"Go," Angie said. "I'd walk you to the door but I don't know when I'll see you again, and I don't want to miss you too much. I ain't a kid, I don't handle it good anymore."

His feet shuffled on the carpet on the way to his room.

"I'll mail Johnny a wedding present," Vic said, but I don't think Angie heard him. Vic leaned over and kissed my forehead — how soft his skin was!

"So long, Joseph." He made a show of taking the Jenny Sutherland painting off the desk and tucking it under his arm. I listened for the sound of the front door closing. Connie continued to snore. He'd made it.

A minute later Angie appeared in my doorway. "You crying?" he asked.

"A little."

"We're both gonna catch it from her, you know. Pretty smart of you, waking me up so we could share the blame."

I wiped my eyes, thinking how Angie and Connie would blame each other when I took off.

Connie shocked us with her reaction to the news of Vic's departure.

"Thought I heard the door slam last night," she said, continuing to spoon coffee into the pot.

Angie and I looked at each other as if we'd just watched a fuse burn to the nub of a dud firecracker.

"That's all you got to say?" Angie asked.

She shrugged. "Whaddya want me to do, cry?"

The next afternoon it was as if the weather were making up for Connie's tranquility with a rattling hailstorm. Angie put on a floppy yellow raincoat and ran to the backyard, ordering me to stay behind. Through the window I could see that the hailstones were the size of mothballs and bounced like marbles.

Five minutes later Angie came back inside with a small basket filled with muddy green tomatoes. At the sight of them I started to cry.

"You killed them!" I screamed. "We worried all summer about the chickens killing them and then *you* did it!"

He wrestled his way out of the raincoat. "If I hadn't done it they woulda gotten smashed."

"Damn it!" I hollered, pounding my fists on the table. He wrapped his arms around me.

"Hey, calm down!"

"I *hate* this place," I sobbed, wondering if I could stand to stick around those few days before Mel's birthday. The strength ebbed from Angie's grip.

"You don't mean that," he said hopefully.

"Lemme *go!*" I kicked at his legs, squirmed my head, wriggled like a fish. Angie recovered his strength, lifted me, carried me to the couch, and tossed me down on my belly. He pressed one hand between my shoulder blades and the other against the back of my head.

What strength, even greater than Vic's! My face was flattened so hard against the cushion that stemless yellow flowers bloomed on the insides of my eyelids. I felt as helpless as those pegged lobsters I'd seen that day at the Fulton Fish Market. Angie relaxed the pressure long enough for me to turn my head aside to breathe.

"You calmed down?"

"Yeah," I gasped.

"Pretty strong for an old man, huh?" he said, recalling my remark during the drive to Roslyn. "Am I hurting you?"

"Can't *move.*"

"That's the idea, but am I hurting you?"

"No."

"All right." He leaned down and put his mouth against my ear. "Your father's coming back, I swear he's coming back, may I be struck dead this instant if he doesn't."

He paused, I guess to give God a chance to throw down a bolt of lightning. Hailstones clattered but that was all.

My muscles relaxed. He let me go. "He's already back and he doesn't want me."

"Ayyyy . . . follow me. Bring the basket." He picked up the *Journal-American* on our way to the wine cellar.

Without wiping off the mud he took each tomato and wrapped it in a generous sheet of newspaper, passing them to me as he finished each one. "Lay them back in the basket," he instructed.

I obeyed. That dirt-floored corner of the basement had a deep, earthy smell that seemed to eat into my lungs.

"How come you hate my house?"

"I didn't mean that, Angie."

"Didn't think so. Be careful what you say. It's not so pretty but she's a good house." He wiped mud off the end of his nose. "When you're mad about somethin', scream about what's botherin' you, not somethin' else."

He took the basket and set it behind some empty green gallon jugs that had once contained Freddie Gallo's wine.

"We'll come back soon," he said. "They'll be red like blood."

I didn't have much time to wait. "*How* soon?"

"Soon."

"C'mon, Angie, how come they'll turn red?"

"Magic." He reached for the string overhead and clicked off the light.

Days later classes started at nearby P.S. 108. They didn't register me, believing my father would be back any day now, so Connie warned me to stay off the street in case the truant officer came around.

271

But I wanted to make one last bottle hunt, figuring Mel and I would need every cent we could scrape together. As I searched I kept looking over my shoulder for the truant officer, not even knowing what he looked like.

It was a big load, around thirty bottles. The glass felt cold in my hand, as if to herald the changing of seasons my skin couldn't yet detect.

I told Nat he wouldn't be seeing me anymore and he wanted to know why.

"My father's coming back to get me," I said. "We're moving back to our old house in Roslyn."

Nat's brow knotted. "I thought you told me he sold that house."

I swallowed. "Yeah, but he bought it again 'cause I told him I wanted to go back." A jingling noise; the coins were shaking in my loose hand.

He believed me, his face loosening into a smile. "That's *wonderful*, Joseph! I knew you weren't really happy around here. That sad little face coming through my door . . . see how everything worked out?"

We shook hands. "My God, that's quite a grip," he said. "The first time we shook it was like a dead fish."

"I was just a kid then."

He shocked me by tipping me two dollars — paper bills, no less. I'd always thought Nat dealt strictly in coins, carrying buckets of change around to pay bills.

Nat patted my cheek. "You buy your father a nice present. After-shave lotion, something nice."

He walked me to the door, something he'd never done before. He had skin the color of bean sprouts grown in darkness. He tilted his face to the sun and shook his head, as if in wonderment of all those people who lay on beaches to soak up its poisonous rays. His eyes were wet, but not from the sun.

"Your father's coming home. Dear God in heaven, what I wouldn't give to see my daddy again." He looked at me. "Come see me when you visit. Don't tell Zip I tipped you, he'll have five heart attacks."

* * *

272

I stopped painting. Mostly I just hung around the chickens, biding time. I liked the idea of having to be on the lam from the truant officer. Good practice for my escape, when they'd all be hunting for me.

Angie and I took away the fence separating the birds from the tomato plants, now that there was no fruit to protect. They attacked the plants so savagely it was scary. Those birds had doubled in size since coming to Shepherd Avenue.

Connie came out with a newspaper wadded full of garbage. She had me dump it in the middle of the yard and instantly the chickens were upon it — tomato and bell pepper seeds and stems, orange rinds, potato peels.

They made a ragged circle around it, bobbing and clucking, occasionally pecking one another. I kicked a clump of food toward the one that would come with me to Patchogue.

"Always hungry." Connie's voice was dreamy, far away. It was strange to hear that tone from her. "You feed 'em and feed 'em and you can't fill 'em."

I heard water running inside, striking a tinny surface. Angie was taking a shower. Dusk: the purple-hued night-lights went on over at the hamburger joint, making it glow like a spaceship.

"Angie says they'd never run away, even if we took the gate down."

Connie snorted, unimpressed. "Why should they? They got it good here and they know it."

She opened the gate and entered the yard, something she rarely did. She crouched, groaning against her bulk, and put a hand to a white bird's tail. The bird jumped forward and lifted her wings but didn't stop eating.

"How come you stay, hmm?" Connie crooned. She touched its tail again. "Hmm?"

"They don't like to be touched when they're eating, Connie."

"Too bad. It's my food, I'll touch 'em if I want."

"Connie . . ."

She ignored me. The shower was still running. "How come you birds hang around, when I got two sons that ran away, one of them twice?"

With a snakelike thrust Connie's hand was under the bird

like a pancake spatula. Her fingers gripped the yellow feet. She held the squawking, flopping bird bouquet at arms' length as she stood.

"Put her down, Connie!" She shook it. "You're *hurting* her!"

Connie studied the bird's face, pinched its food-gorged crop. It tried to peck her. She slapped its head.

"It's sick," she said. "This chicken has the fever."

"*What* fever? She's fine," I said scornfully.

"Oh, no, no, no. Look at the eyes." She grabbed its beak between thumb and forefinger and held the head close to my eyes. "See how black the eyes are?"

"They're always like that, Connie. Put her down."

"I bet they *all* have the fever. Only one thing to do."

Her left hand found the bird's neck, then the right. Yellow feet clawed the air, and with a horrible muffled crunch Connie twisted its neck.

The bird let out a high, thin squeal and dumped a load of white dung down Connie's dress before its wings and neck finally sagged in death.

"That's one."

My screams rang off the buildings surrounding the yard. Before turning to run inside I saw Connie toss the dead bird aside and crouch to reach for another. None of the survivors had stopped eating, even for an instant.

I pounded on the bathroom door, screaming Angie's name.

"Use the toilet downstairs!" he yelled.

I shoved the door open. Soaking wet, Angie was hitching a towel around his hips.

"What the hell —"

"Connie's killing the birds, make her stop oh God God God —"

"Jesus Christ on the cross . . ."

He was in and out of his room in seconds, tugging on pants over wet legs, the towel draped around his neck. I ran behind him. The smell of his after-shave lotion made everything seem even more urgent.

Salt and Pepper was in her hands when we got to the yard.

It was as if she'd been waiting for us to appear before dealing the final death blow.

"Don't," Angie breathed.

When she was through twisting its neck Connie tossed my favorite bird onto the feathery pile, then spanked her hands together before turning to leave the yard. The front of her dress was streaked with dung. It looked like a modern art drip painting.

"Sick, every one of them," she said to Angie in the tone of a doctor. "Nobody wants sick chickens."

He gripped her shoulders. "Are you crazy, woman? Just tell me that, are you nuts?"

She wriggled out of his grasp. "Don't touch me."

"What made you —"

"I told you. They were sick. Get rid of them. Leave me alone." Sentences like telegrams. She went in and the screen door slammed shut.

Angie and I walked into the yard. There was still food on the ground. I crouched to look at Salt and Pepper. She resembled a rain-stiffened handbag. Her eyes were still open, black and shining dully, rosary beads. I stroked the feathers of her wing. It was like touching corrugated cardboard.

Darkness had fallen, and I was alone. "Angie? Angie!"

He was back in a flash. "I just went in to get shoes, take it easy." He put his arm around me. His skin was still wet, and he shivered. I pressed my face to his bare ribs. The flesh was soft and I could feel the xylophone of bones under it.

"Go inside," he said. "Lemme take care of this." But he let me keep my face against his ribs for a while.

"We have to call the cops," I said. "Let's get them to put Connie in jail."

"Shhh . . . go, go inside. Your grandmother's in her room, she won't come out. You won't even have to look at her."

I watched him work from the back window. He took a huge A & P grocery bag and stuffed the chickens into it. He rolled the top closed and went down the block to toss the bag into one of the big trash hoppers at the hamburger joint.

I knew he threw them there, because I couldn't find them

in our pail the next morning. I asked him where they were and he told me, with no bullshit. What was the difference? They were dead. It didn't matter where they were now.

CHAPTER TWENTY-ONE

CONNIE wouldn't leave her room, except to go to the bathroom. She wouldn't eat, wouldn't go near the kitchen. Angie and I ate simple meals like cold cheese cut over hard bread with oil and vinegar dripped over it. He lacked her delicate touch with food, soaking the bread with vinegar. You couldn't eat it.

We watched a lot of television and took walks, unconcerned about any truant officer. We didn't talk about Vic, my father, or the birds. It was as if a natural disaster had robbed us of these things: an earthquake, a tornado, locusts — something we couldn't get mad at.

I made "X's" on the kitchen calendar that marched toward September 12. Angie never asked why.

Sitting on the porch we heard brassy music coming from Atlantic Avenue.

"My God, Joey, the feast! I forgot all about it."

You smelled the feast long before you got to it, the smell of confectioners' sugar on sizzling deep-fried lumps of sweet dough. You heard it first, too, bands composed of neighborhood men playing dented trumpets and trombones and gray-skinned drums.

We broke through the crowd and saw an enormous statue of the child Jesus in a long red gown, a gold and velvet crown on his head. His right hand was held up, palm out, two fingers extended in blessing.

"Throw one our way, we could use it," Angie said.

A man standing on the statue's platform bent over to accept dollar bills from the people. He pinned them to the velvet curtain behind the statue. Hundreds of them fluttered in the breeze.

"Always hated that part of the feast," Angie said, pointing at the money curtain. "God knows where it really goes. That guy'll probably have a new Cadillac tomorrow."

276

Men with huge forearms and V-necked undershirts grilled sausages and peppers on wide griddles, squinting against the grease and the steam. Their chest hair was black and thick, burying the thin gold chains around their necks. Gold horns and miraculous medals seemed to be suspended from nothing between their pectorals.

Brown oil bubbled in a cauldron the size of a kettle drum. The woman behind it skimmed its surface with a big spoon full of holes, shook the *zeppole*, and dumped them into a pan.

Angie held up two fingers. "Don't tell your grandma about this," he warned, unnecessarily — as far as I was concerned, I was never speaking to Connie again.

The lady dropped two in a bag, sprinkled sugar over them and handed them over. The two-dollar tip from Nat was in my pocket. I pulled out a buck before Angie could reach his money.

"What the heck are you doin'?"

"I'm treating you, that's what I'm doing." I made my voice as rough as I could, tires on gravel. The lady gave back ninety cents. Forty-five small bottles, I thought — would I ever get the Deposit Bottle Exchange Rate out of my head?

"You don't have to spend your money on me, Joey."

"I want to," I said, remembering how Nat had told me to spend it on my father. Fat chance. I didn't even bother telling Angie to call me "Joe." What difference did it make now?

Angie shook the *zeppole* bag to sugar them up evenly. "It's just that your father sent you that money so you could buy stuff for yourself."

Oh boy. How long had I been looking for an excuse to tell Angie? With bottle-hunting days behind me, there was no reason to keep it a secret anymore.

"This money ain't from my father," I spat. "I made it all by myself."

He squinted one eye at me, the way his wife often did. "You did? How?"

"Ya know the guy who takes bottles on Atlantic Avenue? Empty bottles?"

"You don't mean Nat the Jew, where Zip goes?"

"Uh-huh. Well I went there too. All summer long. That's

where I was when I wasn't with you, pickin' up bottles. Zip didn't care as long as I didn't go on his turf."

The eye squinted till it was nearly shut, like Popeye's. "So where'd you go?"

I told him.

"Jesus, Mary, and Joseph. And you're alive to talk about it."

I put my hands on my hips, gunslinger-style. "I wasn't afraid."

"You coulda got killed, you know that?"

"So? Nobody woulda cared." I gripped my belt buckle. Angie's jaws clenched. He looked over at the cauldron of oil as if he were trying to determine if it was big enough to boil my whole body. "Nobody woulda *cared*, huh?" he muttered, expecting no answer.

I released the buckle and clasped my hands together in front of my groin, as if to protect it. "I made over forty bucks and I'm leaving, Angie."

He seemed to have been more surprised by the bottle revelation than by this announcement.

"Leaving? Where you goin'?" Not, "Where do you *think* you're goin'?" but "Where you goin'?"

I took the deepest breath of my life, coating my lungs generously with *zeppole* oil vapors. For the absolute *last* time I recited my plan, ending with Mel and me walking off into the sunset. He said nothing when I was through.

"Don't say I can't do it, Angie. I'm really gonna do it and you can't stop me."

He pursed his lips, opened his mouth, and tapped his golden front teeth together, as if they were dentures he had to settle into place. "Forty bucks, huh?"

A gust of wind blew his hair forward. As he pushed it back I looked for streaks of blackness but, like the beard he scraped away, it had gone completely white, seemingly since the start of my escape tale.

But his eyebrows were still jet-black, and they arched into steeples as he said, "You're leaving me, huh?"

I'd have preferred another Phil McElhenny fastball to my head over that little sentence.

"How you figure on gettin' there?" he asked.

"Trains. I know what trains I have to take, it's easy."

"How about if you let me give you a lift?"

So that was his game. "Don't you try and trick me, Angie, I'm really going."

"Oh, I know, I know," he said, his voice thick with respect. "But you're gonna need more than forty bucks if you're gonna hit the road, Joseph. You let me drive you to Patchogue, you'll at least save train fare."

The *zeppole* bag grew greasier and greasier in his hands. He was running out of dry places to hold it.

"Hey," said the lady who sold them, gesturing with the spoon, "you're blockin' my customers here."

We walk-skated from her stand, the street slick with oil. People swarmed past us, eager to play rigged games of chance, buy heros, and go on the rides. Angie and I were the only ones standing still. In that sense we were very much alone out there, more so than we would have been in the house.

I said, "You'll really drive me out there and let me go with Mel and not make me come back?"

He nodded. "If that's what you want, sure." A dim smile. "But you know something, Joseph?" He looked left and right as if to make sure no one was eavesdropping, and then his lips were an inch from my ear.

"*I don't think you wanna go.*" He pulled back and winked, exactly the way he had the first time I met him, in the bathroom. He jutted a cherry-red lower lip and shook his head slowly. "Nah," he said, agreeing with himself, "you don't wanna go."

I still had the ninety cents in my hand. I poured it into my pocket and listened to the coins greet one another. I tried to pull my hand out but it had become a fist, too big for the mouth of the pocket.

"It's Mel's birthday soon, Angie. I want to see Mel. She hates it where she lives."

Angie's hand was relaxed as he held it up the way the statue did. "Fine, fine, you'll go see Mel. You could spend the whole day together, huh? And maybe her aunt'd let us take her back here for a few days, you could play stickball. Who knows? Or maybe you could stay overnight in Patchogue. . . . Hey, Joey,

I ain't trying to tell you what to do, these are just ideas off the top of my head." He patted the top of his head, momentarily flattening his hair. "I shoulda thought of this stuff before, buddy. I'm sorry. What do you say, huh?"

"Call me Joe."

"Right, *Joe*."

"And gimme a *zeppole*."

We bit into them. As I chewed I became confused by a salty taste, and it took a moment for me to figure out that a teardrop had rolled down my cheek and leaked into the corner of my mouth. I threw the rest of the pastry toward the Ferris wheel.

"Hey! You wanna hit someone?"

"I don't care."

Angie licked sugar from his fingertips. It dusted his lips as white as his hair. "Joe, Joe, Joe." Steely fingers massaged the top of my head. "You can't go no place in this world on forty bucks. You mighta lasted two days. Then there's the truant officer to worry about. The *police*. The whole world woulda been lookin' for you two."

I could tell he'd bitten off the word "kids" at the end of that sentence. I pulled his hand off my head and held it by the wrist, the way kids clung to their parents at that feast to keep from getting lost.

"My mother told me if I had a hundred dollars I could go anyplace I want and do anything I want, Angie. I tried to get a hundred but I didn't make it."

His smile was benign. "Forty dollars, a hundred dollars, it wouldn't matter. You wouldn't get far. Either way it's a drop in the bucket."

I let go of his wrist. "You calling my mother a liar?"

He rubbed the wrist I'd held as if he'd just unstrapped a tight watch. "She wasn't a liar, Joe. She was just telling a story to a little boy when she said it. And you ain't a little boy anymore, are you?"

I didn't answer right away. Somewhere behind us a brass band launched into a tune that wasn't recognizable as "The Star-Spangled Banner" until the second stanza.

"No, I'm not," I finally said.

280

His hands went to my shoulders, light as two doves. "Now you tell me something." He tapped the bones over his heart. "What made you think you could just run away like that?"

"My father did it to *me*."

"Uh-huh. Well. A coupla things." He held up a forefinger. "He had a car." His middle finger. "He had lots of money." I waited for the ring finger but instead Angie crossed his flat hands over his heart. "And *he's coming back*. How many times am I gonna tell you this? Like it or not, it's true. And I *know* you like it, in here." He tapped *my* chest. "I'll ask you one more time — what made you think you could just run away?"

I finally knew what he meant. "Nobody . . ."

He nodded, urging me to say it, but I clammed up. He showed me the backs of his hands and twitched his fingers toward his face, a father coaxing a baby to take those first steps. "Come on . . ."

"Nobody said I couldn't."

Cymbals smashed. The national anthem had ended. There was cheering and scattered jeering.

"All right," Angie said, pointing at himself with a jaunty thumb, "*I'm* saying you can't. Okay? Do we understand each other like men or what?"

"Yeah." Was I getting taller or was he shrinking? It seemed we stood eye to eye. All I could do was repeat his name as I grasped his hand. I held it in both my hands, pulling the fingers as if they were udders.

"Cheez," he giggled, embarrassed. We began walking. I let go of him.

"Angie, you're my friend, right?"

He stopped walking. "*Friend?* God, I'm your blood." He tapped a blue vein on his wrist, visible through a clearing in the hairy foliage. "What flows in here flows in *here*." He tapped the kink of my elbow. Warmth flooded my being but I didn't let it get me drunk because there was more to know.

"What I mean . . ." I rubbed the spot where he'd tapped me, as if I'd just taken an injection there. "Suppose you weren't my grandfather. Would you still be my friend?"

"Oh." We started walking again. "Well, let's be honest, I

probably never woulda met you. I never see kids, am I right? But if I *did* know you, I'd be your friend."

"Swear?"

"I swear." He crossed his heart, even though I hadn't asked him to. Like the claw of an earth-moving machine his hand reached toward me, rustily, guided by an inexperienced lever operator.

"Shake."

I squeezed even harder than I'd squeezed Nat. He winked, hesitated, then lunged toward me. The one and only time Angelo Ambrosio ever tried to kiss me, we both nearly busted our noses.

"Jesus!" he yelped, his hands flying up to cover his nose.

I did the same thing. "What'd ya do *that* for, Angie?" I whimpered.

A trombone voice, behind the hands: "For Christ's sakes, I was tryin' to kiss ya." He wiggled the tip of his nose. "Whoa. Well. Least it ain't broken. You okay?"

"I think I'll live."

"Tough guy. That's the last time I'll kiss you, until maybe your wedding day."

We put our heads back and howled with laughter — God, how long had it been since we'd laughed like that? I gave another *zeppole* maker a dime for two more.

"You, ah, ain't tryin' to buy my friendship here, are you?"

I shook the bag. "I just want to treat you, Angie. You let me live in your house and everything."

The Ferris wheel was drawing us. Now, at dusk, white lights glowed all the way around it, and down each of its support spokes. It looked like a giant illuminated spider doing cartwheels.

The ride was fifteen cents — "Up a nickel from last year," Angie noted as I paid the operator, who secured us in place and slammed down the safety bar.

One by one, each bucket seat was filled. When the wheel bore a full load we stopped moving just a notch at a time and spun around smoothly.

Angie rubbed his arms. "We should have brought sweaters.

282

. . . Hey, I could never get that grandma of yours up here. This thing scares her. She's afraid it's gonna break off and roll away. I keep tellin' her if that happens, it's better to be on the wheel — the people on the ground are the ones in trouble!"

He laughed. "Met her at a feast like this one. Know something? I don't think she ever called me by my name. She just talks to me." He pointed at a sausage and pepper stand below. "Look, look at Palmieri. Poor guy never had a wife. Hot food once a year. What a life."

I watched Palmieri walk, munching a hero, his elbows tight to his sides, as if he feared catching diseases from other people. The top of his balding head glistened in the light from the Ferris wheel.

Angie poked me. "Hey. Did your father ever tell you what our name *means*?"

"Uh-uh."

"Ambrosio. Am-*bro*-sia. One different letter, that's all, and it means nectar of the gods, what the gods eat and drink. See? That's your name, your *core*. It's inside you as tight as the pipes I put in all them buildings."

He pointed at Palmieri without looking down. "You could never in a million years be like that guy who lives upstairs. You're gonna taste everything, down to here."

He tilted his face back and slid his fingertips from his chin to the pit of his stomach. The gesture was noble and at the same time sort of effeminate, a princess feeling her own silky skin. Angie tipped his face forward and leaned against the protective bar as if he meant to break its lock and fly toward the horizon, me under his arm.

Our carriage rocked. Change fell from my pocket, sprinkling the people under us, who moments later were above us and then below us again with the turning of the wheel.

"It's only money, Joe!" Angie howled. The man at the controls cupped his hands over his mouth and howled, "Don't rock it!" as we whirled past him.

The wheel slowed down. The operator began unloading passengers, starting with the people behind us. What a break; we'd be the last to get off.

Notch by notch, we traveled upward, and when we hit the peak the whole neighborhood lay sprawled beneath us.

"Connie," he murmured. It was strange to hear; he rarely spoke her name, either. "I'd pay a hundred bucks for her to see this."

"She's not like you, Angie."

"No, thank God for that."

"I like you better."

"No you don't. You like me different. Your father and you and Vic are different but I love you all the same."

"Well, I hate Connie. Don't *you?*"

"You nuts? She's my wife. I love her."

"She killed the birds and they weren't sick, Angie. You know that."

"How you're related to me, you're related to her."

"They weren't sick," I repeated.

He shrugged. "Maybe they were. I ain't a doctor. Maybe she knows more about chickens than both of us."

"Yeahh, sure."

He patted my knee. "You think you hate her but I'm tellin' you, you don't. She had a bad day. That's what you hate." He took my chin between thumb and forefinger to make sure I saw his eyes. "Chickens ain't as important as people. Don't you forget that."

"I know the story about the soup, Angie."

He let go of my chin. "What soup?"

"How the whole fight started because Connie gave me too much soup when I was a baby and her thinkin' my mother tricked him to get married and everything. Vic told me."

Angie's faint smile surprised me. "Vic gets carried away with his stories, sometimes."

"But isn't it true that *one thing* caused —"

"Joseph. Please. Bad stuff never happens because of one thing. You're smart enough to know that, I think. If it hadn't been the soup it woulda been somethin' else."

I pounded the steel safety bar with my palm. "*Why?*"

"Because," Angie said calmly. "Just because. And that's the best answer I can give you."

His eyes, more than his words, got through to me. The wheel groaned, shifted. We went down a notch, paused, went down another notch, each stop punctuated by the sound of the safety bar clanging down on a new set of passengers.

He patted my hand. "You'll see. You'll get older, you'll be surprised by how much you can forgive. If you're smart. And you are."

I didn't like the way he sounded. It was too much like a good-bye. "Next year we'll get Connie to ride this thing," I said.

Angie let his lips flap as he exhaled. "Next year . . ." He gestured vaguely at the sky. "Too far off to think about."

We were a quarter of the way down. "Point in any direction," he said suddenly.

"Why?"

"Just do it. Point, point."

When I'd pointed in all directions he nodded.

"All those places you pointed, I worked there. This whole neighborhood, it's all mine, everything you can see. That clown Ammiratti is nothing next to me."

His shoulders seemed to widen. He tilted his head back for a look at the stars, and then his eyes closed — no, he was grimacing. His Adam's apple jumped, as if with a hiccup. We moved another notch groundward, and as the carriage rocked it seemed strange that Angie should sit with his eyes closed and his face stern for so long.

"Angie? Y'okay?"

Before the wheel could clang down another notch I knew he was dead.

I surprised myself with my composure. As long as we sat up there, demigods above Brooklyn, not even death could get us. I pulled Angie's fingers free from the cold iron safety bar and put his hands on his lap. When our carriage reached the ground and the operator lifted the bar to let us out, I finally started crying.

CHAPTER TWENTY-TWO

PALMIERI took me home, jabbering incoherently the whole way. I vaguely understood that we'd left Angie behind. The next thing I knew I was in my cot, under the covers. Downstairs was the din of voices, visitors comforting Connie.

The next morning it was as if the wall between us had been torn down, never existed. She strode into my room and laid out my dark suit. I took a bath and put it on. Palmieri had to knot one of Vic's ties around my neck because Connie didn't know how to do it.

The funeral parlor was a carpeted room full of people on foldout chairs, talking in loud voices. Sometimes they even broke into laughter. It all seemed like a long, sick joke.

I stayed at Connie's side, and when she moved I even took her hand. Part of me still hated her and we both knew it, but I was the only male Ambrosio around — the role of something or other sat squarely on my small shoulders.

I knelt with her before the coffin, Angie's face powdered pink, his lips crusted, a rosary twined in his hands. He didn't look dead, just made-up. I kept waiting for his tongue to flick at those lips and dot them with bits of chewed sunflower seeds. The worst thing of all was that his hair had been parted by the stupid undertaker in a way he never wore it.

"Neither son here," I heard them moan. "*Neither son.*" Oh, what a disgrace it was.

I felt like telling them all to shut up. How could they put on such performances and then show up at Shepherd Avenue to munch pastries and guzzle coffee?

Grace Rothstein, skinnier and crazier than ever, took over the reins at the house. Angie's death provided her with a perfect outlet for those cooking impulses the demise of her husband's deli had stifled. She made pies, roasted chickens, put up gravies.

A bond developed between Connie and Freddie Gallo's widow, both members of the same dismal sisterhood.

Palmieri came down to sip coffee and pay his respects, though he couldn't hide a selfish worry from his clownish face — would Connie sell the house? Where else could he live so cheaply? I sneaked away from the crowd and lay on Angie's mattress. His room reeked of Old Spice. I went through his closet, where he kept his work shoes and the black lunch pail. I tried on his vest, slid my hands into the pockets and felt little bumps.

Sunflower seeds. I ate half of them and took the rest to my room, putting them in the pocket of my own jacket. Handling them made me feel better.

Deacon Sullivan had become a priest weeks earlier and delivered the eulogy before Angie's open grave. I didn't listen to a word and I doubt that Connie did, either. In the middle of it she pointed to a patch of scrubby grass next to the hole.

"That's where I'm gonna end up."

I had to run off and pee in a clump of bushes next to a tombstone with a black marble hand atop it, the forefinger pointing toward heaven.

I approached the priest after the service. "Father Sullivan?"

I could tell he loved his new title. "Yes, Joseph?"

"My grandfather never really liked you."

His mouth fell open, as if I'd plunged an ice pick into his guts. "I just wanted you to know that," I said casually. "He felt sorry for you, that's why he was always nice when you came to the house."

I walked away from him, a long-denied score settled at last.

That night I flopped on Vic's bed, the first time I'd ever used it voluntarily. It wheezed odors of his sweat, a smell tangy with leather and horsehide fragrances, as if his long hours of ball-playing had permanently leached those elements into his perspiration. I savored the smell, believing I'd seen the last of him. Before him, this bed had been my father's: had it once breathed his dreams, too, odors of watercolors and oil paints?

Downstairs the babble of "mourners" was steady, sort of like the clucking of the chickens had been. They were driving me crazy and I knew there were days of this bullshit to come.

I couldn't take anymore. I knew it was time to leave Shepherd Avenue. I would be going ahead of schedule, Mel's birthday still a few days off. I checked the calendar and saw it was

September 9, my mother's birthday. She would have been thirty-one years old.

I went to the telephone, dialed Long Island information, and asked for the number at Mel's aunt's house, even though I knew she wasn't "alowed" to use the phone. I didn't even know the name of the ogres she wrote about — the operator found the number by tracing it through the return address on one of Mel's letters. The operator said it wasn't quite in keeping with company policy to do it that way but I talked her into it, *whined* her into it.

How often Connie had bitched about long distance phone bills from West Virginia! The bill for this call would come after I'd split, my final insult to my grandmother.

The phone rang four times before an irritated female voice snapped, "Hello!" above a crackling sound. The phone must have been near the stove, where she was frying something.

"Hello, I would like to speak with Mel DiGiovanna, please. This is Joseph Ambrosio calling."

My mother had done a good job teaching me telephone etiquette, but this woman wasn't impressesd.

"What are you, kiddin' me?"

What a voice, a human bugle; I had to hold the phone away from my head to protect my eardrum. I didn't know what to do, so I began repeating the same schtick until I was interrupted.

"I heard ya the first time, I heard ya the first time. *Wait* a minute, willya?" There was a thumping sound as she dropped the phone, then the crackling subsided a bit as she turned the flame down on whatever she'd been cooking.

I clenched my teeth, thrilled by the thought that the next voice I heard would be Mel's. We would talk a lot less awkwardly than we wrote, I was sure.

But no.

"Hello?" It was the aunt again. "You there, sonny?"

"Yes . . ."

"Mel don't live here no more."

I felt nauseous. Sweat beaded up on my arms and forehead. "What?"

"She don't live here no more. My brother in Phoenix took

288

her three days ago." She might have been talking about an old couch.

My lips felt dry and crisp as the paper I painted on. "Where's Phoenix?"

"In Arizona. A long, long way from here." There was triumph in her voice.

I looked wildly around the parlor for a pen and paper, walking in a circle as wide as the phone cord would stretch. "Can you give me her address?"

"I — no, wait, *hey!* You're the little punk who wrote all them letters, ain't you?"

The parlor seemed airless. "I'm not a punk." It took precious breath to say it. "Where's Mel?"

"I ain't tellin'. What for, so youse two can write bad things? You think I didn't see them letters? That last one she tried to send, ho, boy, I wish they had the electric chair for kids."

"What did she say? In the letter?"

"I ain't telling. I don't have it no more, anyway. We used it to light the charcoal last night on the barbeque. We cooked pork chops outside."

Fucking Italians, squeezing food anecdotes into every aspect of their lives! A wild, desperate stab of hope; this woman was lying through her fangs. Mel was in her room or outside or chained up in a corner of their garage, near a food bowl and a water dish.

"Mel's still there, isn't she, Aunt?" I said, not knowing what else to call her.

"No she ain't. . . . *Aunt?* Don't you *aunt* me. I'm not your aunt."

"You tell Mel I'm coming right over. Tonight."

"Hey! Are you crazy? You stay away from our house! Just stay away!"

I raised the phone as high as I could and slammed it down, hard enough, I hoped, to break her fucking eardrum.

The hum of voices downstairs exploded briefly in laughter. Someone, probably Grace, had cracked a good joke. I knew it would take hours for them to clear out.

I lay on Vic's bed the whole time, not sleeping, barely blinking as I stared at the ceiling. Connie went by on the way to her room, and then there was silence. With Angie gone she no longer snored, having lost her collaborator in those nightlong window-trembling symphonies.

I took my bottle bag from the drawer where I'd hidden it. I remembered how Zip had teased me about not being able to carry my chickens with me. Thanks to Connie, that wasn't a problem anymore.

"I'll show her."

Underpants, socks, and shirts went into the sack, and there was still loads of room. The thing breathed a sweet-sour smell from the sticky drippings of all those soda bottles I'd hauled.

I tossed in a few Spaldeens, even though I didn't play stickball anymore, and that seemed to complete the job. I checked under my cot and even slid a hand under Vic's mattress, extracting a stale Milky Way bar. I ripped off the wrapper and ate it, ignoring its chalkiness.

So little to take. How could it be so easy to pick up my life and go? There *had* to be more. I remembered a box of sunflower seeds Angie had opened just before he died. I tiptoed to his room and threw that in, too. I would not eat those seeds. I would save them, the way people save sugared almonds from a wedding.

I took the framed painting of my mother off the wall. The frame made it too bulky, so I took it apart, dismantling the work of my dead grandfather. I winced with the pull of each little nail at the back of it, as if they were being yanked from my flesh. It was a relief when the thing finally fell apart. Frame, glass, and cardboard backing tumbled onto my bedspread. I left it all there and rolled the painting into a scroll. There was a crackling sound as I did that, and when I unrolled it for another look bits of watercolor dust fell from my mother's face, which now had white lines where paint was missing. I had aged her twenty years.

"I'm sorry, Mom."

I hastily rolled it up again, put a rubber band around it and stuck it in the bag. The only thing to get now was my money.

I went to the basement without turning on any lights, knowing every corner, every pipe, every shin-shattering object down there. I clutched the jar to my chest as I carried it upstairs, as tightly as firemen hold babies they pull from burning buildings.

I trembled as I dumped the money onto the bedspread for a final count. The coin level had risen a full inch above the grease-pencil mark I'd made on the jar. No thieves in the house, after all. It came to $43.35, including the paper dollar I still had from Nat's tip. There would have been more, only I'd lost that pocketful of change on the Ferris wheel with Angie. We had laughed over that, I remembered.

There was nothing more to do but go to the bathroom. I had to giggle, however strange it seemed; it struck me that the only similarity between Connie and my mother was that they were always telling me to go to the bathroom before I went anywhere.

I took a leak and didn't flush. I looked at my face in the mirror Vic had broken. The crack ran jaggedly down the middle of it, dividing my face between the eyes and giving me a lightning-shaped scar on my cheek.

Tough guy. I finally looked like a tough guy. I mussed up my hair to make myself look even tougher, but it fell back into place. I studied my cheeks for the slightest sign of beard, but I barely had peach fuzz. Yeah, some tough guy.

Angie's can of shaving cream was still on the sink. I found his razor in the medicine cabinet, unscrewed it, and shook his rusty blade into the wastebasket. I wet my face with hot water, screwed the empty razor shut, shook the can, and squirted shaving cream into my left palm. The odor was dizzying, sending me back to the time I met Angie; for a few seconds I had to grip the sink to keep my balance. I took his lather brush, dipped it into the cream, and painted my face where whiskers would one day grow.

It made my skin tingle, as if from a narcotic. Two yellow rivers cut the cream patches on my cheeks; I was crying. I wiped over the rivers with the brush and then I was okay, calm and steady as I scraped my face with the toothless razor. I rinsed it in a thin stream of hot water, just like Angie used to. My confidence grew with each stroke. The mission was going to be all right.

I floated back to my room, my head a planet separate from the rest of my body, the odor of Rise its atmosphere. I put on my windbreaker, slung the sack over my left shoulder, and hefted the money jar in my right hand.

No more of that damn basement; I would go out the front door. Halfway down the hall I panicked and went back, thinking I'd left something behind. I moved some books on the bureau and saw a pointed white object the length of my middle finger.

It was the feather from Roslyn the Duck, which Connie had stuck in my hair that time. I blew dust off it and stuck it where she'd put it, in the hair at my crown. Indian-style, on feet light enough to leave the tiniest twigs unbroken, I would escape from Shepherd Avenue.

Down the hallway again. I put the sack down and had my hand on the brass knob of the glass-paned interior door when the chandelier snapped on.

"Hey, Yankee Doodle. And where do you think you're goin'?"

I whirled to face Connie, who stood at the other end of the hallway. If she'd been a stranger, her appearance would have scared the shit out of me.

Rage caved in her dentureless mouth even deeper than nature had. Her loose hair hung in serpentine coils over her breasts. Those twisted feet I'd rubbed with sand at Rockaway Beach looked absolutely obscene. The crooked, long-nailed big toes jutted in the air, like the sandals of a court jester. Her skin was the color of her nightgown, the color of macaroni dough. She looked worse than Angie had in his coffin.

I forced myself not to be frightened. "I'm leaving this place." I said it louder than I'd meant to, tinkling the glass chandelier chimes ever so slightly. "I'm running away with Mel."

Hadn't I vowed never to repeat my plan again? I was sick of my own voice.

She stepped toward me. "Why?"

"She's the only one."

"The only one what?"

"Who . . . loves me."

"Madonna mi, *love* he wants." She lifted her massive arm and pointed in the direction of my cot. The flying squirrel curtain of flesh on her upper arm trembled. It must have been like holding up a barbell. Her face showed the strain.

"Get inside."

"No. Good-bye."

I opened the door and stepped onto the black and white tiled area between the doors. A paratrooper, ready to jump into the wind. I had my hand on the main door's knob when I saw something that literally froze me in place.

Connie was *running* toward me. Not walking fast, *running*. All her life, maybe, she'd saved the one sprint her body allotted her for this night. The floor thundered and the panes of the interior door rattled at her approach. It would have been less surprising if the Empire State Building had yanked itself free of its foundations and come after me on brick feet.

I fumbled with the door, got it open, and flashed outside, clutching my goods. Safely down the front steps, I was ready to trot to the el, confident that Connie would stop at the porch.

Wrong. Before the door could bang closed she bashed it open and cleared all the porch steps like a hurdler, hair and nightgown flying. When she landed, her knees bent, the gown flattening all around her like the white part of a fried egg. Her legs are busted, I told myself, but then she stood straight, looked at me, lifted her arm again, and shook a fist.

"GET BACK HERE!"

It was the loudest scream I'd ever heard. Windows went yellow all along Shepherd Avenue. Zip Aiello appeared on his porch in long johns, scratching his cheeks with both hands. Connie crouched, as if awaiting the sound of the starter's pistol, and then she came after me.

I turned and ran. Even as my legs pumped I realized how ridiculous it was to be chased by Connie. Maybe later, on the train to Jamaica, I could even laugh about it.

I peeked over my shoulder and saw that I was losing her. A train went by, in the opposite direction of the one I needed. That was good; usually that meant another was due in the right direction within minutes.

One last peek at Connie. She was tiring even more. Her mouth hung open and she was hunched forward in search of breath. I turned back toward the tracks just in time to feel my foot catch a chunk of broken sidewalk.

The jar and the sack went flying in looping arcs. I heard the smash of glass, then came down hard on my belly. My elbows took the brunt of the fall as a paralyzing tingle ran all the way to my hands. My knees hurt, too. The skid had scraped the pants clean through to the skin.

I shook my head to clear it and saw coins rolling around amid bits of broken glass. The train I needed went by. The sack had landed on the spikes of a wrought-iron fence, where it still hung, its contents spilling. A Spaldeen rolled toward me. I reached for it with a stiff hand but my fingers wouldn't cooperate to pick it up. I watched it roll to the curb, then rolled onto my back to take the weight off my wounded joints.

Connie wasn't running anymore. No need for it. When she got to me her breathing was like the tearing of cloth as the southernmost portions of her lungs, dormant for fifty years, were suddenly being called to work. Zip Aiello appeared, having put pants over his long johns. He took five seconds to survey the situation.

"I'll pick up the money."

A black teenager in a feathered fedora came along, munching on a bag of french fries. He blinked huge inky eyes and shook his head.

"Mutha-*fucka*," he commented. "I dig your feather more'n I do mine." He went away.

Connie's breathing was slowing down but her nightgown clung to her lumpy body — she was sweating, something I'd been forbidden to do in her house! She wiped her forehead in disgust of the fluid her body was surrendering. I stayed on my back like a beetle, elbows and knees in the air. They felt as if they'd been soaked with gasoline and torched. People clustered all around me, most of whom had visited the house earlier in the night. There was a wall of legs in all directions and their tired faces looked prehistoric: I was a wounded animal to be slaughtered, butchered, and hauled back to their caves.

Connie knelt and gripped my wrist as if to take my pulse. With her other hand she smoothed back her damp hair.

"It's me or nobody."

I yanked myself free, feeling the tear of a thin scab already forming at my elbow, and let out a scream that came all the way from my bowels. The people moved back. I gargled on my own saliva, spat it out in an upward spray, and felt it shower my face. I kept screaming at the sky, even as my shoulders were being pressed to the pavement. I opened my eyes to see Johnny Gallo gazing at me in terror.

"Long Island, shut *up* already, for Christ's sake," he begged, but I wouldn't obey. I couldn't. I was even screaming as I inhaled, so it was a sound that could go on all night, all week, forever. I shut my eyes. Johnny maintained a trembling grip on my shoulders.

"It's about time, Doc," Connie said minutes later. I felt the sleeve of my windbreaker being pushed to my elbow but wouldn't look. The pinch of a hypodermic needle: Johnny's hands came off me, to be replaced by many hands under my knees, head, and elbows.

"One, two, three, lift!" said a voice I didn't recognize, and then I was out for good.

CHAPTER TWENTY-THREE

I WOKE up in my cot, my knees and elbows heavily bandaged. There were gauze pads against the wounds, bound in place by strips of adhesive tape even whiter than Roslyn's feathers had been.

I sat up, careful not to bend my elbows or knees. An iodine-colored solution had been swabbed on them before the bandaging. It stained my skin beyond the boundaries of the gauze shields.

Connie appeared carrying a bowl of minestrone, a dish towel under it to protect her hands from its heat. There were no trays in that house. This may have been the first time a meal had ever been served in bed.

"*Eat.*" She put the soup on the night table, and from her apron pocket she extracted a spoon.

I cleared my throat, hoarse from all that screaming. "Who put these bandages on me?"

"The doctor from up the block."

"Where's my money?"

"Downstairs. Zip picked it up."

"I wanna count it."

She went to get it, limping. The doctor really should have treated *her* after that remarkable sprinting. It took her five minutes to return with a clear glass bowl.

I dumped it and counted it. There was eighty cents missing, I told her.

"Some fell down the sewer. . . . So you were a bottle man all this time, eh?"

"Zip should keep his big mouth shut."

I was starving but I didn't touch her soup. Soon steam stopped rising from it. The oil on its surface began to chill and harden around the edges, like ice on a lake at the start of winter.

By the time she came back to the room the chilled oil coating covered the whole surface. I could have dropped a nickel on it without breaking through to liquid.

"Now you're gonna starve yourself to death?"

"I ain't hungry."

She shrugged, picked up the bowl. "I got something for you. Your friend's address in Arizona."

"I don't want it."

"You can make a phone call if you want, a short one."

"I don't want anybody."

I didn't eat the next day, either. Connie phoned the doctor, who said it was okay to take off the bandages. I wouldn't let her do it. The pull of gauze against scab was a sweet pain that made my eyes tear. I kind of enjoyed it and was sort of sorry when the last one came off, except that now it would be easier to move. It was time to dream up another getaway.

And while I tried to hatch a new plot nothing could rouse me, not even the sound of my father's Comet pulling into the driveway late at night.

I feigned sleep. Down the hall I heard Connie's angry shouts

("You and your stupid postcards!"), and then his voice, surprisingly soft and apologetic.

Footsteps toward me; I lay as still as I could. The door opened a crack.

"Don't you wake him," Connie commanded.

"I just want a look at him, Ma."

A stripe of light slashed my face. "My God, he got older." When he finally shut the door I sighed deeply and bit the pillow. An hour later, when their talking died down and he'd gone to sleep in his father's bed, I locked the door.

I didn't even answer in the morning when he tried the knob, then knocked, then pounded on the door. He said my name over and over. I coughed loudly in response but refused to speak. He went away.

At around noon there was a scratching in the lock, and Connie came in. She'd had her own key all along!

I pretended to be reading a book. I had to use the toilet badly and jiggled my foot to relieve the feeling. It didn't work.

Connie's dress, stockings, and shoes were black, as I knew they would be for the rest of her life. Her garb made the catfishlike stripes of white hair on either side of her part stand out more than ever. I could hardly believe it but I suddenly felt a twinge of compassion for her, remembering certain things — the way she'd stood up for me that time in the church with Mel, the times we'd made macaroni together, the paint supplies she'd given me.

But it only lasted a moment, winking out dead like a spark that floats from a winter bonfire.

She put a paper bag down at her feet and sat on the cot. "Well, I don't gotta tell you who's here."

I turned a page.

"He wants to see you."

"No."

She took a breath. "This is what it is. We're all gonna live here. You'll go to P.S. 108, same school your father went to. And *me*," she said in wonderment, as if this had just occurred to her. "Anyhow you have to catch up with the other kids, they're in a week already."

I put the book down. "Big deal. I ain't goin'."

Her hands were folded. "Let him see you."

"No. I hate him. If he comes in here I'll kill him." On stiff legs I went to the closet and took out a Johnny Mize bat. I could barely heft it, but a summer with the Ambrosios had taught me a thing or two about dramatics — for a moment, Connie seemed alarmed.

Then she chuckled. "You can't even swing that thing."

I put it down. "That was him I saw, wasn't it? Don't lie to me, Connie."

She pushed back the catfish stripes. "He was in the city these past few weeks, yeah. Hotel room. But I don't know if it was him you saw."

"It was him. . . . why didn't he come here that day?"

"Don't ask me to understand my son. I didn't even understand my husband." Her voice broke and her hand went to her throat. She was trying to act as if something going down the wrong pipe had made her voice flutter.

"School tomorrow," she said when she was back in control. "Every day you fall further behind."

"Forget it, Connie."

I flopped face down on the bed. My bladder felt the pressure of her hand on the small of my back. I jumped in surprise, but the touch was remarkably delicate, especially coming from a woman so sparing of human contact.

"I'm not smart," she said feebly. "You and me, we didn't always get along so good. . . . It don't matter. I killed your birds, I don't know why I did that, it sure didn't make me happy."

She was sorry. Months earlier I'd never have identified the apology. Her hand moved smoothly up and down my back. My eyes formed wet spots where they pressed into the pillow.

"I miss Angie," I said into the cloth. The words must have been gibberish to her because her hand continued to move steadily.

"When you're ready, come downstairs. You can't stay here forever."

I sat up and looked at her.

"You and me, Joseph, it's wrong for us to be enemies."

298

She left the room. I got up and swung my legs over the side of the bed. They banged into the bag she'd brought.

I stared at it before opening it. I figured it would be some sort of peace offering from my father, a quickie gift to make up for all that neglect. I reached into it and pulled out something firm and roundish, wrapped in newspaper. Slowly, as if I were defusing a bomb, I unwrapped it. When the paper fell away I was holding a tomato coated with dry mud, one Angie had set aside in the wine cellar that day of the hailstorm.

I used the paper to shine it clean. It gleamed a brilliant red.

I unwrapped all of them and rubbed them clean. Sixteen red tomatoes made a dazzling sight, spread out on the white sunshine-splashed bedspread. After I put them back in the bag I went to the bathroom.

The long, steady stream of piss felt like poison leaving my body, and then I went downstairs to see my father.